THE FRIGHTENERS

'Eddie?'

'Yeah?'

'You okay?'

'Yeah, I'm all right, Rennie. Just can't sleep, that's all.'

'You wanna talk? About Tracey and the kids, I mean.'

'No. There's nothing to talk about. They're dead. Just like the people who did it. They're dead, but they don't know it yet.'

'What is it, Eddie? There's something different about you. And it's more than Tracey and the young'uns. Something's happened to you.'

'Get some sleep, Rennie.'

'What's *happening*, man?'

'Not yet, Rennie. Not yet. I'll let you know when it's time.'

About the author

Stephen Laws has acquired a growing and enthusiastic following in the horror fantasy world. His first three novels, *Ghost Train*, *Spectre* and *The Wyrm*, have received the highest praise and established him in the top league of British writers in the genre. Born and brought up in Newcastle upon Tyne, his previous books drew on his knowledge of Northumbria and the North-East, but in *The Frighteners* he has used a broader canvas, carrying his unique talent into an arena that is boundless.

The Frighteners

Stephen Laws

NEW ENGLISH LIBRARY
Hodder and Stoughton

Copyright © 1990 by Stephen Laws

First published in Great Britain in 1990 by Souvenir Press Ltd.

A New English Library Paperback edition 1991

Second impression 1992
Part-title decorations designed by Ray Laws

Printed and bound in Great Britain for Hodder and Stoughton Paperbacks, a division of Hodder and Stoughton Ltd., Mill Road, Dunton Green, Sevenoaks, Kent TN13 2YA (Editorial Office: 47 Bedford Square, London WC1B 3DP) by Clays Ltd, St Ives plc. Typeset by Medcalf Type Ltd, Bicester, Oxon.

British Library C.I.P.

Laws, Stephen
The frighteners
I. Title
823[F]

ISBN 0-450-55450-3

'To put the Frighteners on . . .'

English Gangland/Underworld Slang:
Literally, to extort, to threaten
with physical violence in order to
attain one's ends.

CONTENTS

PART ONE

CARVE-UP

'Is it the mere radiance of a foul soul that thus transpires through, and transfigures, its clay continent?

'. . . man is not truly one, but truly two. I say two, because the state of my own knowledge does not pass beyond that point. Others will follow, others will outstrip me on the same lines.'

The Strange Case of Dr Jekyll and Mr Hyde.
Robert louis Stevenson (1886)

1

'How much do you hate?' asked the madman.

Eddie Brinkburn was squatting at the base of the prison recreation yard wall. He looked up at the owner of the voice. The bulky figure blotted out the sun, casting Eddie into shadow. The voice was hoarse, strained. And even though he could see only a silhouette, Eddie knew that it was Archie Duncan. Great coarse hands with knotted purple veins were hanging at the huge figure's sides, clenching and unclenching. Those hands had once brutally murdered six people.

'How much do you *hate*?' asked Duncan again.

Eddie was sitting with his back to the wall. He had been watching the other cons walking, talking, jogging or simply sitting looking at the sky. Duncan seemed to have appeared from nowhere.

'Not now, Archie.'

Eddie braced his back against the cold wall and levered himself into a standing position, using his good elbow. Even when he was standing, Duncan still towered over his five feet eight. Eddie wiped his lips nervously, running a hand through thick black curly hair. Duncan was staring at him intently, bullet-shaped shaven head cocked to one side, thin spittle hanging gossamer-like from rubber lips. The eyes seemed innocent and childlike . . . and this was probably the most frightening thing about him.

'How much do you . . .?'

Eddie sidestepped and began to walk away, keeping a nervous eye on Duncan lest he should follow. Duncan

11

remained standing, staring at the grey exercise yard wall as if Eddie was still there. Eddie heard him say:

'. . . hate?' as he turned up the collar of his jacket and walked slowly to the centre of the exercise square, regulation shoes crunching on thin gravel. Eventually, he knew, Duncan would move on and find someone else of whom he could ask his question. They were the only words that Duncan ever spoke; the only words that Eddie had ever heard from him, during the first two years of his five-year stretch. Duncan was a lifer.

Shouldn't even be here, thought Eddie as he began to jog on the spot, warming chilled limbs. His left arm, warped and useless, flapped uselessly at his side. Angrily, he took the paralysed fingers and stuffed them into a sidepocket. *Should be in a mental home or a psycho ward or something.*

Little was known of the details of Duncan's crime other than that he had been disturbed while burgling a home and with his bare hands had killed the family of six who lived there. There was no doubt about it – Duncan was subnormal, mentally retarded. And even though he had shown none of that horrifying psychotic behaviour during his stretch, no one wanted to get too close to him in case he decided to give it another try.

A swollen sun edged precariously through its veil of steel-grey clouds and swirling smoke from the industrial chimney on the skyline, beyond the prison wall. Everywhere Eddie looked, he could see grey. The cold grey faces of the incarcerated wandering idly in circles in the prison yard, or bouncing tired rubber balls against the cold grey prison walls. The cold steel-grey of barbed wire mesh. It matched the grey feeling in his gut as he picked his way back across the yard to the farthest wall, hands in pockets.

Rennie Montresor was still sitting where Eddie had left him. His eyes were closed as he drummed out the beat from an inner song on his knees. Eddie stood over him for a while, looking at his dark, lean frame and tight black curly hair. And when those eyes still didn't open, he kicked Rennie's feet. The black man looked up, shading his eyes.

'Turn the music down,' said Eddie. 'You're keeping the other cons awake.'

'Oh, so now you're sociable again, are you? What happened to the bad temper, then?'

'Okay . . . so I'm sorry.' Eddie leaned against the fence, sliding down on his haunches next to Rennie, both of them now looking out into the centre of the prison yard. Rennie continued to tap out the rhythm on his knees, casting one rueful sideways glance at his companion. Eddie saw that glance from the corner of his own eye and, for an instant, it seemed to him that even Rennie's sculptured ebony West Indian face had turned a little grey.

'Archie's on the prowl again,' said Eddie.

'Weird fucker.' Rennie stopped drumming, cracked his knuckles as if it was an important finishing flourish for a specialised musical instrument and breathed out heavily. After awhile, he said, 'Imagine it, Eddie . . .'

Eddie knew what was coming and groaned. 'Not again. I can't stand it.'

'No . . . bear with me and I'll take you there.' Rennie exhaled again before continuing, like a weightlifter just about to make a snatch at a 200-pound bar-bell. Long black-and-tan fingers danced in the air, conjuring up pictures.

'A beach with white sand. Hot sand. The kind that burns your feet unless you got sandals on. Surf. Plenty of surf curling in from a big, deep, green sea . . .'

'Spare me . . .'

'. . . and palm trees, of course. Jamaica without palm trees is like Brixton without petrol bombs.'

'Hah, hah.'

'The heat's coming at you in solid waves as you're walking down that beach. And you press this ice-cool can of Red Stripe against your cheek till it gives you a pain there. Man, you're feeling good. Then this girl . . .'

'No girls, Rennie! I've told you before.'

'Okay, married man. No girls. That was . . . just some tree stump over there, just looked like a girl for a minute. But look at everything else. Ain't you glad to be here?'

13

'You've never been to Jamaica. You were born in London, just like me. Hell, even your parents were born in London.'

'Well, if that's the case — tell me what this is I see before my eyes. The heat and the sun and the sea and the beer. That's real, Eddie. I can smell it. I can feel it. I can see it. That's got to be Jamaica.'

'I don't know why you do it.'

'Escape, man. Escape. They've got us in here — and that's the reality. But they can't take what's in our heads; they can't take away the fantasy. And that's what's going to see us through. I'll teach you. Just give me time. Just a matter of time before you find out that the fantasy is better than the reality. Imagination — that's all you need.'

Eddie spat ruefully onto the tarmac and looked around the recreation yard again.

'Grey . . . just grey . . .'

'No,' replied Rennie. 'Wrong, wrong, wrong. It's green and brown and orange and . . .'

'How much do you hate?'

'Oh *shit* . . .' Rennie clambered to his feet as Duncan stepped in front of them, looking down. He helped Eddie up, too, hooking one hand under his good elbow and hoisting. 'Thought this was a *private* beach,' he said in disgust as they strolled to another part of the recreation yard.

2

Later that night in the cell, while Rennie snored in the bunk below him, Eddie watched the striped shadows of the window's bars creep across the wall.

Grey, grey . . . everything always had to be so bloody grey.

Now at last, the Jamaican heat which Rennie had talked of earlier that day crept like a suffocating blanket over Eddie. He wished that he could shut his eyes and embark on Rennie's fantasy, but he could not. The prison cell was a tomb, and when he shut his eyes he felt as if he were in a stone coffin. Eddie squirmed, feeling the vest clinging to his body; his mouth parched. For some reason, he could taste the smell of petrol in his mouth, and the taste reminded him. Reminded him of . . .

* * *

Eddie had been working under the car for most of the day, fixing the crankshaft on the Audi. Rennie kicked his boot.

'Coffee.'

Eddie grunted and swung himself out from under the car on his maintenance trolley, wiping a grease-smeared face with a rag from his top overall pocket. Upside down, he could see Rennie's grinning face above him.

'Hey,' said Rennie, handing him the cup as he stood up. 'You're even blacker than me.'

'Hah, hah. Bloody comedian.'

'How's it going?'

'Fixed. He can collect it the day after tomorrow.'

'Day *after* tomorrow?'

'Yeah. *He* doesn't know it's fixed yet, does he? That's another day's labour costs.'

'I was right. You *are* blacker than me.'

'He's getting the job cheap, Rennie. You know that. He's a rich fat cat. He can afford it.'

'For an anti-capitalist, you're a hell of a capitalist.'

Eddie laughed, sipped his coffee and gestured around him at the garage: one pit, grease-smeared walls, one 'office' which was basically a plywood cordoned-off section of the garage, ten-foot square and what could only be described as 'sparsely equipped'.

'*This* is capitalism?'

Rennie shrugged in response, and sat down on the workbench. 'Point taken.' He leaned over and switched off the cassette tape that had been blasting out 'Mustang Sally'.

A car horn bleated from the street outside. Three short blasts, one long: a familiar signal.

Rennie banged his cup down on the workbench and stood up quickly, turning his back on Eddie. 'Oh *hell*, Eddie! You're joking, man. Not again!'

'It's money, Rennie. The stuff that pays the bills, remember?' His voice sounded unconvinced and unconvincing. Rennie remained where he was, hands braced on the workbench, looking down and shaking his head. Eddie moved to the double doors as the car horn sounded again: three jabs and a bleat. The doors rolled back and a sleek black BMW slid slowly into the garage, drawing up carefully alongside the Audi.

Rennie was wiping his hands with a cloth as the car's front doors opened simultaneously. Two familiar men in black suits climbed out. The driver was short, wearing sunglasses and a perfectly knotted silk tie. He flicked imaginary dust from his carefully creased trousers with an impeccably manicured hand. His door clicked shut. *Terry Bishop*, thought Rennie, *And Tony Bell. Both Sheraton's people. And that's Bad News.*

On the other side of the car, Tony Bell leaned on the roof,

16

interlocking his ring-studded fingers and smiling at Rennie; a smile of broken teeth, thick-set eyes crowned by an American GI-style crew-cut.

Rennie continued to wipe his hands, slowly and deliberately, as if the muck on his fingers would not come off. The gesture was not lost on the two men. The driver took off his sunglasses, folded them neatly and placed them in his top pocket. His smile was glacial. Rennie's insult would be dealt with in good time.

The garage double doors rattled shut. Eddie returned. 'Hello, Bishop. More work?'

The driver turned slowly from Rennie, maintaining eye contact longer than necessary to emphasise an inevitable confrontation, finally looking at Eddie as he said, 'England needs men like you, Eddie. Good businessmen. Good for the economy.'

'The *black* economy,' said the crew-cut, still grinning at Rennie.

'Exactly, Mr Bell,' countered Bishop.

Rennie threw down his cloth and walked away. Bishop's false smile was gone now. 'There's an attitude problem there, Eddie. Can't say I'm too keen on that. Know what I mean?'

'No, no. It's okay.' Eddie moved to touch Bishop's sleeve. The warning glare, that such unclean hands should come nowhere near his Armani suit, kept him away. 'Really, Bishop, he's okay.'

'But will he keep his mouth shut? If he can't . . .'

'Of course he will. No problem.' Hastily, Eddie turned to the BMW. Brand new, by the look of it. 'Same thing?'

Bishop dusted his lapel. 'Yeah. Number plates.'

'Where's this one from, then?'

'Now, now, Eddie. That's a naughty question, isn't it? Ask no questions, get no lies, eh?'

'Okay, fair enough. Same terms?'

Bishop turned to Bell, hands held out in mocking supplication. 'Is he, or is he not a businessman, Mr Bell?'

'True blue,' said the crew-cut.

'And so discreet. Hopefully that'll stay the way it is. You've done us good in the past, Eddie. And that always means more work and more money in the bank.'

'How hot is it?'

'Hot enough. We need the change of plates for tomorrow.'

'Pretty hot. Okay, then . . .'

3

How much do you hate?

'. . . Pretty hot . . .' said Eddie aloud, and now the heat in the prison cell seemed even more stifling and claustrophobic than before.

'What?' asked Rennie from below in a voice blurred with sleep.

A pause. Then: 'Jamaica, Rennie. Jamaica . . .'

'Yeah.' Rennie laughed quietly and turned back to new dreams. 'It's hot.'

So's hell, thought Eddie.

Tonight, Rennie's dreams of Jamaica were shadowed from the beginning. His golden beach had rapidly become surreal, with the sun turning into an eye; at first glaring, then hooded and closing slowly. As it closed, darkness descended. The sea became flinty; bitter-cold winds swept in, bringing strangled clouds. The waves whispered on the now stark beach, and that whispering echoed in Rennie's head, telling him that he had an . . .

'Attitude problem . . .'

* * *

. . . As the car horn bleated again − three short, one long − Eddie pulled back the double doors and a Mercedes glided into the garage. It was a week since the BMW had been moved on. They had never brought another back so early before: business must really be good. As the car slid to a halt, Rennie played over in his mind the most recent argument with Eddie over involvement with these people.

19

'You said you wouldn't have any more dealings with these guys, Eddie. You promised me.'

'It's good money. You get a good part of it.'

'We don't need that kind of money. We're not running with the street gangs any more. Hell, Eddie, they're *animals*, these people. You know what Sheraton's people did to Johnny Prescott's bar when he wouldn't pay their protection money. They burned the place down. Put Johnny in intensive care with his arms and legs broken.'

'We need the cash . . .'

'They're *animals*, Eddie!'

'Look, Rennie! You're starting to piss me off. There's another way of looking at this, you know. Like — how does *anyone* go about telling them that we're not doing any more work for them? *How*, Rennie? "Thanks, but no thanks, Mr Bishop." Don't you understand — we'd end up in intensive care like Johnny Prescott, or worse. At least this way we're on their good side — and earning good money. So why not take the cash and stop complaining?'

'Eddie . . . Eddie . . .'

And now, as Bishop's latest acquisition slid to a halt and he climbed out of the driver's seat, Eddie hurriedly turned to Rennie and whispered through clenched teeth, 'For God's sake don't make it obvious, Rennie.'

Rennie scowled and turned away into the 'office' as Eddie moved over to the car and began talking to Bishop and Bell. Absently spooning instant coffee into a chipped mug, he looked back to watch Bishop picking imaginary fluff from his lapel as they talked. What the bleeding hell was Eddie doing, getting mixed up with this bunch? Bishop's lot were bad enough, but everybody knew that his extortion racket (with stolen motors on the side) was only one small part of Sheraton's bigger, dirtier criminal organisation. Bishop was a minor 'lieutenant' within that organisation — but still someone to be avoided at all costs. Rennie looked up and saw that the conversation had taken a different, more disturbing direction. The two gangsters' faces were set, devoid of humour; Bishop was poking a finger at Eddie's chest. Eddie was shaking his head, holding out his hands in a pacifying gesture. Bell was joining in now, spitting unheard words through his broken teeth. Quickly, Rennie abandoned his cup and walked back into the garage.

Eddie was wearily nodding assent to something now. Bishop and Bell were smiling, Bishop turning one of his familiar glacial smiles in Rennie's direction as he approached.

'Ah,' said Bishop, 'the hired hand.'

'A partner,' replied Rennie tightly. 'What's going down?'

Bishop sniggered, affecting a pseudo-American accent. 'Going down? Goin' *down*, man? Well where-all-are you from? This is England, man. Not L.A.'

Rennie remained tight-lipped. Bishop finished sniggering and then continued, straightening his tie: 'Your "partner" has agreed to assist us in a . . .' Bishop turned to Bell, as if hunting for the right phrase.

'A "withdrawal" situation,' replied Bell.

Bishop clicked his fingers. 'That's it exactly.' Then, tightly: 'We do so hope that your . . . partner . . . isn't going to cause problems. This is important, Eddie.'

'No problems,' replied Eddie, looking at Rennie in defeat.

I wish I was in bloody Jamaica, thought Rennie before replying, 'No problems.'

Later, when they'd gone:

'What the hell is a "withdrawal" situation?'

'He wants a driver. Me. And you, as a back-up.'

'What for?'

'Look, Rennie. It's worth five hundred. And it's cash we can do with. Tracey needs that operation and that National Health Service waiting list is years long . . .'

'What does he want drivers *for*, Eddie?'

'And you — how the hell are you ever going to afford a trip to Jamaica and trace your folks?'

'WHAT THE HELL DOES HE WANT DRIVERS FOR, EDDIE?'

Angry now, in retaliation: 'All right! All right . . . XL Garage. Joey Siegel's place. They're not paying Bishop's

21

money. He wants the garage done over as a lesson. We're driving Bell and his mate while they do the business . . .'

'Getaway drivers, Eddie? Are you out of your bloody head?'

'What choice have we got, eh? Why the hell do you think I'm still in business? Why do you think I've got away without paying Bishop protection money?'

'But it's getting worse, Eddie. We're garage owners; we're mechanics. Not Bonnie and bloody Clyde.'

'What choice do we have? Going to the Coppers? And then what'll happen to Tracey and the kids? You think I want them getting car battery acid in their faces?'

'But, Eddie . . .'

'No buts, Rennie!' And then quietly: 'No buts. What choice is there?'

Rennie knew ultimately that he was right. There was no choice.

4

How much do you hate?

Eddie toyed with the chips on his plate, prodding them with his fork as he watched his two kids eat their meal. Jane was five, her chin smeared with tomato sauce, one eye on the cartoon show now playing on their television. Blonde hair tatty after a day's play, ready for her bath. Russell was seven, with a face modelled on his mother's: large eyes, delicate chin, full lips. He was whingeing because Eddie had told him off for 'stealing' pieces of Jane's jigsaw just before teatime to make the task more difficult.

Eddie's stomach was curdled into a thick, bilious knot. He pushed the plate to one side and watched as Tracey spooned more baked beans carefully into Jane's mouth.

Tracey was a young, beautiful girl in an old woman's body.

The dark rings under her eyes made him want to go down to the nearest Social Security office and smash their windows in. Eddie watched as Tracey brushed a strand of hair away from her eyes — eyes that seemed too large and glazed these days — as she talked softly to Jane, telling her that Heinz was a magician from Fairyland and that when you ate his beans they made you grow as big as a beanstalk. Eddie wondered whether Heinz had any way of working his magic to shorten the waiting list for the operation that would kill the thing inside Tracey that was killing her. With that thought came a great rage: a rage at the system which had originally promised free health care for all but now quite clearly was a system that

23

discriminated according to the ability to pay. Eddie needed that money *now*.

God knows he had tried to do what the system wanted him to do. Both Rennie and he had grown up in one of the roughest areas of South London. In their teens they had both been prominent in one of the hardest street gangs. They had bucked the system, reaped the profits and taken the punishments. Hell, they had even shared the same probation officer. And it had been Rennie who had convinced him that they were going nowhere, that the only future they had would be doing time inside. He had convinced Eddie that they should make something of themselves, make something of their lives.

Hence, the garage. Hard graft and honest money.

But no matter how hard Eddie grafted, no matter how much he obeyed the system and played by its rules, it still didn't get Tracey the treatment she so desperately needed. He could slave his guts out and it would still be too late. Driving the car for Bishop was going to change all that.

Who gave a shit about the 'fair' system? If playing 'unfair' meant the difference between curing Tracey and letting her suffer, then he was going to play 'unfair'. Eddie pulled the plate back. His stomach was still knotted and bitter with acid. Forcefully, he shovelled the food down and made it stay there.

5

How much do you . . .?

Eddie opened his eyes, sweat streaming down his face. The slatted shadows had crept farther down the wall, widening and sprawling; reinforcing the impression that he was caught in a net, or in some huge spider's web. He became aware that Rennie was mumbling in his sleep below him, twisting and turning uncomfortably in his bunk.

Eddie swallowed hard, wiped his face and rolled back into that sleep which was not really a sleep at all. He was in the garage again . . .

* * *

'It'll just be the once, Rennie. I promise you that. I've spoken to Bishop. He's promised . . .'

'That lying bastard's promises aren't worth anything.'

'We're partners, Rennie. You've got as much say as me in this.'

'Well I say "no".'

'Tracey, Rennie. Tracey and the kids.'

'You twat.'

'And you owe me one. You know that. When those Micks set on you in Curley's Bar, it was me that waded in. No one else stood up for you.'

'So now you're calling in markers?'

'Yeah, if that's what it takes. Then we're even.'

'And no more deals with Bishop?'

'No more deals. That's what Bishop said to me. Really. He thinks the place is getting too hot.'

'You having me on? He really said that?'

'Really. No joking, Rennie, this is the last. Once we've got the cash, I'm giving my share to that private clinic. Tracey'll be okay. And then . . . phfttt! . . . That's it. No more deals.'

'And no more protection money to pay?'

'Come on, Rennie, be realistic. We can't have everything.'

'Okay. The once. And that's it.'

6

Salvador Dali had been given the contract on Rennie's
Jamaican dream. The sea had turned to blood – and there
were glistening oil slicks on the surface. The glistening oil
patches became detritus-ridden pools, and as Rennie wheeled
from one dream to another he saw that these pools were
glistening on the main road beside Joey Siegel's garage.
Headlights reflected in the water, and dirty waves washed
the pavement as each car passed. Eddie lit another cigarette
after he had parked the Audi in the car park opposite the
garage. Rennie was next to him. Tony Bell sat in the back;
grinning, always grinning, running an unnecessary comb
over his crew-cut. A newcomer sat next to him; a young man
they had never seen before, with short blond hair and a face
that was a study in designer video repressed violence: cool
blue eyes, tight-lipped, wearing a reefer jacket and faded
blue jeans. Bell had introduced him briefly as 'Bobby', but
it was apparent from the way Bell treated him that he was
somehow different. Bobby looked young and inexperienced,
yet Bell, a hardened pro if ever there was one, treated him
with an air of careful respect. If that was the case, Bobby
had to be taken at face value.

For twenty minutes, they waited in the car park; in darkness,
no lights. They waited as traffic ploughed waves past them
down the main road, churning up the pools of water from
that afternoon's continuous drizzling rain. In twenty
minutes, there was only one customer. A quiet night.

'Okay,' said Bell, as if at a given signal. The suddenness

27

of the word startled both men in the front. He and Bobby climbed out of the car, chunking the doors shut, and, turning up their collars against the chill wind, they walked purposefully across the car park to the main road.

'So why the hell do they need *drivers*?' hissed Rennie, glad of a chance to talk at last. 'It's pointless us being here. Why go to all the bother of dragging us into this business?'

'They're going to rough him up a little, that's all..Teach him a lesson. Nothing serious. Take the till money. We wait five minutes, then we drive over. They climb in, we take them away smooth.'

'But why do they need us? I don't like any of it. There's no point us *being* here, is there?'

'I don't like it either, but there's . . .'

'. . . no choice, I know.'

Bell and Bobby crossed the main road and walked briskly into the garage forecourt, under the red and green neon sign: 'Siegel's'.

'They're not going to hurt him bad are they, Eddie?'

'No. Just put the frighteners on him.'

They watched Bobby as he pushed ahead, entering the glass-fronted shop with what seemed to be an unprofessional swagger. He moved to the counter. Bell followed close after, closing the door discreetly behind him as if no one would be able to see them through the glass frontage. A small, bald man in a woollen waistcoat suddenly appeared through beaded curtains behind the counter. There was a silent exchange of words between Bobby and Joey Siegel. Now, Bobby was stabbing a pointed finger at Siegel, emphasising his words. Rennie was reminded of Bishop's gesture to Eddie in the garage. But Joey Siegel wasn't impressed or intimidated by Bobby's aggressive manner. Now, he was stabbing a finger *back* at him. Eddie could imagine the conversation: Joey Siegel was a child of the holocaust, he wasn't going to allow anyone to intimidate him into handing over hard-earned money.

'Things are . . .' began Rennie, as Joey Siegel came round the side of the counter towards Bobby.

'. . . going to . . .'

Bobby seized the old man's shoulder and vigorously headbutted the old man on the bridge of the nose.

'. . . turn nasty,' Rennie finished weakly, as a red stain spattered the glass office wall like a thrown tomato, and the old man fell back twitching against the confectionery stand, scattering Mars Bars and Polo mints.

They watched as Bobby dragged him behind the counter by his waistcoat, throwing him to the floor out of sight while Bell moved, calm and unconcerned, to the till, ringing the register and clearing the tray.

Bobby began viciously and silently kicking the old man, each blow provoking a sharp breath from Rennie.

'Okay, okay, that's enough, you vicious bastard. That's *enough*!'

Angrily, Eddie jammed his foot on the pedal and the Audi screeched out of the car park towards the main road.

'Hurry up, Eddie! He'll kill the poor bastard!'

Eddie checked quickly for oncoming traffic and then the car streaked across the glistening black main road, jamming to a halt in the garage forecourt. Eddie remembered Bell's instructions about a 'smooth, early getaway', seeing with anger and disgust that Bobby was still methodically stamping and kicking. He remembered Bell emphasising the need for 'not drawing attention', watched as the kicking continued . . . and then jabbed down hard on the car horn with the heel of his hand. Bell whirled in alarm. The kicking ceased instantly, and Bobby stood back, straightening his tie. Silent, angry words were exchanged behind the glass frontage. Bell threw open the office door and Eddie could see the brimming rage on his face as Bobby hurried through. Both men began to stride towards the car.

And then things began to happen in slow motion.

Eddie saw the movement behind the counter first. It was a young man emerging from the inner office through the glass beads; a man in stained green overalls — obviously a mechanic.

'Andy Siegel . . .' said Rennie, recognising Joey's son;

29

his voice came out slow and dragging, matching the slow motion of the scene.

The mechanic looked down and saw what had been done to his father. He stood paralysed for a moment, mouth open in horror . . . and then he blundered to a drawer behind the counter. Frozen, they watched Bell and Bobby making for the car, unaware of the mechanic behind them. And now the glass office door was being flung open with a long, slow crash — and the mechanic was in the doorway, running, holding up one hand so that Eddie could see that it was . . .'

'. . . A shooter!' Rennie exclaimed. 'God, Eddie! He's got a . . .'

The sound of the first shot was a long, ricocheting *'blat*!*'*, but the bullet appeared to go nowhere. It was not a Hollywood sound effect: it was a shocking, horrifying *flat* sound. Bell and Bobby flinched, looking back and seeing the mechanic for the first time. In slow motion, they tried to run as a second shot punctured Bell's left thigh: a simultaneous explosion of blood and fibre on each side of his leg.

Screaming, he collapsed on the concrete forecourt, hugging his wound.

The mechanic was howling like some enraged animal as he moved forward, raising the gun again and firing wildly.

A third shot punctured the Texaco petrol pump in the forecourt with a loud *'spang*!*'*, spraying a cloud of petrol as Bobby ran for the car.

'Eddie!' yelled Rennie. 'Watch out!'

The windscreen imploded as the fourth shot passed between them, glass flaying hands and faces. Eddie spat blood, brushing glass from his face and hair in time to see, feel and hear the petrol pump explode into a roaring blossom of black-orange flame as a wild fifth shot detonated the spraying petrol. They watched in horror as the billowing cloud of fire gobbled up the forecourt and swallowed the running figure of Bobby. The fireball snuffed into nothingness, but Bobby was running out of the cloud of black smoke which now replaced it.

And Bobby was still burning — a man of flame, burning fiercely as he ran towards them, trailing smoke; his face a mask of melting wax as he ran, silently screaming.

Rennie was uttering short hoarse cries of horror as Eddie slammed into reverse and the car shot out of the forecourt. The burning man collapsed into a pile on the forecourt, the fire dampening now. The Audi screeched back onto the main road, narrowly avoiding an articulated truck. The cold night air felt like fire on Rennie's bloodied face as it blasted through the shattered windscreen. He looked back. Joey Siegel's garage was wreathed in black smoke. Something still burned on the forecourt. And then it was gone from sight.

'Can you see what's happening back there?' shouted Eddie through gritted teeth as they sped north on the highway.

'Great, man!' shouted Rennie in reply, shaking his head. 'This is just bloody *great* . . .'

'Can you see anything, Goddamnit?'

Rennie strained round in the seat to look back, 'Nothing but smoke. Jesus, Eddie . . . that guy had a gun.'

'I saw it. I heard it.'

A chill wind blasted through the shattered windscreen; a cutting rain from the water on the highway sliced into the car. The wind and the rain together were blurring Eddie's vision. And then Rennie started to groan, sinking down into his seat as the sounds of a wailing police siren from somewhere behind reached their ears.

'Maybe they don't know about us,' shouted Eddie. 'Maybe we got away without being seen.' But then he saw the blur of the police car in the rear view mirror, three hundred yards back, but closing the gap . . . and he knew that Joey Siegel's son had telephoned the police and given the car's licence number.

'Now what the hell are we going to do?' shouted Rennie, hands over his face.

'There's only one choice. We've got to lose them, put as much distance as possible between us, then dump the car and make a run for it. They don't know who we are. This car's stolen. Nothing to finger us.'

'Well, get us off this road before they're able to hem us in with other cars.'

'Good thinking.'

Eddie wiped the water from his face. Ahead, he could see the blur of traffic lights. Now he knew just exactly where they were: at the lights ahead was a roundabout; the right exit led to another main road; they could just as easily be hemmed in there by police cars as they would if they continued north on the main highway, or attempted a suicidal three point turn before the roundabout, and headed south the way they had come. But the left-hand exit was a different matter; only four hundred yards on the rough road there and they could turn up into a warren of side streets and back alleys. Once there, they could easily dump the car and make a break for it.

Eddie's eyes flicked from left to right. They were doing 80 mph, but they needed just that little bit of extra time. He tried to assess what lay beyond the ragged grey-green blur of hedges, shrubs and fencing on their left, and then remembered that it was open parkland. Could he cut that corner and head across the open land to the left-hand exit road beyond, avoiding the roundabout altogether? The fuzz would surely never follow him that way. Eddie looked from the highway ahead, to the park, to the highway, to the park . . . And then Rennie suddenly knew what he was thinking, and yelled:

'*Go for it!*'

Eddie eased off the accelerator, checked quickly for other traffic and then swerved from the main highway onto the pavement.

'Cover your face!' he yelled.

The shock jarred them in their seats as the car hurtled screeching across the pavement and ploughed through a deteriorating park fence in an explosion of rusted and splintered boardings. A sliver of wood jammed into the ragged gap of the windscreen; Rennie hammered at it with his hand and it was snatched away over the roof. Both men

32

began to bounce up and down in their seats as the car hit the grassed park area and Eddie jammed his foot on the accelerator. The car roared ahead over the open ground. Rennie had a brief glimpse of an interrupted football match off to his left, and a bunch of kids standing open-mouthed in amazement as their car roared towards the fence on the exit road ahead.

Rennie looked back. The police car had pulled onto the pavement on the main road. He could see its light flashing, but they were not being followed.

'It's worked.'

'Not yet it hasn't,' said Eddie grimly, twisting at the wheel as he gunned the engine forward. 'Come on . . . come on . . . come . . . on!'

Rennie braced himself for Eddie's fresh assault on the fence ahead. Then he saw the rusted open gate. 'Over there!'

Eddie saw it and swerved. Seconds later, the car bounced between the rusted pillars of the gateway and up the slight embankment to the road. Rennie prayed that there wouldn't be any pedestrians up there on the pavement as the car suddenly crested the embankment, swerved screeching, and bounced precariously onto the exit road, Eddie wrestling with the wheel all the while. The sound of the police siren seemed a long, long way away.

'Now all we've got to do is turn into the estate . . .'

A car horn blatted angrily behind them as Eddie crossed lanes and headed for the nearest right-hand turn into the estate. He could see a car up ahead, travelling towards them. But this was no time for the highway code, no time to give way politely to traffic on the right. Eddie jammed down hard on the accelerator and swerved sharply in front of the oncoming car. Rennie gripped the dashboard for support, seeing the look of horror on the other driver's face as he slammed on his own brakes.

'Done it!' shouted Eddie as the car roared into the side road.

A young woman was pushing a pram across the road directly in front of them.

There was no way that Eddie could stop to avoid the collision.

'Oh my *God* . . .'

Eddie pulled the steering wheel sharply to the left; saw the look of fear on the girl's face, yanked harder again at the wheel . . . and the car flashed by her, the draught of its passage whipping her hair across her face. Was that a baby crying in the pram? thought Eddie almost dreamily, Or is it the sound of the tyres? as the car *whumped* onto the pavement on the other side of the road, bounced . . . and ploughed explosively through a stone garden wall.

There was a four-foot drop on the other side of the wall. The car nose-dived into it, engine racing, shattered bricks flying. When the car connected with the ground again after its swan dive, Rennie saw the bonnet buckle instantly as the radiator grille embedded itself in garden soil. He saw it all happen in a dream; saw himself leave his seat on impact, saw himself flung through the ragged aperture of the windscreen and bounce on that bonnet. He bounced . . . and flew away, into a dark place.

The car stood on its snout for what seemed a long, long time. Eddie was trapped behind the driving wheel, which had been shunted forward into his chest on impact. His left forearm and hand were somehow entangled in that bent steering wheel.

That's not right, he thought, as the car began to topple over, wheels racing in empty air. *My hand shouldn't be bent like that, my arm shouldn't look twisted like that* . . . And then the car slammed all the way over onto its roof.

A great black steel door crashed shut in Eddie's mind. There were no dreams.

* * *

But he was dreaming now: dreaming of the crash . . . and of babies crying, police sirens wailing, tyres screeching and of words . . . loud, echoing, stentorian words . . . words which became . . .

7

The Judge's words echoed in the stark, brick prison cell which was also Eddie's sleeping mind; a cell within a cell within a cell:

'Edward James Brinkburn. The jury have found you guilty of aiding and abetting in a particularly vicious robbery, a robbery which resulted in the garage proprietor — Mr Siegel — suffering appalling injuries, leading to partial paralysis. Mr Siegel's business premises also suffered considerable damage. I hope that you will have had time to reflect during these proceedings on the consequences of your actions. I am advised by the Chief Medical Officer's reports that as a result of the crash, following a police chase, your left arm is temporarily paralysed. Similarly, two of your accomplices in this particular attack did not emerge from the incident without paying the price of their vicious and premeditated actions. Anthony Everett Bell and Rennie Montresor have already received sentence for their parts in this crime. Robert Sheraton will not be answerable for his part in these proceedings until he is discharged from intensive care.

'It is now my duty to ensure that the public at large are protected from men such as yourself, men who — as members of an organised criminal syndicate — have no compunction about resorting to the most hideous and brutal violence to attain their ends — in this case, a cowardly and vicious assault on an honest and respectable businessman.

'I therefore sentence you, Edward James Brinkburn, to serve a sentence of five years' detention at Her Majesty's pleasure . . .'

'*How much do you hate?*'

'Tracey!' Eddie sat bolt upright in bed, face glistening with sweat, gasping for breath. 'Oh God . . .' And then, quietly, as he lay back in what felt like his coffin, 'I'm sorry, Rennie. Why didn't I listen to you?'

'*How much . . .*"

8

'How are you, Eddie?'

'I'm okay, sweetheart.'

'How's your arm? Getting better?'

'Fine. Getting the feeling back now. Might be able to help Rennie in the workshop soon.'

'How are they treating you?'

'Not so bad. I've got Rennie to talk to. It's worse for him 'cause he's black. He gets some stick sometimes. Not when I'm around, though.'

'I was reading . . . reading things in the newspaper . . . about some of the things that happen in prison. Bad things, Eddie. Men going with men and stuff. In America . . .'

'This isn't America. Don't pay any attention. It's not like the television or the movies.'

'Oh God, what did you *do* it for, Eddie?'

'Do you really have to ask me that, Tracey? Don't you think . . . now, come on . . . don't cry . . . it's okay . . . okay . . . We needed the money to go private. To get you off that waiting list for the operation . . .'

'But it would have been *dirty* money, Eddie!'

'I don't care what kind of money it would have been. It would have got you that operation. I wanted to look after you, love.'

'I need you outside, not *inside*. God, Eddie. The kids need you. Why d'you *do* it? Why? All we had to do was wait. You could have looked after the kids when I'm in hospital. But now you're here and I'm . . .'

'I know . . . I know . . . *fuck* it!'

'Be quiet. They'll hear you.'

'You're only twenty-eight, for Christ's sake. It's not fair. Just not fair.'

'Heart bypasses aren't so risky these days. The doctors at the Welfare were telling me.'

'Yeah . . . but what about the bloody waiting list?'

'Only three months to go now, Eddie. That's all . . . just three months . . .'

9

In the machine shop, sliding underneath the Governor's car, Rennie also slid into another of the fantasies which had kept him sane for the past eighteen months. Rennie was that super-cool, black dude from the old series "Mission Impossible"; the guy who was the electronics, mechanical expert; the guy who could put a bug in a can of beans or turn a Sony Walkman into a quadraphonic stereo-system with two spoons, a bent penny and the spring out of somebody's biro. And now, Rennie the supercool dude was under the Governor's car, pretending to fix the exhaust but, in reality, cutting a secret compartment into the bottom of the car. Rennie could envisage it clearly. He and Eddie would both slide under the car tomorrow, hoist themselves into the secret compartments and lie tight. Then, when the Governor drove out of the prison and into town on his way to the 'Annual Lock-'em-Up Convention', they would pop up on either side of him.

'Put your foot down hard, Governor. This is a "Mission Accomplished".'

'What?' said a passing pair of legs.

'Nothing,' replied Rennie, grinning.

The legs vanished and Rennie continued, playing and replaying the fantasy over and over again for better effect. This was a good fantasy. He would keep it for future use.

Two more pairs of legs appeared in his line of vision: one clearly in a prison warder's fabric; the other, the grey jeans of a prisoner.

Grinning again at this fantasy, Rennie returned to his work.

'Where's the spade?' said a voice.

'Maybe he's under the car,' came the reply.

Rennie's grin faded. A new feeling crept over him. Something was going to happen. He was going to hear something he didn't want to hear. The safe part of him urged that he should make a noise, any noise, so that the owners of the voices would know that he was there. But then the owner of the first voice, the prison guard, said:

'Naw. I think I saw him up on level seven chewing the fat with Brinkburn.'

And Rennie knew that it was now or never, if he wanted to get out of this safely; all he had to do was bang his spanner on the exhaust pipe or scrape the undercarriage trolley he was lying on. But another voice, just as scared, but more to do with survival, made him stay quiet. If something bad was in the air and he didn't get to know about it, how could he avoid it and survive?

'So what's the deal, Mr Fisher?'

Fisher! That bent bastard . . .

'There's a possibility that the guy who does it and doesn't get fingered might have probation brought forward.'

'No offence, Mr Fisher. But it seems to me we've heard that story before. I think what's needed is something more practical.'

'Like?'

'Like a grand outside waiting for the guy on release. A numbered account. With interest, of course?'

That's Toddy Brooks. I'm sure it is.

'That's a possibility.'

'And we need to know who the instruction comes from. Gives more credibility to the sub-contractor to know who his contractor is, if you know what I mean.'

'I know what you mean. The instruction comes from Tony Bell in Wandsworth lock-up . . .'

Oh, God no . . .

'. . . on behalf of Sheraton.'

Oh Bloody Hell, NO!

'Sheraton wants Brinkburn frightened . . . and damaged.'

'What, just for fucking up a garage job? Didn't know Sheraton's mob cared so much about hired men. Maybe I should get myself shot in the leg like Tony Bell.'

'Bell's got nothing to do with it. It was the other guy on the job – Bobby.'

'Oh yeah? And who's he?'

'Sheraton's younger brother.'

Rennie felt as if his stomach was going to crawl up through his torso and out of his mouth. He swallowed to control the nausea, eyes tightly shut.

'Bloody hell,' said Brooks. 'What's Sheraton's brother doing on a street job? Guy like him should be spending his time in penthouse suites or on a bloody yacht in the Med somewhere, not getting his hands dirty on something like that. Sheraton's people pay *other* people to do jobs like that . . .'

'That's the point. Kid felt he needed street cred.' The warder laughed. 'Sick of doing nothing, he said. Sick of the quiet life. Felt he needed some experience of action on the street. So he muscles in on a street job without letting his elders know and ends up getting fried. Third degree burns. Intensive care. Nasty.'

'I get the picture, Mr Fisher.'

'Reckon Bobby Sheraton looks like something out of a horror film now. Tony Bell reckons it was Eddie Brinkburn's fault, so Sheraton's taken his word for it.'

'Eye for an eye?'

'Fifty-fifty. Sheraton also wants Brinkburn to keep his mouth shut about the car operation aspect.'

'And what about Montresor?'

'Damage him as well. Nothing serious. Just enough to make him keep his trap shut.'

'A grand, Mr Fisher? Plus my commission, of course.'

'I think that'll be okay. I'll get word back to Bell in Wandsworth. You got somebody in mind for the job?'

'Leave it to me . . .'

The legs disappeared.

Rennie breathed out slowly and carefully, waiting for a full ten minutes before he slid out from beneath the car on the far side, beside the machine shop wall. Peering over the bonnet of the car, he could see no sign of Fisher or Brooks. The other prisoners in the machine shop were carrying on with their work, supervised by the warders. Wiping his hands, Rennie flitted round the car and down the centre aisle. At the far side of the workshop, he could see Mason, Security Warden for the workshop, standing at the security check-out. Work here was for the cons who kept their noses clean, and it was Mason's job to search each person passing in and out, before and after work. Any prisoner violating the rules by trying to smuggle material in or out could never expect the privilege of working here again. For many of the cons who were used to working with their hands — Rennie included — the workshop was *the* place to be, the only place where he could do real work, the work he had been used to on the outside; and he valued that work above all. It was the only place where he had *purpose*. There was no way of knowing now whether Fisher had discussed Rennie's whereabouts with Mason. Fisher was bent — everyone knew that — but Mason was straight; so perhaps there was nothing to worry about.

Rennie first steeled himself and then breathed out again heavily, trying to expel the tension which had coiled up inside him. Then he gangled down the centre aisle, past the lathes and the other machines, towards Mason. He tried to whistle and then immediately gave it up when he couldn't find the spit.

Mason looked up from the security gate. Rennie grinned, feeling the strain of that forced smile on the corners of his mouth. He held his arms wide for a body search as Mason stepped towards him.

'Clean, Mr Mason.'

'Not from where I'm standing, Monresor. More oil and gunge on you than on the Governor's car.' Mason smiled as he began the usual routine, patting Rennie's side pockets and around his waist, clearly not wanting to dirty his hands. The smile was enough to relax Rennie. 'Okay, go and wash.' Mason unlocked the cage and Rennie strolled easily through. At the end of the corridor, he ran to the showers, checked them out — there was no sign of Brooks amidst the cons who were showering there. Casting anxious glances at the security cameras set into the corners of the shower-room and wondering whether Fisher was up there somewhere watching him, Rennie showered quickly and vigorously.

He could still smell the fear on his skin when, later, he headed quickly for Level 21 to tell Eddie what he'd overheard.

10

Eddie and Rennie walked slowly round the perimeter fence of the recreation yard.

'So Sheraton wants to put the frighteners on us . . .'

'What the hell are we going to do?'

'Maybe we can put the record straight. Tony Bell's given Sheraton one side of the story. He was the one who allowed Sheraton's brother to go along on that job, and kept quiet about it. He knows what happened. And he knows that we didn't screw anything up. He's told Sheraton a load of fucking rubbish to cover his back. We've got to make sure that our version of the story gets fed back.'

'We could just go to the Governor. Tell him what's going on. Maybe we'd get solitary for a while, some protection.'

'What, you mean in E Block with the child molesters and the perverts? No way. I'd rather take a hiding than do that.'

'Well, maybe that's the answer. Maybe we just sit tight and wait for it to happen. Let them do it . . . get it over with. We lose a few teeth, get a couple of broken ribs. Maybe that'll keep them happy.'

'Maybe . . . maybe . . .'

11

'Come in, Brinkburn.'

George Frobisher, Prison Governor and true believer that criminals are born and not made, gestured to the seat in front of his mahogany desk. Eddie noticed that Frobisher, as usual, was avoiding any eye contact with him; as if criminal tendencies were somehow contagious and could even rub off on the Governor himself.

Eddie heard the office door being closed gently behind him by his escort warder as he crossed the worn carpeted floor to the proffered seat. Faded Victorian prints adorned the plain pastel walls. Eddie wondered whether Frobisher pined for the good old days when institutions were places of real punishment with no interference from bleeding heart liberals or social reformers. He sat down.

Frobisher seemed more nervous than usual today. Fidgeting with the papers on his desk, he finally appeared to give up on them before shoving them into the top drawer of his desk. Then he sat back, sighed, and knotted his fingers in a cat's cradle. The ancient office chair creaked as he rocked back and forth, eyes still down.

He looked up. For the first time, he looked directly into Eddie's eyes. He gave a tired, tattered smile, exceedingly worn at the edges. Eddie did not like that look.

'Something wrong, Mr Frobisher?'

Frobisher cleared his throat. The smile was more like a grimace. 'I don't think there's really any easy way to say this, Brinkburn. I'm afraid that you must prepare yourself for a very bad shock.'

'Yes, Mr Frobisher.' Eddie was surprised to hear his own voice. It came out automatically, from the grey nauseous pit which had been his stomach. Something bad . . . something very, *very* bad was going to happen. The room was suddenly even more claustrophobic than his prison cell. He could feel the walls and ceilings pressing in on him, their monotonous grey smoothness threatening to suffocate him as he heard Frobisher say:

'I'm afraid that your wife and children have been killed.'

There was a long and empty silence.

'Killed?' *Surely that wasn't my voice*, thought Eddie. 'Killed.'

'A household fire. I'm really terribly, terribly sorry.'

'Sorry . . .?'

'I don't want to prolong this for you, Brinkburn. But I must tell you everything I know at present. It's only right, I think. A police investigation is presently ongoing. It would seem . . . seem . . . that a petrol bomb was thrown through the front window of your council flat. Your wife and children were upstairs, I believe. By the time the fire brigade arrived it was too late to do anything. The flats were ablaze and it was impossible for anyone to get to your family.'

'Family . . .'

'Are you all right, Brinkburn?'

'*All right? Yes . . . all right . . .*'

'The police are investigating, as I say. I believe that they may wish to interview you today to find out if you have any idea who might have done this. To find out if you know of anyone who holds a grudge against you or your family . . .'

'*Grudge.*'

'Brinkburn? Are you sure you're all right? Water? Can I . . .' Frobisher's voice was coming from a faraway place; distant, far away and echoing. The room was suddenly very, very dark. There was a buzzing in Eddie's ears.

Now, strangely, he was being led away by the same guard who had brought him to the Governor's office, although

46

he had no recollection of leaving the room. They were walking back along the corridor and the guard was talking to him. The words failed to register. The walls of the corridor were crowding in, sharpening and shrinking as they walked. Somewhere, Eddie could hear a new, familiar voice; a voice coming from the same dreadful pit. It was Archie Duncan, the madman, and he was saying:

'*How much do you hate?*'

They turned into the corridor leading to the engineering block, feet clattering and echoing. Fellow prisoners passing them seemed to be staring at Eddie, as if they could somehow sense that his real world had disappeared and he was now living a dream. The guard was still talking, sympathetically by the tone of his voice, but none of the words registered with Eddie as they walked along. Archie Duncan's voice faded into a whisper and was now replaced by another.

'*We've gotta watch out, man,*' said Rennie. '*Sheraton wants to put the frighteners on us. I heard it. Under the car. We've gotta keep together . . . gotta keep near the guards during recreation . . . gotta . . .*'

'*How much do you hate?*'

Rennie was standing outside his cell on the catwalk, looking down into the central part of the prison, when he saw Eddie and his escort guard coming back through the security gate below. For some reason, the guard was holding him by his paralysed arm, almost steering him, and Eddie was letting him do it. The guard was talking earnestly but it seemed as if Eddie was too preoccupied to take any notice. Instinctively, Rennie knew that something very bad had happened. Perhaps Eddie had told the Governor about the threat? Maybe that was it. Maybe Eddie was being taken into custodial care, transferred to another block. That must be it. Eddie was looking up to the catwalk now as they drew nearer.

Rennie hurried down the nearest flight of iron stairs to meet them. Walking towards them, he felt his stomach lurching as the details of Eddie's white and clearly shocked face became more apparent. Eddie's glazed eyes saw him at last, freezing Rennie in his tracks.

There was a terrifying distress behind those eyes which only confirmed in Rennie's mind that something very, very bad indeed had happened.

'Hiya, Eddie. What's happening?' Rennie's own voice sounded cracked, its attempt at nonchalance a complete failure.

'Move along, Montresor,' replied the guard tersely. His tone only served to underline the electric tension in the air and the glacially distressed yet savage look behind Eddie's eyes.

'How much do you hate?' said Eddie.

'What?'

'Out of the way, Montresor,' said the guard again. 'Brinkburn's on his way to the Infirmary.'

'They killed them, Rennie. Tracey . . . and the kids. My . . . my . . .'

'Tracey?' Bile crested in the back of Rennie's throat. 'Russell and Jane . . .?'

'Montresor! Get the hell out of the way, you black twat, or I'll have you on remand!'

'They killed them, Rennie. Killed them. *Killed them!*'

The combination of ice and fire behind Eddie's eyes had suddenly exploded. He lunged out with his good arm, pushing the guard away from him. Rennie stepped back in alarm. He could see that something inside Eddie had cracked: there was no recognition in his eyes; no recognition of where he was, no recognition of Rennie himself. The guard lunged back and seized Eddie's wildly flailing arm.

'Brinkburn! For God's sake . . . Brinkburn!'

Rennie retreated further, unable to assist. The horror of Eddie's words had enveloped him. Tracey and the kids were dead . . . dead . . . dead . . .

Other warders were running to assist now as Eddie and the guard collapsed in a struggling heap on the tiled floor. Eddie was shouting hoarsely; long wordless yells of pain, anguish and rage.

When they finally carried him away to the Infirmary, Rennie walked slowly to the toilet block, found a cubicle and began to vomit out the horror which had accumulated inside him.

12

Rennie's sleep was tormented again by fever dreams.

And in those dreams, he was in Eddie's house. It was autumn, and night was creeping.

Eddie was saying goodnight to the kids, standing outside their bedroom doorway. Rennie stood not far away in the small passageway that Tracey always referred to jokingly as 'the hall'. He was swirling the ice cubes in his glass and listening to Eddie.

'You going to give 'em hell at the match tomorrow, Russell?'

'Yeah. You coming to watch?'

'Try and stop me.'

'Can I come too?' asked Jane.

' 'Course. Every team has to have a mascot.'

Rennie smiled and turned his attention to the other conversation, taking place in the kitchen. Tracey and Florinda were in there, fixing something to eat. He had met Florinda at a nightclub. She had been the only black woman there and he supposed it was inevitable that he should eventually talk to her. She worked in a hairdressers' and had been *born* in Jamaica, for crying out loud. They had got on like the proverbial house on fire. He had listened to her laughter and decided that he liked that laughter a lot. He listened to her now, laughing with Tracey . . . and liked that sound, too. He liked the conversation that Eddie was having with the kids. He envied Eddie. Maybe soon, he and Florinda . . .?

'Russell wants to ask you something,' said Eddie, patting

him on the shoulder. 'Night, kids.' He moved back to the kitchen and the sound of laughter.

'Night.'

'Night . . . Rennie?'

Rennie entered the small bedroom, gave Jane a quick peck on the cheek in the lower bunk and then stood up again to lean on the frame of the upper bunk where Russell lay.

'Yeah? What is it, soldier?'

'What's it like being black, Rennie?'

'Same as white, son. Why do you ask?'

'Ahmed and Rani are always being picked on by the big kids at school. Ronnie Washburn says it's 'cause they're black and they should go back to their own country. But they say they were born here and this *is* their country.'

'And they're right. When you get older you'll probably hear more white people saying that — kids *and* grown-ups. But skin's skin and it doesn't matter what colour it is, it's what kind of person you are inside.'

'Do white people sometimes not like black people because . . . well, because . . .'

'Come on, Russell. Spit it out.'

'Well . . . daytime's . . . kind of white . . . and night-time's . . . black, know what I mean?'

'No.'

'Well, what about black magic and white magic?'

'Oh, I see . . . you mean the good guys wear white and the bad guys wear black.'

'Darth Vader's all black.'

'So . . . because I'm black, I'm the bogeyman?'

'No! I don't mean that at all, Rennie. It's just what Ronnie . . .'

'Don't listen to any of that bad stuff, son. Like I said, it's what you are on the inside that counts — not the outside.'

'Why do people think that black means bad and white's good.'

'Good and Evil. Black and White, eh?'

'Yeah.'

'Sometimes, Russell, there's no black *or* white in this world.'

'Rennie?'

'Yeah?'

'Are there . . . things . . . in the dark?'

'We still talking about black folks and white folks?'

'No. I mean . . . are there vampires and monsters and things in the dark? For real? Like on the videos?'

'No, son. There's nothing like that in the dark. That's just storybook stuff.'

Darkness engulfed Rennie's dream.

And it began again.

13

It had taken three men to hold Eddie while two more strapped on the 'restraint'. Alone in an isolation cell, he had fallen asleep, drugged and exhausted in his strait-jacket.

On the first three occasions that he emerged from that sleep, he had begun to scream again, requiring more sedation each time.

Now . . . days and nights, sleeping and waking, had lost their meaning for him.

This time, when he awoke, he did not scream.

The room was grey, like everything else in the prison. And he became aware of a tremendous quiet inside himself. Whatever had been making those screaming noises had gone away. Disembodied voices were talking to him, although he could see no other people in this grey, grey room.

'Hello, Brinkburn. Hello . . .? We've given you something to quieten you down.'

'You're in shock, son.'

Shock?

'In the circumstances, there won't be any charges because of your . . . outburst.'

The voices blurred in and out of hearing. Seconds, minutes or days passed . . . there was no meaning to the passage of time. When his consciousness refocused, someone was feeding him with a spoon as if he was a kid again or something.

'Listen, Brinkburn. I've never done no one any favours in here.' He did not recognise the voice. 'But I'm going to do you one now. Word was out that you and Montresor were due for a good kicking 'cause of what happened to Bobby Sheraton. But things are different now. You understand? You listening?'

'. . . listening.'

'Sheraton's brother is dead, Brinkburn. You hear me? *Dead*. He died in hospital. So there's been a change in orders now. You're not just due for some punishment, they're going to kill you. Laverick's got the contract and he's been told to . . .'

'. . . kill . . .'

'Like I said, no favours. But what they done to your kids was, well . . . I got kids myself. Take my advice, Brinkburn. Get yourself into max security. Get Frobisher to do it. If he won't, then break a screw's head so they'll have to send you there. But do it. Do it!'

'Now then, Brinkburn,' said another voice. 'How are you doing?'

The first voice was silenced.

He never heard it again.

14

Rennie shuffled down the queue for food in the main area between cells on the ground floor. He had no appetite again today. Eating was a purely mechanical function, an excuse to leave his cell. The vegetables and meat on his plate had been overcooked and looked like steaming sludge.

He found a seat and placed the tray in front of him, looking at the food as if deciding what to do with it. He began to eat.

It had been three days since Eddie had been taken to the Infirmary. Despite Rennie's enquiries about him, the screws had been keeping tight-lipped about his condition.

Eddie, you bloody idiot. Why didn't you listen to me? What the hell did you have to get involved for . . .?

This was no time for recrimination. Rennie looked idly back to the queue . . . and saw Eddie.

He was nearly at the front of the queue, letting the con on the other side of the table slap the sludge on his plate.

'Eddie?' Rennie began to rise, clearing a space for him to sit at the table.

Eddie was walking towards him, face set and expressionless.

'Good to see . . .' began Rennie.

And then Eddie veered away from the table and headed for another.

Rennie stood up, leaving his food behind, and following him. 'What's wrong, Eddie?' He saw Eddie sit down at another table across the way, lift his fork and begin to eat. Rennie walked over. Now, he could see that Eddie was sitting directly opposite Toddy Brooks. And Toddy was looking distinctly unhappy. He continued to shovel food into his mouth, head down. The other cons were doing their best to ignore both men as Rennie drew level and placed a hand on Eddie's shoulder.

'You okay, Eddie?' Eddie did not look up. Keeping his eyes fixed on Brooks, he asked:

'Where's Laverick?'

'How the fuck should I know?' returned Brooks, keeping his head down.

'Where's Laverick? I don't see him eating here. Tell me where he is, Brooks.'

'Maybe . . . maybe he's in the shower-room, or something. Him and his boys been on special duty again. They always clean up there, you know that.'

Eddie carefully replaced his fork, eyes still on Brooks.

'What do you want Laverick for . . .?' began Rennie. But Eddie was standing up now and turning away from Rennie, heading for the metal staircase leading up to the other levels. Rennie followed close behind. 'Eddie, for God's sake. What's wrong with you?'

Mason was standing at the foot of the staircase, keeping an eye on the cons as they ate. Rennie saw Eddie walk right up to him and stop. He moved to follow, but there was a restraining hand on his arm. It was Frederickson. 'Just get back to your table, Montresor.'

Eddie saw movement at Brooks' table and looked over as Fisher, the bent screw, motioned with one finger and Brooks left the table to walk over to him. They began to talk quietly, Brooks watching Eddie over his shoulder.

The whole chain of events was beginning to take on a horrific and inevitable pattern. Rennie could feel the fear in his guts as Frederickson pushed him back to his own seat, and he heard Mason ask:

'Where do you think you're going to Brinkburn?'

'Shower-room, Mr Mason. Haven't been showered in three days.'

Fisher walked quickly over.

56

'You know the procedures, Brinkburn,' said Mason.

'Please, Mr Mason. I stink.'

'Perhaps we can make an exception in your case,' said Fisher, coming up behind. Mason looked at Brinkburn again, grunted and stepped aside. Eddie began to ascend the metal staircase. Mason moved off, leaving Fisher standing there.

Rennie watched Eddie climb those stairs, watched him reach the first landing and then turn right; listened to his footsteps ringing on the metal. He looked back at the other cons, all getting on with their meals, all unaware or uncaring. And then he looked at Fisher. He was watching him . . . and smiling. Fisher raised his hand and beckoned with one finger, just the way he had done to Brooks. Sick to his stomach, refusing to think of the consequences, Rennie stood up and walked slowly over to him.

'Brinkburn's not in his right mind, is he, Montresor?'

'No, sir.'

'No, sir. That's right.' Fisher smiled again. 'I'm in a good mood today. You'd better go after him and make sure he doesn't piss his pants.'

'Fisher, you . . .'

'*Mr* Fisher, black boy. You want to say something?'

'No . . . Mr Fisher.'

'Good. Better catch up with your friend. Don't want any accidents, do we?'

Fisher stood aside. Quickly, Rennie began to mount the stairs.

15

Eddie could feel the steam of the shower-room on his face like some kind of cloying death mask. The face was not his, reinforcing the out-of-body sensation he had first experienced in the Governor's office. He kept walking; the hollow tapping of his shoes on the tiled floor seemed like distant echoes – they were not his feet at all. He passed the racks of weight-training equipment that Laverick and his boys were so keen on and reached the end of the row of changing-cabinets, just as he heard the crash and clatter of the washroom door behind him. Distantly – in another dimension, perhaps – he seemed to hear Rennie shouting . . .

'For God's sake, Eddie. They're going to *do* you, man! Get out of here . . .'

. . . and then a cry of pain.

Without looking back to see what had happened, Eddie turned the corner and stopped. They were all here in the main tiled area which gave access to the showers themselves, as he had known they would be. Laverick was sitting on a wooden bench, naked except for a pink towel around his white, flabby middle; carefully combing thinning hair to his balding pate. Laverick's boys were all here. Latham and Taylor were leaning against the cabinets, fully dressed, talking and smoking; they looked up in surprise. Beyond, Eddie could see Dunn in the showers, still soaping his body, wreathed in that cloying steam. Laverick looked up and smiled when he saw Eddie.

'Well, look who's here.' The smile broadened into

something that was anything but a smile. 'Saved us the trouble of looking you up, Eddie. Very considerate of you.' He began to rise. Latham and Taylor moved forward on either side of him. Latham flicked his cigarette end to the tiled floor. Eddie saw it fizzle in a pool. From outside himself he watched them come. He was made of stone.

* * *

Frantically, Rennie had tried to reach Eddie before he could enter the shower-room. But Eddie had ignored his pleas, staring ahead and walking like some kind of screwed-up zombie or something. Eddie had pushed through the shower-room door which had crashed against the inside wall. Now he was inside the washroom, where Rennie knew that Laverick and his men would be. Eddie must be trying to commit suicide. There were no prison screws here: this was Laverick's place. The door slapped shut behind Rennie as he called Eddie's name, in time to see him turning past the changing-room cabinets into the shower area. Rennie moved forward . . . and then something smashed him to the floor from behind.

Rennie looked up from the cold, tiled floor, tasting salt in his mouth. Angel — one of Laverick's 'minders' — loomed over him, smiling.

'Can't get in without a tie, son. This is Mr Laverick's establishment, you know that.' He grinned.

Rennie tried to clamber to his feet. Moving quickly, Angel placed a foot on his chest and pressed down hard, pinning him to the floor. 'Now you wouldn't want to interfere would you, Mr Montresor? Mr Laverick and the lads are in there. I'm sure they'd rather you didn't interrupt them. They'll get around to you in due course, son. Just be patient.'

Rennie looked up a Angel's grinning face.

* * *

Laverick paused, running the comb across the threads of hair smeared to his scalp, eyes still fixed lasciviously on Eddie. Latham and Taylor were on either side of Eddie now, their casual manner failing to conceal the threat and the fact that Eddie could no longer turn and run for it.

'Little bit of a commotion going on back there, Eddie? Seems to me like I heard the spade's voice.' Unblinking, Laverick raised his voice, echoes bouncing from the tiled walls: *'You got Mr Montresor back there, Angel?'*

Distantly: *'Yeah!'*

'Then bring him along for the party.'

Distant, but getting louder: the sound of someone being dragged like a bundle of rags along the tiled floor to the showers.

Eddie watched and listened. The dream continued. He watched Laverick look over his shoulder and smile. The dragging, slithering sound was closer now, right behind Eddie. A kick. A grunt of pain.

'Black sod . . .'

Laverick moved past Eddie's left shoulder, joining Latham and Taylor at the cabinets, both of them grinning. Laverick began to pick at his teeth.

Still made of stone, Eddie became aware of Rennie crawling on the tiled floor at his feet, clutching his chest where Angel had kicked him. More than anything, Eddie wanted to bend down and help him. But something told him that the time was not right yet.

'Laverick . . .' Rennie spat blood onto the tiles, grimacing and looking up. '. . . you can't do it. You can't kill him in here and get away with it . . .'

Laverick looked at his sycophants. Prompted by his odious smile, they began to laugh.

'Kill, Mr Montresor? Strong words. This isn't a kill, it's a bloody suicide.'

Laverick looked back at Eddie, still smiling. But now, his smile was fading. Something about the way that Brinkburn had casually strolled into the shower-room, when he must know by now what was in store for him, was beginning to unsettle Laverick in a peculiar way. If Brinkburn knew what was in store, why wasn't he hiding away somewhere; keeping out of sight, or crawling to the screws to protect him? Why the bloody hell had he just walked in like that? Brinkburn's inexpressive stare remained fixed on Laverick. He didn't seem to care.

'Anything to say?' Laverick's irritation was turning to a kind of unease.

'You can't do it, Laverick.' Rennie struggled to a sitting position. 'You're gonna have to do me as well. Nobody's going to believe in two suicides.'

'Shut your face, Montresor! A double suicide's easy enough to arrange. Lots of pipes in here on the ceilings to hang things from. Easy enough to spread the rumour that the pair of you were gay. Same business, same crime, same cell . . . oh yes, the same cell: we all know what goes on in there after lights out, right lads? Terribly depressing in here for two sensitive gayboys. What else could they do but have a lover's pact? Say goodbye to it all.' Laverick looked back at Eddie, a man standing like a statue. 'Well? Like I said before – any last words?'

Laverick took a step forward. Eddie could see the others moving in on either side, on the periphery of his vision.

Laverick's single step forward provided the trigger, the moment Eddie had been waiting for. In an instant, a series of thoughts flashed across his mind: a National Health waiting list that was too long, Tracey, the kids, two years in prison loving them and not being able to be with them. And then Eddie lunged forward to meet Laverick, head-butting him with a jarring smack! across the mouth. A grunt boiled up from Laverick's innards and back again as his hands flew to his face. He staggered back, bent double, blood seeping like molasses between his fingers in string-like traces. For a long instant, Laverick's cronies were frozen in place, the sudden attack taking them completely by surprise. Laverick straightened again, staggering, a gurgled croak of horror and pain bubbling into a red-mouthed scream of rage when the hands moved away from his face and he saw the scarlet, sticky handfuls of broken teeth.

'You . . . you . . . *Shtring him UUPPP!*'

Inertia had taken possession of Eddie again. His rage and horror had been vented in that one moment of brutal violence. He stood, trembling, hands clenched at his sides, as Latham and Taylor moved in on him at last. He could see Latham's fist coming but was powerless to avoid it. The world tilted. He hadn't felt the blow at all, but now he was lying on the tiled floor looking up, and all hell seemed to have broken around him. Dazed, he became aware that Laverick was yelling . . .

'Don't mark him, you idiotsh! Jusht shtring the fucker up . . . Shtring him up!'

And now there was another high-pitched screaming and a flurry of movement. Turning, Eddie saw that Rennie, still prone beside him on the floor, had lunged upwards and grabbed Angel firmly by the balls. He was hanging on grimly as Angel contorted, hugged himself double and clawed at Rennie's unrelenting grip as he toppled in slow motion to the floor, face white and teeth clenched. Then there were hands on Eddie's neck, hauling him up from behind. The inertia dissipated as he felt his windpipe being closed and blue and white sparks began to dance behind his eyes. He lashed out backwards with his good arm; once, twice — a third time, and he had connected with someone's ribcage: Another gasp of pain and the grip was gone. Dunn was running naked from the shower towards them, slipping on the tiles and falling *slap* to the floor as Eddie swung a wild and uncoordinated punch at Laverick's flabby white figure. Surprisingly agile for his bulk, he dodged it, towel falling from his waist to reveal shrunken genitalia, but not agile enough to avoid Eddie's flailing form behind that punch as their bodies collided. The impact flung Laverick backwards over the wooden bench, spindly legs thrashing. Eddie swung back, rage now replaced by a sickening fear in his guts. Rennie was hanging onto Angel's balls, shrugging up tight on the floor as Latham aimed a kick at his head — missed and caught him on the shoulder. Something hit Eddie in the side, pain exploding in his ribs. He doubled over as Taylor withdrew his fist, grabbed a hand of Eddie's hair and swung another punch which hit him on the ear. Unable to use his paralysed left arm, which flapped lifelessly at his side, Eddie head-butted Taylor in the ribs, grabbing him around the waist with his good arm as they crashed backwards against the cabinets.

* * *

Fisher looked back over his shoulder, checking the door. Then he looked back at the security camera screen, smiling. He turned down the sound reception until the clashing, clattering echoes were only a series of small, tinny reverberations, and licked his lips: This was good. This was *really* good. He adjusted the axis tilt on the camera and focused the zoom.

Better than television, laughed Fisher. Leaning forward, he opened the main console beneath the camera screen, reached inside and yanked out a wire. The image on both screens sparked and died. 'Lights out, Mr Brinkburn,' he said aloud, closing up the console and leaning back in his seat. In ten minutes, after it was all over, he would report the breakdown.

* * *

Rennie clung on tight to Angel, realising that this was the only chance he had to help Eddie and himself. Resisting Angel's clawing hands on his tightly clenched fist, he could see the others laying into Eddie. The intended 'cover-up' was blown now: no gay suicide scene. Blood had been drawn and now, Rennie knew, Laverick and his men only wanted to damage and kill with no thought for future consequences. Angel's face was a ghastly white; he was making little baby noises, on the point of unconsciousness. *Come on, you bastard!* thought Rennie. *Pass out!* He squeezed harder, savagely. Angel spasmed, his knees jerking inwards into a tighter foetal position. One knee drove spasmodically upwards, accidentally hitting Rennie under the chin. Stars exploded behind Rennie's eyes; white pain and light flooded his mind. Blurring in and out of unconsciousness, he registered what was going on in the shower-room only in a series of disjointed and fragmented images, as if his mind was tuning in and out of the same television channel. Angel was now completely unconscious, the unbearable pain of Rennie's grip having sent him over. Rennie struggled to an elbow, fell into a brightly lit chasm again and rolled over . . .

Taylor was kneeling behind Eddie, holding him by the arms. Eddie was in a sitting position, while Latham jabbed a vicious punch at his face. Eddie, semi-conscious himself, turned his head. Latham's fist scraped his jaw and connected with his shoulder. Cursing, Latham pulled his fist back, grabbed a handful of Eddie's hair and prepared to deliver the *coup de grace* . . .

'No . . .' Rennie's entreaty turned to a strangled retch . . .

Another hand appeared from nowhere, impossibly large, seizing Latham's whole fist as he drew back for that final punch. Latham grunted in alarm as he was pulled back with terrific force, struggling round from his awkwardly dragged position to see his unknown assailant. Rennie struggled round too, not believing, and Latham started to scream in pain as his fist was slowly crushed. A voice said . . .

'How much do you hate?'

Archie Duncan loomed monstrous and gigantic above Rennie, perspective distorted. Latham pawed at the huge fist which held his and Rennie heard an echoing and unmistakable *crunch* of bone as the grip slowly intensified.

'How much . . . do you . . . hate?' Duncan asked again.

Taylor flung Eddie aside and launched himself at the hulking apparition. There was a thud and slap of flesh as Taylor connected with the giant, the impetus of his charge bundling the three protagonists away from Rennie's line of vision. Another *slap*! as bodies hit the cold, tiled washroom wall. Rennie whited out again, reaching for Eddie. Beyond, Laverick was pulling himself to his feet, chin bloody, eyes stupid.

'Eddie?' Rennie retched again and heard a *clang*! from

behind. He turned awkwardly to see Archie slamming Taylor against a pipe mounted on the wall. The pipe ruptured, suddenly enveloping the three struggling bodies in a gushing cloud of steam which billowed and swamped Rennie, obscuring his vision. He rubbed his eyes and saw Latham rolling out of that hissing cloud towards him, hugging his shattered hand. Rennie blurred out of his television station again, seeing a pair of bunion-ridden feet appearing slip-slap in his line of vision, feet that could only belong to a returning Laverick. In slow motion, just before the white-out, he saw one of those feet glide towards him, felt no physical connection, but knew that he had been kicked in the face.

Rennie slid away. He was flying, through clouds which hissed and boiled and asked: 'How much . . . do you . . . hate?' His mind refocused, and he realised once more where he was − still in the shower-room, not in the sky. The boiling, billowing clouds were from the broken pipe. And the words were being spoken by Archie Duncan. Those clouds were rolling apart long enough for Rennie to see . . .

Eddie on his knees, one good hand braced on the floor, the other hanging limp; looking up, hair dishevelled and matted with blood; a thin stream of saliva hanging like a thread from his mouth. Above him, Archie Duncan was standing in familiar pose: hands rigidly at his sides, eyes staring. There was no sign of the others.

'Do you hate?'

Breathing heavily, Eddie's face registered pain, exhaustion and then . . . slowly . . . rage.

'Do you *hate*?'

'Yes . . .' croaked Eddie at last, face grimacing. 'Yes . . . *Yes, Goddamnit! I hate! I fucking hate! Hate, hate, hate, hate!!!*'

A great cloud of steam gushed around Archie as his face spread into a broad smile; a smile revealing rotten teeth; a smile that bore testimony to some wretched madness, not humour.

Eddie was shaking, breath coming in great racking sobs. 'I . . . hate . . . hate! HATE, HATE, HATE!!'

Archie was leaning downwards and forwards, through the steam, reaching for Eddie. Puzzled, still stunned, Rennie saw the strangely glazed look on Eddie's white face, blood creeping down from his hairline, mingling with the sweat and the steam on his brow. 'What . . .?' began Rennie as Eddie reached slowly up for Archie's hand.

A spasm in the guts cramped Rennie again and he hugged himself, fighting down the bile, teetering on the rim of unconsciousness. He fought back, shook his head the way he'd seen it done in the movies and wished he hadn't when the pain crashed in a wave around the base of his skull. He looked up again: the steam was hissing and gushing, filling the shower room in a surreal billowing of white.

'Where the hell *is* that bastard?' came Laverick's voice from somewhere in the steam. Rennie became aware of three indistinct forms thrashing through the clouds towards them, choking and gasping. 'I want them all dead! Do you hear me, Latham? Find them, Taylor . . .' In a matter of seconds it would all begin again, only this time Rennie knew that the great hulk in front of him would not be able to help. Both he and Eddie were finished, half-beaten to a pulp. And the great grinning giant was taking Eddie's hand, the rotten smile spreading and spreading. Rennie grimaced, expecting to hear the crunching of bone and Eddie's screams.

But something else was happening.

Something which Rennie could not explain. Eddie was smiling, eyes glazed, grin spreading. And Eddie's eyes were somehow reflecting the light in the shower-room, taking on the same maniacal gleam as Archie's. Looking from face to face, Rennie could see that both faces now held that look of glacial madness. There was a noise, which at first seemed to be the hissing of steam, but was now assuming its own identity. It was a crackling, oscillating howling which built in intensity as Rennie watched. Something was happening to Archie's eyes.

Archie's eyes were now somehow gone, the sockets filled

with a powdery white light which undulated and cast black garish shadows on his face; as if his head had become a bloated Halloween turnip, lit from the inside.

'Eddie . . .?' began Rennie again, looking back at him.

Eddie's eyes had vanished, too. The same boiling white light was spilling from his eye sockets onto his cheeks. He was still grinning. And now, behind Archie and Eddie, Rennie could see two forms emerging from the clouds of steam beyond.

'Got them!' said Taylor. 'Got the fuckers!'

'Cream the bashtards!' said Laverick through broken teeth. 'I want them *dead*!'

Rennie had time to see that one of the silhouettes was holding a length of pipe, taken no doubt from the broken bracket on the far wall from which the steam had come gushing. He watched as it was raised above Eddie's head with a hideously deliberate slowness, just as the howling, oscillating noise became too much for him. He clasped his hands over his ears, trying to yell at Eddie, trying to tell him to duck.

As the sound swelled to an unbearable pitch, there was a loud SNAP! as if something had been switched off. The 'snapping' had an instantaneous effect on Rennie. He felt his consciousness slipping away irretrievably. He had slid from bad dream to bad dream, but this latest dream was one he was glad to get away from. None of it made any sense as the white-out faded to a deep gulf of blackness. Archie's eyes. Eddie's eyes. The glowing light. The identical look on their faces. The noise that had threatened to burst his eardrums. He was better out of that dream. But the last part of this particular dream was probably the worst part. The noises he heard just after the loud snap and his final descent into oblivion horrified him more than anything else he had heard or seen and he was glad to be away from them.

Those horrible noises, fading to nothing as he faded away from the hellish shower-room.

Those horrible *tearing* noises; those wet, ripping noises.

But worse.

The screaming that accompanied them. The sounds of men screaming desperately and hoarsely and in mortal agony. The pleading and the crying and the animal-like sounds those men made as the ripping went on and on and on . . . Rennie faded away completely to a safe place.

16

Archie stood for a long time, head down, waiting. When it was time, he moved to the steam valve and turned it slowly and methodically until the clouds of steam had faded to nothing from the ruptured pipe. When the steam stopped, he stood back, head still bowed and waiting again.

After a while, he moved back to the centre of the shower-room, pushed aside a wooden bench and reached down. Hoisting Eddie's limp form effortlessly, he slung him over his right shoulder like a sack of potatoes. Squatting once more, he grabbed the black man by the collar and stood up slowly, as if performing some elaborate weight-lifting exercise. The collar ripped but held firm as Archie stood, drawing up the limp form until Rennie's head was at shoulder height. Stooping quickly and flicking Rennie over his left shoulder, Archie straightened smartly again, shrugging the black man's body farther over his shoulder until the balance was right. A white man on his right shoulder, arms and legs dangling; a black man over his left.

Archie moved slowly and purposefully across the shower-room, skidding once in a dark pool beneath him. Halting to regain balance, he went on again slowly. Head down, burden still dangling limply, he walked down the length of the changing area to the main door.

It opened.

Somewhere behind him, the steam valves began to turn again and the washroom filled with steam once more.

Archie went out into the corridor. There were no sounds, no echoing voices, no clang and clatter, no bustling activity.

No movement. No guards to stop him and ask what was going on. No querying looks from fellow prisoners. No one. Nothing. Archie kept walking, footsteps ringing and echoing. The walk to C Block took thirteen minutes. In that time, he traversed four corridors and passed through two manned security barriers without obstruction or challenge.

At the main corridor to C Block, he stopped, head down and waiting. After a while, he continued through the main service area, ascending the steel staircase leading to Level 21 of the first catwalk. Turning smartly left at the top of the corridor, he walked half-way down and stopped outside Cell 223.

He turned to face it.

After a while, it opened.

Archie entered.

The room contained two double bunks and a sink unit. Frosty lights spattered the one cell window, which was barred. Carefully, he leaned down until Rennie began to slide from his shoulder. Just at the point where the black man was beginning to fall, he nudged his shoulder inwards and the impetus shoved Rennie in the right direction. He sprawled across the lower bunk. Then Archie took Eddie in both hands, like a father with a small child. Gently he raised him to the top bunk and laid him on it, carefully arranging Eddie's head, arms and legs into a sleeping position. He stood back, looking at Eddie. After a while, he leaned down again and arranged Rennie's body in the same position.

He stood back, head down. And waited.

He walked out of the cell, back down the corridor. He descended the silent staircase to the service area and continued down the main corridor to A Block, silently passing the security barrier. After ten minutes he had reached Cell 344. He stopped in front of it as he had done with the previous cell, and when the door opened, he entered.

The door closed behind him.

Archie waited for the sound of the closing door and

moved into the centre of the empty cell. He braced both hands against the small communal bench and pushed it up against the far cell wall, beneath the barred window. Grunting, he clambered up onto the table, first on all fours but then rising until his face was level with the window. He reached down to his waist and unhooked his leather belt — a belt which he should not be wearing. Passing the belt round one of the window bars, he secured it with the buckle and wrapped the other end twice round his bull-thick neck, taking the loose end tight in his other hand to keep it in place.

Then he kicked the table away from beneath him in one savage gesture.

17

Eddie struggled from a dream world of broken glass, only to find that splinters seemed to be embedded behind his eyes. The rolls of barbed wire which crawled with animated and deadly intent through rolling clouds of steam now seemed to have wrapped themselves around his brain.

Hangover, thought Eddie. *That's all. It's a hangover.*

His eyes refused to open, the pain biting behind his eyes and coiling looplike around the base of his skull.

It's Sunday morning. I was out last night with Rennie on the town. We had too much to drink, as usual. Now all I need is a couple of Solpadeine and a good breakfast. He smiled through the pain, eyes still closed, pushing himself up on one elbow. He took a sniff at the air, expecting the smell of bacon and coffee; the sounds of Tracey in the kitchen, the kids playing with their toys in the living room.

'Tracey . . .'

The air smelt cold, sharp with the tang of disinfectant. Eddie's stomach curdled and the hollow horror of his surroundings flooded his soul. The fact that he had called Tracey's name and she wasn't there — was dead — filled him with an anguish he had fought to hide from. Bile rose to his throat and he clasped his hand over his mouth, seeing for the first time the ragged cuts on his knuckles and the dried blood. When he moved, his entire body ached; his legs, his good arm. The jagged glass stabbed into his optic nerves again as he finally swung down from the bunk to the cool tiled floor. The cell zoomed in and out of vision as if through a focusing lens. Eddie grabbed for the bunk to steady himself.

Rennie stirred, groaning. Eddie could see that there was blood on his mouth; thick, like lipstick. There was another dark stain on the side of his blue shirt.

'Rennie . . .' He swallowed his voice. It had come out *wrong*, like some other person's voice, not his own at all – somehow hollow and echoing. Rennie began to push himself up from the bunk. Eddie watched his look of puzzlement spread and grow.

'What the hell are we . . . we . . . doing *here*, Eddie?'

Eddie started to say that he could not remember anything. And then it hit him hard. The recollection swamped and absorbed him, his stomach shrivelling as he clutched the iron bunk frame and fought not to collapse.

The shower-room. The boiling clouds of steam. The knowledge that Laverick and his cronies were going to kill him at last, but now he didn't care. He didn't care, because there was a chance that he might be going where Tracey and the kids were. And then he had seen that face emerging from the clouds of hissing steam – Archie Duncan's disembodied, mad face rising like the head of some swollen cobra. Eddie was mesmerised by those glittering cobra eyes, now burrowing somehow with a new and unfathomable intelligence that had never been there before, as Archie asked . . .

'How much do you hate?'

. . . his voice blending with the steam in a sibilant release. And now, in response, the two years of incarceration, Tracey's long and wasting illness, her death, the kids, the threat of being beaten to death: all these things had swelled in Eddie's chest until he was shaking in an uncontrollable rage, a rage which was somehow recognised with glee by Archie's glittering cobra eyes. The rage swelled until it must burst physically from Eddie's chest.

And then Archie's eyes had changed.

A howling, undulating, exultant sound had filled Eddie's brain.

And something had *jumped*.

Something had jumped from Archie's eyes. Something invisible but real; something intangible but very, very alive. And it had jumped from Archie's eyes to Eddie's eyes. He had felt them bulge in their sockets as whatever it was had entered them, swarming into his brain. His rage had turned to fear as the unknown force swarmed deep into the secret recesses of his consciousness. At that point, he had fainted.

Now, teeth clenched, Eddie staggered to the basin and turned the cold tap on full, savagely grabbing a scooped handful of water and throwing it at his own face, shaking his head. Behind him, Rennie was climbing groggily from his bunk.

'What are we doing here, Eddie? What the hell happened? Last thing . . . last thing I remember is . . . us getting totalled by Laverick's mob.' Rennie retched. 'My bloody head! What happened, Eddie? How . . .?'

Eddie turned, cold water running from his face, soaking his shirt front, and began to say: 'Archie . . .' And then the alarm bells sounded: claxons echoing down cold, tiled corridors; the sound of warders' clattering feet in the corridor outside; cell doors being slammed shut; shouted orders, prisoners being shunted into their cells.

Rennie moved towards their own cell door. Eddie saw a fleeting glimpse of a blue warder's uniform beyond and then the door was slammed fiercely shut, the sound stabbing fresh hollows of pain in Eddie's eye sockets. Rennie rushed to the door.

'What is it, Mr Frederickson? What's going on?'

Frederickson's face appeared in the door window. 'Washroom showers. Sounds like someone's been done in . . .' The grilled window was slammed savagely shut.

Rennie turned back to Eddie − slowly now, as his own memory returned.

He remembered the eyes.

18

When Frederickson 2134 and Donaldson 5467 reached C corridor, they at first thought that there was a fire. Smoke was gushing through the doorway of the shower-room. Andrews 9855 was just ahead of them and they saw him dragging Phillips 3456 from the doorway as they ran to help. The cons in the immediate vicinity had been moved away.

'Who sounded the alarm?' asked Frederickson.

From the floor, Phillips was coughing and gagging. 'Fisher reported a fault in the security cameras . . . I checked . . . and . . . and . . .'

'We need the fire fighting . . .' began Frederickson.

Phillips was shaking his head emphatically, hardly able to speak. 'No . . . no . . . not a fire . . .'

Donaldson peered into the smoke-filled washroom and realised that it was not smoke, after all.

'Steam pipe . . .' gagged Phillips. 'No fire . . . steam pipe . . . broken . . . and . . . and *Oh, God, God*!'

'What the hell's the matter with him?' asked Frederickson, leaning down to take his arm and then sharply backing off as Phillips convulsed and a stream of vomit was coughed onto the floor.

'In there . . . in there . . .' gagged Phillips. 'I don't believe it . . . *in there*!'

'Stay with him,' Frederickson said to Andrews, taking out a handkerchief and pushing it to his lips. Donaldson followed him into the billowing clouds of steam in the shower-room.

'Shouldn't we wait for . . .' began Donaldson, but it was

too late; Frederickson was swallowed up by the hissing, gushing steam, and Donaldson followed close behind until he could see the grey silhouette in front of him again. The air was heavy with vapour. 'Frederickson,' he called, 'we don't know what the hell's in here. We should wait. There might be a con in here with a knife or something.'

'In that case it's gonna be a con with a broken face,' said the grey silhouette ahead. 'Okay, fun's over! Who's in here? Come on out. We're giving you a chance.' Frederickson coughed and sputtered 'This bloody steam! Donaldson, where the hell's the steam valve in here?'

'In the shower section, I should think,' said Donaldson. 'Up ahead.' He joined him, wafting away clouds of steam with one hand and keeping the other closely over his mouth as they moved forward together. Behind them in the corridor, the sounds of the claxons and the alarm bells suddenly ceased; the only noise now the empty clack of their shoes on the wet tiles, the hissing of the steam and their coughing and spluttering as they moved. Donaldson looked back, unable to see the doorway, wishing that he had been professional enough to question Phillips more fully about what to expect before he had followed the foolishly rash Frederickson. Donaldson knew that every move he made was calculated to gain credit in the Governor's eyes, and if there was any credit here, he wanted a share in it. Let Frederickson forge on ahead if he wanted. If there was some bloody maniac up ahead with a knife or a lump of pipe, waiting to brain the first warder who happened along, then Frederickson could have the privilege of going first.

'Come on out,' called Frederickson again. They had reached the end of the locker corridor, leading down to the shower area. Now Donaldson could see that the steam was emanating from a broken pipe on the far wall. 'Over there. I'll get it.' He moved off through the steam to where he had seen a pressure valve about fifteen feet away. He stepped in something soft and his foot skidded. Quickly regaining balance, he reached the pipe. The valve was scalding hot. Using his handkerchief as an improvised glove, he began to turn the valve. Immediately, the steam began to snuff out from the broken pipe. He continued to twist, seeing Frederickson's figure becoming clearer and clearer from the shoulders downwards. At last, the clouds of vapour ceased to gush and water began to drip from the rent in the broken pipe. The air was filled with a haze which was now beginning to dissolve, gauze-like, swirling away to nothingness.

There were dark pools on the floor, still indistinct because of the vanishing steam. Dark pools . . . and irregular, contorted bundles . . . bits and pieces of something. Donaldson strained to see.

'*OH, MY GOD!*' choked Frederickson.

At last, Donaldson could see what it was that lay torn and strewn all over the shower-room floor. The horror of it refused to register; he just stood looking as Frederickson reeled to the shower cubicle and emptied his stomach as Phillips had done earlier.

At last, the horror did register. But only when Donaldson recognised his skidmark and saw what it was that he had stood on — and when he saw the remains of that disembodied eye, smeared over the toe of his boot like a squashed oyster.

19

CONFIDENTIAL REPORT:
GOVERNOR GEORGE FROBISHER:
HRH HEADLEY PRISON:
File 897/453
INITIAL REPORT PENDING FULL ENQUIRY
AND POST MORTEM.

The purpose of this report is to advise of an incident which took place at the establishment today at ll.35 am. It does not constitute fully substantiated evidence but is intended to give a preliminary indication as to the nature and scale of the event. Investigations are proceeding. It is appreciated that this report will not appear on the official record or files in accordance with normal practice and subject to the judicial system. Hopefully, I believe that I can give information which will bypass the usual procedures and 'tie up' the situation fairly effectively.

At ll.15 am, Warder Phillips 3456 was securing corridor 5 of 'E' Wing in accordance with normal supervision procedures and received a radio alert from Warder Fisher 4765 on duty in the Security Monitor Room that security cameras in the shower-room had malfunctioned and advising that he should investigate. Warder Phillips ascertained on arrival that there appeared to be smoke emanating from the shower-room (see File 675). Investigation revealed that this was steam, not smoke. Five dead bodies were subsequently discovered in a dismembered state (see File 676). Preliminary post mortems are about to be carried out on the deceased.

As previously notified, identification of the prisoners proved initially impossible on discovery of the incident since there had been considerable disfigurement and dismemberment. Although full details will of course be made available to the formal investigation and coroner's court, it is worthwhile recording at this preliminary stage without prejudice that evidence indicates that Archibald Junior Duncan took his own life shortly thereafter by hanging in his own cell. Further, that blood and tissue samples taken from Duncan's fingernails and mouth confirm that the murders were committed by him. The severe breach in security which failed to detect the shower-room incident and allowed Duncan to return to his cell undetected past three manned barriers, is still under investigation. I would also like to refer the Investigating Committee to my memorandum of 26th June 1986 (FMcl/239) reiterating a previously expressed view that Duncan's psychiatric case history made it inappropriate that he be incarcerated at Headley; moreover, that a specialised psychiatric institution would be the appropriate detaining body. You will recall that your response was to point out the current overcrowding problems experienced in general throughout the penal institution . . .

'We were *there*, weren't we?' Rennie finished poking his side with his index finger, sure that a rib must be broken. So far, he hadn't passed any blood in his urine.

'Of course we were there.' Eddie lit a cigarette, leaning back against the cell wall, exhaling blue smoke.

'But there's so much I can't work out. When I passed out, they were just about to kick the living shit out of us. I mean, they were going to *kill* us. And then Archie . . . it was Archie, wasn't it?'

'It was him, all right.' The blue smoke of Eddie's cigarette reminded him of the gushing steam in the washroom.

'And Archie's eyes.'

Eddie looked up sharply. It was as if Rennie had been reading his mind.

'What about them?'

'I dunno. They were . . . kind of . . . glowing, or something. So were yours.'

'It was the steam, that's all. The light was funny in there.'

'So what happened after I passed out?'

'How should I know? I passed out myself. Next thing I knew I was in here again with you.'

'If that's the case . . . how the hell did we get back here? Nobody saw anything, Eddie. Nobody.'

'It was Archie. It must have been him. You heard what the other cons and the screws were saying. Archie finally blew his top. Everybody's been waiting for it to happen. And it's bloody lucky for us that he did it when he did. We were going to end up dead in there. You know that.'

'Where the hell did he come from?'

'It doesn't matter. He just *did*. God knows why we're still alive. We're lucky he didn't tear us apart the way he did with Laverick and the others.' *No man could do what Archie did*, said a little voice in the back of Eddie's mind. 'Afterwards, God knows why, he took us back to our cells.' *How could he? How could he do that unnoticed? How could he get past the screws?* 'His mind was gone. Who knows what his reasons were? And then he went back to his cell and topped himself.' *Why didn't he kill us?*

'I just don't get it . . .'

'Count your blessings, Rennie. We should be dead and we're not. We could have been implicated in Archie's carve-up. And we're not. Let's just be grateful we got away with it.'

'You're right. I suppose you're right.'

Why am being so defensive? Why don't I believe a word of what I'm saying? asked Eddie's little voice.

21

The rain was falling in a dense spray, rinsing all colour from the carefully planted trees and shrubs of Headley Cemetery. Dense grey clouds boiled in the sky, allowing no clear light. The grass hissed around unkempt gravestones, begging to be noticed. Next to Row 43, beneath a willow tree, a small knot of people stood in the rain listening to the intonations of the vicar as the last coffin was lowered into the grave.

No remand. No remission for good behaviour. You've got more than a life sentence. You've got an after-life sentence. You and the kids.

How much do you hate? Archie had asked. And Eddie remembered the flood of rage in the shower-room at the point of death. The rage was still there. He could feel it. But it was buried deep down and distant. It wasn't coming through now with heat. It was cold, hard and flint-like. It spoke to him directly. It told him that he had been buried and that Rennie had been right all along. He had gone along with Sheraton's mob for the ready cash. But they had wanted him heart and soul. He had gone along with them because he needed the cash for Tracey and the kids. But, in prison, he had first been denied his family for five years. Now, he was denied them forever. Sheraton's people had killed them. And they had tried to kill him, too. The time for silence was over. He had kept his part of the bargain by keeping his mouth shut. All that was history now. He had nothing left to lose. The cold ice part of him told him that it was time to talk to the Governor; time to split on Sheraton and do as much damage as possible — limited though that could be. It was time to earn the remission he had been promised. But above all, it was time to get out of prison and begin his own, newly formed plan.

He would destroy Sheraton and everything he stood for. He would personally crush his empire, bring it to ruins. He would personally kill Sheraton with his bare hands . . .

Eddie was wearing a blue prison mackintosh. Water coursed in rivulets down the plastic runnels of the mack from his rainsoaked head. He was unaware of the fact that his accompanying guard had taken off the handcuffs when the first of the small coffins had been lowered into the first grave. Eddie watched as Tracey's coffin bumped from sight. On his left, he knew that her parents were standing beneath a large umbrella; husband supporting wife. He had not acknowledged their presence since there was no love lost between them − not even in their shared grief. He knew that they blamed him for the deaths as surely as if he had been the one directly responsible.

Eddie had no idea who the other mourners could be. Kids' teachers, perhaps? He didn't know. Just as the rain was rinsing all colour from the scene, it seemed to have rinsed all emotion from him, too. He couldn't feel anything. Nothing touched him. He was a dead, hollow shell. The vicar's words seemed jumbled and meaningless. Somehow, the drabness of the funeral and the corroding rain reminded him of the times he had stood in the prison yard and everything had seemed so grey. This was even more intense. He found himself looking around at the trees and the shrubs; the cemetery railings. Looking for a meaning. And he realised that, even from here, he could see the south wall of Headley Prison; just a grey brick patch of wall in the distance, visible between the branches of faraway cemetery trees.

Now he could find that meaning. Death was a prison, too.

He had been put away into that concrete block for years for something he hadn't done. Tracey and the kids were being put away now − also for something that they hadn't done. In fact, they were completely innocent of any crime.

Wouldn't even fiddle the Social Security, she was so honest.
The drab, rinsed-out rain colours matched exactly the drab
non-colour of the prison itself. He had been buried in Cell
223, Corridor 9. Tracey and the kids were being put in Plot
12, Row 14. *Just like a prison. But there's no probation for
you, love.*

He didn't have time to be dead yet. There was a great
deal to be done. He looked down on the coffins for the last
time, and felt the guard's hand on his arm.

'Time to go, Brinkburn.'

'Yeah . . . it's time . . . it's time . . .'

22

'You wanted to see me, Brinkburn?'

'Yeah. I think you know what it's about.'

'I really was very sorry to hear about your family. It couldn't have been easy for you while you were in here, but . . .'

'Yeah, I know. But . . .'

'And if you're here to say that you're prepared now after two years to tell us about your involvement with Sheraton's organisation, then I can't guarantee you the same promises that were made both before and after your conviction.'

'You said . . . everyone said . . . that if I told you everything, my contacts, everything . . . it would reduce my sentence, maybe even give me early probation.'

'That was then, this is now.'

'I want to hurt Sheraton.'

'I know that. But you don't have a bargaining position any more. You really are . . . always were . . . a small cog in the machine, Brinkburn. You've spent two years in prison being faithful to scum.'

'It wasn't that. Not being *faithful*. Not that at all. I was scared for Tracey and the kids. I kept my mouth shut because they said they would hurt them while I was inside if I didn't. Now they've done it. And I'm gonna hurt them now.'

'Talk away, Brinkburn. I'm not guaranteeing anything. And I'm sure you're aware that Sheraton's contacts inside will also know about it eventually. There's nothing I can do about it, you know that. I can't guarantee your safety.'

'I can't be hurt any more. I want you to make it known that I've talked. I've got my own protection now.'

'I can't guarantee . . .'

'You're going to have a dream tonight, Mr Frobisher.'

'What?'

'You're going to keep having those dreams until my early parole comes through.'

'Bad dreams come from guilty consciences, Brinkburn. You're the one who should worry about bad dreams.'

'The first one will come tonight.'

'I'll pass on a report of our conversation, Brinkburn. Someone will be interviewing you soon.'

'Every night until I'm out, Mr Frobisher.'

23

Frobisher heard a voice that, for the past twenty years, he had only heard in his dreams. He knew that he was dreaming now, because he could hear Judith's voice so clearly. He was floating in smoke against a grey expanse; the smoke becoming shrouds of tattered nightgown. There was music playing somewhere, but unlike any kind of music he had heard before, on instruments that did not exist; formless and drifting, like the tattered nightdress. Judith's voice called his name over and over again; drifting away, echoing . . . and returning again with greater and greater insistency; as if that voice was on the end of a swing, each time it drifted farther away on the upswing, it returned closer and more insistent on the downswing. It was a voice he had loved so much, the dearest sound he had ever heard . . . and he wanted so much for it to go away.

'George . . . sweet George . . . my George . . . George . . .'

He strained to change the dream, but the voice remained; twisting and drifting in and out of consciousness, shrouds of that torn nightdress drifting against his dreamscape, impossibly large and small by turns; drifting like underwater weeds in the current of his dream.

'*George!*'

Frobisher sat bolt upright in bed, fear clenched in his teeth. Judith's voice had suddenly seemed to yell directly into his ear. It had been filled with threat and a completely uncharacteristic malice. He exhaled, breathing out the night-time spectres. Wiping a hand across his sweating face he could see by his wristwatch that it was 3.30 am. A sheet was wrapped around his legs in a great coil of linen. There were no blankets on the bed: he must have kicked them off onto the floor. Black-blue shadow lay heavily on the walls and ceiling.

Frobisher thought again of his beautiful Judith. Her pale face and long, curled ginger hair; her pouting lips, the lisp, her green eyes. He had been deeply in love with her. And she had loved him. Much more than that bitch of a woman whom he had married and who had eventually left him. Judith had been kind, generous, affectionate − and very good to him in bed. But she had also been his niece. She had been sixteen, he had been forty. And she had become pregnant.

When he had told her that she must have an abortion, and that she must not tell anyone about their relationship (it would ruin him), she had run away. Two weeks later her body had been retrieved from the river. His secret was safe. But how much he missed her.

Something moved in the bedroom corner; beside the door, in the black, wedge-shaped shadow between the door and the wall.

Frobisher struggled to unwrap his legs from the enshrouding sheet, suddenly feeling straitjacketed and vulnerable. Somewhere deep within that corner-shadow he had seen a glimpse of white fabric. It reminded him uncomfortably of the ragged shroud he had seen in his dream.

'Geoooorrrgggeee . . .'

The slow, dragging, *wet* voice was not from a dream. It was no remaining echo from his nightmare. The voice had come from the corner, from the shadow. And something in Frobisher's stomach seemed to crawl. Even though he knew he was not dreaming, he still willed himself to be awake. And when that limp, white hand emerged from the shadows and beckoned to him; oh God, how he wished he was asleep.

There was something else there in the dark. Something

beyond that cold, disembodied white hand; something that coiled and twisted. Undulating and turning, like snakes or weeds or . . .

It was hair.

Locks of flowing red hair that curled and twisted like the underwater weeds in his dream. The hair framed something white and featureless which Frobisher knew must be a face but, oh God, he didn't want to see a face that had been ten days in the water as the hand reached out again from that mirror-lake of blackness and the figure finally glided out of the pool of dark. Frobisher clenched his hands to his eye sockets, pressing his palms deep. He looked again, shaking his head to clear away the nightmare weeds which still seemed to cling to his mind.

She was still there. And now she was at the foot of the bed. Her nightdress swam in streamers around her white legs, her slender waist, her breasts. But he had been wrong about her face: it wasn't eaten by the fishes. She was smiling, the smile occasionally masked by the streamers of hair which performed the same exotic dance as the dress around her body, teased by wind or water or both. Her skin was a deathly moon-glow white; her lips black-red. Her tiny, pointed teeth were carved from pearl. She was smiling and he knew that she wanted him, just as she'd wanted him on the night before she disappeared. She held her arms wide and moved round the bed, smiling down.

Frobisher was aroused, in spite of the impossibility of the situation, denying the logic of this dream within a dream. He moaned, struggling to move away across the bed on his elbows. Her marble-white face was hypnotising. It *was* Judith . . . and yet it was not. He was fascinated; attracted and repelled. But above all, he was feeling aroused as Judith sat on the edge of the bed beside him and the sudden downward tilt in the mattress dispelled the notion that this was all a dream. An alabaster-white hand skimmed the bed like some white fish hugging the riverbed, passing over the tangled sheet around his legs, hunting for ingress to the warmth. It found a gap and Frobisher drew breath sharply, captivated by Judith's glacial smile; dark, dark lips parting, tongue darting between her teeth. The coldness crept to his groin and Frobisher gasped again as his manhood was enclosed. Raising himself on his elbow, shuddering, he lifted his head for Judith's hungry kiss and probing tongue.

And then Judith opened her mouth wide and retched into his face; a spewing, howling gush of salt-water and seaweed.

Frobisher screamed, clawing at the green-black strands of weed as it gushed from her mouth and encircled his head, clawing away across the bed. Judith stood up, slime and barnacles and small crabs erupting from her mouth in one long, continuous torrent, splattering on the sheet. Frobisher lashed out in horror as an eel squirmed from her mouth and slithered towards him across the bed. Judith's spew trickled to a halt and she began to laugh. It was a hollow, horrifying laugh of dank and filthy drains.

Frobisher scrambled from the bed, the sheet now matted in seaweed and river filth, small living things squirming and writhing within its folds. In horror, he looked back at Judith. Her laughter gurgled away like dirty rain down a waterspout. Now he realised that his first impression of her from the shadows had been right. He did not want to look at her . . . but could not turn away.

Her face was the face of a corpse: dead and ten days in the water. Her features were white and bloated; one eye milk-white and with no iris, the other eye gone . . . eaten by the fishes. Within the empty socket, a small hermit crab had set up residence, its spidery legs scuttling on the bony edges of the skull. Her hair was matted with seaweed. And her body . . .

Judith shrieked with laughter again and flew away backwards into the air, arms held wide. Frobisher shrank back against the bedroom wall in shock as Judith continued her upward ascent, her pale, bloated body slamming into the upper corner of the wall near the ceiling with such force that it caused a splash of water. Filthy rain pattered to the carpet. Her gaze remained fixed on him, the malevolent stare eating into his eyes.

Oh God, am I awake or asleep . . . Oh God . . .?
'You're dead,' croaked the thing from its perch.

Still looking at him, still with that dead smile on her face, Judith began to scrabble up towards the ceiling, her back still pinned to the wall. She reached the upper corner and continued moving, now crawling towards him face-down, like some hideous fly on the ceiling, legs doubled up to her waist, her elbows somehow stuck to the ceiling like spindly fly legs as she began to inch across the ceiling to where he stood. Frozen, Frobisher watched her come, water dripping from her sodden body. She brushed against the light-fitting and it began to sway, throwing crazy, horrible shadows as she continued to come, now more like some hideous spider than a fly, creeping towards the fly which remained trapped in her web in the corner.

!!!I WANT TO WAKE UP!!!

Judith screeched, flinging herself from the ceiling above him, arms spread wide, seaweed hair flying.

Frobisher found the scream inside as the thing enfolded him in its wet shrouds. He collapsed to the floor, vomiting in fear and horror as dead white lips clamped on his own . . .

But now the shrouds were somehow no longer wet and alive. Sobbing, he lashed out and they tumbled aside.

Judith was gone.

For a long time Frobisher just sat and looked at what had attacked him. Then he looked back at the bed. There was no seaweed, no crabs, no eels, no pools of stagnant seawater. He looked back at the floor, and the shroud which he had thrown aside.

It was no shroud.

They were the missing blankets from his bed.

That was all.

Nothing else.

Something scampered over his hand in the darkness, and this time Frobisher went on screaming over and over again.

24

'Eddie?'

'Yeah?'

'You okay?'

'Yeah, I'm all right, Rennie. Just can't sleep, that's all.'

'You wanna talk? About Tracey and the kids, I mean.'

'No. There's nothing to talk about. They're dead. Just like the people who did it. They're dead, but they don't know it yet.'

'What is it, Eddie? There's something different about you. And it's more than Tracey and the young 'uns. Something's happened to you.'

'Get some sleep, Rennie.'

'What's *happening*, man?'

'Not yet, Rennie. Not yet. I'll let you know when it's time.'

25

'So who's your minder, black man?'

Rennie stood up slowly from the car engine, wiping his hands on the cloth. The voice had come from behind him. He turned.

There were two of them – Brooks and Turnbull. Turnbull was looking back over his shoulder, keeping an eye out for the supervising warder in the machine shop while Brooks did the talking. Turnbull was slouching, hands in pockets, chewing gum. Brooks looked Rennie up and down, cocky and arrogant.

'Charmed life or something?'

'What do you want, Brooks?'

'Pretty heavy scene in the showers last week, wasn't it? Big Archie cracking up like that and totalling Laverick and his lads. Some of the screws have been saying that he fried 'em up with an electric cable or something. So badly done over they couldn't tell which piece belonged to who. Do you believe that, black man?'

'I believe everything I'm told in here. I believe you've got to watch your back.'

'Yeah? Well that's the only way to be, isn't it? Thing is . . . I know that there were two other people in that shower-room when it happened. Two people who were due for a bit of a kicking. Now how do you suppose those two got away with it? How come they could just walk away with no one even knowing that they were there?'

'You've got a big mouth, Brooks.'

'Thought you should know – it ain't over yet, black man.

Not by a long chalk. In fact, if anything, things are even worse for you two now. Don't see how you're gonna get out of here at all, actually. Lessen it's feet first in a wooden box, know what I mean?'

'I know what you mean,' said Eddie from behind.

Brooks turned as Turnbull began to fidget. Eddie seemed to have appeared from nowhere, from behind one of the machine crates. He leaned against the crate and Rennie felt glad that he was there. Glad, but still afraid of that new look in his eyes. That strange, dead look.

'Well, just thought we'd let you know how it is, Brinkburn. Do you a favour, like. Sheraton's lads getting done over like that — it's not good for public relations, know what I mean? Doesn't look good in the slammer if the hard lads can't do what they're being paid for.'

'Who did it, Brooks? Who torched my house?'

'I don't know nothing about that, son. Nothing. I just pass messages on, that's all.'

'Like the message you passed on to Fisher about finding someone to put the frighteners on us.'

Rennie saw the look of panic on Brooks' face. 'Who told you that? I never done nothing like that!'

'Yes you did,' continued Eddie. Slowly he pointed down beneath the car. 'Next time you're setting somebody up, make sure you check under the car.'

'Look . . . look . . . I've done you a favour. I've told you Sheraton's mob still want to lay hands on you. Can't do fairer than that, right?'

Brooks backed off, still keeping a wary eye on Eddie.

'There's a bad dream coming your way tonight, Brooks. You too, Turnbull. A real bad one.'

26

Brooks lay on his top bunk, hands linked behind his head, staring at the ceiling. Below, Turnbull was snoring like a buzz-saw. After five years in the same cell, it didn't bother Brooks any more, although at the beginning he had often threatened to smother Turnbull with a pillow if it kept up. No, tonight it wasn't Turnbull's snoring . . . it was something about the way Eddie Brinkburn had spoken to him and, in particular, the look on his face.

In his eyes.

Brooks had seen that look before, and had spent most of the remainder of the day trying to recall it. In his sleep, it had come to him and the realisation had woken him with a start, so that sleep was now impossible.

He had seen that look before in Archie Duncan's eyes.

Crazy Archie Duncan, who had spent most of his time inside walking around like some huge, hulking, fucking zombie, asking everybody, 'How much do you hate?' The same Archie Duncan who had killed a family of six and who, by all accounts, had torn Laverick and his guys to pieces in the shower-room, before killing himself.

There's a bad dream coming your way tonight, he had said, and something about his voice, combined with the look in those eyes, was deeply unsettling.

Below Brooks, Turnbull snored and mumbled something in his sleep before turning over.

'Bad dreams?' said Brooks to himself. 'The worst bad dream I know is getting on the wrong side of Sheraton's mob. So if anybody has to worry about bad dreams, it's you, Brinkburn . . .'

Something moved underneath Brooks. He raised himself quickly onto one elbow. Something hard had moved under the mattress.

'Pack it in, Turnbull.' Obviously, Turnbull had stretched in his sleep or something, and had bumped the bottom of Brooks' mattress.

Brooks felt the movement again: a hard ridge in his mattress, moving across the width. He rolled over and looked over the edge of his upper berth down to where Turnbull lay.

'I said . . .'

Turnbull lay on his front, mouth open, still snoring. He was nowhere near the bottom of Brooks' mattress. The movement came again: a hard, rolling ridge underneath him. In an instant, he had a vision of a live rat inside his mattress eating the stuffing. With a short hoarse cry, he vaulted from the top bunk and landed on the cold cell floor with a smack of bare feet. Turnbull remained comatose, lost in his heavy slumber. *Lazy sod,* Brooks reached back and pulled away the covers from his mattress. He poked with one hand and waited. Nothing. He moved back to poke it again and this time he saw the undulating movement in the mattress itself.

'Fucking *rats*,' he said aloud in outrage. 'Fucking prison is full of . . .' In indignation, he began to move towards the cell door. He was going to hammer on that door until the warder came and moved the bloody thing out of his mattress. And then he was going to get in touch with his lawyer and sue the bastards. Something *ripped* in his mattress and Brooks looked back. What he saw there froze him into immobility.

Something had pierced the mattress from within, something very sharp which glinted metallically but which Brooks could not make out. The thrust of whatever it was had created a vee-shaped mound and now this mound was traversing the mattress from head to foot, the entire length of the bed, with a long and deliberate *riiiippppp*. Brooks started as the bed sheets were somehow twitched away from the mattress to land in a heap on the floor. Turnbull continued to snore, unaware of what was going on above him. Brooks began to blink nervously, not sure what the hell was going on as the mattress began to split open down the middle where the cut had been made; peeling away from the centre like a fish being filleted. Wads of stuffing began to fall from the sides in a tumbling curtain of foam and kapok.

'What . . .'

Something was now forcing the metallic cross-frame within the mattress and the bed frame itself to bulge outwards through the huge rent in the mattress. Brooks could hear the *ping!ping!ping!* of the metal strands snapping under the pressure. Turnbull moaned and turned over. Brooks started to say that he should get out from there, when his attention was caught by the mounds of stuffing which had come from the mattress and which were lying on the floor.

The stuffing was moving.

It was wriggling and writhing like something alive.

PING! Brooks flattened himself against the cell wall as something flew out of the mattress, whirling across the room. It hit the cell door and clattered to the floor. It was a piece of flattened wire from the bed frame. And as Brooks watched, it began to move.

Like a small silver snake, it uncoiled, flattened and writhed on the floor . . . like something in a flame. And Brooks could only watch as it twitched, end-over-end, to the foot of the cell door. Recoiling again in alarm, he gazed fascinated as it flew upwards towards the cell door and jammed in the ridge between the door and the wall. It began to uncurl again and then, like a wasp burrowing its sting, began to wriggle into the almost non-existent gap. Finally it stopped, with three-quarters of its length burrowed between the door and the wall. Wide-eyed, Brooks turned to look back at his bunk. The stuffing on the floor beneath Turnbull was still alive, still wriggling, bunching itself together somehow, tidying itself up. It was a huge blob of wadding now and to the awe-struck Brooks, it looked as if something was somehow *kneading* that wodge of stuffing, turning it into something . . .

Turnbull turned over in his sleep, still unknowing . . . and Brooks felt his flesh freeze as the mattress on the bunk above him finally peeled completely open and something which had been inside it *sat up*.

In the dark, Brooks could see that it was the size and length of a man . . . but not a man. Somehow . . . something had taken the insides of that mattress . . . the wire and the springs and the metal . . . and created the facsimile of a man. It was a wire-cage of a man . . . a tailor's dummy . . . the wire-cage of a man awaiting its coating of *papier mâché* to give it proper shape and substance. And as Brooks watched, the wireman turned on one elbow and looked at him with a face that had no features, only wire strips and tufted plastic. It had no eyes, just the hollow indentations where the *papier mâché* would go. It had no features at all . . . but it was watching him nevertheless; leaning on one elbow and looking at him in a manner so casual that it was terrifying. Below it, Turnbull snored again and turned face up. The thing above looked down at him.

In that moment, Brooks knew what was going to happen. There was a horrifying inevitability about it, but there was absolutely nothing he could do. He was in a nightmare, and the logic of nightmare would determine that he had to stand, frozen, and watch . . . watch . . . watch . . .

He watched as the wire man thrust its long, tubular, wire-framed arm down through the mattress and fastened its metal fingers over Turnbull's face. Turnbull awoke, trying to scream. But he could not scream. The wire fingers were clamped tightly over his face, clamping his mouth shut. He began to make urgent moaning sounds, the sounds someone makes when the dentist has touched a nerve with his drill . . . as the fingers tightened. Brooks wanted to turn and face the wall, to end this dream, to turn away from the horror of it and wake up in his cell, in his bunk . . . with no silently monstrous wire man. But he could only stand and watch as crimson streaks began to flow in a criss-cross, ever-spreading network over Turnbull's face and across his widely bulging eyes. The wire man braced its other arm on the upper bunk frame and began to pull. Slowly, like a thrashing, flapping fish caught on some monstrous angler's line, Turnbull was raised in the air towards the mattress above. He began to claw at the wire arm, his feet thrashing and banging against the sides of his own bunk as he was drawn higher and nearer to the wire man above, and as Turnbull's head finally vanished into the torn interior of the mattress, his hoarse cries turned to horrifying whoops of terror as the wire man's head also burrowed into the hole in the mattress to meet its rising catch.

Brooks was suddenly free of his horror and flung himself at the cell door.

'Help! *Help!* HELPPP!!!'

He hammered with the flat of his hands on the bare door, not wanting to turn round when he heard those slow, wet ripping sounds and Turnbull's voice rose to a high-pitched scream; a scream that issued through teeth that were clenched firmly shut. His hands ached badly, and he hoped that the pain he was suffering in this dream would wake him up; wake him up to find that it was time to get up, time to slop out and go down for something to eat. On the other side of the door, he became aware of movement and the muffled sound of a warder's voice. He hammered on the viewing hatch. Beyond, he recognised the familiar voice of Thirlwell, the warder.

'What the bloody hell's going on in there . . .?'

'*For God's sake, Mr Thirlwell . . . OPEN THE DOOR!!*'

Turnbull's screaming had stopped. Even though Brooks continued to hammer on the door, he could still hear the rustling and *glugging* noises behind him. He also heard the fumblings on the viewing hatch and Thirlwell's curses when he could not open it. And then, with horrifying certainty, Brooks knew that the animated piece of metal he had just seen wedging itself between the door rim and the wall had somehow rammed itself into the fabric of the door-lock and curled around inside it so that it could not be opened. And with an even more horrifying certainty, Brooks knew before Thirlwell began fumbling with his keys at the lock of the door, that no matter what the warder did, he would not be able to open it.

Behind Brooks, there was the sound of further scuffling and movement. He turned, mouth open, hands aching, a feeling of fear lodged deep above his buttocks, like a piece of that metal burrowed deep into his spine. He turned.

The wire man had climbed down from the top bunk and was standing facing him, weaving slightly, hands held stiffly at either side. Through it . . . through the maze of wires and plastic and tufted metal which constituted its ribcage and thorax, Brooks could see the huddled form of Turnbull, sprawled back in his own mattress again, dark splashes on the whitewashed wall and on the ragged blanket. Fluff floated in the air. Where Turnbull's face should have been, there seemed to be an indeterminateness . . . a formlessness of red; a chaotic jumble of which he could make no sense. And when Brooks looked at the wire man's head, he immediately realised what had happened to Turnbull's face.

The wire man had taken it.

It had peeled his face from his head . . . and now the wire man had smoothed it down over the wire frame. It had found the living tissue that would be its *papier mâché* face. It grimaced with Turnbull's face, mouth yawning wide and hollow — and then it opened its eyes.

There were no eyes, just hollow spaces. The jumble of movement around the feet of the wire man, which was the somehow animated wadding and stuffing of the mattress, was now moving upwards . . . and Brooks did not have to look to know that the wadding was crawling up those legs, wriggling into the wire frame and giving the wire man his own substance.

The wire man grinned at Brooks and wagged a disapproving, tubular finger. It turned to the lower bunk again, and somewhere, in a different world . . . perhaps in the waking world . . . Brooks was distantly aware of sirens and of pounding on a door. Somewhere, someone was trying to break into his dream — but could not. The wire man leaned down and began tearing the clothes roughly from Turnbull's body. First the vest, bloodstained and torn. The wire man stuffed it roughly into his thorax. Then Turnbull's trousers . . . the same. When Turnbull was completely naked, the wire man took the dead man by one leg and pulled him from the bunk, discarding the ruined wreck of Brooks' former cellmate on the floor like a huge white, plucked chicken. Turnbull's ruined face continued to leak onto the floor. And now the wire man looked back once, only briefly, to see if Brooks was still watching . . . before it began to rip the lower bunk mattress apart with taloned, metal hands. It began to grab handfuls of the stuffing and wadding . . . thrusting it deep inside its chest cavity, stuffing it down. It continued . . . until its entire wire-framed body was filled with the stuffing of the two mattresses and Turnbull's violated body.

And then it stood up . . . whole and full-bodied and substantial . . . and turned back to Brooks again. It smiled with Turnbull's dead and torn white face.

And began walking towards Brooks.

27

'Hear about Bell?' asked Rennie.

'No . . . no . . . what?' returned Eddie.

'Some of the other cons were saying that he topped himself. Found him hanging in his cell by his belt.'

'Just like Archie Duncan, eh?'

'No way that Bell would top himself like that. It must have been somebody else.'

'Yeah . . . that's what I think, too. Maybe somebody sent him a bad dream.'

'What?'

'Nothing. Maybe it was Sheraton. He tried to get us for what happened to the kid brother. Maybe he got to Bell as well.'

'Sounds about right.'

'One less shit to get even with. Listen, Rennie . . . I want you to be careful when you get out tomorrow. You've done your time. And there might be people waiting for you on the outside, know what I mean?'

'I can handle myself. You're the one who needs to keep his nose clean in here. You've still got another eighteen months to go . . .'

'No, Rennie. I'll be out of here well before then. There's a lot of things I have to do. You find Florinda and . . .'

'She's gone, Eddie.'

'I don't . . .'

'I got a letter. She says she can't handle it any more. Gone off with some . . . businessman, or something.'

'I'm sorry, Rennie.'

'Okay . . . okay . . . okay, I'll sort everything out on the outside. The garage, everything. It'll all be waiting for you.'

'I've done my waiting, Rennie. Believe me, I'll be out sooner than you think.'

28

'What did you mean about dreams?'

Frobisher had been nervously toying with his pencil when Brinkburn was first ushered into the room. Now that the warder had been dismissed, Brinkburn stood in front of the Governor's huge mahogany desk and noted the change that had come over him in the last few days. He looked gaunt. There were hollows under his eyes; the eyes themselves seemed glassy and betrayed the lack of control upon which Frobisher had always prided himself. He was looking at Brinkburn with a feverish intensity, waiting for his answer. Eddie was not sure that he could give him one.

'Dreams?'

'You know very well what I mean. Last time we . . . spoke . . . you told me that a bad dream was on its way and that they would keep on coming until you were out of here. What did you mean?'

Eddie thought: *How the hell should I know what I meant? I know that I said it . . . and I know that I meant it. But it wasn't like me speaking at all. All I know is that I want to be out of this bloody place. And I also know that when I said you were going to get bad dreams, I knew that you would. Just the same as Brooks and Turnbull.* But all Eddie said was: 'Did I say that, Mr Frobisher?'

'Don't play games with . . .' Frobisher composed himself, carefully placing the pencil back on his blotter lest he should snap it in half and betray just how shattered his nerves were. For a long moment, he looked up at Brinkburn and Eddie tried to read the emotions there, tried to make sense of the jumble of confusion that was taking place behind his eyes.

'What about early probation, then, Mr Frobisher? Do I get it?'

'I'm not the good fairy. I don't just wave a wand and the doors open.'

'Then the dreams are going to keep on coming.'

'Don't talk to me like that! Who the hell do you think you are?'

'They're going to keep on coming and they're going to get worse.'

'I'll break you in here, Brinkburn. I can see to it that you'll never get out . . .'

'And yet you can say with equal certainty that you can't get me an early probation. What do I believe?'

'You'll never . . .'

'Judith is angry, Mr Frobisher. She doesn't like being dead. She wants you to share being dead with her . . . forever.'

Frobisher began to shake — an internal tremor that he fought to contain. Without realising it, he picked up the pencil from the blotter and broke it. His face had gone grey. He looked suddenly very, very old.

'How . . .?' The words sounded like dead things coming up to the surface. 'How . . . did you know about Judith?'

'She told me,' replied Eddie. *What the hell am I saying? Who the hell is Judith!?* 'And if she has to come back from that dead, watery grave again, she won't be at all pleased.'

Frobisher looked as if he was going to be sick. His hands fidgeted over the broken pieces of pencil-like withered crabs searching for bait. He looked down at the report on the blotter before him: a report on the gruesome remains of the two prisoners who had been found torn to shreds in a locked cell. First the shower-room murders, now the two in their cell . . . and standing in front of him — Brinkburn — the man who was sending him the dreams of Judith that would certainly drive him mad. Frobisher knew at that moment without any doubt that the man before him was responsible for the mayhem that had descended on his prison. The

Council of Inquiry could ruin Frobisher's career. He had to handle it very carefully.

'Get out, Brinkburn.'

'Out,' said Eddie. 'That's a nice word.'

And somewhere deep inside himself, Eddie seemed to hear that word repeated; as if spoken by another voice; in excited expectation.

Out!

PART TWO

THE
FRIGHTENERS

'My devil had been long caged, he came out roaring.'

The Strange Case of Dr Jekyll and Mr Hyde.
Robert Louis Stevenson (1886)

1

Rennie lit a cigarette and flicked the match out of the car window. He had been waiting in the driveway leading up to the prison for over an hour; too early, he knew, but he had wanted to think about Eddie and somehow he had been unable to do that properly back in the flat. So he had left early, arrived at the prison and waited for that full hour, hoping that it would concentrate his thoughts.

Eddie was different. But different in a way that Rennie could not understand. There was an easy way to understand it, of course: Tracey and the kids. Losing your wife and children all at once was bad enough, but losing them *that* way was surely enough to send anyone over the top and into the laughing academy. But there was somehow more to it than that. There was something down inside, deep down behind his eyes, that Rennie didn't like. It was an alien thing. Over the years, he had got to know Eddie's moods, his way of life, the way he thought. They shared a business together, for crying out loud, and socialised together, too. You couldn't spend most of your life knowing a guy without getting to know exactly how your partner operated. There had always been a *simpatico* feeling between them. But after the incident in the shower-room . . . and Rennie had finally concluded that he would never figure out what the hell had happened there, or how they had come out of it alive . . . there had been a new *strangeness* about Eddie. After his own release from prison, Rennie had faithfully visited Eddie at every opportunity. And he had observed that strangeness gradually becoming more and more apparent. At first, it had merely seemed like thoughtfulness. Rennie had presumed it all to be a result of losing Tracey and the kids, followed by nearly being totalled. A feeling of guilt and bereavement and, yes, hate. But there was infinitely more to it than that. Now and then, he had found himself watching Eddie during visiting times, suddenly realising that he hadn't been listening to a word that he, Rennie, had said. Rather, he had been sitting there listening to some strange internal voice, nodding occasionally as if it had told him something that made sense.

Rennie sat back in the driving seat, trying to put all the pieces together; all the experiences; trying to weigh them up and come to some sort of sense. But he was still no further forward when the wicket gate in the large main doors opened and Eddie stepped out carrying his suitcase, wearing the same clothes he had been wearing on the day they'd put them both away. With genuine surprise, Rennie remembered that it was the same suit Eddie had worn on the day he had married Tracey in the city's Registry Office. Somehow, and again for reasons that made no sense, it seemed appropriate that he should be wearing that particular suit on this particular day.

The door closed and Eddie stood for a moment, looking around. Rennie watched him range over the looming grey expanse of the prison wall, the driveway, the sky. Even from this distance, he could see the smile on his face.

Eddie whirled back to the prison, pitching his suitcase at the walls. The case bounced back from the concrete and slapped to the ground. A pause — and then Eddie retrieved the suitcase and looked back to where Rennie sat in the car. Rennie gave a 'toot' on the car horn. Eddie picked up his suitcase and began to walk over.

Same guy, same way of walking, same sideways way of holding his head. But there's something else about him now, something that's been done to him by the prison. The time he's spent inside has done something to him that I don't much care for because I don't understand it. And then, bitterly: *I'm a selfish bastard. How the hell do I know how*

110

I'd feel if it was my wife and kids? Wouldn't I be changed? Wouldn't it screw me up, as well?

Eddie reached the car, climbing in when Rennie pushed the door open for him. He slung the suitcase on the back seat and sat down heavily in the front, still gazing ahead. Rennie looked at him for a long while as Eddie continued to stare at the prison wall.

'Out,' said Eddie at last.

'Yeah,' replied Rennie. 'Out and about.'

Eddie turned and smiled. And now it seemed that all Rennie's uneasy thoughts about the change that had taken place in Eddie were fantasies. It was a smile he remembered well of old. He grinned broadly, smacking Eddie on the shoulder and leaving his hand there. Eddie took it around the wrist, squeezing hard.

'Let's get pissed,' said Rennie.

'Good idea. But first, I want to see the garage and the house.'

'Ah hell, man. What do you want to do that for?'

'To remember. That's all.'

'You been out thirty seconds and you want to . . .'

'Please, Rennie.' And Rennie could see that there was a definite plea there. 'Just one look, that's all. Then back to your place, okay?'

Rennie looked hard into his eyes, scarching for that alien glint behind them. The prospect of that look was there, but it was not there in itself. Not yet.

'Okay, man. Okay. Just one look.'

The car roared out of the gravel drive, away from the prison and the Bad Dreams that were left there.

2

Rennie lit another cigarette and tried to look away from where Eddie stood, trying to give him some kind of privacy, some kind of respect while he paid his own last respects.

He scanned the council estate on his left. There'd been an attempt to landscape the place at intervals with young saplings, to detract from the predominantly grey concrete and the faceless, featureless buildings. But local kids had taken exception, or else they had provided an amusing diversion from the boredom . . . and now the saplings were broken or bent under continued assault. A ragged blue plastic bag had caught in the branches of the tree nearest to Rennie; it fluttered and rattled in the wind like some kind of distress signal. Beyond, kids were playing football on a rough patch of ground where a couple of council houses had been demolished. Rennie listened to the distant yells, curses and encouragements. It reminded him of the time Eddie had wildly taken that car from the main highway, through a dilapidated fence and across open parkland in their bid for escape. Kids had been playing football then, too. Somewhere, a radio was playing. A young mother was shouting that it was time for Gavin to come in for his dinner.

At last, Rennie looked back to where Eddie stood.

He hadn't moved in more than twenty minutes. Still standing there on the cracked concrete pathway leading up to the front door, Eddie was looking up to the upper flat where he had lived. The building seemed more like a concrete bunker than a place for people to live in. It had once housed four families; two upper flats, two lower flats. It was now totally unoccupied, perhaps itself awaiting demolition. The windows had been boarded upstairs and down, and Rennie could see the black smears of soot from the windows bearing testimony to the fact that the place had been ravaged by fire, and that people had died there. The graffiti artists had also been around. There were splashes of orange, green and yellow paint on the lower walls, none of it decipherable. The block was flat-roofed, designed by architects who had not apparently taken account of the fact that rain in England often fell vertically and who, no doubt, were still puzzled as to why water collected on those roofs, poured down onto tenants' heads and made flats uninhabitable because of wet rot.

It was a strange shrine.

Rennie had just decided on another cigarette, when Eddie turned and walked back to the car.

Silently, he climbed in. Rennie could not bring himself to look at his face.

'Okay . . .' said Eddie in a cracked voice. 'Now, the garage.'

Rennie flicked his cigarette end out of the window. This was something else he had been dreading for some time. 'There's something else, Eddie. Something I haven't told you. About the garage . . .'

'It's been fired as well?'

'Yeah, but how . . .?'

'I thought so. Let's go.'

3

No one had bothered to board up the garage.

Both double doors had collapsed during the fire; the side windows had exploded in the heat and, at the last, the roof had caved in. Only four ravaged walls remained; within . . . a charcoaled mass of beams, fallen masonry and twisted, blackened metal, all welded together in glue of molten tarmac and rubber.

Eddie sat in the car, looking. Rennie had finally managed to sneak a look at his face. It was expressionless.

'Sheraton,' he said at last.

'Or kids. It happened two weeks before I got out. Police said it was deliberate.'

'Sheraton,' said Eddie again. 'No doubt about it.'

'No evidence.'

'Don't give me that. We don't need evidence. It was Sheraton, all right. They think we're all burnt out now, Rennie. All burnt out. Well . . . they've got another think coming.'

Rennie saw something in his eyes, then.

Something that looked like fire.

4

Eddie sat in the upholstered chair facing Rennie, watching as he twisted the cap of a bottle of Bell's and poured two large whiskies. He looked around the room again: small with flower-patterned wallpaper, two upholstered chairs and a sofa. The potted plants that adorned the window sills and shelves were dying from thirst, their brown leaves hanging lethargically. The faded blue carpet had seen too many pairs of feet; there was a yellow stain under the formica coffee table where someone had spilled a chicken curry years ago. The uncleaned windows were spattered with pigeon dirt on the outside, giving a view over the concrete jungle of a council housing estate, six storeys below.

'Not as salubrious as the last place I had, but it serves the purpose.'

'You sure no one knows you're here?'

'Listen, mate. The last thing I wanted when I got out of the pokey was Sheraton knowing where I lived. We're safe up here. Nobody knows.'

'Good.'

'Get on the outside of that,' said Rennie, handing him a glass. Eddie took it, savouring the sight of the whisky swilling around inside before taking a large mouthful. It burned and then warmed on the way down. Rennie followed suit.

'Good stuff, eh?'

'The best.'

The whisky warmed Eddie's gut and reminded him of something: something intangible that seemed important. He hunted for it, suddenly realising that it was because it felt related somehow to what had happened to him in prison. Something had come into him, something that had 'jumped' from Archie into his eyes and settled deep into his gut like a living thing. The whisky was like that, warming him from the inside out. Except that the thing which had seemed to burrow down into Eddie, too deep for him to find now, was born from cold, not from heat. And the coldness was always in there, deep down. Now he realised that he felt different again, very different from the way he'd felt inside prison. Inside, the 'feeling' had been frustrated. It had been waiting for something, impatient for it. Now, it was more satisfied. It had got what it wanted.

It was . . .

'Out,' said Rennie again, lifting his glass.

Eddie smiled and did the same. 'Out.' He drank.

'I know it's early days, Eddie.' Rennie flopped back into his seat, running a calloused hand through his hair. 'But we got to think about the future. About the business.'

'Burnt,' said Eddie flatly.

'Yeah, but we're insured. Don't forget that. I got in touch with the insurance people. Twelve grand, that's what we get. More than enough to get a new place and start again. Just as well we were insured against "Acts of Violence". Bastards tried to suggest it was to do with riots . . . which we're *not* insured against . . . until I came heavy on 'em.'

'I don't know, yet.' *It hasn't told me what it wants.* 'I just don't know.'

'You're living in a dream, man. You've got to snap out of it. Look . . . I know you're just out and I know you need some time to rest up, relax, have a good time. I'm going to make sure you get it. But after that, we've got to do some serious thinking about the future. We've got to get on with our lives.'

'Dreams,' said Eddie, swallowing another mouthful of whisky. 'I ever tell you about the dreams I used to have in prison, Rennie?'

Rennie sighed, giving in for the moment. 'No.'

'Good dreams, Rennie. Really good. I used to dream about Tracey and the kids. They used to come to me. In the cell, after you'd gone. Tracey would sit on the end of the bunk and the kids would play in the cell. Really nice dreams. She'd tell me about how she was and how the kids were doing and it really made me feel good. But more than dreams, Rennie. That's the thing, man. They were . . . well, I know this sounds crazy . . . but it seemed as if they were really there, you know? And those dreams came most every night. Really nice. Made me happy.'

' 'Course they did.' Rennie wasn't smiling any more. Gazing down into his glass, he looked like the saddest man on earth. Eddie wasn't watching him; his eyes were fixed on the dirty window and the darkening sky beyond.

'Those were good dreams. The Bad Dreams were reserved for other people.' Eddie looked back. 'Ever had Bad Dreams, Rennie?'

'This past three years been like a bad dream, man.'

'No, I mean Bad Dreams at night. Dreams like you're awake. But you can't wake up from them.'

'Yeah, I had Bogeyman dreams before.'

'Bogeyman?' Eddie laughed. And Rennie decided that he did not like the sound of that laugh. There were traces of that alien glint now in Eddie's eyes. Rennie looked away as Eddie continued.

'Remember how worried you were about me? Remember how you didn't want out, 'cause you thought Sheraton's hard men would do for me?'

'Yeah, I remember. After that fucking shower-room carry-on, how could I forget? I'm still surprised you're in one piece, you lucky bastard.'

'You're a good friend, Rennie. Best friend a man ever had. But you needn't have been worrying. You see . . . after that bust up, when Archie Duncan stepped in . . . I've got this . . . special . . . I dunno . . . *talent*. Yeah, that's what it is: a talent. The other cons, including Sheraton's lot, kept well away from me. Do you believe me?'

'Believe what, Eddie? You're not making a whole lot of sense.'

'I could give them *dreams*, Rennie! Yeah! Bad dreams. I could send them dreams that could scare the living daylights out of them. But the dreams were like . . . like the flipside of the nice dreams I got. The Bad Dreams. Those dreams . . .' Rennie was disturbed at Eddie's agitation as he continued. '. . . they can . . . *turn real*, Rennie. I know it sounds as if I've gone crazy, but it's true. I can turn those Bad Dreams real. It's as if I could see inside the con's head, see what's in there and send him his own gift-wrapped, living-breathing nightmare. Remember Brooks and Turnbull? Remember Fisher? Even the Governor, Rennie! How the hell do you think I got out so early? I told him he'd keep getting those dreams until I was out. Well . . . now I'm out.'

Eddie drank again, breathing deeply. Rennie watched his other hand grasping at the arm of the chair. He seemed to be steadying himself. He drank again, draining the glass, and Rennie leaned across to refill it. 'Those Bad Dreams can turn real, Rennie. And when they turn real they can . . . do damage.

'The other cons kept away from me. They kept away because I could put the Frighteners on them. Now that I'm out, I'm going to put the Frighteners on Sheraton and his mob. I'm going to have my revenge, Rennie. I'm going to make Sheraton pay for everything that he's done. For Tracey and the kids. And for you and me. I'm going to make him wish he'd never been born.'

'You sound cracked, Eddie. You know that?'

Eddie looked over at Rennie, straight in the eye. The *look* was there, and it chilled Rennie to the bone. He gritted his teeth and decided that he was going to stare Eddie out. He was not going to look away from that malevolent glint. The glint mellowed and now Eddie was laughing as he drank again.

'Cracked? Yeah, maybe. I know how it sounds to you. Just out of the clink and Mad as a Fucking Hatter, eh? Well, the proof's in the seeing, Rennie boy. I'll just have to show you things to make you change your mind. You're going to help me. You're going to help me every step of the way. And it starts tonight.'

'Look, man. Let's just relax. Have a talk. Kill that bottle. We can talk about all this tomorrow . . .'

'Tonight, Rennie,' said Eddie. And this time, he was not smiling. 'Got a telephone?'

'Not yet . . .' Rennie poured himself a drink and turned away, downing it quickly and not wanting Eddie to see how unnerved he had been by the look in his eyes. 'Can't afford one.'

'Maybe just as well, then. Wouldn't want to be traced back here.' Eddie finished his drink and stood up. 'Nearest public telephone box?'

'One in the corridor outside. Another downstairs on the corner of the street.'

'Okay . . . okay . . . I want to use the one in the street first.'

'I don't understand . . .'

'Back in a minute. Got a call to make.'

Rennie threw down another triple after Eddie had left.

5

Frankie Laine — no relation to the ballad singer but secretly proud of the association — straightened his bow tie in the mirror and returned to the plush, leather-covered chair in his office. Beyond, business was . . . as they say . . . booming. Laine's casino had taken a small fortune this week. Some kind of Chinese festival week, so the Chinese punters were even keener than normal to spend their cash at Frankie's place. Special Chinese dishes had been made available on the restaurant menu, all heavily subsidised by the gambling take. Even after the massive cut that Sheraton always took from the establishment, it would still leave Frankie with a more than healthy bank balance and the certain knowledge that the 'insurance money' (a euphemism for 'protection money') would keep his premises safe from firebombs and broken limbs.

He pulled open the top drawer of his desk and looked again at the photograph. Each new starter at Frankie's place had to provide a photograph in the appropriate dress before they could expect to be croupiers. The girl he was now looking at (blonde, extremely attractive and with *bosomus maximus*) had just begun her job tonight. He had been watching her for a while, and he looked forward to the special post-interview with her in the privacy of his office, which he always insisted on with new staff. Just a little something to prove to him how committed she would be, how much she could be trusted. Frankie licked his lips, shut the drawer again and leaned back.

The telephone rang.

Nonchalantly, he swivelled his chair in a lazy arc, scooped up the receiver and cupped it against his ear, grinning broadly in expectation of the night to come.

'Hello, Frankie. This is Eddie Brinkburn.'

Frankie sat forward again, holding the earpiece tighter, grinning more broadly now.

'*Mister* Brinkburn!' There was an unmistakable taunt in his voice. 'First time I've ever talked to a dead man. A little birdy told me that you'd got out today.'

'Nice to know the grapevine's still as effective as ever, Frankie.'

'Yeah. And somebody important's very interested in meeting you. One or two old debts to settle.'

'Yes, I certainly have. And you're going to help me, Frankie. In the meantime, I need some ready cash.'

The 'beeps' on the public telephone began and Frankie began to laugh uproariously as he heard another coin being shoved into the slot.

'You certainly sound short of cash, Eddie!'

'How much do you have in ready money?'

'Expecting a loan, Eddie? Sorry, can't oblige. But if you tell me where you are, I can send somebody over to talk to you about it.'

'I reckon you must make about three or four grand a night in takings. I'm not greedy, I'll take three thousand.'

'I don't believe you, man. Still got a sense of humour after all . . .'

'You'll close at 3.00 am with half an hour for counting up. I'm going to give you a telephone number. You're going to ring me at three-thirty and we'll arrange a collection point.'

'And why am I going to do that?'

'Because if I haven't heard from you by three-thirty, I'm going to put the Frighteners on you.'

'The frighteners? And how do you intend to do that, Eddie? Pardon my curiosity, but as you can hear over the telephone, my knees are knocking in terror.'

Eddie gave him the telephone number. 'I suggest that you write it down. You've got until three-thirty.'

Frankie burst into laughter again. 'You're out of your skull, Brinkburn.'

'No doubt you'll be telling Sheraton's people about our conversation, giving them the telephone number so that they can trace it. I'll save you all some trouble. It's a public telephone box in Windsor Street. Anybody hanging around there at 3.30 waiting for me to answer the phone will also have the Frighteners put on them.'

'Tremble, tremble. Thanks for the info . . .'

'Three-thirty, Frankie.'

Click.

6

'Okay, Eddie. So what's happening?'

Eddie sat back with satisfaction, pointing at his empty glass. As Rennie poured out the refills he told him of the telephone conversation.

'Bloody hell, man! You been out less than an hour and you're setting yourself up for a major hiding.'

'Worried?'

'Course I'm bloody worried! Those guys inside tried to do us, Eddie! Now we're outside, we're even easier meat. Now we're out, we've got to get out of here, away from London. Start again where nobody knows us. Lie low for a bit. Now you're just laying yourself open again . . . leaving *us* open!'

'Take it easy, Rennie. Believe me. I know you think I've cracked. But ride it out, man. Just trust me. Nothing's going to happen to us. Don't you see . . . the only way we can be safe, really safe, is to hurt them. Hurt them so bad that they'll think twice about touching us. Frankie's the first. He'll provide us with the readies.'

'And how the hell does that happen? How are we going to lean on him? Send him one of your Bad Dreams?'

Eddie sipped his drink. 'In a manner of speaking.' He looked out of the window, smiling. Rennie groaned, running his fingers through his hair.

'Let's wait and see, Rennie. By now, Frankie will have made his telephone call. He'll have told Sheraton's mob all about it. They'll have the telephone number now, and the Heavy Squad will probably already be on their way. In . . .'

Eddie looked at his watch. '. . . about twenty minutes, Windsor Street will be well and truly staked out. Nobody's going to be able to get in and out of that street without Sheraton knowing about it. They'll all be sitting there, waiting for me at three-thirty.'

'And then what?'

'Like I said . . . let's wait and see.'

* * *

Frankie finished off his pint of lager with an angry flourish. His euphoric air of expectation had worn off abruptly. His post-interview interview had not quite gone as planned. The new croupier had slapped him good and hard in the face when his intentions had been made plain after closing time. He slammed the empty glass down on the blotter of his desk and spun the swivel chair hard.

'Bitch!'

He checked his face in the mirror, still rosy after the slap. Adjusting his tie, he returned to his seat, stopped its creaking rotation and sat down again, opening the bottom right-hand drawer and taking out a bottle of brandy and a fresh glass. After a swallow, he looked at his watch. Three-twenty-five.

There was a knock on the door.

'Come in.'

Frankie's accountants entered. Duncan Jenkins was short, stocky and bull-headed, looking like a well-to-do professional darts player. He carried the case containing the notes from tonight's 'take'. His partner, Billy Tavistock, had a pock-marked face that looked as if it had been the target for Duncan's 'arrows'. Stooped and gaunt, he was carrying the loose change from the till, and it was very apparent from the look on his face that he did not care for the man behind him, who was now closing the door. Frankie could understand that dislike. Keith McLeish was one of Sheraton's financial advisers, a synonym for someone who stood watching eagle-eyed while Frankie's boys counted the takings — just to make sure that Frankie wasn't trying to fiddle Sheraton out of any 'insurance money', since it was calculated on a percentage-of-takings basis. McLeish shut the door and leaned against it; black suit, black tie and a face that had seen so much street action that he didn't have eyebrows any more. There was just enough intelligence in those eyes to make one aware that not only could he do damage to a person's limbs, but he could do it in a very creative and permanent fashion. He watched as the other two walked round the desk while Frankie leaned back and opened the safe in the wall behind him.

'How much?' asked Frankie, smiling insipidly at McLeish.

Billy opened his mouth to speak, but Jenkins answered before him, making Billy look like some unnecessary ventriloquist's dummy.

'Three and a half grand.'

'Eddie Brinkburn should think about entering for "The Price is Right". He almost got it right.'

'We've got our own little game show lined up for Eddie in Windsor Street,' countered McLeish.

'So I hear.' Frankie watched as his own men placed the money reverently in the safe. 'Nice of Eddie to leave me five hundred, wasn't it? What do you think, Keith? Your lot going to help me bear the loss?'

'Consider our services tonight free of charge, Mr Laine. Mr Brinkburn won't be asking for any of our money again.'

Frankie slammed the safe door shut and spun the dial, grinning again.

7

Pat Hudson earned big money working for Sheraton's organisation. He had been employed for six years and now had his own place, a nice car and enough money to do what he wanted, when he wanted. His place within that organisation was a 'Management Operative', which meant that when the management directed that he persuade an awkward customer that he or she should, after all, be paying Insurance Money to avoid his or her head being kicked in, then he went out and kicked that particular head until it saw sense. It was a skill that he had learnt early on when he worked the streets, and it was nice to have this particular talent recognised by such a big-time organisation. He shouldn't really complain about the conditions of service, bearing in mind the lucrative salary. But he was complaining tonight.

Kicking somebody's head in was one thing; sitting out here in a scraggy park overlooking Windsor Street, freezing your arse off, was another thing altogether. He had arrived on time, just as he'd been instructed, but he was more than a little pissed off to find that he had arrived first and would have to stay there, without a hip flask (he should have thought ahead), while all the other sods took their time arriving. The park was littered with old newspapers, some containing the remnants of last night's fish and chips. The stunted trees which bordered the park were suffering the onslaught of neglect and kids' vandalism. He wrapped his overcoat tighter around him. There was a chill wind blowing across the park. Beyond the park railings, in Windsor Street, he could see the telephone box that he'd been told to watch. No one had used the fucking thing since he'd arrived. He clapped his hands together against the cold, cursed again, and wished there was a trades union for disaffected 'management operatives' within Sheraton's organisation.

The sound of a car approaching drew his attention to the side street which bordered the park and also led down to Windsor Street. He recognised it straight away. Terry Bishop – the Car Expert. Pat grinned. Terry Bishop had a special interest in Mr Brinkburn. After the Petrol Station rumble, Bishop had lost an important operative, first temporarily to prison, and now for good and by methods which no one had been able to work out. Perhaps tonight, scores would be well and truly evened.

The car slid to a halt in the shadows of the side street. Rubbish whispered around its wheels. Pat cursed again. At least Bishop and his new colleague could sit in the warm, listening to a stereo. He turned to look back at the telephone box. No one could pass by him unobserved. Pat shoved his hands under his armpits for extra warmth, huddled back against the freezing park bench and tried to ignore the cold which crept up his spine.

8

Singing 'High Noon' in a flat and wavering monotone, Frankie Laine checked his watch. It was three-thirty. He grinned, taking a sip from his glass of brandy. He lifted the glass in a toast to his accountants, Tavistock and Jenkins, and to McLeish, sitting opposite his desk, all with glasses in their hands. Frankie felt good tonight. He had done Sheraton a very big favour purely by chance. (After all, Eddie had chosen *him* to telephone that night, no one else.) Now things could only bode well for him. Perhaps there might even be a cut in the percentage deal? Who could tell? So Frankie had broken open his drinks cabinet and allowed his good feelings to blossom into free drinks for all. Even for McLeish, the evil bastard, who even now was sitting with a stupid grin on his face as he poured a fifth scotch into that battered and ugly face of his.

Billy Tavistock thought only of getting home. It was three-thirty in the morning, for crying out loud. He had been on the go all day. But if Laine was in a good mood, it was best not to spoil it. Jenkins had nowhere particular to go; he was happy enough to stay and drink himself into oblivion, if that's what Laine wanted.

'Three-thirty,' said Frankie, raising his glass again. 'And here's to Mr Brinkburn in his telephone box waiting for a call that isn't going to come.'

'And to a nice little surprise for him,' said McLeish, returning the toast.

'What was that?' said Jenkins.

'What?'

'Back there in the casino. I thought I heard . . .' And this time, they all hear the crash and tinkle of broken glass. McLeish reacted first, kicking himself leisurely away from the desk, eyes still fixed on Frankie with a look that asked: *Is this genuine trouble or just one of your boys?* Frankie knew that it was a look of bravado; the look of someone keen to live up to his reputation given the right circumstances. It was an act but an act which could be proved as the real thing if necessary. Frankie shrugged in reply and stood up.

'Shouldn't be anyone in at this time. We all locked up, Billy?' Tavistock nodded nervously.

Another crash; the sound of a bottle, perhaps, falling from a shelf.

McLeish swaggered to the office door, straightening a tie that didn't need straightening. Tavistock and Jenkins kept back, quite willing to allow the hired man to deal with any intruder.

Blue velvet blackness lay on the casino, the only illumination coming from the strobe lighting over the bar at the far side. On their right, a restaurant section had been separated from the gambling floor by plastic trellis work, so that diners could watch the punters losing their cash in comfort. On the gambling floor itself there were six tables: two for cards and four long green baize tables with roulette wheels. The counting up office was on their left, like a small post office with a grille window.

But the casino itself was empty. There was no sign of an intruder; no evidence of where the noise could have come from.

McLeish swaggered out of the office, stepping down into the velvet darkness of the gambling floor, keen to prove to the others that he could damage anyone skulking around in the shadows very badly indeed. Behind him, Frankie leaned on one of the trellised arches beside the restaurant section and lit a cigarette, smiling. He was enjoying McLeish's floorshow and felt genuinely sorry for any poor fucker who might be there. In the office doorway, Frankie sensed rather than saw that Jenkins and Tavistock were skulking timidly, keeping out of the way and not wanting to get involved. He smiled again, blowing smoke from his nostrils and watching it drift upward, sucked in towards the gentle *whup-whup-whup* of the propeller-shaped fan hanging from the ceiling, as it turned slowly and lazily. Beneath it, McLeish began to look under the gaming tables.

Nothing.

And then Frankie recoiled as another unseen bottle crashed to the floor behind the bar. McLeish straightened up and strode purposefully towards the source of the noise, now with a curious Frankie behind him. There was still no sign of anyone. Could somebody be hiding behind the bar counter?

McLeish reached the bar, braced his hands on it and leaned over to look.

'Okay. Come on out . . .' Frankie saw McLeish look up again and then from left to right. Obviously, there was no one behind the bar.

From nowhere, a bottle exploded on the bar between McLeish's braced hands.

McLeish lurched backwards, hands trying to protect his eyes from the spray of flying glass and liquid. Frankie stopped in his tracks, the smell of strong liquor in the air. He watched McLeish brace himself again for some kind of action, shaking glass fragments from his hair . . . and then both men froze, as this time they *saw* a bottle of vodka fall from one of the bar shelves and crash on the floor out of sight. They took two quick steps backwards as another bottle flew from its perch and shattered on the bar, scattering glass. And then another and another. McLeish turned to say something to Frankie.

And then all hell erupted.

Rows of bottles leapt from the shelves, one after the other in a rapid successive blur, shattering and splashing on the bar-all apparently yanked from their perches and smashed by an invisible hand. Frankie clung to the trellis work and felt something there. It was a pulse; a warm, pulsing

130

sensation as if a generator below ground somewhere had been switched on. Overhead, he became aware that the propeller-fan was beginning to speed up, rotating faster and faster: *whup-whup-whup*.

'What the hell is going on, Laine?' McLeish grabbed him by the lapels, saw the look of utter surprise there and turned back again as the sound of tearing cloth and the squeal of bending metal rent the air.

The green baize cloth on the casino tables was being torn off by invisible hands, ragged folds of it ripping and flapping into the air like tattered rags.

A great wind had descended on the casino. Betting chips and spirit glasses began to fly through the air as Frankie pulled away from the trellis, fighting to get past McLeish and back to the office as the howling wind tore at his clothes, snatching away his breath.

McLeish grabbed for a table that was bolted to the floor, tie flapping wildly around his head like the green baize streamers on the gaming tables, rubbery jowls rolling as if from G-force. Frankie grabbed for the trellis again, spinning round and fighting against the sudden great suction which was dragging him towards the centre of the floor. Glasses and bottles continued to crash behind the bar.

Squinting against the wind, hanging on for dear life, Frankie watched a roulette wheel tear itself free from a table and flip end-over-end into the centre of the floor. At last, he could see something there.

It was a whirlwind: a spinning vortex of air stretching from the floor to the ceiling; now visible because of the broken glass, detritus and shreds of cloth which spun within its centre. Frankie could see that all the debris flying through the air was being absorbed into that miniature tornado. The green baize cloth was being torn from the tables and sucked inside; sprays of broken glass were quickly whipped into the vortex. Two roulette wheels were now whirling in there somewhere.

In amazement, he watched as the tubular frames of two of the chairs bolted to the floor on his right began to writhe

131

and contort as if some invisible strongman was trying to tear them apart. An arm *spanged*! away from the main frame, buckled screeching as if in a flame; then snapped and flew away end-over-end into the whirlwind. The strip-lights overhead exploded in brief flashes of blue light and sparks before being torn from their mountings, twisted wiring and broken filament whirling away into the vortex.

A blur of movement on his right made Frankie duck instinctively, thinking that something else had torn loose from its mountings on its way to the centre of the whirling vortex of air. But then he saw that it was Tavistock and Jenkins, dashing through the restaurant section on the outskirts of the wind, racing in terror past the bar, towards the exit. Frankie saw them shielding their faces from the flying glass until they reached the main doors. They began to heave and tear at the handles . . . and Frankie knew with awful certainty that they would not be able to get out; that the doors were somehow locked and that it had to do with the appearance of this whirlwind in the middle of his casino. He looked back to McLeish who was struggling to hold onto the table, and then past him to the whirling vortex of debris, broken glass and green baize.

There were *two* vortices there now – and they were somehow taking shape.

Overhead, something crunched and snapped. Frankie ducked again as the propeller-fan tore loose from its mounting in the ceiling and zipped savagely through the air, instantly becoming absorbed into the swirling mass of one of the whirlwinds. Deep within the vortex, the propeller continued to spin vertically, *whup-whup-whup*. In horrified fascination, Frankie began to make sense of the shapes that were being constituted by the wind and the debris.

They were man-shaped.

He had been desensitised over the years to any real degree of instinctive or intuitive feeling, but he knew now, without doubt, that he was in the presence of something evil. It evoked a purity of instinct that he had never experienced before. The man-shaped things within the whirling vortex

132

were the essence of a deep evil, whose presence was now crystallising the moral wretchedness he had embraced for twenty of the thirty years he had lived. He cried out to the wind that he had always wanted to be good, but he hadn't been allowed. He cried out for a second chance. He cried out for the ability to live his life again. And he knew that it was too late.

The whirlwinds shrivelled away to whispers of air.

Now Frankie could see the man-shapes properly, could see how they had been created. He began to cry, great floods of tears coursing down his face.

McLeish hadn't seen them yet. His attention was fixed on Frankie's bawling tears, puzzlement on his own face. He turned to the far side of the casino where Jenkins and Tavistock were banging and yelling at the mysteriously locked doors; he turned back to where the whirlwinds had been. And then he, too, saw the shapes.

They were both similar in a horrifyingly haphazard manner.

Hulking, man-shaped monstrosities, but too tall; weaving from side to side, flexing what constituted their 'arms' like great shambling bears, their hunched shoulders nine feet from the floor. Behind him, McLeish could still hear Frankie blubbering like some great baby and wondered what kind of Halloween trick was being pulled here. An elaborate trick, that was for sure, because the things on the casino floor had been created from the broken glass, torn baize and debris that moments before had been flying through the air. The heads were a tangled mass of green cloth, papier-mâchéed into a rough, distorted approximation of human faces. Without eyes. The bodies were compacted and mangled remnants of tubular chair frames, splintered wood, shattered filament tubes and garbage. McLeish watched one of the forms lift a claw-like hand to its face, as if curious. And he could see that the horribly encrusted hand was composed entirely of broken, coloured glass from the shattered bottles which had flown from the bar. The thing next to it seemed to be breathing, and when McLeish looked more closely, he could see that there was a gaping cavity in the walking garbage heap's chest. And deep within that ragged crater was the propeller-fan, still lazily turning on its side *whup-whup-whup* – occasionally spitting out shredded paper or crunched, broken glass which seemed not to fall away, but to be re-absorbed into the mass of the thing.

'Nice fucking trick . . .' said McLeish. And then wished that he hadn't said anything. Because the things turned their heads in his direction, as if blind but now aware of where he was by the sound of his voice.

The man-shapes began to shamble towards him.

Frankie's anguished cries reached a new pitch of intensity. Beyond, Tavistock and Jenkins began to shout hoarsely for help as they threw themselves at the casino doors with a renewed and desperate vigour.

McLeish took two nervous steps back as the man-things slowly came on, and fired a nervous glance back at Frankie, as if looking for some kind of play-acting on his part, as if expecting that he would suddenly cease his crying, jump up and yell: 'Hey, McLeish. Neat trick, huh? Come on, boys, take off the costumes and let's all have a drink. Got to admit, Mac, had you going there for a bit, eh?'

But Frankie did not jump up. He just went on crying as if his life, or any prospect of being saved, had been taken away from him. And now, in anger, not wanting to give in to that horrible feeling in his guts, telling him that these things were things of nightmare, not subject to a boot in the groin or a broken glass in the face, McLeish picked up one of the tubular chairs which lay at his feet and had not been sucked into the vortices, swung it savagely around his head and flung it at the nearest of the approaching things.

The chair hit the thing full on the chest with a smart snap! and then *stuck*. McLeish goggled as the chair was greedily swallowed into the thing's bulk, reconstituted . . . and made larger. The thing reached the steps leading up to the restaurant floor, and for the first time McLeish remembered the gun in his inside pocket. It was there for show, the tell-tale bulge to remind Frankie and his boys that he worked for Sheraton, and that he meant business. He had never used it, although he knew how. As he pulled it out, he became aware that Frankie was blundering away through the restaurant on all fours, still crying and bawling. The second thing turned lazily, head cocked, listening as Frankie reached the bar and staggered to the casino doors to join Tavistock and Jenkins.

The first thing began to mount the stairs towards McLeish.

'All right, pal. How's this for a party game?'

McLeish steadied the revolver with both hands, the way he'd seen it done on *Miami Vice* on the television. 'Just one more step.'

Unconcerned, the thing took another step.

McLeish squeezed the trigger. He was shocked by the savage, barking bite of the shot, magnified by the acoustics of the casino; more shocked when half of the thing's 'face' blew away in a spray of cardboard beer mats, shredded green baize and betting chips, and then when the damaged head began to squirm and undulate as detritus and garbage began to crawl up from the innards of the thing's chest. Reconstituting like living matter, it filled in the gap which the bullet had blown away until, in seconds, the head was complete again. McLeish fired again, directly into its chest. The bullet passed through, the hole quickly filling up again like a footprint in a swamp. *Miami Vice* pose now gone completely, McLeish jerked three more shots into the man-shape, seeing the bits of rubbish flying away as holes were punched into it, holes which were quickly filled and reconstituted. It stepped forward to meet him, arms held wide . . . and McLeish broke for it and ran the way that Frankie had gone, down the restaurant towards the bar.

But the second man-shape was waiting.

Hands of broken bottle-glass fastened on his throat and side. Eyes bulging, scream constricted, McLeish saw his blood spurt in a fractured geyser from the ruins of his throat, slopping like thick soup over the thing's tattered arms and his own shirt front. He felt himself being manhandled around to face the thing, scooped from the floor and lifted into the air, green glass fingers burrowing into his side and taking a ragged fistful of his internal organs. Pain had gone now in that fraction of a second, replaced by a sad and dying curiosity, as the thing, expressionless and dispassionate, forced his head towards the crater in its chest. Eyes filming through a blood-red haze, McLeish felt strangely comforted by the *whup-whup-whup* of the slowly rotating propeller-fan in the cavity, even though he knew that he was to be fed into it as if into some surreal sausage machine.

Neat trick, was his last thought before the blades began their work under the remorseless pressure which continued to push him in.

* * *

'It's your fault, you bastard!' yelled Tavistock, hunting around for something . . . *anything* . . . not sucked into the maelstrom, which would allow him to hammer down the casino doors. Frankie was on his knees beside them, clawing at the doors, looking back frantically over his shoulder to see that the man-things were . . . doing something . . . to McLeish something he didn't want to see. The spell of regression which had been forced on him by the things' appearance was suddenly transformed into anger that Tavistock should talk to him like that. He jumped to his feet, grabbed the accountant by the lapels and threw him back at the doors.

'What do you mean, *my* fault?' he screamed.

Tavistock fought back, grabbing Frankie's lapels in an equal fury and terror, wisps of hair flying from his balding pate, now not giving a damn who thought he was boss in this hell-hole of a casino. 'Your fault, you stupid bastard! Your fault! You should have given him the bloody money . . .'

Eddie Brinkburn. He had completely forgotten about Eddie and his threats: *'Give me the money, Frankie. Three-thirty on the dot. Because if you don't . . . I'm going to put the Frighteners on you.'*

'The Frighteners . . .' said Frankie aloud, letting go of Tavistock who was now yelping and leaping away from him in terror. Frankie looked back. One of the man-things was coming towards them, across the casino floor. Effortlessly, with one hand, it scooped up one of the tables in its way, heaved and ripped. The table was torn from its bolts in the floor and crashed over to one side, allowing the thing easy passage. The other thing was shambling down the restaurant towards them. It was holding one of McLeish's legs, having fed the rest of his body into the mincing machine in its chest. As it walked, it continued to push McLeish's lifeless form into itself. Behind it, Frankie could see a trail of minced McLeish running from the thing's legs. Tavistock scrambled away from Frankie, hammering at the doors again and yelling hoarsely. Frankie's bladder emptied at last as Jenkins dodged maniacally back and forth between the two approaching things, trying to find some way of running between them, caught in a trap.

'Not me, not me. *Oh, God . . . NOT ME*!' Jenkins suddenly skipped to the right of the thing approaching across the casino floor, bent low and headed back along the side wall towards the counting-up office.

Frankie could see at once that he could never make it; he watched, eyes staring, mouth open, urine gushing down his inner thigh.

The man-thing seized Jenkins easily by the throat, the scoop of its spade-shaped, broken-bottle claw catching him directly under the chin and lifting him high into the air like some bizarre angler catching a human fish. Jenkins, jaw clamped shut, emitted a high-pitched keening scream which quickly died away as the thing held him up directly before its non-face and watched the life bubble out of him. And then it discarded him behind it in one downward swing of its arm, Jenkins sliding from its hand like a joint of beef dropping from a butcher's hook.

Tavistock continued to hammer, screaming, at the doors, but Frankie could only stand and watch as the thing which had killed Jenkins finally paused, ten feet away from them, standing silent, bloodied arms held at either side, non-face staring down at them. It was waiting.. n Frankie's left, the *whup-crunch-whup* of the other thing grew louder. Not wanting to look, but looking anyway, he first felt the shadow of the second thing over him and then saw it stop six feet away on his left, towering over the two men and looking down. In its left claw it still held McLeish's foot, the leg protruding from the bloodied crater on the thing's chest — the last vestige of Sheraton's hard man.

'. . . hello . . .' said Frankie in a little boy's voice, smiling upwards at the thing in a helpless plea.

The thing pressed the leg deep into its torso: *whup-crunch-whup-crunch*. Fascinated, still smiling his rictus of a smile, Frankie saw the bottle-green claw push McLeish's shoe into the propeller-fan, and began to sing . . . 'Ten green bottles hanging on the wall, ten green bottles hanging on the wall. And if one green bottle should accidentally fall, there'll be . . .'

. . . as the slowly turning blade inside the thing also minced the 'fingers' of its own spade-shaped claw. Still singing as Tavistock's screams reached a new pitch, Frankie saw the broken glass fingers reconstitute from the thing's wrist; the broken, mangled glass quickly replenished as the hand withdrew from the cavity. Behind it, McLeish had become a fifty-foot glinting trail on the restaurant floor.

The second thing's shadow loomed large and Tavistock's screams flew to a high falsetto, but Frankie didn't look. He didn't want to look, he only wanted to sing . . .

'. . . ten green bottles . . .'

. . . as Tavistock's whining screams were borne upwards and away from him, dwindling to a liquid gurgling. Frankie felt something warm and wet splash across his shoulder, but all he could do was sing and look up into the non-face of the thing that had minced McLeish.

'Ten green Brinkburns hanging on . . . Brinkburn . . .'

'*Three thousand by three-thirty, Frankie. Otherwise I'll set the Frighteners on you . . .*'

'ALL RIGHT! EDDIE! ALL RIGHT! I'm sorry! God,

I'm sorry!' Frankie was yelling up at the face of the thing, as if it was somehow Eddie himself there, huge and vengeful and bloodied, glinting in the dark like some gigantic scarecrow. 'You can have it! Honest, I'll get it now, from the office. All of it . . . not just the three thousand, Eddie. I don't want any of it! It's all yours!'

The thing lifted its bottle-green claw in front of his face.

'I'm sorreeeeeeee, Eddieeeee! I'm sorry! Please don't . . .'

And then Frankie saw that the thing was pointing sideways and backwards towards the office.

'Yes, yes, yes . . .' Frankie bowed and scraped around the gigantic figure, his gaze fixed on that deadly hand, nodding furiously, waiting for the glass fingers to swoop down on him. 'Yes, I'll get it . . . get it . . . get it . . .' He scrabbled frantically back across the restaurant floor, skidding on the trail of slime that had been McLeish.

Time had lost is meaning. In a jumble of activity, Frankie seemed to watch himself blunder into the office, crash across the room to the safe, fumbling with the dial. He couldn't remember the combination, but somehow the automaton with his face and body, which was fiddling with the dial, could. He opened the safe, grabbed handfuls of notes, IOUs, bonds . . . everything . . . and began to cram them into the briefcase on his desk. When the safe was empty and the briefcase full, he scooped it up and scrambled back into the casino.

Holding it before him like a sacrificial offering and a shield, he blundered across the devastated casino towards the two massively dark and weaving shadows by the doors.

The doors were open.

The things stood silently, like sentinels, on either side of the doors.

Cringing, Frankie approached. Outside, he could see the litter-strewn pavement of the back alley. A wind was gusting, blowing rubbish into the nightclub as Frankie held out the suitcase, burbling as he shambled nervously towards the two things.

'It's all here, Eddie. Every bit of it, I promise. I don't

want any of it. It's all yours. But please don't kill me. Please
. . . please . . . please . . .'

Now standing directly between the two things, bent over
double and with the suitcase held over his head to ward off
those terrible hands, Frankie waited for death to come. He
knew that if he dared to pass through the casino doors and
out onto the pavement, they would swoop down and take
him. But death did not come as he shambled through the
double doors, aware that the wind outside had suddenly
transferred to the casino itself. The whirlwinds had come
back, and Frankie realised that the broken glass and the
rubbish and the green baize were flying in the air again . . .

He stepped out on to the pavement and took six halting
and fearful steps without looking back. What if the things
shambled out into the night behind him? Was it a cruel trick?
Were they going to let him get this far and then . . .?

Screaming hoarsely, in full command of his urine-soaked
legs, he took off down the back alley like a bat out of hell.

Behind him, the air was filled with flying gauze, tinkling
glass and rubbish.

The two huge shadows on either side of the casino doors
began to diminish in size.

9

Parked in Windsor Street, just below the high-rise where, six storeys up, Eddie and Rennie were drinking whisky, Forster and his three men sat watching the telephone kiosk, a hundred yards away, on the corner of a grimy side street. Forster sat in the passenger seat, next to Mickey, who had been driving. In the back, the other two were playing cards. Mickey looked at Forster and smiled before turning back to the telephone box. Forster cracked his knuckles.

Standing in the doorway of the kebab shop, Rooney could see Forster's people in the car, and he wished the bloody kebab place was open. He could smell the grub from the all-night Chinese takeaway at the other end of the street and it was making his stomach growl. To make matters worse, he knew that his old boozing buddie, Charlton, would be in that Chinese takeaway right now, probably getting stuck into some Chinese chicken and chips while he watched the telephone box across the road. Why the hell couldn't the kebab shop be open? He was starving. Why the hell couldn't he have been given the Chinese takeaway stakeout instead of Charlton? Hardly bloody fair. Rooney clapped his arms round his sides to ward off the freezing air and hoped that the fella they were waiting for, whoever he was, would make his telephone call soon, so that they could move in and take him. After that, he could get home to the wife and kids for a super-early breakfast. God knew why Sheraton's lot wanted this bloke so badly, but want him they did.

'Not even a bleeding bag of crisps,' said Rooney aloud.

He slouched back against the kebab shop window, straining to see inside to catch any sign of movement. 'Hurry up and make your telephone call, willya?' he said to the night. 'I'm bloody hungry.'

10

Eddie stood at the window of the apartment block, six storeys up; looking down at the street, hands braced on the window sill. Somewhere behind him, Rennie was foraging in the refrigerator for something to eat. Down below lay the graffiti-ridden warren of streets, the neon wash from the Chinese takeaway on the pavement. Eddie saw tattered plastic bags snared on the spines of rusted railings, flapping desperately to be free. He saw boiling black clouds, heading his way, full of brooding rain to come. But even as he looked at all these things, he knew that something else — something inside him — was looking down at those streets. It was as if he was scanning the streets on behalf of the thing inside. When it found what it was looking for, it would let him know. He continued to scan the streets, puzzled.

He turned away from the window, looked back to the kitchenette; listened to Rennie slamming the fridge door, banging open a cupboard. He turned back and looked down again.

And then he knew what it was the *feeling* inside had been hunting for. As he'd looked down into those streets, he had found it — a series of details, insignificant in themselves, but which now suddenly made sense. He scoured the streets again, picking up each of the details he had seen and initially overlooked.

A man, sitting alone in the darkness of the park beyond the telephone kiosk.

The front bumper of a car parked in the side street of that park.

The car parked directly below him, facing towards the telephone kiosk.

The man standing in the doorway of the Chinese takeaway, eating from a steaming foil tray.

The shadow of the man in the kebab shop doorway.

Eddie looked at his watch. It was three-twenty-nine.

He smiled.

'Ten green bottles . . .' he said, staring out of the window onto the street below.

'What?' Rennie was now at the end of his tether, seriously questioning Eddie's state of mind. His impatience was showing. 'Look, Eddie. For God's sake, man, what the hell is going on here? What . . .?'

Eddie turned from the window, one hand fluttering in uncharacteristic weakness to his brow. His face was ashen, beads of cold sweat on his face. Rennie moved quickly forward and took him by the elbow, fearing that he might collapse. Eddie clung to the hand that grasped him; he suddenly looked so old. His breath was hoarse, as if he was having difficulty breathing.

'Sit down.' Rennie guided him back to the sofa. Eddie slumped down, hand covering his face, as Rennie bent to pour more whisky. He pressed the glass into Eddie's fingers. 'I'm going for a doctor.'

'No!' Eddie pulled himself into a more attentive posture, wiped his face again and swallowed a mouthful of whisky. Then gently, '. . . no . . .' When he looked back at Rennie again, he seemed to have regained some of his old composure. He smiled.

'I know what you're thinking. Know you think I've cracked up. It's okay. I can understand how all this must look. You've got to be wondering what's going on. Sometimes I wonder what the hell it's all about myself. But you don't have to worry.'

'So tell me. Come *on*, man. From what you say, there's a street full of hard men down there, all waiting to mince us. You've set us up for a real fall, Eddie.'

'I've set something up all right. But we're in no danger. Believe me.'

'Convince me.'

'I've got something. I don't know what the hell it is. I suppose you could call it a . . . new . . . *power*. I can do things, Rennie. Things you wouldn't believe possible. I can get us anything we want.'

'And how do you do that?'

'I can put the Frighteners on people.'

'You're not talking sense again.'

'Remember Archie Duncan?' Rennie nodded. 'Remember what happened in that washroom? You said so yourself . . . you couldn't understand how we got out of there in one piece. One minute we're there, nearly totalled, and the next we're back in our cell. And Sheraton's boys are splattered all over the place. Well . . . something happened then, Rennie. *Something* happened.'

'What?'

'There was something *inside* Archie. I don't know what it was, or how it came to be there. But there was something . . . something that was somehow locked inside him. It *jumped*, Rennie. It jumped out of him and into me . . . and it had something to do with the way I was feeling. Archie kept asking everyone how much they hated. Remember that? That's all he could say: "How much do you hate?" Well, at that time, right at that moment . . . I hated everything the way nobody's ever hated in their lives. And . . . whatever, it was . . . my hating that way made it able to jump out of Archie and into me.'

'Hold on . . . hold on . . . This is too much all at once. First things first. How the hell did we get *out* of that shower-room, Eddie? What the hell happened to Laverick and the others?'

'The power, Rennie. *The power*. It jumped from Archie to me. It's what saved us. It made Archie kill Laverick and his friends for us. And then Archie carried us out of there.'

'Oh yeah? Past those security barriers, and the screws . . . and the cons? He just carried us all the way back to our cell without anyone seeing and just dumped us there without anyone seeing?'

'That's right. It was the power. There's no limit to what it can do. I can feel it inside. I can do things with it, Rennie. I can make things happen with it. I can *use* it.'

Rennie slumped back into his chair and drained his glass; he felt hopelessly depressed about this conversation, as if he was being drawn into Eddie's own neurosis and confused mindgames.

'Show me, then,' he said at last.

Eddie looked up, eyes glinting 'What?'

'I said, show me.'

'I'll show you soon, when Frankie turns up with the money we need.'

'No, Eddie. I don't mean then. I mean now. I want to see what it is that you can do.'

'What, here? But there's nobody I want to . . . want to . . .'

'Want to hurt? Is that what you were going to say? Nobody here to hurt?'

'Yeah . . . I mean, no . . . I mean, okay. I think I can show you something.' For a while, Eddie sat staring into space, swilling the whisky around in his glass. His gaze transferred to the ceiling, as if he was working out some kind of complicated puzzle. 'Listen, Rennie. I'm not . . . completely sure how this stuff works. I mean, I don't tell it *exactly* what to do, if you know what I mean. All I know is that when I want to persuade someone to do something, or if I want to . . .'

'Hurt somebody?'

'Yeah, well, there's people need hurting, Rennie. Never forget that. Like I was saying, though . . . if I want things to happen, I can do it by . . . *thinking* in a particular way. Once I've done that, I leave the power to it. The Frighteners take care of the rest.'

'So show me, Eddie.'

Eddie began to smile. 'It's happening already. You just haven't noticed yet.'

Rennie started to feel something then; an insubstantial feeling at first, but growing in familiarity and unpleasantness. He shuffled in his seat, remembering that he sometimes felt like this when he was working under a car. If he spent a lot of time under there, with the oil and the heat on his face, it seemed as if he might suffocate. Not that he was claustrophobic, not at all; but sometimes that feeling meant that it was time for him to get out from under the car, maybe have a coffee or a beer or a chat with Eddie for five minutes before he started again. That feeling was on him now, and he could see that Eddie was enjoying it.

'What . . .?' began Rennie. And then Eddie smiled again, slowly pointing to the chest of drawers at the other side of the room, beside the television. Rennie followed his pointing finger, feeling that prickling touch of sweat and oil all over his body and believing now that something was actually going to happen.

'Look,' said Eddie.

The chest was three drawers high, with cheap porcelain figurines on top. And as Rennie watched, the bottom drawer began to slide open by itself.

'How . . .?'

'Just watch.'

The drawer stopped.

Something began to crawl out.

Rennie half-rose in his chair, shrinking away from the sight as if a poisonous snake was slowly slithering out of that drawer.

But it was not a snake. It was white . . . and crumpled . . . and made of cotton. Shaking his head and glancing at Eddie just long enough to see the latter grinning widely at what he considered a neat trick, Rennie looked back to see that, somehow, a crumpled white shirt was being pushed out of the drawer. No, not being pushed. Not pushed at all.

It was crawling out by itself.

A sleeve twitched over the side, feeling downwards until the cuff had reached the carpet. Now, with a rough fumbling sound, the rest of the shirt began to follow. The second

147

sleeve looped over the rim of the drawer and reached down to the carpet. Both sleeves scrabbled forwards over the carpet as the remainder of the shirt finally flopped free from the drawer onto the floor.

Standing now, Rennie could see with a feeling of mounting unreality that all the clothing in that drawer was somehow alive.

The shirt wriggled sleeve-over-sleeve across the carpet towards him and . . . oh, God . . . he didn't want it to touch him. As if somehow sensing his innermost thoughts, it stopped, furling runnels of movement fluttering up and down its length; alive but waiting. The rest of the drawer's contents began to flop and twitch onto the carpet, squirming and writhing. Rennie saw his ties there, twisting and weaving like exotically patterned snakes. His T-shirts, vests and pants coiled and contorted together on the carpet, like snakes making love. Sweat was coating Rennie's back now as the other two drawers quickly slid open and the contents were disgorged, writhing onto the floor, a ridiculous squirming mass of laundry. But ridiculous though it was — and Eddie seemed to be enjoying the clothes show immensely — Rennie could find nothing to laugh at as the jumble of clothes on the floor began to *compact* together.

'Clothes maketh the man, Rennie,' grinned Eddie.

The tail of the first shirt was opening up as if air was blowing through it, even though there was no draught of air in the room. In a jumble of movement that was also somehow horribly obscene, the contorted mass of squirming clothing began to force itself into the shirt, filling it with substance and mass.

Rennie gripped the arms of his chair, wanting to get away from this bizarre spectacle, but unable to move. His wardrobe door flew open. Something whipped in a blur across the carpet towards the activity in front of the chest of drawers. By the colour of the material, he could see that it was a pair of his jeans, now being held on the floor by invisible hands as more clothing began to force itself into the trouser legs. The jeans flipped over and connected somehow with the shirt.

And then the thing stood up.

It was the size of a man. A shirt, stuffed full of Rennie's dirty laundry, attached to a pair of jeans, also stuffed full of linen and dirty underwear. Headless, handless and without feet, it stood in front of the chest before them, weaving from side to side like some obscene puppet.

'Seen something like it on TV ads when I was inside,' said Eddie casually. 'Clothes get together and wash themselves. Cut out the middle man. Literally. You must have seen it.'

Rennie looked back, just as the thing took two wavering 'steps' forward into the centre of the room.

'No!' Rennie held out his hands. 'Eddie, whatever in hell it is . . . stop it!'

'Nothing to be afraid of. He won't harm you.'

The thing stopped, weaving.

'Can't you . . . feel it, Eddie?'

'Feel what?'

'That fucking thing is . . . *dangerous*. Can't you feel it, man?'

'Oh yeah, it's dangerous. Just looks like a bunch of clothes, but it's dangerous all right. Good, eh?'

'Send the bloody thing away, Eddie. Please.'

'It's not going to . . .'

The thing stepped forwards towards Rennie again, sleeves raised.

'Where are *you* going?' Eddie snapped. 'Enough!'

The shirt and trousers crumpled in on themselves, collapsing inert on the carpet. Now, the laundry was simply the pile of dirty clothes that it had always been.

Anger turned quickly to puzzlement on Eddie's face. Then the puzzlement was wiped away, to be replaced by humour as he turned to look back at Rennie. 'Convinced, Rennie?'

With trembling fingers, Rennie groped for his whisky glass and drained it.

'I don't know . . .'

'What to say? Not surprised. Took me a while to get used

to it in prison.' Eddie poured himself another drink. 'I don't know how I can call them up. But I can. They don't have a personality or anything, that much I know. They're just like . . . machines . . . I tell them what to do . . . and they do it. In their own way, of course. I just let 'em get on with it.'

'You tell them to kill, Eddie? To *kill*?'

'No. I tell them what I want. And they go and get it for me. If they don't get what I want, they do what they have to do. There's a choice.'

'Some choice.'

'And what choice did Tracey and the kids have, then?'

Eddie stood up and moved to the pile of clothes in the middle of the carpet. He began to poke them about with his foot. Then he moved back to the window and looked down onto Windsor Street, hands braced on the sill. Rennie poured more whisky, glancing from Eddie to the pile of clothes. He wondered just who the hell had been let out of prison. Was it Eddie?

Or was it somebody . . . or something . . . else?

11

A whirlpool of dead leaves rattled down the centre of Windsor Street. A sheet of dirty newspaper took flight like a trainee banshee, cavorting with the leaves before being expelled into higher air, drifting upwards and away into the night. Beyond Windsor Street, the city was in its dead sleep. In the whispering street itself, nine wakeful minds shared the same thought: they wanted to be home in bed, not sitting on park benches or in cars waiting for some two-bit loser to turn up and step into a telephone kiosk. The same nine minds wished to hell he would get on with it. It was past the time he was supposed to show. And the same minds had already decided that if the loser still failed to show after another half-hour, then they were all going back to bed anyway. He was only one miserable little shit trying to be a little bit too cocky. Enquiries could be made tomorrow and in the next few days. There was no way he could hide in the city without someone in the organisation getting wind of where he was. When that happened, they could move in, pick him up and turn him over to Sheraton . . . or better still, just finish the bastard off. Leave him hung up and bleeding from a lamp post or something . . . whatever Sheraton wanted. But please let this bitter cold, God-awful night be over and done with.

And then a ragged figure turned the corner into Windsor Street from the direction of the post office; bulleted round the corner as if he'd been bodily thrown, staggered, clutching a briefcase to his chest, and began to run down the street towards the telephone box. Nine people sat up alert. The figure's breath was streaming around its head in the cold early-morning air. Its shirt tail was hanging out and its trousers were torn. Gasping, tottering and staggering, the figure bounced against a rough stone wall and across the street, colliding heavily with the park railings. For a second, it leaned there, gasping for breath . . . and then pushed itself away and headed directly towards the telephone box.

'Wait for it,' said someone in the BMW.

'Wait until he's in the box,' said another voice in the vehicle parked by the side of the park.

The figure in the kebab shop doorway blended away into the shadows as the figure passed him. Likewise, the figure in the Chinese takeaway.

The figure slammed into the telephone kiosk, struggled with the door and clumsily pulled it open, blundering inside with the suitcase.

Two car engines started up. The men in the park, the kebab shop and the Chinese takeaway stepped out of the shadows and began walking towards the telephone box: an isolated pool of light in the darkness. Two cars slid slowly into Windsor Street, gliding through the shadows.

Six storeys up, a silent figure watched the shadows converge, and smiled. The figure moved back from the window.

Inside the telephone box, the telephone rang; the shrill peals stabbed through Frankie's mind, threatening to upset the control of his bladder again. Fumbling desperately, he snatched the receiver to his ear, breath hoarse, full of effort and impending tears.

'*Hello, Frankie. Been a naughty boy, haven't you? Have you got the money?*' asked Eddie from the public telephone box in the corridor, six storeys above.

'Yes! Yes!'

'*But you're not alone, are you?*'

'I'm alone, Eddie! I'm alone . . .' And suddenly, Frankie remembered what had been planned by Sheraton's mob; remembered the reception that had been organised for Eddie while Frankie was to have been safely at home in bed. Now

152

wanting to puke in fear, he became aware of the shadows that were converging on the telephone kiosk. 'Not me, Eddie! Not me! It was Sheraton. Honestly, Eddie. You know that! But look . . . I've got your money. All of it and more! You can have it!'

Click!

'Oh no, Eddie! Don't hang up! Please!' The receiver fell from Frankie's trembling fingers, clattering and rattling on the inside of the kiosk, around his knees. He groped at the glass of the kiosk, feeling the shadows drawing closer and now seeing that a whirlwind of leaves, rubbish and newspapers seemed to have appeared in the middle of the street. His heavy breathing on the glass began to mist over the approaching shadows. Frankie's bladder let him down for the second time that evening. Again, he began to cry.

12

Forster grinned when he saw Bishop's car glide round the corner of the park and turn into Windsor Street ahead of him. Right on time. Nice and neat. Just the way that Sheraton liked to have things done. Smooth and efficient. His own car was gliding towards the telephone kiosk from the other direction down Windsor Street. In the back, Bob and his mate had stopped playing cards, sitting forward attentively now, straining to see the dim form crouching in the telephone box. Forster cracked his knuckles again and looked out across the park to see a hunched figure walking slowly towards the railings. Pat Hudson, no doubt. Charlton and Rooney were starting to cross the road now.

'Easy,' said Bob from the back seat, popping a peanut and chewing loudly.

The car engine coughed and spluttered. Forster felt a tremor from the engine run the entire length of the car's frame. Mickey twisted the choke; the car donkeyed, emitting a strangled coughing sound.

'Oh, shit . . .'

Forster looked up towards the kiosk again, hoping that Brinkburn wouldn't hear the car's approach and do a runner. If they lost him because of a faulty engine, Forster didn't fancy the prospect of having to make explanations to his superiors. He had been told to check the engine out and make sure that nothing could go wrong. If he screwed up now . . .

The engine spluttered again, coughed . . . and died.

'Oh, shit!' Mickey twisted the choke again. The engine

protested. Strange noises began to come from under the bonnet. 'What the hell's wrong with it?'

The car glided to a halt. Mickey considered the possibility of using the starter again, but couldn't risk alerting Brinkburn.

'What's going on?' asked Bob, leaning forward over the passenger seat, eager to get on with the business.

'How the hell should I know!'

The engine began to make more strange noises. Mickey banged his hands on the steering wheel, straining to see ahead. The other car also appeared to have stopped. Bishop and his man for the job, Cussler, were climbing out — still about thirty yards from the telephone kiosk.

'Okay. We get out here and walk.'

They climbed out of the car.

And then things started to happen.

Pat Hudson stepped through the park gates onto the pavement leading towards the telephone box and cursed aloud when the epaulette on his overcoat snagged on one of the railings.

Charlton saw Rooney emerge from the kebab shop and begin to cross the street. He smiled, and dropped his empty silver foil tray into the rubbish bin on the pavement. His smile vanished instantly, when something cold and hard in the rubbish bin seemed to grip his hand and hold it there.

Forster recoiled in alarm from the car bonnet: something inside seemed to groan, like the slow rending and twisting of heavy metal. Mickey and Bob looked at the bonnet in puzzlement too, as they heard a *spang!spang!spang!* sound from inside, and the bonnet slowly, almost reluctantly . . . began to lift.

Bishop and Cussler turned away from the telephone kiosk, distracted by the sudden activity ahead of them at Forster's car.

Rooney froze in the middle of the road, watching, perplexed, as Hudson struggled to free his raincoat from the park railings and Charlton seemed to be wrestling with something in the rubbish bin on the pavement. In the street ahead, something seemed to be happening at Forster's car. The bonnet was lifting. The bonnet was lifting and . . .

. . . and Forster goggled in amazement at the car engine inside, which seemed to have taken on a life of its own. It was writhing and contorting. Wiring, valves, tubes and pistons were twisting themselves out of shape . . . wrenching themselves apart in an agonized screeching and squealing of rent metal and torn wires. Sparks jumped out of the engine onto the pavement. Mickey and Bob sprang back. Forster turned, looking back at Bishop and Cussler as they stared, holding his arms wide as if to say, *How the hell should I know what's going on?* He turned again to the engine. It was alive. Alive and . . . rearranging itself. From the park, someone screamed and, turning, Forster saw . . .

. . . that the person screaming was Pat Hudson. He was somehow snared on the park railings. But the railings now seemed to be much more than just railings. The metal spikes were *bending* towards him, and Forster heard one of them tear itself free from the metal framework with an echoing *clank*! and a shower of rust before bending, point-inwards, towards Hudson, who seemed to be trapped in the embrace of a grille of rusted and spiked railings. Forster couldn't make out what the hell was happening to Hudson in his barbed straitjacket, and . . .

Rooney watched in horror and amazement as Charlton seemed suddenly to be yanked head-first into the rubbish bin. He started to move forward, unsure what to do in the face of such a ridiculous sight. Charlton's legs began to kick and thrash; his cries were muffled . . . and Rooney didn't know whether to start laughing or what when . . .

. . . the barbed, rusted railing plunged directly into Hudson's chest with an audible *whump*! pinning him back against the barbed cage of the other railings as they continued to snap apart, bend inwards and impale him there in a snakes' nest embrace of twisted iron. A dark pool began to spread around Hudson's feet as he slumped, still held erect by the puncturing spikes. Bishop and Cussler suddenly had Browning automatics in their hands; they were crouching low, looking urgently around to try and locate the source of this bizarre attack. Rooney knew now that it was no longer a laughing matter as . . .

. . . Forster's eyes bulged wide in disbelief as the thing which had been born under the bonnet of his car, from the compacted and mangled innards of the car engine, tore itself loose and stood up, its shadow towering over him. It was vaguely man-shaped; a swaying tower of contorted wiring, broken valves and metal tubes. The engine itself had been twisted and shaped into the monstrous form before him; as if Leonardo da Vinci had been given the raw materials of the car engine, and from them had fashioned an anatomical likeness of some bizarre man. It looked down on Forster. From the horrifying *mélange* of wiring, metal and torn rubber that was its head, it smiled a hideous smile of broken valves and dripping, hissing black oil. Forster looked up at it, awestruck and unbelieving. And then the thing lashed out with one of its rough steel arms.

Forster's head whirled in a liquid arc across to the other side of the road, wedging between two park railings, quickly dying eyes looking out sadly across an upside-down park. His body slumped twitching to the road. Mickey and Bob scrambled in horror to the pavement, now also with guns drawn from under their coats. Mickey fired first. The bullet passed straight through the engine-man as it began to clamber out from under the bonnet and shattered the car windscreen. The thing was big; impossibly big to have ever fitted under that bonnet in the first place. Bob began to fire blindly, too, uttering small, hoarse cries as he did so. Bishop and Cussler began to skip nervously back towards their own car. On the far side of the road, the ridiculously bizarre sight of Charlton, still stuffed head-first to the waist in the rubbish bin, was now smothered and very, very dead. An excited yammering came from the Chinese takeaway; the lights went out and the blinds were hurriedly drawn.

Mickey fired again, and this time the bullet ignited something in the car. There was a soft *whump*! as petrol caught fire and blue, bunsen-like flame began to spread liquidly around the bonnet, creeping up the twisted wiring and tubular legs of the engine-man as it finally pulled itself free and stood erect and weaving in front of the car. Its nine-feet tall frame was now wreathed in blue flame, surging in its see-through innards, its legs and its arms. As it moved, a lake of fire moved with it from the car along the tarmac. Its body squeaked and groaned; its expressionless, chaotic face turned to look at them. Behind it, Forster's decapitated body began to burn. Rooney could take no more. He turned and fled from the hellish scene, quickly followed by Forster's third man.

Bishop and Cussler clambered back into their car as the thing walked slowly and purposefully towards them, each step a grinding of metal on metal. The car screeched into reverse; hurtling back, it smashed across a pavement and into a shop frontage, righted itself and snarled away. Mickey and Bob, flattened against the park railings, began to edge away past the burning car and corpse as the engine-man watched Bishop's car disappear. Inside the telephone kiosk, the man who was most definitely not Eddie Brinkburn was screaming hoarsely, as the engine-man turned its slowly burning body to look at him. And then it looked past him, unconcerned about the screaming man in the box, to the two men who were scrabbling to get away. Flecks of burning petrol had landed on Hudson's corpse as he hung from the park railings.

'What do we do? What the hell do we *do*, man?!' screamed Bob. Mickey stood next to him, both men unwilling to move towards the burning figure in the middle of the street . . . or past the corpse which hung on the railings. They had seen those railings come alive, they didn't want to pass too close in case the same thing started to happen again.

The engine-man turned as Bishop's car vanished into the night and began slowly to stride back towards the burning car.

Bob fired one shot; it screamed ricocheting through the twisted metal and off into the night. He skipped across the road, in front of the car and its lake of burning petrol . . . jumping across the flames and heading for the other side of the street. Mickey drew himself back, ready to make the same break for it.

And then the petrol tank finally fractured and erupted, just as Bob passed the front of the car. The roaring, deafening blast flung Mickey back against the railings; he fell forward again to the pavement. Momentarily, the car had vanished in a seething fireball. Struggling to his knees and scrabbling to find where his gun had fallen, Mickey looked back to see that the wreck was now wreathed in billowing orange flame and oily black smoke. Unconcerned, the engine-man had now reached the wreck and, innards groaning and squealing as its makeshift joints protested, it bent down into the flame and the dirty smoke, reappearing moments later with the burning bundle of what had once been Bob in its twisted metal hands. It held the burning body aloft in front of its face, its head turning from side to side to examine it. And now it let him drop once again to the burning pavement, still holding one of his arms, like some hideous child of the gods hanging onto a favourite doll. It turned to look round again. And its gaze fell on Mickey.

Forgetting the gun and the possibility that the railings might turn into snakes again, Mickey scrabbled to his feet and ran back towards the telephone box and the man who was sobbing inside there. He hurtled past, running away from the nightmare and praying hard that this was all just a dream, that it had never happened.

The thing turned to watch his progress, dragging its burning doll with it. Mickey vanished into the night.

At last, the engine-man turned back to the telephone kiosk.

Inside, Frankie was huddled on the floor, flames from the burning car reflecting in the glass. Crouching in his own excrement, he began to yell again at the top of his voice in fear and terror as the telephone started to ring. Not wanting ever to become involved in anything ever again, just wanting to stay at the bottom of that telephone kiosk forever,

Frankie knew that he had to answer that telephone; knew that if he didn't, then that . . . *thing* would come over for him. He scrambled back to his feet and grabbed the receiver.

'*Still there, Frankie? Good. Now . . . bring the money up to me. You know Windsor Court, don't you? The high-rise on the other side of the street? Bring it up to No 43, sixth floor. And quick! Before people start to wake up.*'

'Yes,yes,yes,yes,yes,' said Frankie, reverently replacing the receiver, seizing the briefcase and blundering back out into the smoke-wreathed street. Hopping across the street, giving the burning wreck and the makeshift man a wide berth, he scampered through the main doors of Windsor Court. Curtains were beginning to twitch as he passed. Somewhere in the night, he could hear the sound of approaching police sirens.

Outside, in the street, the thing in front of the car wreck watched him vanish inside. It let go of Bob's burning arm, finally consigning his body to the flames. It looked down into the rolling flame and smoke and bowed its head, almost sadly.

And then it fell apart.

Torn metal, twisted tubing and burning junk collapsed in a shower of sparks into the roaring orange flame and gushing black smoke.

13

'Did anyone see you?' asked Eddie, leaning casually against Rennie's drinks cabinet. He looked composed, completely in control.

Standing in the centre of the room, composure a thing of the past and looking more like a meths-sodden derelict than a casino owner, Frankie clutched the briefcase to his chest. His clothes were torn, mud splattered and stinking. The smell of excrement and urine was overpowering.

'Nobody. No one. Not anyone.' Frankie's eyes were fevered; permanently haunted now by the things he had seen at the casino and in the street. Outside, the police sirens had reached Windsor Street and even six storeys up, blue light was flashing against the windows opposite.

'Got the money?'

Frankie held the briefcase out before him; again as if it was some sacrificial offering, or his only guarantee of returning to the plush and confident life he had enjoyed before 3.30 am that morning. Eddie grunted, pushed himself from the cabinet and calmly took the briefcase away, dropping it onto the dining table and flicking the clasps.

Rennie had watched everything from the window. First Frankie's frantic arrival at the telephone box, then the encroaching heavies and then the bizarre nightmare of death and fire and things that couldn't be. The burning orange flame from the exploded car had reflected on Eddie's face as they both watched . . . and to Rennie it seemed as if he was looking at a mask: a lifelike mask of Eddie Brinkburn; a mask that hid something alien.

Rennie had waited with Eddie until Frankie had hammered frantically on the door, had watched as the man who had once with such disdain refused him admittance to his casino, had shambled into the room smelling like a sewer, with nightmares ingrained behind his eyes.

Eddie finished counting the money, smiled and clicked the briefcase shut.

'Only wanted three thousand, Frankie.'

'It's all yours, Eddie. Every bit of it.'

Eddie tut-tutted, walked back to Frankie and pushed a wad of notes into his torn coat pocket. 'Three was all I asked for. That's all I should get, isn't it? Don't want to get you into further trouble with Sheraton. You spend it. Buy yourself a new suit.'

'Sure . . . sure . . . whatever you want.'

'Now I'd like a little information. Just a little . . .'

'Eddie.' Rennie stepped forward from the window. Frankie's eyes, once so contemptuous, swivelled to Rennie, waiting for an instruction — *any* instruction he could carry out, anything to please. Eddie looked up.

'If he's staying here any longer, let him use the bathroom and get cleaned up. I can't stand the smell.'

Eddie laughed and pointed to the bathroom.

'You heard the man, Frankie. Five minutes. And no shit on the floor.' Frankie scuttled subserviently away, deferentially closing the door behind him.

'Now what?' asked Rennie at last.

'Wait and see. Just a couple of minutes. All part of my plan, Rennie. Frankie's going to help us out.'

Rennie bowed his head, shaking it, running his hand over his eyes. 'Too much, Eddie. All of this. Far too fucking much all at once. I need some time to sort it all out.'

'I know, I know. But it's okay. Everything's under control. Really. It's okay. You'll get used to it, Rennie. Honest. I promise.'

'Clothes that come alive . . . robots or something out of car engines. And *you*, Eddie. I don't even know if you're *you* any more! I look at your face sometimes and it's . . .'

162

it's like you're not even someone else . . . more like you're *something* else! Not even human, maybe.'

'Look, Rennie!' Eddie strode forward angrily, stabbing at him with one finger. 'I *need* you, man. You're going to be part of this. We've always stuck together. For years! I owe you a lot. You got done over just as much as me for that petrol station business. It was three years of your life, too. We're not letting Sheraton get away with it. Those bastards took three years out of your life, three and a half out of mine — and they fucking murdered my wife and kids, Rennie! They killed them! Burned them!'

'I know that, Eddie. Take it easy. I know that.'

'Now that this has happened to me . . . whatever in hell it is . . . I'm going to use it. *We're* going to use it. And we're going to make Sheraton and all those other bastards pay for what they've done.'

'Just us, Eddie? Me and you and your walking clothes and Meccano kit?'

'You can't imagine what I can do. I've just started, Rennie. I'm just getting the hang of it. It's getting bigger and stronger. I can feel it. We're going to bring Sheraton's empire down. We're going to smash everything they've got.'

In the bathroom, they heard the toilet flush and then the bathroom door clicked open. Frankie shambled back into the room. The smell was not appreciably improved. His eyes seemed glazed now.

'Here he comes,' smiled Eddie, his ferocity now subdued. 'Keep those doggies moving, eh, Frankie?'

Frankie tried to laugh; a hollow rictus which looked ghastly.

'Now then, Frankie. You're going to do something for me, aren't you? You're going to let me have some names and addresses of the people in Sheraton's little organisation. People like yourself — know what I mean, Frankie?'

'Please, Eddie. Don't. Sheraton'll have me totalled . . .'

'Now, now, Frankie. You don't want me to put the Frighteners on you again, do you?'

'I'll tell you anything you want to know, Eddie.'

'Good boy. Begin.'

163

14

Frankie sat patiently in the outer hall for three hours, like
a dutiful child. At the end of that time, Eddie popped his
head round the living room door and told him that it was
okay now, the police appeared to have cleared off. There
had been a knock at the door a couple of hours ago: the
police conducting door-to-door enquiries, no doubt, about
the incident downstairs in Windsor Street, but no one had
answered . . . and after a while they had gone away.

Frankie nodded dutifully, eyes glazed; then he left quietly,
closing the door submissively behind him. Head down, mind
somewhere else . . . in a place free from nightmares . . . he
shambled to the lift and pressed the 'down' button. He
believed that he was asleep, that at the proper time he would
wake up at home, with his world secure and everything back
in its proper order and perspective. He did not believe in
the world through which he now stumbled; did not believe
in nightmarish walking garbage men which ate people up
and spat them out in little pieces, nor in metal men that
climbed out of car engines amidst flames and smoke, nor
in public litter bins that ate people and park railings that
turned into snakes. It was a dream that he had believed in
for a while, but when he had finally recognised it as such,
he had opted out from believing anything ever again in this
nightmare world, until such time as his alarm clock would
ring and he would find himself back in his plush bedroom.

Frankie looked up and saw by the lights above the double
doors that the lift was at Floor 2 and climbing rapidly to
meet him at Floor 6. He had to admit that this was one of

the most detailed dreams he had ever experienced. As the light climbed, he wondered what the consequences would be for him in the waking world if he really had given Eddie Brinkburn all those names and addresses — particularly since there were many which he was not supposed to have, but which he'd picked up to keep him a half-step ahead in his dealings with Sheraton's organisation. Of course, in the real world his life wouldn't be worth a fart; but in his dream world everything would be okay. The Number 6 light *pinged*! and the double doors opened. Frankie laughed at the detail of the dream and stepped inside.

Still laughing as the dream turned into a nightmare of falling, he plunged seven storeys through the suddenly-vanished lift floor. All dreams snapped into an eternal blackness when his body hit the rubbish-strewn concrete paving at the foot of the lift shaft.

The lift light *pinged*! again, like the sound of some strange cash register ringing up receipt of another soul. The double doors closed. The sound of slowly groaning, rending metal echoed in the lift shaft as the rolled-back floor began to roll itself into position again. Fluted-metal flooring straightened out, fastening itself back into its proper place, re-acquiring the tensile density of steel; rivets popped back into sockets. A series of hollow clanks and groaning metal. And now the floor was no longer alive. It was a lift floor again, just like any lift floor, sturdy enough for its quota of fifteen passengers.

The lift descended to ground level.

15

'Bishop? I'm telephoning on behalf of Sheraton. I understand we've had a little trouble with Mr Brinkburn.'

'No problem! Absolutely no problem! We've got a special squad out in the field right now looking for him.'

'Four of Sheraton's people are dead, Bishop? And you say there's no problem? No problem . . . with cars blowing up and the police sniffing around now. This is beginning to sound more like a Charles Bronson movie.'

'I know, I know! They screwed up. No doubt about that. Seems as if there's other people involved.'

'Who?'

'Apart from the spade . . . Montresor . . . we don't know. But he must have got himself a small army or something.'

'Sheraton's not happy, Bishop. Not happy at all. Mr Brinkburn is a little fish. And he's making Sheraton look a fool.'

'I've got people on . . .'

'You're being held personally responsible for sorting this matter out. Do you understand?'

'Yessir!'

'Mr Brinkburn and his friends are to become history. Immediately.'

'Yessir!'

16

'Good evening, sir. Have you an appointment?'

She was about forty-five, respectable-looking and with a coiffure that looked carved out of cheese. Her make-up had been carefully applied but had been overdone, giving her face the overall appearance of a smudged photograph. She looked as if she should be serving behind the counter of a small village post office.

'Yes, my name's Burns.'

'Ah, yes. Mr Burns. You're expected.'

She held the door wide and he stepped slowly inside. The lobby could have belonged to a seaside lodging house: dark oak panelling on the walls, the smell of dried flowers and carpet freshener; a well-worn, russet brown carpet on the floor which stretched away up the long, shadowed staircase. Indeterminate Victorian prints gazed grimly down from the walls. Somewhere above a radio was playing, and he heard a woman's throaty, almost derogatory, laughter coming from one of the rooms on the upstairs landing. On his left, a door opened and an elderly gentleman in a pin-striped suit emerged. He thanked the young woman in the dressing-gown who had opened the door for him, smiled and collected his briefcase and umbrella from the Victorian coat-rack beside the main door, acknowledging the newcomer's presence with a slight, professional nod.

'Goodbye,' said the coiffured woman as he stepped out into the street and she closed the door behind him. 'Please come again.' She turned back to the new arrival. 'I believe you have been recommended to us, Mr Burns?'

'Yes, that's right. Mr Laine gave me your address and the recommendation.'

'Aha, Mr Laine. A frequent and well-respected customer. And now that you're here, Mr Burns, do you have any particular requirements?'

'Yes, I do. I want you to close down the brothel. And I want you and all your girls to leave London.'

'I beg your pardon?'

'I want all business associations with Sheraton's organisation severed. You'll find, I'm sure, that there's more than enough business in other parts of the country under different 'protection' regimes. Try Newcastle . . . or Glasgow. I'm sure you'll find that business up there will be just as good.'

'You're not police . . .' The woman's tone had changed now. The cultivated accent seemed to have vanished.

'No, I'm not. But your place has to be closed for business by 6.00 pm this evening. And you all have to be on your way.'

'I'm paying good protection money to avoid this sort of thing. I've got the best.'

'Yes, I know. Sheraton. But as of 6.00 pm tonight, your association with Sheraton ends.'

'Get the sodding hell out of here! I've had threats from the likes of you in the past. All it's going to take is one telephone call and . . .!'

'You'll have Sheraton's people over to kick my arse. Yeah, I know. But you've got until six tonight. Don't forget. Because if you do, I'm going to have to put the Frighteners on you.'

'Get out of here, you scum!'

'With pleasure. And by the way, if you're making that telephone call . . . the name isn't scum, or Burns. It's Brinkburn.'

17

The fat, balding man slammed the office door shut to block out the sound of lorries shunting in and out of the factory and the echoing shouts of the workforce. Clutching at the source of the raging indigestion which always seemed to ravage his gut in the afternoon, he belched, farted and moved back to his desk.

'Tell me again,' he said nervously, lighting the same cigar for the fourth time.

'I've told you everything,' said the tall man in the faded overalls, removing his feet from the fat man's desk and sitting up in his chair.

'So tell me *again*.'

'I answered the phone 'cause you were having a crap. This guy says, "You've got an hour to burn all the drugs you've been shipping for Sheraton." So I act dumb, as if I don't know what the hell he's going on about. I tell him that we're a freight service . . . express delivery . . . and who the hell is he, anyway? He says, "I know that you've been shipping drugs for Sheraton as a sideline for over two years. As of now, it stops. And everything you've got has to be burned! Every last bit of it." So I'm starting to sweat a little, 'cause no matter who he is, he's guessed right − or been told − about the drugs business. I'm not sure if this is a proper threat, or one of Sheraton's mob testing us out or something . . . so I still play dumb. I tell him to fuck off and stop bothering people when they're trying to do an honest day's work. I say I'll have a trace on the 'phone like you see in the movies and we'll have the police onto him. So he just laughs and says: "This has got nothing to do with the police. This is something that I'm taking care of myself. As of now, you've got fifty-seven minutes left to burn everything, otherwise I'll have the Frighteners put onto you".'

'The Frighteners? That's what he said?'

'Yeah, exactly.'

'Then what?'

'Then he says, "Tell Sheraton that Brinkburn called".'

'Brinkburn?'

'Yeah.'

'Make a telephone call.'

18

London Evening News: November 15th

Police and Fire Brigade were called out early last evening to attend a fire which broke out in a boarding house owned by Mrs Doris Sharp in Elmtree Road. No one was hurt in the incident, but residents were forced to evacuate the building which was completely demolished by the fire. The police have not ruled out foul play, as there have been as yet unsubstantiated reports of intruders who may have been in some way connected with the outbreak of fire. It is also understood that police enquiries have been commenced in respect of the nature of business conducted from Mrs Sharp's boarding house. Vice Squad officials refused to comment at this stage.

Daily Standard: November 16th

The Fire Brigade is still attempting to control a fire which broke out at Reighton's Freight Agency in London's dockland early this evening and which is raging out of control, resulting in thousands of pounds worth of damage. It is understood that the entire freight stock of the company has been destroyed by the fire.

19

'Mrs Sharp? This is Eddie Brinkburn. I got your "new" telephone number from a working acquaintance, shall we say. Don't hang up on me if you know what's good for you.'

'I won't, I won't! Listen . . . I'm sorry. I should have done what you wanted. But for God's sake . . . *for God's sake* . . . don't make those things come back again. I don't know what they were, but I never want to see them again. I'll do anything you say, anything at all. I'll move . . . that's it! I'll do just what you wanted. I'll move and take all of my girls with me!'

'That's just fine, Mrs Sharp. Pity that you didn't take any notice of me when we first had our little talk. But there's one thing I need from you . . .'

'Anything, anything at all.'

'Good. I want some names, addresses and telephone numbers. I know that you have lots of them, Mrs Sharp. All of the other madams . . . pardon me . . . ladies in the trade. All of the "boarding houses" paying protection to Sheraton. Do you understand?'

'They'd kill me . . .'

'Not if you're far, far away. And you don't want to see my friends again, do you?'

'Oh God, no! All right. I'll tell you everything you want. Just give me a minute to get my address book out . . .'

'Good girl.'

20

'Reighton?'

'I told you. No comment. My bloody business burned down. And I don't know how. Check with my insurance people if you want, but leave me alone. What more do you want? I was lucky to get out of that place alive.'

'This isn't the newspapers, Reighton. This is Eddie Brinkburn.'

A pause.

'Are you still there, Mr Reighton? I suggest very strongly that you don't hang up, and listen to what I have to say. Do you understand me, Mr . . .'

'*What in the living hell were those things?* I saw them . . . I *saw* the bloody things. But I couldn't believe it. Pieces of junk welded together . . . or garbage . . . or something. One of them tore Ernie Freeman to pieces right in front of me. Into pieces . . .'

'It's nice to know that they made an impression.'

'Then they set fire to my place. What the hell were they, Brinkburn?'

'Never mind. Just listen to what I say.'

'Look, it wasn't me who phoned Sheraton's people. It was Ernie Freeman. Honest.'

'Then he got what he deserved, didn't he? Now it's up to you to stay on my good side, Reighton. Because you don't want the same thing to happen to you, do you?'

'No, no, no! Okay . . . okay . . . take it easy, Brinkburn. Just ask me. That's all. Tell me what you want.'

'Names, addresses and telephone numbers. I want to

173

know everything there is to know about your dealings with Sheraton. Everything. Do you understand?'

'But they'll . . .'

'Kill you? Well . . . I won't tell them if you don't. And I'm sure that you're quite good at keeping secrets, aren't you?'

'Don't . . . don't send those things back, Brinkburn.'

'I won't. As long as you start talking.'

'All right. I first got involved back in '82 . . .'

21

Bishop was nervous.

Nervous because he didn't know whether everyone who had survived the encounter in Windsor Street would stick to their agreed stories. Nervous because he still couldn't rationalise what had happened. He had been effectively in charge of the operation and it had been made very clear to him that any failure would be his responsibility. Pat Hudson, Charlton, Forster and Bob were dead, the manner of their deaths so bizarre as to be beyond any rationalisation. And that . . . *thing* . . . climbing out of Forster's car — how on earth could he report back to Sheraton (that equally terrifying figure whom he'd never seen) about *that*? If he told the truth as it had happened, no one would believe him and he'd be finished: finished with Sheraton, finished with breathing, finished with life. So he'd driven around to Rooncy's place with Cussler, found him there shaking with fear and too scared even to open the front door. Cussler had eventually been forced to shoulder-charge it down. Once inside, they'd killed a bottle of whisky and come up with a revised version of what had happened, to protect their necks. It had been a trap. Brinkburn had been waiting for them with a gang of hard men no one recognised, really well-organised professionals. Brinkburn had arrived (not Frankie — oh God, don't say anything about Frankie Laine) and they had moved in. That's when Brinkburn had given the order and his men had moved in on the set-up, knocking out Bishop's people. That was the story — and they had to stick to it. Nothing about machine men or snake railings.

There was bound to be a feedback from Sheraton's contacts in the police force on the nature of the deaths, of course. But, with luck, they'd get away with it. All they had to do was keep to the same story.

Since that time, he had also been charged with finding Eddie Brinkburn and squashing him flat. But none of his people in the street had been able to find anything out; not a sniff of Brinkburn or his friend. And Bishop was painfully aware of the mounting list of brothels, half-way houses and drugs factories which were being burned down.

Bishop realised that he had been nervously playing with the executive pencil on the blotter in front of him and hastily dropped it, smiling nervously, sitting back and looking round again. Even the surroundings made him nervous. It was the first time he'd ever been asked here and he felt intimidated by the plush and intensely formal executive board room.

It looked like the board rooms he'd seen on television — in *Dynasty* or *Dallas* or something; oak-panelled walls, chandeliers, a floor-to-ceiling window overlooking the city below. A deep-pile red carpet that swallowed the sound of the footsteps of anyone walking on it. A long, highly polished teak table in the centre of the board room with identical blotter pads for each of the thirty places. The murmuring hubbub of the people sitting round that table served to make him feel even more uneasy; he could sense that everyone there was also desperately trying to conceal their own uneasiness. From his own seat, half-way down on the left, he scanned the faces. Sober, dark suited, neat ties; balding, respectable businessmen all — but all in the employ of Sheraton apparently. All somehow connected with this great glass building which had 'Solperan Inc' in gold lettering above the main entrance door downstairs and in scroll lettering on the door of the board room, but which should really have read 'Sheraton Inc'. Why the hell was he here? Why had he been telephoned and told to attend? He'd never even heard of Solperan Inc before, knew nothing of the internal machinations of Sheraton's 'business'. Why should he be trusted to such an extent now? All he did was run the car racket and protection aspects; surely a piffling, minor part of what he knew to be a major criminal enterprise.

He exchanged a nervous glance with the fidgeting, oily businessman next to him and went back to fiddling with his pencil. What the hell was this guy into as part of Sheraton's business chain? Prostitution? Protection? Drugs?

The double doors of the board room opened and the murmuring stopped. Two almost identical heavy-set men in sober business suits and with faces that concealed any tendency towards civilised behaviour, entered and opened the doors wide on either side. They looked like boxers at a funeral.

'Be upstanding please, gentlemen,' said one of the bereaved boxers with a strong Cockney accent. Seats bumped on the thick red pile of the carpet. The company rose in unison, Bishop slightly late but quickly catching up and nervously straightening his tie.

Sheraton walked into the room.

'No one told me . . .' said Bishop in awe, under his breath.

'What?' whispered the fidgeting, oily businessman next to him.

'Sheraton. No one told me.'

'Told you what?'

'That she's a woman.'

Sheraton strode briskly yet somehow fluidly the length of the room, head down, black tresses of hair hiding her face. The boxers closed the doors and followed closely behind. Bishop noticed that one of them was carrying an oblong cardboard box about two and a half feet long. The other held a pile of business files.

When she reached the head of the table, they stepped in front of her and pulled out the seat so that she could take her place.

Bishop examined Sheraton closely, refusing to believe that she was a woman, that she could possibly be the Head of the Corporation, the mention of whose name frequently had underlings peeing in their pants. The same Sheraton who could command the life and death of everyone in the organisation or anyone who proved to be a nuisance. The same Sheraton whose younger brother had been hideously burnt in the petrol station affair. To Bishop, she seemed more like a cosmetic sales adviser or one of the models they used to push soup on television. Dressed in a dark blue business suit with ankle-length skirt, a white blouse with ruff and with designer spectacles Sheraton looked no more dangerous than an Avon Lady.

She looked up from her papers abruptly, took off her spectacles and placed them on the table. Her face was striking – beautiful even – but not in a gentle way. There was a certain sharpness to her features, the angle of her face, and an aquiline nose dissipated any hint of softness. She was certainly a very attractive woman; even in such intimidating circumstances, Bishop found himself responding to her sexually. He guessed that she was about thirty-five.

Sheraton looked up again. Bishop fancied that he could see the green of her eyes even from where he stood. Expressionlessly and carefully, she appraised the ranks on either side of the table. Somewhere, someone coughed and shuffled. Appraisal completed (her gaze swept over Bishop without apparently registering anything – for which he was profoundly grateful), she smiled – a smile of even white teeth in an expression so deadly, Bishop could almost feel the bite.

'Please sit down, gentlemen.' Her voice was soft, but assured and confident.

Bishop began to find the whole scene ridiculous, although he was reluctant to let this feeling override his innate nervousness. He sat down with the others.

'Thank you for coming. Please smoke if you wish.'

In response, half a dozen cigars emerged from inside pockets, lighters flared, blue smoke drifted across the table. Somehow, with amusement, Bishop could only view the

178

image of these men with their cigars and the woman at the top of the table from a phallically symbolic point of view.

'There's only one item on the agenda.'

Sheraton looked up, like a schoolmistress expecting a shouted answer to an easy question. None was forthcoming.

'Eddie Brinkburn.'

Bishop's smile died in his teeth.

'We've all read the newspapers. We're all in the same business. And we all know what's happening.'

Oh shit . . .

'In the space of one week, four brothels have been burnt down. Three drug warehouses have been destroyed — two burnt out and one blown up; God knows how. Three administration sections of the East Bank have been wrecked, with confidential distribution information taken. At the present count, twelve operatives have been killed. Eddie Brinkburn, gentlemen. Eddie Brinkburn.'

Not my fault. Not my fault . . .

'Now how is this happening? I ask myself.' Sheraton picked up her spectacles again with an immaculately manicured hand. 'The single biggest corporation of its kind in the country. An amalgam of three disparate criminal organisations, with a strong family history, all brought together into a streamlined, efficient, state-of-the-art executive empire by my father, and inherited by me with control and organisation intact. Massive manpower and resources, links so deep nationally and internationally that we can't be touched by the law, the Government, anybody. With our roots firmly embedded in every single organised criminal activity in the city. And yet . . . and yet . . .'

Sheraton started to walk slowly round the table, her minders dutifully following. Again, the image of a schoolmistress talking to erring children overpowered Bishop; as if she was delivering a lecture now.

'. . . and yet . . . one little man, one pathetically little man, can somehow do all this. A little man who . . . changed numberplates on stolen cars, I believe. A mechanic. One little man and his ethnic friend who botched up a very minor

179

operation which maimed my brother. One little man who managed to total not one, not two, not three . . . but *seven* men contracted to make sure that he never got out of prison alive. One little man who can organise sufficient muscle to trash two casinos, four brothels, three drugs factories and two office blocks. Now we have the police sniffing around us, gentlemen, eager to find the chinks in our armour now that we're under attack by this *little man*. It's all very embarrassing. Very embarrassing indeed. Not only is this making us look foolish countrywide — but we're also beginning to look foolish internationally. Oh yes, our Common Market friends, and particularly our American friends, are beginning to wonder whether we're losing control. They're asking questions. Questions like — is this a gang war? Is there a new bid for takeover? How big is this new, dynamic and challenging organisation? Does it present a real threat? And if it does, perhaps we should be trading with *them* rather than Sheraton. Now this is a situation which I find particularly displeasing. Because no one in my employ — no one *here*! — seems able to tell me where Mr Brinkburn and his black batman are, how they're getting their information, and who's providing them with their muscle. Depressing, gentlemen. Depressing . . .'

Sheraton passed behind Bishop, followed by the minders. He felt the hair prickle on the back of his neck and his scalp; but he was already feeling relieved. He had surely botched the frame-up of Brinkburn in Windsor Street, but there were bigger, more important concerns at stake: other people had made mistakes, other things had been happening — the guys sitting around this table had all failed to track Brinkburn down. He wasn't alone in his failure. And there was safety in shared blame to this extent. Sheraton passed on, head down, still delivering her lecture.

'. . . and I don't like to be depressed. Because my depression turns to anger. And I'm sure that you won't want me to be angry.'

You won't like me when I'm angry, thought Bishop, thinking of the Incredible Hulk's famous line and now feeling not quite so agitated as before. He could listen to this woman ranting if she wanted to, there was no threat involved after all. They were all guilty. Brinkburn was clever, really fucking clever — they had all underestimated him.

Sheraton stopped at the end of the table, head down again; thoughtful. Behind her, the two minders also stopped. With perfectly manicured hand under her chin now, still thoughtful, she beckoned to the man holding the parcel. He began to unwrap it. The entire attention of the audience was on the parcel as Sheraton continued:

'We all know that there are certain rules in this game, gentlemen. My rules. I don't have to remind you all that my word is law — if you'll pardon the dramatic cliché. When I instruct that something is done, then my will shall be done on Earth as it is in heaven — *or* hell.' Sheraton began to retrace her steps again, still with head bowed. The parcel was open now; the minder placed the empty wrapper and box on the table. At last, Bishop could see that he was holding a cricket bat. The boxers followed behind her. 'When I said I wanted Brinkburn dead — that *is* what I wanted. And you've all failed me in that respect. That's not good, gentlemen. That's not adhering to the rules. That's *not* cricket.' Sheraton stopped behind Bishop again, half-way down the table. 'Brinkley!' Opposite Bishop, a fat balding man, with a shirt that looked too tight and a bow tie like a crippled butterfly stapled to his neck, started in his seat, almost swallowing his cigar.

'Yes, ma'am?'

'You played cricket in your younger years, didn't you?'

Puzzled, Brinkley replied: 'Yes, ma'am.'

'And you abided by the rules, didn't you? You played the game according to the rules? No foul play?'

'Yes, ma'am.'

Bishop tried to suppress a grin. Brinkley — a complete stranger to him, as were all the board room's occupants — was turning purple under this oblique interrogation. Sweat was instantly beading on his brow; his eyes were boggling. Bishop was beginning to enjoy it — particularly since the object of Sheraton's attentions was someone other than himself.

'Have you heard of Al Capone, Brinkley?'

'Al Capone . . .' Brinkley's voice was a hoarse gasp. It choked away. '. . . yes . . .'

'Of course you have. An American gangland leader in the 1920s. You've seen the films, read the books. Did you know, Brinkley, that he once convened a meeting of his operatives — just like this one — when he found out that one of them was letting him down? And do you know what he did?'

Brinkley tried to reply, but his voice had died in his throat.

'To punish the offender — and to teach the others a lesson — he beat that man to death with a baseball bat.'

Bloody hell, thought Bishop, watching Brinkley's face turn even more purple, his eyes fixed on the cricket bat.

'Well, that was America,' continued Sheraton. 'This is England. And you let me down, didn't you, Brinkley?'

Brinkley's eyes were starting from his head, his body beginning to shake.

'Well, in this organisation that's not cricket. When I give specific instructions, I expect them to be carried out. Right, Bishop?'

'Right . . .' said Bishop, now realising that the spotlight had been suddenly shifted to him, grin dying on his face and half turning in sickening realisation.

Sheraton snapped her fingers, face suddenly ablaze with fury. The boxer with the cricket bat swung it in a vicious, heavy arc. The impact on Bishop's head sounded like a perfect-six, lifting him bodily forward across the table. His false teeth skittered over the polished wood in a spray of blood and spittle, a gaping crack from below his right ear peeling across his Brylcreemed hair, spilling bright pink brain tissue. A tide of black-red blood spread swiftly like treacle from Bishop's twitching, instantly dead body. In horror, the other board room occupants drew back gasping from the table.

'Any resemblance to Al Capone,' said Sheraton icily, 'is strictly intentional. Move him.'

182

The two boxers hauled Bishop's body from the table, leaving bits of him behind on the polished wood. They began to drag him towards the door.

'Resume your seats, gentlemen. The . . . mess . . . will be cleared away.' Sheraton walked slowly back to her seat at the head of the table. Somewhere, someone was desperately trying to hold back the urge to vomit.

'I hope that my point is made clear. Find Eddie Brinkburn. Find him now and terminate him. I will not brook any more failure. That concludes the business of this meeting, gentlemen. You are dismissed. And I'm sure that you won't disappoint me again.'

22

'Now what?'

'Now they'll send the professionals to get us — since none of the people in Sheraton's operation can touch us. They'll pay big money now.'

'We'll never get away with it, Eddie. We've had it.'

'No we haven't. We can go anywhere and do anything. Anything. They can't touch us.'

'I wonder whether you are crazy. You think you're . . . an untouchable. Is that it?'

'Untouchable? Yeah . . . yeah . . . I like that.'

23

Rennie had been trying to dream of Jamaica the way he'd dreamed of Jamaica when they'd both been inside. But tonight, he couldn't even get an untainted view of those beaches or that sky — Salvador Dali seemed to have a permanent foothold in the foothills of his dreams. At times, it seemed as if he'd been partying with that other crazy painter guy (What was his name? Bosch? Yeah — Bosch). And between the two of them, they'd turned Rennie's dreamplace into a Hell of their own making. A place where beautiful sunsets had become bleeding rents in the sky, the sea itself a lake of blood from the wounds. And when Rennie tried to conjure up the beaches, there were dark, ribboned things like flapping sheets scampering on it which he didn't want to see up close. There were ragged scarecrow things in the trees. Each time that Rennie tried to find his dreamplace, these things sensed that he was trying to get back into the dream, sensed where he was and began to come for him — and he was forced to withdraw before he was obliged to see what manner of things they were.

He awoke, sweating.

For one terrible second, he believed that he was back in his cell; he believed that everything that had happened, everything that he had seen since his release and Eddie's release, was nothing but a bad dream. The feeling lasted no longer than that . . . and he wasn't quite sure as he lay in the dark, bathed in sweat, whether he was glad or not. A part of him wished that he was back in that cell with Eddie. Maybe, then, his world could be replaced with some sense of order, some sense of sanity. Everything that had taken place since that time had been more than a nightmare. He had seen the things that Eddie could do; had witnessed first hand the talent that mad Archie Duncan had given him — though neither he nor Eddie knew what it was, how it worked, or where it came from.

Rennie turned over to face the bedroom window. Eddie was in the next room, probably deep in sleep and dreaming up new ways of hurting Sheraton. To say that Rennie was afraid was an understatement. He had listened to Eddie's telephone calls; listened to him extracting information from the terrified people on the other end. He had watched him staring out of the window, face almost mask-like, afraid to ask what he was thinking, how he was able to conjure these things up . . . things that defied logic. But he knew that they were real and he knew that Eddie could do what he said he could do. He had seen those dirty clothes scrambling around on the carpet, for crying out loud. He had read the newspaper headlines when they were delivered, watched Eddie's smiling face as he read out the latest report of a burnt-out warehouse or building, savouring the between-the lines statements of the misinformed press. He knew from the way Eddie talked about it that he really was intent on rubbing out every last vestige of Sheraton and his empire. But how long could it possibly be before Sheraton found them in their tatty rented flat? They were on their own. They couldn't possibly survive. How the hell was he going to talk Eddie out of his revenge campaign? How much would it take to slake his thirst for revenge? How much longer before they could cut and run . . . maybe use the money that Eddie had extracted from the frightened to enable them to start again somewhere else — on the continent? Or how about Jamaica? No . . . that wouldn't be possible . . . would it . . .?

Rennie turned away from the window and the shadow stripes of the sky. Eddie was standing in the doorway, apparently still groggy from sleep. He shuffled into the room.

'Eddie? What's up . . .?'

And then Rennie screamed and leaped backwards out of bed away from the door and towards the window. The thing in the doorway was not Eddie. It had no head, no hands . . . no flesh. It was a tumbled, rumpled tangle of Rennie's clothes: his jacket, his shirts, his bedlinen — all tangled together in the same nightmarish way that he'd seen before. Rennie uttered another hoarse cry of terror as the clothes-thing shambled across the room, sleeves outstretched and groping for his neck, cotton feet whispering on the carpet pile.

'*NO!*' Eddie's hoarse voice sounded from the doorway.

But the shambling clothes-thing still flew across the bed at Rennie's throat. His hands flew up to protect himself. Shouting, he beat out with his hands, waiting for the thing to wrap itself around him, to suffocate him, to strangle him, as Eddie yelled again: '*I SAID NO!*'

The thing wrapped itself around Rennie. But the bedlinen . . . and the jacket and the shirts . . . were limp . . . they came apart in his hands, falling in a tangled heap to the floor. Breathing heavily in panic, Rennie threw the crumpled non-animated clothing to the carpet and stood in it in horror, still looking down as if this was some sort of trick; that it might suddenly take on form again at his feet, seize him around the ankles and begin . . . slowly . . . to . . . climb . . .

Rennie kicked at them in disgust. The jacket flew across the room. Eddie caught it and flung it behind him, still wiping sleep from his face.

.'You okay?' he asked.

'Okay? *Okay*? For God's sake, Eddie! What the hell are you doing, man?!'

'Dunno, Rennie. Sorry . . . I was asleep . . . dreaming . . . It shouldn't have . . .'

'I thought you said this stuff was under control! I thought you said you could handle it.'

'I can handle it!'

'Then what the bloody hell was all that about? That thing was going to kill me . . .'

187

'It wouldn't have killed you. You were okay . . .'

'And if you'd stayed asleep? What then? What if you hadn't woken up and stopped it?'

'I'm sorry, man. I don't know how it happened . . .' And Rennie saw on Eddie's face as he said those words that he did after all know now how the thing had manifested. He slumped down on the edge of Rennie's bed, head in hands, shaking away the last remnants of sleep. 'I need a drink or something.'

Rennie sat beside him 'How, Eddie? What happened?' Eddie looked up, sleep going at last, and slapped Rennie on the shoulder. 'It was the dream, son. The dream. I dreamed that you'd betrayed me, that you'd walked out and gone to Sheraton. Told him where I was. That's it . . . just the dream. Somehow, I must have conjured it up in my sleep.'

'You think I'm going to turn you in to Sheraton?'

'No, no! It was a dream, that's all. Just a dream.'

'Eddie. That thing would have killed me.'

'It wouldn't . . .'

'You don't know that! What the hell is going to happen next time you have a dream like that?'

'I won't. Don't worry. I've just got to be careful, that's all. From now on, we sleep in the same room, okay? Nothing's going to happen like that again, I promise. But if anything does start to happen . . . you'll be able to let me know.'

'Unless it gets me around the fucking throat and chokes off my voice, man.'

'It won't. I'll set up an alarm by the bed. Something to wake me up just in case.'

'This is a nightmare, Eddie. When's it all going to end?'

'It'll end when Sheraton's wiped out. Sheraton . . . and everything that he's got. I'm going to hurt him, scare him. Yeah . . . I'm going to scare the bastard to death.'

'And after that?'

'After that . . .' Eddie's face clouded.

'You can't see anything after that, can you?'

Eddie grabbed up a handful of clothes from the floor angrily, terminating the discussion. 'Try and get some sleep. Nothing else is going to happen like that. I promise. I'm in control.'

'Yeah, Eddie. If you say so.'

Eddie walked towards the door, Rennie's clothes in his hands. When he reached the door, he turned back again. He was looking down at the bundle of clothing. He looked up, almost guiltily.

'Better pack your . . . things. Tomorrow we're leaving here.'

'Where do we go, Eddie?'

'A place I know. A place where they can't get to us . . . and we can make our plans.'

'Is there any place like that? A place where they can't get to us?'

Eddie smiled, looking down again at the clothing in his hands. It was the shadow of something else — whether humour, or sarcasm, or wistfulness . . . Rennie could not tell in the darkness of the bedroom.

'Oh yes . . . this is a place where our dreams can come true.'

Rennie wondered just what sort of dreams Eddie had in mind.

24

The car was a blue Volvo, hired from Plymouth Dealers under a false name and with forged identification papers, which had been taken from a terror-stricken foreman while he stood watching his warehouse burn — a warehouse which had been a clearing-house operation for Sheraton. The car had been hired for one day only: to be picked up from the central depot at 9.30 am and due for return by 9.30 pm.

It would never leave the depot.

A booking clerk had placed the order and taken care of the necessary paperwork. He had then passed on the information that Eddie Brinkburn had been into the office and wanted a car. The clerk had gambling debts — substantial debts; debts which were now no longer tolerated by the management of his local casino. It had been made plain to him that he should pay back what he owed within a week or the prospects of any future fatherhood on his part would be rendered null and void. There was no way, on his pay, that he could pay back the sums he owed. But fortune had eventually smiled on him. Lady Luck had come round again. He knew that Brinkburn was wanted badly for an unspecified reason; had seen the photographs circulating at the casino; knew how important it was that Brinkburn be found. On impulse, he had taken one of the photographs. And then, on the morning that Brinkburn had walked in with his false papers, the clerk's heart had leaped into his throat. Sensing that his gambling debts were now a thing of the past, he had passed on the relevant information to the casino management. By return telephone call, he had advised that the Volvo was to be collected from the underground car park beneath the office at 9.30 am, had given the registration number and had himself been advised to keep everyone out of the car park between 9.15 am and 9.45 am and — oh yes — his credit was good. Very good indeed.

25

Michael Gallagher was good at his job. Better than that — people gave him credit for being the best. He took an interest and professional pride in his work Some people toiled all day behind a desk or in a factory; Gallagher was a works foreman for a local government engineers department. But in his spare time, he earned more money on one of his specialist jobs than he could earn in a year as a foreman.

He killed people.

For money. Specifically, for Sheraton Incorporated. His time in the army had been good training.

It was all very simple, really. He was given a name, a photograph, a location and ten thousand pounds in used bank notes. He sussed the place out beforehand, picked his spot and did the business. Just like the movies, really. Easy as pie. No hassle. And one of the good things about his reputation, he felt sure, was because, damn it all, he even looked like a hit man; just like one of those cool Mafia-type hit men on the television. His looks seemed perfectly allied to his part-time profession. He even wore those cool sunglasses to aid with the impression.

Cool, man.

Right on.

Let's *hit* the mother . . .!

Gallagher chuckled and checked his watch. 9.20 am. He sat in his car: a Corsair — rented with false ID, of course — shadowed and hiding under a concrete eave of the underground car park; a sleek black shark lurking in an underwater cave, waiting for prey. From where he sat he had a perfect view of the staircase door, the concrete ramp and Brinkburn's Volvo. No matter where Brinkburn appeared, he must be spotted — if not by Gallagher then by the three other men he had sub-contracted for the job. For normal 'hits', Gallagher was content (and secretly proud) to carry out the job himself; nice and simple, one shot in the head. But this time, Sheraton had been very specific — they wanted at least four men; they wanted Brinkburn *very* dead. No subtleties. No worries about the repercussions, the media newshounds, the public outcry. No one-shot.

Normally, Gallagher liked to work alone. Other helpers meant less security; and even though he'd used these guys before in similar circumstances when Sheraton needed someone puréed rather than simply killed (and they had been professionally up to the mark), he still didn't like to use them. Still . . . orders were orders . . . cash was cash and, for reasons known only to Sheraton, the fee on his particular hit had been substantially increased.

Eddie Brinkburn.

Who the hell was *he*, anyway? What could he have done or what threat could he pose to Sheraton's corporation? Not Gallagher's job to ask, of course, but tantalising questions nevertheless. Gallagher scanned the car park again; pinpointing his own people.

Fallis. Thin, tall, short black cropped hair. Bad body odour and teeth. Sitting in a Ford Capri above the ramp looking down, probably chewing his nails. Eyes flitting rat-like from staircase door to Volvo. He cradled a Kalashnikov AK 74 in his lap; the short, close-quarter combat version favoured by Russian helicopter and tank crews in Afghanistan. A full, banana-shaped clip was already inserted, with a second clip taped onto it for speed reloading.

McGuigan. Ginger-haired. Glaswegian. One eye gouged out in a pub brawl years ago, now replaced with a glass eye staring vacantly at the ceiling while the other eye remained fixed on the Volvo from where he stood in a concrete alcove below the ramp. One hand under his long brown overcoat was holding in place a Remington pump-action shotgun, barrel pointed to the ground. It was loaded with heavily charged solid lead slugs.

Norton. Bearded. With a nondescript blank and featureless face. Devoid of eyebrows, watery eyes without colour. Pallid. Like someone ten days in the water. A man who could pass in a crowd. A man who could put a screwdriver under your ribs in a crowded street and walk calmly away without ever being seen. Sitting in an Allegro somewhere to the left of Gallagher, with a Czech CZ 75 9mm pistol in his inside pocket.

Fallis, McGuigan, Norton. And Gallagher. All wary of their past associations in this line of work. But all capable of doing the job. Gallagher sometimes wondered in his more idle moments where their future together lay. More specifically . . . what would happen when their usefulness ran out or if it became necessary to implicate each other in one of their past deals? How could things turn out then? He'd often thought, after a six-pack of Becks Bier, that they were all − the four of them − somehow bound together. Functioning at present, when necessary, as a peculiar team; but all destined for something, something that fate had in store for them. Simply put, it was an association that could not last forever. It had to end eventually. And he felt sure, when that time came, when it became expedient to have each other out of the way, they would probably have two options: fight it out among themselves . . . kill each other if necessary; or be taken out by the very organisation that paid them so well at present. Any attempt at banding together, any union to avoid that day, was absolutely impossible. It involved a degree of . . . what? Civilisation? And that was something, despite their cool professionalism on the job, that they didn't have. One day . . . one day . . . Gallagher shook himself from his split-second reverie and rechecked his watch.

It was 9.30 am.

He scanned the underground car park again: the cold grey concrete barriers and ramps, the shadowed recesses, the silent cars. Pinpointing each of the three men once more, he turned to look back at the staircase entrance. As if somehow perfectly stage-managed, Gallagher saw an indistinct blur move into view behind the glass panels of the door. And then the door swung open and Eddie Brinkburn stepped into the car park.

Perfect timing, Mr Brinkburn, thought Gallagher, squeezing the wax earplugs into his ears – knowing that the others would be doing the same – checking out his own sub-machine gun. It was a Uzi Israeli model, sewn into a rig in his coat, and could fire 600 rounds per minute. Very soon, there was going to be a lot of unpleasantly loud echoes.

The door crashed echoing behind Eddie and for a second he stood there in the shadows, looking round.

Every right to be wary. Don't take any chances. Never know who's hiding in the dark, do you, Mr Brinkburn? Now . . . come on. There's no one here, is there? That's it. Everything's quiet. Everything's safe.

Eddie found the blue Volvo he was looking for and began to walk slowly towards it. His gait was unsteady as he moved, slightly limping.

Too much drink, son. Well . . . I don't blame you. Got a lot on your plate . . . Lot of people looking out for you. Want to do you damage. Never mind. Pretty soon, you'll be beyond all that.

Eddie limped to the Volvo, shoulders rounded, gait awkward. With one hand leaning on the roof of the car, he fumbled in his jacket pocket for the keys, still looking slowly around at the shadows. Gallagher and the others, from their darkened places, watched him open the door and climb clumsily in. The door slammed. The engine coughed into life and the car began to nose out of its recess.

The car park suddenly echoed to the sound of roaring engines and screeching tyres. Gallagher stamped his foot down hard and screeched up to the side of the Volvo, just as McGuigan's Allegro roared down the concrete ramp and screeched to a halt in front of the Volvo, hemming it in.

195

Gallagher swung out of the car, sub-machine gun held at hip height, and saw only a blur of movement to his right and left as Fallis and Norton emerged from their hiding places. The timing was perfect, accurate and deadly with neither of the four in their own line of fire and the Volvo and its occupant now stalled between them.

At the moment that Gallagher opened up with his own submachine gun, the others began to fire as well.

The Volvo was suddenly alive with disintegrating movement. The windscreen, side windows and rear window blew out instantaneously. The tyres exploded and the Volvo slumped like some great metallic beast, brought down in mid-charge by a hunter's gun. The bodywork was alive with whirling, fist-sized holes; sparks danced and screamed from the punctured frame. Cordite swirled in the air, hemming the car in like fog. Glass, torn metal and burning plastic exploded in every direction to the sound of a roaring, echoing tornado.

And within the car, Eddie Brinkburn twitched, jerked and blew apart like a sack of offal.

The roaring of the guns finished simultaneously; crashing echoes dying away in the stone cathedral-like passages. Gushing steam from the disintegrated engine and radiator flowed up over the riddled roof of the car. Four figures moved slowly and spectrally through the fog created by their own weapons towards the car.

Gallagher swung the sub-machine gun into his left hand, holding the warm metal against his side. With the other hand, he leaned over to the passenger door and yanked the handle. The door came completely away from its hinges with a screech. Gallagher thrust it aside with a clatter, bent down and looked in.

Not only was Eddie Brinkburn dead, he was (as Sheraton had ordered) very, *very* dead indeed. What remained was thrust back in the seat, head thrown back and mouth wide open in a dying scream. The top of his head had gone, his jaw hanging by a thread of cartilage. One arm had been blown off. It lay on the back seat, ragged and grasping. The torso was riddled with gaping holes. Brinkburn must have had newspapers stuffed into his shirt for some reason because shredded pages of the *Sun* and the *Guardian* were hanging out of the rents in his body. Even now, shreds of newspaper were dancing in the air like snow.

'Good job,' said Fallis as Gallagher became aware that the others had reached the car and were peering in through its shattered windows at their handiwork. Gallagher didn't reply as he looked at the ruined, riddled corpse in the driver's seat. Something about the newspapers and the ruined face was disturbing.

'Where is it?' asked Norton.

'What?' said McGuigan.

'Bloody funny, if you ask me.'

'What?'

'No blood. There's no blood.'

And Gallagher realised what it was that disturbed him. No blood anywhere. Not a drop of it. Just a torn, ragged bundle and spilled newspapers and a face that was somehow too grey. Gallagher leaned in to prod the corpse, to move its head so that he could look at its face. He was saved the effort.

The dead face turned and looked at him.

The top of the head was gone, yes; but Gallagher knew at once when it turned its face to him that the thing in the car had never been human. The hollowed places in the head where the eyes should be had never had eyes. It was a *papier mâché* head; a grey paste and paper head that did somehow look like Eddie Brinkburn from a distance, but was most definitely *not* Eddie Brinkburn up close. The ragged, bullet-ridden coat contained no real body as such. It had been stuffed full of rubbish: newspapers and empty yoghurt containers and cereal packets — the entire contents, in fact, of three rubbish bins behind the car rental agency. And as the thing moved forward in its seat and the grey paper jaw dropped into its lap, Gallagher — astounded — heard someone say . . .

'*What the fucking hell is THAT . . .*'

. . . but could only watch stunned as the garbage innards of the thing in the seat spilled out across the dashboard and its one remaining arm, with a hand and fingers fashioned from jagged tin cans, reached for him.

Still astounded, professionalism gone in the face of something that could not possibly exist after what they'd fired into that Volvo, Gallagher noted with wonder that the tin can hand still had a Heinz baked beans wrapper on it and that the red stuff on it was tomato sauce, just before the fingers closed on his throat. The pain began . . . and his own red stuff began to mingle with the tomato sauce.

The ragged arm on the back seat twisted, curled and flew through the shattered side window at Norton. McGuigan cried out and tried to pull away, but somehow his coat was caught in the car door. Fallis' gun gave one short blurt of roaring noise as he attempted to level it, at what he knew not. The bullets stitched a pattern harmlessly on the concrete overhead as something whipped from the dashboard, something like torn dash wires. It coiled swiftly around his arms.

Screaming began to echo in the car park now. The car was alive again. But this time it genuinely had a life of its own. This time it wasn't the tearing screaming impact of the shells from the Kalashnikov, the sub-machine gun or the pump shotgun that made it squirm and fasten and tear and wriggle and feed as it did.

Soon, the screaming had stopped. The car park was silent.

Three minutes later, in the booking office upstairs, a cleaner, screaming, came across the ticket clerk. He was slumped backwards in his chair, debts fully repaid, throat cut, eyes still staring at what had shambled into his office to collect the keys for a blue Volvo.

PART THREE

THE
HOUSE ON
LIME STREET

'This was the shocking thing; that the slime of the pit seemed to utter cries and voices; that the amorphous dust gesticulated and sinned; that what was dead, and had no shape, should usurp the offices of life. And this again, that that insurgent horror was knit to him closer than a wife, closer than an eye; lay caged in his flesh, where he heard it mutter and felt it struggle to be born, and at every hour of weakness, and in the confidence of slumber, prevailed against him, and deposed him out of life.'

The Strange Case of Dr Jekyl and Mr Hyde.
Robert Louis Stevenson (1886)

1

It was almost dawn.

A red sun was creeping over the city skyline, revealing the same bleeding canyons and slashes in the sky that Rennie had been dreaming of the previous night. The sight of the sun's stealthy progress behind the black silhouettes of factories, office buildings and dilapidated high-rise flats made him feel nervous. As if that sun was a great eye, looking for their hiding place. As if the difference between his waking world and this new world of Bad Dreams had blurred . . . and with the blurring, there seemed to be promises of darker waking and sleeping dreams to come. Hurriedly, he followed Eddie out into the street, looking anxiously from side to side as they made their way to the *cul-de-sac* at the end of Windsor Street, where his car was parked. There hadn't been much to pack . . . only two suitcases each of rumpled odds and ends. It made Rennie creepily uncomfortable to know that the clothes-thing which had rushed at him the previous evening was also locked up in one of the suitcases.

Their breath streamed in clouds around their heads as they moved, the sounds of their footsteps ringing briskly on the pavement as they walked along the deserted street; the noise seemed somehow to proclaim their position to any and all who might be waiting for them. The wind whipped round the corner of Windsor Street. In the middle of the street was a black, burned patch where Sheraton's car had caught fire and exploded. On the other side of the road, rags of plastic shopping bags had snared in the railings of the park like a banshee's washing strung out to dry. Those were the same railings from which they'd had to cut one of Sheraton's men. Even from here, Rennie fancied that he could see a dark stain on the pavement where the man's blood had leaked away and the Council operatives had been unable to remove it.

Rennie looked at Eddie ahead of him, also glancing to left and right as he walked. They reached the end of Windsor Street, turning into the *cul-de-sac*. Rennie looked back at the scene of the recent bizarre and surreal devastation that Eddie's Frighteners had brought. The street reminded him of something . . . and now he knew exactly what it was: it was like a deserted stage in a theatre, an elaborate, scruffy, dingy and deserted stage where a horrific drama had been played out. Rennie felt that he himself was playing a part in all this, but as to his eventual role, the meaning of it, he had no idea. Only an agitation akin to dread; a dread that something even bigger was on the horizon, creeping closer like the bloodstained canyons in the sky overhead, as the ball of blood that was the sun crept higher and the silhouette of the city stood out in starker contrast.

They reached the car, slinging the suitcases into the boot. It was the same battered Citroën that Rennie had picked up cheap on his release from prison. He still remembered the joyous days he had spent under that car when he'd first bought it: his first chance to work on a car outside the prison, using his skills for his own purposes. The bloody thing was so souped up he felt sure that he could even give Nigel Mansell a run for his money. Minutes later, with Rennie driving, they turned out of Windsor Street, away from that grim stage-set and, at Eddie's behest, into the main road. Rennie felt better now that they were moving away from the flat. It had come to feel too much like another prison for him: the same claustrophobia, the same feeling of isolation and waiting. He checked the mirror a dozen times to see if they were being followed. When he was convinced that they were not, he heaved a sigh of relief, grinned and turned to Eddie in the passenger seat.

'So where's the safe place?'

'In the country. Just keep driving and I'll tell you how to get there.'

'So why the mystery? You going to tell me where it is, how you found it?'

Eddie grinned. 'Yeah, a mystery. That's the thing with you, Rennie. Always need to have everything cut and dried. Need to know the ins-and-outs of everything. Well . . . I'm not going to tell you.' He grinned again. 'Not until we get there.'

Rennie looked at Eddie's eyes in the rear view mirror. For the first time in a long time, he seemed to see vestiges of humour there. It made him feel good and he grinned himself.

'Okay. You're the boss as usual. Just give me a clue.'

'A clue? Okay. Let's say that this is a place I dreamed about when I was inside, after you got out. Just like you used to dream about Jamaica, even though you've never been there. A place that I was told about.'

'Another con told you?'

'A clue, you said. If I tell you any more, it'll be more than a clue.'

Rennie grinned, feeling better and better the more distance flashed under the wheels between themselves and Windsor Street.

2

They drove for an hour, leaving the city far behind. On Eddie's instructions, they wove and wound from main road to minor road, from highway to cart track. Even the place-names on the signposts they passed began to sound foreign to Rennie after a while. And as they drove, he wondered at Eddie's powerful recall without the use of a map. He was convinced that another con had somehow given Eddie the information about this 'Safe Place', wherever it was . . . but if that was the case, Eddie must have spent most of his remaining time in prison memorising how to get there, because he never once used their own road map. This could not be a place Eddie had known about before they'd been sent down; in prison they'd spent most of their work time and leisure time together. Rennie would have known about it sooner or later. As far as he knew, Eddie had never been this far out into this neck of the woods before. And there were times when, looking at Eddie's face in the rear view mirror, he gained a particular impression: even though Eddie knew where to go on their quest for the Safe Place, the surrounding countryside was just as new to him as it was to Rennie.

They were now well out in the country. There seemed to be a forest on Rennie's right as they drove, although he had no idea where they were or what it was called. On their left, bare fields. Over near the horizon, the sun's valiant attempt to burst through smothering grey clouds appeared to be a lost cause; its early morning brilliance was now smothered to an early evening dull grey.

'Here,' said Eddie, indicating a signpost at the side of the road which pointed down a track into the trees on the right.

Rennie shrugged, indicating right even though the road behind him was empty. He veered towards the turn-off, impressed by Eddie's precise geography of this unknown part of the country. Now, he could read the battered and corroded sign: '*Lime Street*'.

'Lime Street?' he asked as they turned into it, the car beginning to bounce up the rutted track that led between the dark, shadowed trees. '*This* is a street?'

'Used to be,' replied Eddie, smiling secretly and pointing into the trees to left and right. 'If you look close you can see where there used to be houses.'

Rennie peered into the gloom between the tree boles as they continued to bounce along the track and saw that Eddie was right. The remains and ruins of houses *were* in there, set back behind the trees. Here a red brick wall, covered in weeds and returning gradually to the earth. Over there, a crumbling chimney stack. Farther on, he saw another house, its roof caved in and weeds and moss creeping over the ruined window-sill.

It was unnerving. These ruins should be the ruins of country cottages, or gamekeepers' houses, or tool sheds or something. They should be the ruins of *country* houses. But the ruins that Rennie was looking at as they continued on up Lime Street were different. They were the ruins of red brick, closely crowded houses that belonged on a rundown council estate. Rennie had grown up in streets just like that. He was no architect, but he recognised the type of house straight away. He and Eddie had played in streets like that when they were kids, back in the 1950s. These kind of houses just didn't exist in the country. They were city houses. It made his flesh creep to think that they were so far out in the wilds and here was . . . well, a *street*, for crying out loud. A city street which had somehow been uprooted from the city and transplanted way out here in a forest. A dead street. A street which everyone had abandoned and left to the forest . . . the forest . . .

That was another thing, something else that Rennie didn't like about this street as they drove on and the overhead branches swept lower, scraping the car roof. To get that size, those lime trees must be hundreds of years old, and yet they were growing in and around those ruined houses, those back yards, those crumbling chimney stacks and those yawning black windows, in dense profusion. Those houses must have been built in . . . what? . . . the 1930s; red brick houses for council tenants, just like the ones he knew. How could that be? Two-hundred-year-old trees growing right out of the foundations of those fifty-year-old houses? Even as Rennie scanned this eerie deserted street, he fancied that he could see one of the lime trees growing right out of the middle of a house without a roof, its branches settled over the eaves where the roof should have been. In the blackness behind those ruins and those gnarled and infested trees, he fancied that he could see other houses, other ruins, stretching back to who knew where.

The darkness was becoming more intense, and the ruined street between the trees kept on and on and on . . . How the hell could a street even *be* in there among the trees, like that?

They reached a crossroads.

'Turn left. We're nearly there.'

'Where's "*there*"?'

'You'll see.'

They turned into the trees. Rennie could see that they were driving over weed-covered cobbles. On either side now, overlaid with blankets of choking grass, he could see the remains of pavements. *Crazy*, he thought. *A street. Right smack in the middle of a forest. Doesn't make any kind of sense.*

The darkness around them was almost complete, the ruins at right and left now mere outlines in the rustling, swaying branches of the limes. Rennie toyed with the idea of putting on the headlights and was reaching for the switch when Eddie said, 'We're here.'

Ahead, through the tunnel of shadows and trees which

206

was Lime Street, Rennie saw a patch of grey. He stepped on the accelerator, eager to be out of this unhealthy place. The grey rushed to meet them and suddenly the car broke from the dark avenue of Lime Street and into an open tract of land.

Rennie guessed that the open area, surrounded on all sides by the forest, was about a mile in diameter. The shadows of clouds raced each other over the open space. A fence stretched away to right and left, waving holes torn in the mesh here and there. They were on some kind of cinder track now as Rennie drove on, and at last he saw, in the middle of the open ground and about two hundred and fifty yards away, the object of Eddie's attention.

Beyond the rusted fence, past a sea of weeds and strangled grass, stood a House.

At first Rennie thought it was some kind of castle; there seemed to be two turrets emerging from it, piercing the boiling grey clouds overhead. The shape and size of it was indeterminate, the grey brick structure merging inchoately with the grey density of the trees beyond.

'*This* is it?' asked Rennie.

'Home,' replied Eddie. 'Let's have a closer look.'

Rennie swung the car into the gravelled drive. 'There's a gate ahead,' Eddie told him.

'You've done your homework,' said Rennie. Eddie grinned.

When they reached it, the gate itself was swinging slowly in the wind on one hinge, the hollow poles screeching in protest. When the gate swung to its apex, Rennie cruised the car through and they headed up the tangled avenue of weeds towards the House. Now Rennie could see that the place wasn't a castle, as such, after all. More like one of those posh country places where skint earls allowed goggling tourists to ferret around on Sundays for the extra cash. But as they drew nearer, he could see that the building was in some disrepair.

It's got a face, he thought.

Vines and creepers were crawling over the frontage, trying

to smother the House. Maybe at some time, someone who cared had taken the trouble to trim the strangling vegetation in its suffocating ascent. But that had been a long time ago. At ground level, the sprawling, choking vegetation had been hacked away from the windows: the rapidly fading light glinted dully on scum-grey glass, like faded and dying eyes, as they looked out at the approaching car through ragged gaps in the greenery. Above the ground floor the vines, like veined cataracts, were creeping across the windows, blinding them. Rennie saw a flurry of activity in those upper reaches of the House's face: a flock of tattered black birds erupted from the vines and scattered into the sky. They reminded him of the torn black plastic that always caught in the skeletal trees in the dirty urban streets he had known; and of the horrifying, ragged black shapes that had lately invaded his dreams of Jamaica.

There were statues of some kind by the driveway up to the House, also smothered in weeds, obliterating their detail. An ornamental stone fountain appeared to have been choked by those same weeds, and had eventually died of thirst; but not before vomiting a scum-covered pool into its basin-like bowl; a stained grey cherub gloated obscenely over it.

There was a flight of stone stairs leading up to the main entrance, once ostentatious, now as overgrown and semi-derelict as the rest of the House.

As the car drew nearer, Rennie could see that someone was standing on the steps, obviously waiting for them, flanked on either side by weather-worn stone lions on pedestals. At first, he thought it was a woman in a pink dress — he could see material flapping in the wind — but then he saw that it was a man, a man in a pink dressing-gown. He moved to one of the stone lions, placing a hand on its flank as if it was some kind of gigantic pet, and as the car finally drew up to the entrance, Eddie said . . .

'This is it.'

Rennie stopped the car at the foot of the overgrown stairs. Now he could see that the man was about sixty or sixty-five. He had longish yellow-white hair, one side of which appeared to have been carefully combed, the other standing up in the wind, as if he had been sleeping on it and had just woken up to welcome the car. Under the dressing-gown, tied in the middle, Rennie could make out blue striped pyjamas. The man was smiling broadly. He began to descend the stairs.

Rennie switched off the engine and looked at Eddie: 'Okay, when do I get to find out how you know about the place and who the old guy is?'

'You're too impatient. All in good time.'

The old man lurched to the bottom of the stone stairs and staggered to the car. He was wearing tattered pink slippers. For some reason his smile was gone now, replaced with a look of anger and puzzlement. Eddie wound down the window as he reached the car on his side.

'You're the one,' said the old man, in a refined Oxbridge voice.

'Yes,' replied Eddie.

The old man nodded, scanning the interior of the car as if for other hidden passengers, quickly examining every inch of it. For a moment, his gaze rested on Rennie; then he nodded as if this was also somehow what he had been led to expect.

'Wrong colour,' he said.

'What?' asked Rennie.

'Wrong *colour*.'

'Great. I drive hundreds of miles to a crappy old house and all I get is more racial abuse.'

'No, no, no . . .'

The old man shook his head extravagantly, like a child. 'The car. Your car. It's not the right colour. Not what I've seen. The car I saw was blue, this one is black.'

'Yes, well, it would have been blue,' said Eddie. 'But the blue one is . . .' Eddie turned to look at Rennie, grinning at his friend's puzzlement . . . 'the blue one's full of holes.'

'All right, all right,' said the old man, 'but it's not what I was expecting, that's all.'

Looking at the old man's wild blue eyes . . . eyes that were somehow much too young to be in such an old head — and listening to his refined cackle, Rennie knew that he must be completely out of his head. A complete eccentric. A whacko. But what the *hell* was going on?

'Can you drive?' Eddie asked. The old man nodded. 'And you've got somewhere to put the car?'

The old man nodded again.

'Then put it there and come back. We'll be inside.'

Rennie watched as the wild pink dressing-gown flapped round the front of the car towards him; he turned back to Eddie to demand an explanation — only to find him already climbing out of the car and heading for the stone staircase. The old man began to jab Rennie repeatedly in the arm.

'Come on, come on, come on . . .'

Now angry, Rennie slapped out at the old man; he shrank away, almost cowering, eyes wild and frightened. Ashamed, Rennie climbed out of the car.

'Are you sure you can *drive*, old man?' he asked, moving after Eddie.

The old man dodged round him, not taking his eyes off him. He climbed into the car. 'Not the right colour,' he said again, accusingly. '*You're* the right colour — but the car's not.' The old man's voice degenerated into inaudible grumblings. Rennie winced as he threw the gears into an awkward screech. The car donkeyed away and then swerved round the corner of the House, out of sight, ragged pink driver twisting at the wheel.

Shaking his head, Rennie turned back to see that Eddie had reached the top of the stairs and was standing with a hand on one of the lions, just as the old man had done, proprietarily, as if the thing was some bizarre pet. Rennie hurried to join him. Grey clouds boiled around the 'turrets' of the House, shadows swarming over the staircase and the lions.

'The time for explanations is *now*!' said Rennie as he reached the top, but Eddie was even now walking through the stone portico that fronted the House. Two solid oak doors gave access; they were wide open and Eddie, raincoat swirling, strode straight inside. Rennie cursed and followed, hearing the tone of Eddie's footsteps change as they met marble. Anger was beginning to fill him. He felt once again as if he had become part of a strange, bizarre dream where everyone and everything but him within that dream had its own warped logic, but a logic that evaded the dreamer himself. He didn't want any more of this logic, or at least he wanted to be given the pieces of the jigsaw that fitted, to have the key that would give him access to the reasons for Eddie's new powers, for homicidal things made of garbage and empty clothes that could kill, for this decrepit old House and the mad old man.

They were in a grand entrance hall. Not only was the floor marble, but the walls and colonnades, too. A massively cobwebbed chandelier hung overhead, like a prop from a Roger Corman film. A marbled, grime-coated staircase led away upstairs into darkness. There were at least five oak doors in the hall, giving access, no doubt, to other equally decrepit and semi-derelict rooms. Overhead was a weather-stained, criss-cross skylight. Eddie stood in the centre of the hall, looking around and smiling. Rennie caught up with him, grabbed him by the arms and spun him round.

'Eddie! I've had just about as much as I can take. Give me answers, give me . . .'

He inched back, letting go his grip on Eddie's arm. In the cold, marble darkness of the hall, he could no longer see Eddie's face. He was seeing the face of something else: glittering feral eyes in a face blacker than shadow, a putrescent face that was somehow dead yet living. There was movement on that face; a swarming, shifting, horribly animated movement, like a nest of snakes or worms or . . . And then the cloud passing overhead moved on; cold, grey light unfurled in the hall and the illusion was gone.

The face was Eddie's − of course it was, and any hostility that might have been there was also gone. Eddie smiled . . .

'Answers?'

Still disconcerted by what he thought he had seen, Rennie cleared his throat, fumbled with the collar of his jacket and

211

said: 'Yeah . . . yeah . . . that's what I want, Eddie. You can't keep me in the dark all the time.'

'The dark?' Eddie smiled again, and within that smile Rennie could still discern a trace — an echo — of that horribly bizarre and hostile face that seemed momentarily to have been there. 'Okay, Rennie. Okay. But I just need to look the House over. That's all. I promise that if you bear with me while I suss the place out — see if it's what we need — then I'll tell you everything that's going on. Okay?'

'Okay,' said Rennie grudgingly, turning again as the sound of scampering footsteps announced the arrival of the old man in the pink dressing-gown. 'But first — who the hell is *this*?'

Eddie smiled again as the old man began to hop nervously from foot to foot in his pink slippers. 'This — ' Eddie waved his hand in introduction '. . . is Lister.' The old man smiled broadly, nodding his head eagerly like a child.

'Where . . .?' began Rennie.

'We've never met,' replied Eddie.

'Shit! More bloody puzzles . . .'

Eddie held his finger to his lips. 'You promised. No more answers until after the House inspection.'

'Come on, then,' said Rennie. 'Let's get on with it.'

Eddie gestured grandly to the old man. 'Lead on, Lister.'

3

It was obvious that the House had not been lived in for some time. Some of the windows had been broken by wind or storm, and dead leaves had made dry, crumbling piles on the floorboards. The little furniture remaining had been covered by soiled dustsheets. The wind moaned in long-empty ornate fireplaces. Ancient paint had cracked and peeled from the ceilings and from the walls. Strips of faded wallpaper hung in tatters. Furred things scurried in the rubbish every time a door was opened.

There were six rooms on the ground floor, with an ancient and decrepit kitchen below. The pans and kitchenware on rusted stoves were shrouded with cobwebs. They examined the cellars under the house only briefly as there was no light down there, no electricity anywhere in fact. Rennie had a glimpse of wet stone arches and tunnels before Lister shut the cellar door again. The first and second floors also had six rooms each, all bedrooms apparently. Pigeons exploded through the broken windows in one of the rooms, scattering more dead leaves.

After the inspection, they descended the marble staircase again and Eddie walked ahead into what he had identified as the main drawing room. Rennie followed, shaking his head. Lister remained in the doorway.

Eddie walked over to the bare window bay at the far side of the room, braced his hands against the wood panelling and exhaled. Rennie could see the look of naked enjoyment there and watched as Eddie began to feel the wainscotting, hands greedily exploring the wood, stroking the grain. He laughed – a secret, knowing laugh and turned back to Rennie as if hoping that he was sharing his enjoyment. Rennie's blank expression only seemed to make him laugh the more. He stood back from the wainscotting, pulling the raincoat tight around his neck as he moved into the recess of the bay window; he stood in the grey shafts of light and looked out at the sky.

'Answers,' said Rennie at last. 'You promised me answers.'

Eddie looked back again, the grey light reflecting in his eyes as if they were made of glass; that distant and alien mask behind his face was always present.

'Okay, Rennie. Answers.' He turned and sat on the window ledge. 'This is more than an empty House. Something really important happened here. In its time, over the centuries, this place has been burned and rebuilt three times. It's never been a . . . popular . . . place. That's history. But in recent years, it's been home to something much more . . . interesting.' Eddie's attention seemed to fade momentarily.

'Yeah?' said Rennie, prompting him to go on.

Eddie returned from his brief reverie, picking up enthusiastically now. 'Because of its location and its seclusion, an important party bought this place from a hard-up earl who was desperate for the cash.'

'An important party?'

'Very important. In fact, you probably can't get more important.'

'Who?'

'The Government, Rennie. The Government.' Eddie stood up and began to walk back and forth in the window bay as if delivering a lecture. 'The acquisition was handled very discreetly, as they say, and with absolutely no publicity. This place really suited their purposes, Rennie. They wanted it for a very special project. A project the Government didn't want anyone to know about since it . . .' Eddie closed his eyes, a look of concentration on his face, as if trying to remember important facts committed to memory a long time

214

ago. '. . . might be construed as an attack and infringement on the democratic rights of the individual.' It sounded like a quote. 'You've seen the newspapers, Rennie. You know they don't like what's happening in the streets. The "them and us" syndrome; the advantaged and the disadvantaged. You remember what it was like for us. We grew up in the streets. And they're hard streets . . . hell, they've always been hard streets for people like us. But the people at the top, the people who are half to blame for what's happening in the streets anyway . . . they don't like what they see now. Crime rates climbing sky-high. Street riots. Violent crime on the increase; street muggings, rape, murder. Tie all of that in with overcrowding in prisons and it's no surprise that people in high-up places might get around to thinking about solving the problem "at source"; not by changing the system − but by changing the *people*.'

'How the hell can you change people?' People are people are people . . .'

'Bear with me. Like I said . . . the Government bought this place. And they set up a special unit here. A unit of scientists funded by the Government to investigate . . . patterns of behaviour . . . and the anti-social tendencies of the undesirable element in society. There was a large injection of funds; some of the best brains in the medical and psychological professions were involved. And what better way to conduct . . . experiments . . . than in a place like this? Really out of the way; out of the public eye. And what better guinea pigs to work on than the anti-socials they already had direct access to and control over: the criminal element themselves? They went to the prisons, Rennie, for the prisoners. That's it, Rennie. They set up their examination unit here and they experimented on long-term prisoners. They probed their minds in a way that's never been done before. Murderers and rapists. Child molesters and firebugs. Maniacs and psychotics. All Government sanctioned. But all extremely illegal, of course. A right-wing reaction to the social problem. Find out what it is that makes them that way, find out what it is that produces this kind of behaviour, and eradicate it. A subtle lobotomy. Tigers into lambs. And then release them back to prison; back into society, maybe.' Eddie snorted derisively. 'Good way to ease the overcrowding in prisons. No criminals. No need for a place to put 'em away, right?

'But . . . over a period of years, their research took them out of the . . . scientific . . . world, and into another area altogether. It took them into the world of . . .' Eddie started to laugh. He made an exaggerated fanfare sound and said in a mock stentorian voice: '. . . the Twilight Zone!' His laughter dwindled away. He cleared his throat; and now there was no humour on his face at all as he said:

'It took them into the world of the spirit.'

'You're going to lose me here, Eddie . . .'

'Look, it's simple. I don't know how they did it, but as they continued to experiment, they found out that people are . . . are . . .' Eddie struggled for the words. '. . . more than just flesh and blood and food and water and shit and . . .' He smiled again 'More than *just* human. They found out something that all those Holy Joes have known for thousands of years. They found out that there's a capacity for Good and Evil in all of us; not just all that talk about social pressures and frustrations and greed and ambition. Not that sort of stuff. But Good with a capital "G", Evil with a capital "E". There's an undeveloped *spiritual* side to us, Rennie. They tapped into that. They found out where these forces were . . . deep . . . deep down in our minds. And as their work developed, they found that they could . . . eradicate the Evil Side . . . wipe it out completely . . . wipe it out spiritually. And leave that person completely different. Not good exactly, but at a stroke they were able to take away all the stuff deep down in their minds that made them the way they were. The "Jekyll and Hyde" effect, they called it. And they churned out hundreds of cons from this place: docile, happy, balanced. Didn't matter what the social pressures on 'em had been. Upbringing. Psychological pressures. All that stuff. Didn't matter. They'd changed their *spirit* − but they didn't really know

216

how they'd done it. So they kept on delving and experimenting. They were excited, Rennie. Really excited. For the first time, they had proof of a spiritual side to man.

'Then they tried out their experiment on Archie Duncan.'

'Duncan? What . . . you mean the fat maniac who pulled us out of the showers?'

'The one and the same,' replied Eddie.

' "Do you hate? Do you hate?" ' He smiled ruefully again.

'But I don't understand . . .'

Eddie held up a hand. 'Archie Duncan was one of the guys they experimented on. He had a mental age of six. You know the story. While he was burgling some place, something inside him snapped. He ended up killing a family of six. They put him away for life in a prison when he should have been in a mental ward. They decided . . . that he was a fit case for treatment here, so they did the business on him. But something happened. Something bad. Their experimentation on Good and Evil had released a kind of . . . energy. A psychic energy. As they'd been wiping the Evil out of all those others, it hadn't just been leaking away to nowhere. Its energy had been building up; leaking out of everyone they'd experimented on over a period of years. And it had been accumulating *here*. Here in this House. Invisible. They bled it out of the cons and it . . . seeped . . . into the walls of this House, into the wood and the stone and fabric of the building.' Eddie moved to the wainscotting again and ran his hand over it, looking around again: at the walls, the floor, the ceiling.

'When they got around to Archie, there was a sort of . . . I don't know . . . I suppose that you could call it a "feedback". There was an overload of energy; temporarily it took on form. It *jumped* out of the fabric of the building where it'd been accumulating. And it jumped into Archie. His mind couldn't handle it. He went berserk. He killed three people in here . . . scientists.'

Eddie walked to the centre of the room. 'Maybe he did it in here. I don't know. But the result was pretty

217

instantaneous. The Government had never really been convinced about the results of the experiment. They never had any real evidence. The fact that none of the cons who came away from here ever committed another offence, became model prisoners and the whole lot . . . well, that made no difference to them at all. And when the key scientists started spouting off about how they'd made some kind of breakthrough from the physical side of science into the area of the spirit . . . the soul . . . well, that was too much to swallow as well. Archie going berserk only served to seal the fate of the entire operation. Potential scandal as well, of course. They took fright. Potential bad press of secret Government research, unlawful experiments on prisoners, the threat to individual rights . . . all that stuff. The plug was pulled on the operation . . . and they pulled out.'

'But it didn't end there, Rennie. It didn't end. You see . . . all that "energy" was still inside Archie. It jumped into him, but it couldn't get out again. It was locked in there, locked in his six-year-old mind. And that's exactly where it stayed all those years he was inside . . . looking for a way to get out of him.'

' "Do you hate?" ' said Rennie. 'That's all he used to say . . .'

'And that was the key! It needed some kind of really powerful force to connect with. It needed a surge of . . . of . . . okay, *hate* . . . something really powerful that it could jump into. I don't know the hows or the whys of it . . . that was the way it was. And that's why Archie stumbled around the yard all the time, looking for it. Looking for the right kind of person generating the right kind of powerful emotion so that it could get out of him and be free. Get out of Archie's child mind and into an adult mind.'

'In the showers,' said Rennie, quietly. 'When Laverick and the others were going to "do" us. I saw it. I saw the Thing that was in Archie, saw it in his eyes just before it . . .'

'Just before it jumped. I know. I hated then, Rennie. I really fucking *hated*. I didn't care about anything any more.

218

I didn't care if I died. But I hated, all right. And the energy that was in Archie found its connection, found its way to get out. It jumped into me.'

'But it's . . . God, Eddie . . . It's *evil*. You said so yourself. All the evil stuff that came out of those cons over the years, seeped into the House here. It's in you, now.'

'Evil? What the hell does that *mean*? It means nothing, Rennie. Nothing. It's energy, that's all. A negative energy if it's used the wrong way. But I'm not using it the wrong way, am I?'

'Christ, I don't know. I've seen you do things. I've seen that look on your face. Sometimes it seems that you're not even human any more.'

'*I'm* not evil, Rennie. You've seen that, you know that. I'm wiping evil out, man. I'm destroying it. I'm destroying all the evil that Sheraton stands for, can't you see that? You've seen what they do. You've seen the child pornography, you've seen what they do on the streets. Well? I'm wiping it all out. I'm scouring those streets. I'm washing all the filth out of the gutters and drowning it in the sewers where it belongs. How can what I'm doing with this . . . this power . . . be evil? I'm in control of it. I can make it do what I want. You've seen that.'

'Oh yeah, I've seen your Frighteners, all right. Too bloody close. You remember those clothes doing the handjive? If you hadn't been there . . .'

'Okay, that was a mistake. But I'm in complete control now. I promise. It took a while to learn how to control it, that's all. Now that I'm in charge, I can make it do anything that I want. Bear with me . . .'

Rennie shook his head, wiping a hand across his face. 'I don't know, Eddie. This is so much to take.'

'I *need* you, man.'

'How the hell do you know all of this stuff, Eddie? How did you find out about this in prison? If this business was so secret, how come you know all about it?'

'I didn't find out in prison.'

'Then where?'

Eddie laughed again, hugging the coat to himself and returning to his seat on the window ledge. In mock drama, he flung his arms wide to embrace and indicate the very room they were in. 'I didn't really know *all* of it . . . or how all the pieces fitted together . . . until now!' He began to laugh again. Rennie wearily shook his head, crossed to the window bay and sat on the same sill that Eddie had been using.

'I know how it sounds,' continued Eddie, 'but it's to do with the power that's in me. The fact that I'm in the place where it all started has brought it all to me. Before that, in prison . . . back at your place . . . it all came in dreams. Bits and pieces. I saw this House in my dreams; how to get here, everything. But now I know. I know it all. The House has told me. The limes outside . . . the trees . . . they tell me everything. I know it sounds crazy, but it's true.'

'And the old man . . . Lister. What about him? He was talking as if he was expecting you. As if he knows who you are.'

'The old man? He's a caretaker, that's all. He's out of his skull. He's been here for years. Once the Government scientists moved out, the place reverted to some kind of trust; by that time the earl had buggered off. Now, no one's interested in the old place any more, no one can afford the upkeep. I'm surprised it hasn't fallen apart already. There's still power here, though, Rennie. Some of that energy is still in the walls. I can feel it. It didn't *all* jump into Archie. Given time, I can take all the energy out of here into me, make me stronger. Get rid of Sheraton completely. I think it's the power that's still here that makes the old man know things. I think he can tune into it . . . or perhaps it tunes into him. Whatever, he's crazy. And he doesn't matter. But he'll cook our meals and look after us here. Because this is where we're going to stay for a while. Away from the city, away from Sheraton. The city isn't going to be a good place for Sheraton's people over the next few years, I can promise you that. Bear with me, Rennie. Bear with me until Sheraton, and everything that name stands for, has been wiped out.'

'And then what, Eddie? What happens after Sheraton's gone?'

'After that, anything. We can have anything . . . literally anything we want. Isn't that worth waiting for?'

'Maybe it is. Right now, though . . . I need a drink. Hell, I need a *bottle*!'

Eddie laughed loudly, the sound of his voice reverberating in the empty room, bouncing from the corners until it filled the room with echoes.

'Lister!'

'Yes?'

The old man had been standing in the doorway, nervously hopping from foot to foot, listening to their conversation.

'Where's the booze?'

The old man giggled. 'There's plenty of that here. The wine cellars underneath run for miles and miles and miles. Nobody's been down there for a long time, so . . .'

'Go get a crate. The best you can find.'

Lister tugged at a forelock which had long since gone, and backed out of the room as if he was in the presence of Royals. 'Have you a preference?'

'Anything,' said Rennie. 'Any *colour* you like. Red or white.' To Rennie, getting drunk seemed the best option open to him after the most recent lunatic developments and Eddie's wild story. He looked over at Eddie, who was standing in the bay window again; staring out through the grimy, bird-splattered windows into the crowding darkness of the lime trees and the vast brooding canopy of a darkening sky. Rennie started to speak, intending to invite Eddie on a bottle hunt; then he saw the distant look on his face — another alien look — another expression he had never seen on Eddie Brinkburn's face before, albeit less horrific than the last. *Ah, the hell with it*! Rennie turned and followed the beckoning, white-haired fool in the pink dressing-gown.

4

Eddie searched in the city in the new found way he could, spreading himself wide in the darkening sky as in a dream, letting the wind spread his essence over the buildings, the office blocks, the shops, the factories, the landmarks. All of it lay before him. The city belonged to him. It had no secrets. No dark or filthy corner was hidden from him. He was the wind, he blew litter over bloodstained pavements, rattled at casements and caught fleeting glimpses through grimy panes of street-sour beldams selling their wares on soiled bed linen. Rising high above the city within the industrial smoke gushing from the throats of cancered chimneys, he looked down and saw everywhere the influence of Sheraton; everywhere the tainted effect, the evil pulse in the veins of this monstrous living metropolis. But nowhere could he find Sheraton — the man he sought above all others. The man who killed Tracey and the kids; the man who had sought to kill him.

Sheraton . . . Sheraton . . . where are you, you bastard? Why can I touch those around you, why can I get to them, but not to you? How are you hiding from me? Sheraton . . . Sheraton . . .

5

Barbara Sheraton stood in the bay of her penthouse apartment, twenty-two storeys high, looking out across London. The curtains were open, the window before her stretched from floor to ceiling, fifteen feet of uninterrupted glass. She sipped at the glass of bourbon in her hand, pulling the silk dressing-gown together at her throat. She was unconscious of the glass before her, the only barrier preventing a twenty-two-storey fall to the glittering traffic below. She tried to nurture the feeling which she usually experienced on nights such as this, standing in this spot: the feeling that she was floating high above the city and seeing everything there – its heart and its soul belonging to her. The darkening skyline, the silhouetted metropolis, the streets: all property of the Establishment. It was the great English myth. The Establishment, the Government, did not rule the city. She did. She fed it. And she lived from it. When aspects of it stepped out of line, she punished it. It was her city. She alone had the power of life and death; and neither politician, nor priest, nor saint or demon, lived or breathed in the city but by virtue of her permission. Her father and brothers had all died in the bloody aftermath of the Kray Brothers' decline in London's underworld, when the various family factions had fought for supremacy. Her father and three brothers had pulled the disparate threads of disorganised crime into a truly organised operation. They had died in the process – leaving her to preside. She had clung to her leadership by virtue of the same cold-blooded and uncompromising rules of the family legacy which had been left to her. Queen in a man's world. Chairwoman of the Board — a carefully structured and powerful empire. Squabbling between rival factions at street level had become a thing of the past; all unified now, all part of one organisation — Sheraton's organisation. Minor internal conflict was dealt with summarily; the 'Honour Among Thieves' dictum taken to its most logical, constructive and businesslike end. But now . . .

Now, out of nowhere, a threat to the stability of Sheraton's organisation had emerged.

'One man,' said Sheraton aloud, still looking out over the city. Eddie Brinkburn.

An insignificant man. A man whom she knew only from a prison photograph, taken unlawfully from his prison file.

'A garage mechanic, for God's sake.'

Sleep had been fitful for her over the last two weeks. Her dreams were 'uncomfortable'. No matter what the subject-matter; no matter how realistic or surreal, they all contained one uncomfortable element — Eddie Brinkburn. The shadow of the garage mechanic was always there on the outskirts; as if he was somehow on the fringe of every dream, wanting to get inside, but unable to do so. Brinkburn . . . the man who had invaded her world and her dreams. How? *How*? The man *had* to have contacts and some kind of operation behind him to be able to put the frighteners on so many people in her own operation. Reports back on the various incidents had been garbled, making no sense. How was this happening? There had to be more to this than the mechanic. Maybe after all this time under corporate control, there were factions within her own organisation which had decided to make a bid for power. It was only a matter of time before she found out. Enquiries were being made. But in the meantime, the attacks were continuing. Her international colleagues were continuing to make noises and she had promised an early resolution. *Brinkburn — one insignificant little man. The man who's trying to get into my dreams.* The man who can't be killed. The man who killed . . .

224

'Bobby,' said Sheraton aloud, voice choked.

Beautiful Bobby. The only man she had loved. Bobby with his beautiful blond hair and beautiful body. As she stood looking out into the night, Sheraton closed her eyes and could still remember what it felt like when they had made love, could still remember the firm dampness of that body when they'd moved together, could still feel what it was like when he'd moved inside her and he'd made her come as no man had done before or since.

'Brinkburn! Where are you?'

Bobby. Beautiful Bobby. Her lover.

Her beautiful baby brother.

Sheraton remembered that day in hospital. She'd stood at the foot of the bed, mascara in rivulets across her cheeks, as she'd looked down at him. He was swathed in bandages from head to foot like a mummy, head completely covered but for one eye, an eye also blurred by tears. Bobby's breath came harshly in ragged gasps from the slot-like aperture beneath. Tubes wired in and out of his body. Third degree burns on ninety per cent of his body. Long days and nights in agony.

'Why'd you do it, Bobby? Why the hell did you *do* it? A street job, for God's sake. A cheap little petrol station robbery!' Sheraton watched him struggle in agony to answer but no voice could emerge from those scorched lungs. 'What were you trying to prove? Dad . . . and the others . . . they all died to give us the business. Didn't that mean anything? You would have had it all eventually. I won't be in charge forever. I *needed* you, Bobby. You didn't have to prove a fucking thing!' Sheraton turned from him, unable to watch him gasping to answer, wiping the mascara from her face. 'If it wasn't for the fact that you'd *ordered* that little bastard, Bishop, to take you along, I'd have his head cut off.' Sheraton took deep breaths, restoring control to her voice, not wanting the two men outside − her bodyguards − to hear her reacting emotionally. She turned back again, now moving swiftly to the bed. Bobby was gagging, trying to reply; like a man drowning in his own spittle.

'Be quiet,' she instructed. 'You've got to get better. Do you hear me?' It was an order. 'You've *got* to get better. I want you healed. I don't want a single scar. I don't want a single burn.'

His young skin, muscles taut, the exciting moist dampness on his chest as his fingers hungrily kneaded her breasts.

'I need you to be the way you were.' Sheraton sat on the edge of the bed, ignoring Bobby's gasped intake of breath at the pain of her weight on the mattress.

The taste of his tanned skin. The smoothness. The taut muscles. The taste of his penis.

'I don't care what it costs. I want you back.'

She remembered the simple words they used to use before love-making; those simple but delicious words that were an invitation to the other to begin.

Come on, baby. Make it hard.

She looked again at Bobby's bandaged body; at the raw and traumatised eye staring through that bandaged slit.

Make it hard.

On the other side of the door, Sheraton's minders moved closer to listen as the soft, bitter sounds of weeping reached them.

'What's that she's saying?' asked one.

'Dunno,' replied the other. 'Sounds like . . . like . . . "Make it hard" . . . or something.'

Three days later, Bobby had died.

And Brinkburn, Sheraton had decided, was absolutely responsible.

'Bobby . . . beautiful Bobby . . .' Sheraton finished her drink, the familiar feeling of hate for the garage mechanic building up inside her. There was a vast puzzle to be solved; many questions about the hows and the whys and the wherefores. She remembered the time when that feeling of loss and hate had been so bad that she'd made it known how *pleased* she would be if someone took it upon themselves to pay Mr Brinkburn back in kind by burning the people he loved. The job had been done — and for a little while the loss and the hate had been sated. Something

226

for the garage mechanic to think about before she gave the order for *him* to be burnt.

She looked out into the night again.

The anger was coming back with full force. She remembered giving the order that Brinkburn should meet with an accident in prison. First, the warning; then, after Bobby's death, the order for a more permanent accident. Her execution warrants were *always* followed through. Not so with the mechanic, apparently. No one could — or *would* — touch him. How? How was he doing these things? Who was helping him? On the skyline, Sheraton could see a rose-coloured tinge. The distant sounds of an ambulance and fire engines racing to a fire somewhere. Perhaps another of her warehouses or business operations was burning down.

'How?'

Sheraton whirled from the window, flinging her glass across the room. It shattered on the wall.

The door opened swiftly and her minder, Sewell, entered quickly, ready for action. Short and squat, with shoulders as broad as a Sumo wrestler, Sewell had proved on more than one occasion how useful he could be with a cricket bat — or, indeed, any blunt object.

'Everything all right, ma'am?'

Sheraton pulled her dressing-gown tight round her waist. 'Yes. Give me another drink.'

Sewell crossed to the drinks bar in the centre of the room, needing no further instructions. Two ice cubes. Neat bourbon from the decanter. Expressionless, he carried it to her. Sheraton took it, taking one swift sip and then looking back at him with appraisal.

'How long have you been working for me, Sewell?'

'Three years, ma'am.'

Sheraton nodded, sipping again. 'I want you to do something for me.'

'Yes, ma'am.'

Sheraton drained the glass, handing it back to him.

'Hurt yourself, Sewell. I want you to hurt yourself for me.'

Sewell remained expressionless, hooded eyes giving no hint of emotion. His bull head, short cropped hair and midnight-shaded jowls seemed incongruous set into the tight white collar, the bow tie and dinner jacket.

'Did you understand, Sewell?'

'Yes, ma'am. In what way?'

'It doesn't matter. You choose.'

Face still expressionless, Sewell's grip tightened on the empty glass. Sheraton looked at it, smiling. With a grinding snap, the glass shattered in Sewell's fist. His face remained impassive. Blood began to seep through his fingers.

'Will that be all, ma'am?'

Sheraton smiled again. 'Yes, Sewell. That's all.'

When the door closed again, Sheraton was back at the window. She felt better now, more in control, as she looked out over the city – her thoughts now full of her father and brothers fighting for power and control in London's gangland in the wake of the Krays; the juggling for power. Her father and brothers; now all dead – even the baby, Bobby – all eventually killed in pulling together one single organisation from the disparate and desperate street fighting, the different 'families'. The Sheraton Empire – a vast and powerful conglomerate ruling London's Underground with its roots firmly embedded in the Establishment. But now . . . now . . .

The rose-coloured glow on the horizon seemed to have grown and somewhere out there in the night, she could still hear the distant and mournful wailing of fire engines and ambulances.

'Brinkburn . . . where are you . . .?'

* * *

'Sheraton . . . Sheraton where are you, you bastard?'

6

Days passed.

The old man was made to rig up two camp beds in the room in which Eddie had told Rennie about the Government experiments. Rennie never asked where the old man slept, but he became their unkempt butler. The kitchen below stairs was big enough to cook meals for armies . . . maybe it once had . . . and the old man cooked for them there, too. Rennie never asked about money − the old man didn't seem to need it. When they were hungry, he was despatched and he later returned with the food they required. Each time, that food was supplemented by two or three bottles of cobweb-smeared bottles of wine from the cellars below. No doubt an excellent vintage, but Rennie cared nothing for that. It tasted good and it made him feel good.

For the first time since his release from prison, he and Eddie talked.

They talked of the old times and the good times. They relaxed, they laughed. And it seemed at last that Eddie had been right all along: he was in control after all. The alien looks behind those eyes became a thing of the past. It was a good feeling. At first, those shadows threatened to return when the old man brought in newspapers . . . Heaven knew where from. In the headlines, Rennie could see that the war being waged on Sheraton's empire was continuing. Reading between the lines, he could see that the Frighteners were still at work. But after a while, even those shadows dissipated. Eddie was doing what he said he would do. He was using his new-found power to destroy Sheraton's evil. The catalogue of burnt warehouses, street gang warfare, drug and pornography exposés filled the pages. Each newspaper greeted the arrival of a new age, of a time when the forces of law and order . . . strangely absent from the newspapers in terms of any initiative action . . . were finally gaining a foothold in the way that the Government had promised and predicted. The Evil in society was being rooted out. It was being destroyed. And on such occasions, when the headlines proclaimed this fact, Eddie would hold the newspaper up to Rennie, smile and say . . . 'You see?'

* * *

Rennie awoke from his dreams of the Caribbean beach — the dreams which had kept him sane during his days in prison; dreams which no long contained flapping, ragged things. Eddie was right. He was in control; everything was going to be okay and even Rennie's dreams appeared to be convinced.

He stretched in the camp bed which the old man had provided from his apparently inexhaustible domestic supplies. Moonlight was showing through the bay windows. Rennie turned to look.

In the bay, Eddie was also asleep in a camp bed. He seemed restless; twisting first one way and then another. Through sleep-blurred eyes, Rennie watched him lean out of the bed, propping himself on one elbow and staring up at the bay windows and the calm blue-white light of the moon.

'I'm getting smaller.'

'What?' Rennie couldn't be sure that he'd heard him right. 'What did you say?'

'. . . smaller . . .'

Eddie rolled back into the camp bed, pulling the coverings up around his neck. Instantly, it seemed, he was asleep again. Rennie watched him for a while, puzzling. The moon had been shining on Eddie's face when he'd spoken; he'd looked spectrally white and somehow, Rennie thought, terribly vulnerable — almost childlike. There had been a

230

look of puzzlement there; a look of concern that spoke more of a child than an adult. Somehow — for reasons Rennie could not discern — there seemed to be something important about Eddie's expression, something important about his dream-like words: '*I'm getting smaller.*'

'Just dreams,' mumbled Rennie. He too turned over again, returned instantly to sleep and to his dreams of an unknown Caribbean beach. The sun was high, the waves rolling in on the shore without sound. Someone was standing a little way along that beach and, as Rennie drew near, he saw that it was Eddie. He was looking out to sea and he had the same puzzled, moon-bleached expression on his face. He turned slowly as Rennie approached.

'I'm getting smaller,' he said again.

'No you're not. You're just the same,' Rennie heard his own voice reply.

'No.' Eddie turned and began walking into the sea.

7

They had spent two weeks in the House on Lime Street when the craftsmen and the furniture began to arrive.

For two weeks, they had eaten and drunk and slept . . . and talked of the old times. Rennie's fears had gradually subsided. Eddie was okay. He was in control. On the Friday evening, Eddie had told him to expect arrivals on the following day. Further than that, he had refused to be drawn. He had just smiled . . . and it was a smile of control. In recent times, any hint from Eddie of a 'surprise' would have filled Rennie with trepidation. But not this time. Rennie had got himself drunk again on the rare vintages from the cellars below the House, and was awakened by the sound of someone coming in through the main entrance doors. Somewhere, a car horn was sounding. He struggled from sleep, climbed roughly out of the camp bed in the palatial drawing room to find that Eddie was gone . . . his camp bed neatly folded up and placed on the window-sill of the bay. Rubbing his head, Rennie staggered into the hall.

There was a furniture van outside and four workers were carrying crates through the doors and placing them in the hall. Rennie moved to the entrance, to find that there was not one, but *three* furniture vans.

'Where do you want this stuff, then?' one of the men asked. Rennie ignored him, hurrying off on a search for Eddie, or Lister. He found Eddie in the master bedroom upstairs. He was standing and watching three men unpack a crate, while a team of plumbers and electricians fitted out the room.

'Here they are,' said Eddie simply when he saw him. 'Our visitors.'

In the space of the next two hours, the House on Lime Street was crawling with plumbers, electricians, furniture removers, carpet layers and other tradesmen.

When Lister had brought them breakfast from the bowels of the House and they were standing watching a team of men clear away the brambles and scrub from the drive, Rennie asked simply: 'How?'

'From the city.' Eddie replied through a mouthful of sandwich. 'You know how.'

'The Frighteners.'

'The Frighteners. It's a question of . . .' Eddie laughed '. . . making offers that can't be refused. This is where we're going to live, Rennie. This is the base of our operations and I want it to be in "the style to which we will become accustomed" . . . to coin a phrase. We don't have the cash in our hands. So . . . people are doing us favours after our friends have been around to visit.'

'Bloody hell, Eddie, but you're taking risks. I mean . . . all these guys . . . all this stuff from the city. Somebody somewhere is bound to talk, bound to mention to somebody in the know where we are. You'll blow our cover, give away where we are.'

Eddie smiled again, calmly finishing his sandwich. 'After all this time, Rennie. And you still don't know how well I can put the Frighteners on people.'

'Okay, okay. But I still think you're taking a risk.'

'No risks, son. No risks at all. Believe me. We can have anything we want. Fear's our most powerful weapon.'

* * *

The House on Lime Street breathed with a new life.

The drawing room where Eddie and Rennie had drunk wine and laughed about the old days, the place where they slept and where Rennie had come to believe at last that his friend was not, after all, turning into some kind of monster with monstrous powers . . . this was refitted first. Carpets

233

were laid, the walls painted and papered, the ceilings cleaned, the bay window torched, stripped and revarnished. New paint, new life and new warmth. They continued to eat and sleep there . . . this time on deep and comfortable sofas. Lister . . . the old man . . . still slept wherever it was that he slept. And in the meantime, the craftsmen continued to refurbish the House.

Rennie watched the men work and fought down the urge to chat with them, simply to talk to them, to find out who they were and where they came from; which firms they represented. He felt an affinity with them, a sense of *belonging* that he'd not experienced for a long time. He was a garage mechanic, after all. He was a man who worked with his hands. Those hands, his skill — they had earned him a living before Eddie had foolishly become involved with the small wheels of Sheraton's business empire. He longed to connect, longed to hear them talking about their jobs, their wives, their lovers, their kids. He longed to be a part of that machine again, longed to be part of that system. But of course, he could not talk to them; was forced to remain aloof and distant. Too much of a risk, too much chance of giving things away when he talked. Despite Eddie's reassurances on the ability of the Frighteners to keep mouths shut, he was still wary of what he might say in an unguarded moment. So . . . he continued to watch them at work through windows and from safe distances. When one of the workmen's cars broke down in the drive and he called several men to help fix it, that was the biggest trial of all for Rennie. Without thinking, he was almost out of the door and down the drive towards the car. He resisted, opened another bottle of Lister's expensive plonk . . . a seemingly endless supply . . . and drank again.

Eddie was in control. Of that, Rennie had no doubt. But he was a quieter man now. 'Things on my mind,' he once said to Rennie, when he commented on it. 'Things to work out. Plans to make. Sometimes . . . my mind's somewhere else.'

'In the city?' Rennie asked.

'Yeah. In the city. Like I said, Rennie. I don't tell these things what to do . . . but I can *be* there somehow. I . . . point them in the right direction.' Eddie took a drink from Rennie, smiled, and said, 'I'm getting bigger, Rennie. They're getting more powerful as we get closer to wiping Sheraton out . . . and I'm getting Bigger.'

And Rennie remembered the night when Eddie had woken up and said: 'I'm getting smaller.' And although he still couldn't understand why it should be, he knew that it had been important. Still . . . what matter? Things were okay now.

8

'When, Eddie? When are you going to get to Sheraton and get this whole business finished?'

'You think I don't want to end it, is that it?'

'Sometimes I wonder, yeah. Sometimes I wonder just how far you want to take this . . . revenge. You're destroying Sheraton, Eddie. Just like you said . . . but I wonder.'

'I can end it when I want, Rennie. I promise you that. I could end it today if I could find Sheraton. But I can't. His power base is too great. I'm attacking from the outside in, I've stirred them up all right. They're all absolutely terrified. And I'm getting there bit by bit, piece by piece. I just can't get to Sheraton yet. But I know I'm on the way. As Sheraton's empire falls apart, it's like peeling layers away from some big rotten cake. Sheraton's at the centre of it. If I could get straight to him, make him pay, then that would be the end of it. But I just can't yet. As soon as I do . . . as soon as Sheraton and his empire are finished . . . then I'm finished, too. I promise.'

9

By the end of the second week, the House was fully refurbished.

Each room had been redecorated and refitted; the plumbing and the electrical systems had been overhauled and were working perfectly. Some of the renovation work still remained to be completed — the damp-proofing, for instance. The kitchen . . . Lister's domain . . . had also been refitted, although Rennie did not know how or when they would ever need to use it. He had got used to Lister's bacon sandwiches and rough cooking by now.

At the latter end of that second week, the security firm arrived.

A private security firm. Fences were erected around the House (electrified fences, at that) and a 24-hour dog patrol, with a checkpoint at the front and side gates. Rennie watched them erecting those fences around the estate. Beyond the mesh, the lime trees still kept vigil among the shadowed ruins of the strange street that formed the drive back to the main road.

On the last night of the refit, Eddie sent Lister down into the cellars for a couple more crates of wine. On his return, Eddie announced their house-warming. Lister was the barman.

'A toast!' Eddie held up his glass. Rennie was lying on the sofa, already into his second bottle of wine. 'Me and you, Rennie. Me and you.' They drank.

From the sofa, Rennie said, 'It's a long way from lying under bloody cars.'

'I'll drink to that.' Eddie crossed the room to a corner beside the drinks cabinet; there was a leather case there, which Rennie had never seen before. 'Know what's in here?'

'Surprise me.'

'Remember working on the cars? Remember lying in the freezing garage underneath 'em? What kept you going? You remember?'

Interested now, Rennie sat up.

Eddie opened the leather case. It was full of records. He swooped down, pulled out an album and tossed it like a frisbee across the room. Rennie struggled to catch it without dropping his wine glass. Some of the wine slopped, but he managed to catch the record. It was 'Mustang Sally'.

'Riiiiight! You sneaky bastard. When did you get these?'

'I'm the Man, remember. So now we've got music for the party.'

'Yeah, but no player.'

Eddie smiled and pointed to the other corner. Rennie had never questioned why there were curtains hanging there. He struggled to his feet, reverently laid the album on the sofa and crossed to the curtains, pulling them back. It was a CD player with speakers. Whooping, he hurriedly checked that the speakers were connected . . . they were . . . and set about placing them properly in the room, at either side of the sofa. Seconds later, the album was playing at top volume. Lister continued to grin from behind the bar, as if he could not understand what was going on, but was pleased to be part of it anyway. He laughed when they laughed, but did not seem to know what they were laughing at.

'Just keep the bottles coming, Lister,' said Rennie. 'You understand?'

Lister nodded . . . and grinned again.

* * *

Rennie woke at two-thirty.

He was on the sofa, empty wine bottles at his feet. The lights were still on and the turntable gave a soft thump-click, thump-click as the stylus turned lazily on a finished record.

238

Rennie's head felt bad, fuzzy and full of broken glass. He looked around, squinting at the light. Eddie and Lister were gone.

He struggled to his feet, swaying. He should know better. Getting drunk on beer or spirits was one thing . . . he was used to that . . . but he had never developed a resistance to wine. And now, it was paying him back for his over-indulgence.

'Eddie?' He looked around again. Maybe Eddie had drunk himself into oblivion somewhere behind the sofa.

He checked that there was no one there, then crossed the room and stepped out into the hall. There was a soft blue light creeping through the fanlight above the entrance doors now, light coming from the newly installed standard lamps outside. For the first time, Rennie felt as if he was staying in some lavish hotel, not an empty country house in the middle of nowhere. He also felt secure in a way that he'd never done before — maybe it had something to do with the electric fence and the dogs and the guards on the perimeter.

Those guards were strangely uncommunicative, never speaking, never acknowledging any waved greeting. Rennie presumed that the dogs were Dobermanns; whatever, they were savage-looking bastards. But no matter how remote and peculiar Eddie's security firm were, they made Rennie feel safe. Looking around for any sign of Eddie, he wondered idly how the guards out there managed. Who provided them with food and drink? Where the hell did they sleep? Maybe Lister provided the same kind of service for them that he provided for Rennie and Eddie inside the House. Anyway . . . who gave a damn? Rennie moved to the staircase, resting a hand on the cool wood of the banister.

'Eddie?'

His voice drifted away upstairs. There was no answer.

Rennie turned and began to think about looking in one of the other reception rooms. Then he heard the noise, and his attention drifted upstairs. He strained to listen again, and this time it came louder than before. It was unmistakable: the sound of a woman's laughter, low but clear . . . and coming from one of the rooms upstairs.

'Eddie? You cunning bastard . . .' Smiling, Rennie began to ascend the darkened staircase, gripping the banister rail tightly for support lest his balance be affected by the wine. A woman! Here at the House. And judging by the sound of her laughter, Eddie was having himself a really good time. It made Rennie feel good, too. Since Tracey's death, Eddie had never referred to women, had not felt or, indeed, had any contact with a woman . . . since his release from prison. Maybe he was making up for lost time now. It was just another sign that Eddie was normal again, that this special power he had acquired from Archie and from the experiments that had taken place inside this very house, were under complete control.

'Could have told me,' Rennie said aloud as he ascended. 'No need to be sneaky about it. We're both human.' He reached the top of the staircase, and the sound of a woman's voice and laughter was absolutely unmistakable. Now he could also hear Eddie's voice, low and almost inaudible. They were in the main bedroom. Rennie stopped. What the hell was he doing? Was he a Peeping Tom or something? His curiosity had brought him this far, but that was it. Eddie had somehow found himself a woman, he had sneaked away to be alone with her . . . and why not? Rennie decided to go back downstairs, have some more wine and try to kill this grotty feeling before returning to sleep. Time enough for questions in the morning.

And then he heard the other noise. He had just turned, about to descend again, when he heard the sound of children's laughter. Low, giggling laughter. And there was more than one child. Rennie turned back, listening again: just the sound of Eddie's voice and the mysterious woman's voice. Could he have been mistaken? No . . . there it was again. A little girl's voice, surely. And a boy's? Rennie moved up to the bedroom door; faint light spilled from underneath onto the landing carpet. A shadow passed. What the hell were a woman and kids doing in there?

240

Discretion now forgotten, Rennie quietly opened the door.

Eddie was sitting on the edge of the bed. There was a small girl . . . about five years old . . . on his knee. At his feet, a boy . . . about seven years old . . . was playing on the carpet. And next to Eddie, watching him delight in the kids, was a woman. She looked up, smiling, when Rennie opened the door. And, of course, he recognised her immediately.

At first he thought he must be dreaming, that he was still downstairs on the sofa drugged with wine, and that he had only thought he'd woken and gone in search of a missing Eddie. That was surely the best explanation. The light in the bedroom was low . . . only one lamp glowing on the bedside table next to Eddie. The other figures were in shadow, but they were all unmistakable.

It was Eddie's dead wife, Tracey.

And Eddie was smiling and laughing . . . and playing with his dead kids, Russell and Jane.

Tracey was still smiling; a smile which seemed to be saying: *Isn't this nice? Isn't he a good father?* and she looked back at the children as Eddie finally noticed that Rennie was there. His expression seemed clouded; not completely clear because of the stark bedside lamp on his face . . . but Rennie again felt that dreadful feeling that he might be looking at the mask he had seen before. But then Eddie smiled and said, 'Come on in, Rennie.'

'I don't understand . . .' Rennie stepped into the room. The children looked up now and saw him. They smiled, too, and continued playing as if this was the most normal thing in the world. Tracey, Russell and Jane . . . all dead for more than six months. Burnt to death in a council flat. Killed by Sheraton's people because Sheraton's stupid fucking brother had got himself totalled in a 'bust' that neither Eddie nor Rennie had any business being involved in.

'What's to understand?' said Tracey.

But now Rennie could see that something wasn't right here. At first, his sense of logic had rocked and then tried to assume a normality, had tried to say there must be a logical reason for dead people being here. Maybe they'd

241

never been dead at all. But now, when she spoke and leaned farther forward into the light, Rennie could see what he didn't want to see.

They weren't real.

Tracey was a thing of cloth, a thing of sheets and bedspread and towels. She was only something that looked and sat and talked like Tracey, something that had a patterned paisley face which was a perfect likeness but was not her at all. The children were the same: made from bits and pieces, the bed linen and the draperies and the curtains . . . and whatever was lying around in that room. The Tracey-thing put a hand of cloth onto Eddie's knee and smiled again. There were no eyes. 'Nothing to understand, Rennie,' she said, face still fixed on Eddie. 'We're back, that's all. One happy family again.'

Rennie recoiled, uttering a sound of disgust.

'One happy family,' repeated Eddie. 'They're not gone at all, see? I've told you before. In prison. They first started to come and see me there. They come to see me here now. And they keep me happy. What's wrong with that, Rennie?'

Rennie kept backing towards the door. Eddie's face was wrong. He was talking like someone in shock. His eyes seemed far away.

'But they're . . . they're not *real*.'

'They're as real as I can make them.' Eddie's voice began to rise in anger. 'Don't tell me what's real, pal. What I want to be real *is* fucking real . . .'

'Language, Eddie,' said the Tracey-thing. 'Not in front of the kids.'

Eddie patted her head, eyes still fixed on Rennie. 'Sorry, love. But he should realise who's in charge here, that's all. And when I say something's real, then it's real. Isn't that right?'

The Tracey-thing nodded.

Rennie reached the door again and could feel his stomach starting to revolt at the wine that was still inside. He could feel his gorge rise. What he was seeing was *wrong*; it was wrong in a dreadful, terrible way which he could not describe

242

but which was threatening to result in an eruption from his stomach and throat at any second. He whirled away from the family scene and staggered to the staircase.

'Never forget that, Rennie!' Eddie shouted from behind him. 'What I make is real. It *is* real!'

Rennie puked, his hand flying to his mouth. Vomit sprayed around his fingers. He gulped back and staggered to the banisters, grabbing the rail to steady himself. Lost in the nightmare, he blundered down the stairs.

Behind him, he could hear the bright, mocking laughter of a happy family.

10

Rennie hungered to return to more pleasant dreams.

Waking up and going to look for Eddie had been a mistake; finding the things which posed as Tracey and Eddie's children belonged to nightmare. Everything was wrong again, and Rennie wanted to go back — back to the sofa, back to sleep, back to the dreams. He wanted to awake again on the sofa with his headache to find Eddie asleep in the bay window as usual. He dived back into sleep.

The House was alive. He knew that now, in his new dream. He was still lying on the sofa; the wine bottles at his feet were a glittering pile of broken glass. The walls were wet and running, like the walls of a cave. The moon was shining through the bay window, just as it had done before the House was refurbished and Eddie had said those strange yet somehow meaningful words. The sofa was a raft, apart from the House, and Rennie knew that he must stay there and not venture from it. The House was alive . . . and it was hostile. It had been asleep for a long time; now that Eddie was back, had come back bearing its gift of power, the further power that lived in the walls had been reawakened. Rennie clung to the sofa but . . .

The dream shifted. He was no longer in the drawing room. He was in the library on the other side of the hall and he was sitting at a desk that was too small for him. It was dark, the moonlight was still shining in shafts through the window. He was not alone. The library was a classroom now and there were rows of desks behind and in front of him, desks built for seven-year-old bodies. And as he looked around, he saw that there were children sitting at each of the desks, uniformed and silent, their features hidden by the dark. It wasn't natural for children to be sitting so still and so silent, but they were. Rennie looked ahead, past the silent children, to the front of the class. There was a larger desk up there and a blackboard. Chalked words were written on it, and although he could not read what they said in the darkness, he knew them to be obscene words; words that shouldn't be on a blackboard in a children's classroom. He became aware of an air of expectancy in the class, but it was not emanating from the pupils: they seemed somehow distanced, like dummies, not alive at all. But there was a pregnant atmosphere nevertheless.

Something or someone was coming.

A shadow stepped forward at the front of the class, from the darkened alcoves.

He could see no details, except that it was obviously adult . . . and a teacher. He could see the mortar-board and the flowing black gown. The figure was holding a cane and, without looking back, it slashed out at the blackboard, rap-rap-rapping briskly at the obscene chalked words, drawing the children's attention to them. As one, the darkened children's heads lifted and looked. It was obscene — this teacher should not be showing these kids things like this . . . Rennie wanted to rise from his seat and shout at him, wanted to go down to the front and knock him on his back. These kids were in his care and he was doing more than betraying that trust — he was corrupting them.

Rennie's anger boiled and swelled. If only he were free to act, he would do something about the bastard down there. He'd teach him about betraying his trust and . . .

. . . and suddenly, he *was* free to move. He stood up, hearing the small chair screech back in the silence of the darkened classroom. No one turned to look at him, but the shadow-master at the front of the class stepped forward expectantly. Rennie could still see no details of the figure, but now something else was coming over him; another feeling. His first reaction had been one of outrage and anger.

Now, as the figure stood and waited for him to walk forward to meet it, he felt another emotion. And that emotion was fear.

He was dreadfully afraid of that figure up there, and the last thing in the world he wanted to do was to go to the front of the class and see what it was.

He struggled to wake from the dream as something, some immutable force, made him step into the aisle between the desks. He was walking to the front now . . . and he struggled to fight against the impulse. He didn't want to be in this dream any more. He knew that the dark face up there was smiling . . . and God, oh God . . . he didn't want to see what the face was like. The shadow stepped down and began to swirl up the aisle to meet him; a ragged flapping shadow, a monstrously tall, ragged cloak-thing. Rennie screamed.

The dream changed again.

He was still in the classroom. The children still sat, facing front, faceless and shadowed. But the ragged, swirling, teacher-thing had gone. In the logic of nightmare, he could sense that its presence was no longer there. Now, he was standing by the windows, in the moonlight, looking at a rectangular table . . . also illuminated by the moon . . . and he could see that it was a laboratory bench, the kind of bench that public school kids might work at in a chemistry lesson. There were glass jars on it, a row of them. He moved closer, to see that they were specimen jars. There were things under the bell-domes, things that the children must be experimenting on. Rennie had never seen human organs before, but he knew that was just what they were — heart, liver, kidneys and . . . in one of the bottles, curled and asleep, a premature baby; asleep, but its eyes were open and staring, like a fish.

There was no terror here, not in this part of the dream. But there was a *wrongness*, a feeling of distress that these things should be allowed to exist. Rennie was not completely in charge of his emotions in this dream, and whereas he wanted to find the anger he had felt earlier, he could not achieve it. He was not being allowed to use it. He was helpless now, but disgusted . . . that the children should be working on these things.

Something moved in one of the bottles.

Rennie's attention was forced back. And now he knew that the things in there — the disembodied organs — were all somehow still alive. Twisting, writhing . . . trying to get out of those belljars. He could also see that the shadow faces of the schoolchildren were turning in unison to look at the movement.

'Don't look!' he shouted, but he knew that they couldn't hear his words.

The lids on the belljars were rattling; the things inside were trying to get out. Rennie struggled to act, his limbs like lead; in slow motion he reached for the rim of the bench, felt the cool grain on his fingers. The kids mustn't be allowed to see these living things, to experiment on them. He heaved at the bench, heaved and lifted in slow motion, praying that the force which dictated his actions within his dream would allow him the strength and the power to do what he had to do. The bench slowly tipped over. The glass belljars began to slide from the table, the things inside now livid and frenzied with squirming movement as the belljars crashed to the floor in explosions of splintered glass and obscene, noxious fluids.

'Die, you bastards, die!'

Rennie flung the table aside; it juddered into the window bay. The children were still looking, still examining the spot where the belljars had fallen and smashed. Rennie stepped round to get a better view of the wreckage. What he saw there was more horrifying, more disgusting . . . and more distressing . . . than before.

Amidst the shattered, splintered glass and the slime-ridden pools of chemical, the disembodied organs were *embodying*.

The heart, the liver, the intestines, were squirming and mating, melding and organising. They were all combining to become *whole* again, to create something new in an obscene, repulsive frenzy of squirming matter. In the midst of it all, the premature baby was trying to find its own place,

247

scrabbling and twisting and grabbing like a child in a revolting playpen of snakes.

In horror, Rennie wanted to kick out at that disgusting mess; to scatter the nauseating organs apart, stop them from becoming whole. But the presence of the child within that horrible compacting mess prevented him from doing so. He recoiled from the scene, yelling at the kids to look away. They ignored him, their attention riveted on the terrible couplings taking place on the floor. He skidded in a pool of slimy chemicals, staggered round to the front of the class, shouting, shouting, shouting. And as he reeled round the teacher's desk, he saw the chalked scribbles on the blackboard again. They were still completely alien to him, making no direct sense, still the most obscure things he had ever seen. Suddenly, like a veil parting, he knew now in close-up that the words had to do with the horrifying melding of organs that was taking place on the floor. There was a direct connection. And this was his chance. If he rubbed out those horrible scribblings, he could stop it all and end the horror. He whirled towards the blackboard, hands raised.

And the terrifying black teacher-thing stepped out from the shadows directly before him, ragged shroud-arms wide to embrace.

Shrieking, Rennie awoke from his dream.

He was not in the drawing room. He was on the library floor. And in his hand, he was clutching a pencil-shaped piece of chalk.

Shouting hoarsely in horror and revulsion, he flung the chalk away, blundered out of the room into the hall and through the main entrance doors to the drive.

11

It was a chill morning.

After an hour and a half standing by the hedgerow in the drive, Rennie could feel the cold seeping into the marrow of his bones. His breath rose in steaming clouds around his face. He clapped his hands together, hopping from foot to foot on the spot. But he could not and did not want to go back into the House.

His mind had been racing. What the hell was real and what the hell was a dream? He wasn't sure that he could be sure about anything any more. Eddie and Tracey and the kids . . . was that a dream? The school class and the scribblings and the bottles and that . . . that horrible bloody thing . . . was that a dream? The chalk? The sleepwalking? Maybe it was the wine. Maybe he had been hitting it too hard when he wasn't used to that kind of booze. He didn't know. But he didn't want to go back into that place until he'd sorted himself out, no matter how cold it was outside.

Two of the guys on security patrol with their Dobermanns passed him. He recognised neither of them; their faces were muffled completely with dark scarves. They were even wearing dark glasses at this time of the morning. In keeping with the super-cool, efficient image, no doubt. Rennie acknowledged them with a wave of the hand as they passed on, but they ignored him. He knew what he must look like.

He turned back to the hedgerow, gazing back at the House; at the rising towers and the crumbling brickwork. Some of those windows *did* look like eyes. Was the bloody place watching *him*?

The main entrance doors opened.

Eddie appeared at the top of the stairs, coat flying in the wind, flanked by the lions on either side, their bristling manes frozen in stone. To Rennie, it looked like a perfect portrait, as if Eddie had always lived here. He seemed perfectly at home. He saw Rennie and descended the stairs, hands thrust in pockets, black coat swirling behind him.

Rennie watched him come; could see the look of apology on his face before he drew level. *At least*, thought Rennie, *it's a* human *look*.

Eddie stood in front of him for a long while looking casually, almost nonchalantly, around the newly developed estate. At last, he turned to Rennie and said:

'Come on, Rennie. Come back inside. It's cold out here.'

'Fuck off.' Rennie pulled his jerkin collar tight at his neck.

'What's the matter?'

'You *know* what's the matter.'

'Last night?'

'Yeah, last night. What the *hell* was going on? What *were* those things?'

'Look . . . I was drunk. And lonely. It's not the first time.'

'But those things aren't natural. For God's sake, Eddie. Tracey and the kids are *dead*. What are you doing?'

'Don't give me that! She wasn't *your* wife . . . and they weren't your kids. They were mine. Why the hell are you so offended, anyway? All right . . . they're dead. But when I use my . . . my power and bring them back like that, I'm not so alone any more. The grief doesn't eat my guts so much. It takes away the pain.'

'Those things aren't *real*, man. No matter what you said last night. They're . . .'

'They're real enough for me.'

'That's sick. You know that? Really sick. And I expect they're real enough to kill, if you want them to. Just like your other Frighteners.'

Rennie was unprepared for Eddie's sudden swirl of movement; the blow connected with the side of his face. He fell awkwardly onto the gravelled drive, senses swimming. When he looked up, Eddie was nervously leaning down to help him. There was confusion and guilt on his face. *More human emotions?* thought Rennie again. He slapped out at the proffered hand, knocking it away, and struggled back to his feet, massaging his jaw.

'Great, man. *Great*.'

'I'm sorry, Rennie. Really, I didn't . . .'

'Why stop there? Go on. Do it. Put the Frighteners on me. Am I getting in your way now, too? Go on . . .'

'I'd never do that. You know I wouldn't.'

'Oh yeah? Like that night back in the flat when my fucking clothes nearly strangled me just 'cause you had a bad dream.'

'That's not fair. I wasn't in control. I am now.'

'You keep telling me that, Eddie. But who *are* you?'

'What?'

'Who *are* you, man? Sometimes I look at your face and I don't know what you are any more. Who are you? Who the hell's in there behind your eyes?'

'It's me . . . *it's ME*!' Eddie banged a fist against his chest, *mea culpa*. 'Look, Rennie. I'm sorry I snapped. But for God's sake . . . give me a little bit of space. All right, I know how it must have looked to you last night. I know how weird this all is. But where's the harm in what I did? I miss them, Rennie. I need them. And for a little while I can have them back. Who am I hurting? Who?'

'I don't know. Sometimes I think I don't know anything any more . . .'

'Come on in. I'll find Lister and we'll have something to eat.'

251

12

They ate. And during that breakfast, with Lister as cook, servant and attendant, they did not speak of the event. But it was always there. After the last mouthful, when they both sat back and looked at each other, it was still there in their eyes.

'Are you going to do it again?'

'Is it so important?'

'I don't know. I just . . . just don't like having the fucking things around. I've seen what they can do.'

'These aren't dangerous. I promise you. Come on, man. Indulge me. I don't do it often, just when things get too much.'

'But I don't understand, Eddie. It's not *them* . . . it's not Tracey or the kids.'

'It doesn't matter. I can make the fantasy real now. Hell . . . everything's a fantasy.'

'So now you're a philosopher.'

Eddie laughed dryly. 'No, I'm not that. But believe me, Rennie. I make the fantasy real . . . and it helps. It helps.'

They spoke no more of it.

It was another lazy day for Rennie. Eddie's display of emotion was real . . . it was human . . . even down to the punch on the face. In a way, Rennie welcomed that blow; had welcomed the look of regret, the look of confusion. It reminded him that Eddie was human after all. And it shoved that alien mask behind the face . . . which Rennie had seen and feared . . . farther into the background. Maybe Eddie was right. Who was he to question what he was doing?

252

Later in the afternoon, when he came across Eddie standing at his usual spot in the bay window of the drawing room, looking up into the sky, he wondered just what in Hell Eddie was doing now in the city; just what errands the Frighteners were engaged on, just what nightmares Sheraton's people were enduring. Yes . . . it was a wild and terrifying power. And yes, at the beginning it had seemed that Eddie was barely in control of it all. The whys and wherefores of that power were beyond Rennie. But if Eddie could control and channel it, and if he could keep those hellish things in check, then maybe everything would be okay after all.

13

Rennie drank more wine from the seemingly endless supply that Lister brought from the cellars. He was drinking too much and he knew it. But when his belly was full of the best vintages, things seemed better than they had before. The nightmares of the previous evening seemed far away. When sleep came at last, there were no nightmares. But there were dreams.

Dreams of Florinda. Beautiful, lost Florinda.

He awoke at three-thirty, bathed in sweat. Someone was standing in the doorway.

Alarmed, he was half out of bed when a voice said:

'It's okay, Rennie. It's me.'

And Rennie knew the owner of that voice straight away. 'Florinda?'

The shadow in the doorway moved into the room and Rennie turned away from it, holding his hands to his head. 'Oh God, Eddie. You sick, sick bastard.' Emotions raged and swelled within him, impossible to sort out immediately. Revulsion, fear, betrayal, and yes . . . loss. 'How the hell can you do this to me, you bastard?' The shadow moved closer. Rennie refused to look.

'Don't blame Eddie. He just wants to show you.'

'Keep away from me.'

'Don't hate me. Don't turn me away.'

'I don't hate you . . . I don't . . . Oh *fuck*! . . . You're not real. You're not Florinda.'

'Look at me, Rennie. Look at me and tell me I'm not real.'

Rennie looked up. There were tears in his eyes. He was hurt and lost and afraid, but he had to see. One way or the other he had to see. The shadow moved into the moonlight.

It *was* Florinda.

He could see her beautiful ebony body; her beautiful classical face and flowing black hair; the white of her teeth, her smiling lips. And he could see also how she had been fashioned.

It was black lace, all of it, black lace.

Her eyes were closed, and Rennie also knew that if she opened them . . . there would be no eyes there, only hollow spaces. He knew that she was keeping her eyes closed to complete the illusion. And that illusion was complete. She was beautiful; a perfect living image fashioned from lace, and clothed in a lace nightgown.

'Am I so horrifying?'

Tears coursed down his cheeks, his throat was constricted.

'God, Florinda. I can't . . . I don't . . .'

'How could I hurt you, Rennie? I love you. I always did.'

'You left me. You left me for that bloody businessman.'

'But I'm back. And Eddie's brought me back. It can be the way it was before. I promise you.' Florinda reached the end of the bed and sat next to him. The mattress gave under her weight; real weight, real substance . . . not a thing of lace at all. And Rennie marvelled at the illusion . . . wondered what was inside that lace exterior which so perfectly gave the illusion of limbs and skin and her oh so perfectly contoured face. She reached out to touch him, and Rennie couldn't find it within him to inch away from that touch. He was hurt — by her presence, by the fact that Eddie had conjured her up to teach him a lesson, but most of all by what she had done all those months ago when she had walked out of his life. When her touch came it was . . . not surprisingly . . . a touch of black velvet. But it was a loving touch, a tender touch . . . and Rennie allowed her fingers to caress the contours of his face, down to his lips. Almost involuntarily, he kissed those fingers.

'You see?' she said. 'I'm real. I'm not a fantasy at all.'

Rennie groaned, feeling a familiar heat; a heat that had disappeared when Florinda had left. 'Oh, Eddie . . . you bastard . . .'

'Eddie doesn't matter to us. Forget him. There's just you . . . and me . . .'

The shadow leaned forward and kissed him. A kiss of velvet. Time dissolved, reality dissolved, and Rennie turned to hold her. Eddie was right: the fantasy was reality. Florinda *was* real. And in that knowledge, the heat overwhelmed him as Florinda's urgent velvet kisses inflamed him.

They slid back onto the bed.

'God, Florinda, I've missed you.

'Love me, Rennie. Love me.'

Resistance swam away.

The night enfolded them.

* * *

Rennie dreamed again when his love was spent, slipping away into a drugged sleep. It was an instant slipping away; a release which he had been awaiting for a long time.

He dreamed that he was back in the library.

It was night again, and the same moonlight was shining through the bay window. But this time there were no rows of desks with silent, faceless children. There was no blackboard with its obscene chalked messages; no flapping, horrifying ragged thing teaching the class.

This time, the room looked like a hospital room or a scientific laboratory. There was a bed where the front of the class had been; a strange bed, with straps and wires and drip-feed tubes. There was equipment here, too: computer terminals; charts on the walls. At first, the bed had seemed empty, but as Rennie drifted forward, he could see that there was an occupant. A large man, strapped to the bed; those leather straps on his thighs and arms. He was struggling furiously and although Rennie could hear nothing, he knew that the man was screaming.

Rennie drifted closer, aware now also that there were

white uniformed people on either side of him, also moving closer. And it was these people — doctors? — of whom the large man was afraid. The man jerked his head up to look at him in abject terror, screaming soundlessly.

It was Archie.

Archie Duncan.

* * *

The shock of the familiar face jolted Rennie out of his dream. Daylight crept under his eyelids; he squinted to keep it out, aware now that he was lying naked on his bed.

There was black lace beneath him; a bundle of black lace and cloth and paper and . . .

Rennie rolled from the bed, throwing the stained black lace away from him into the corner. The love he had given last night, the discovery and the release . . . all of it was false and cruel and sick. His fantasies were sour and hollow.

'You bastard, Eddie.' Tears streamed down his cheeks, emotion choked in his throat: 'You . . . bloody . . . bastard . . .'

14

Rennie walked.

Wrapped up in his overcoat against the cold morning air, he walked down the driveway of the House to the main gate. Two of those strange guard dogs saw him coming and silently watched his approach. The guards at the gate did not have to restrain them, nodding in token recognition from their muffled scarves as Rennie walked past them and down the road towards the trees. There was a fresh wind this morning. It hissed among the lime trees as he walked down the centre of the road. Thin sunlight peeked out between thick grey clouds and as the trees grew denser he began to see the ruins of houses on either side of Lime Street.

After a while, he stepped off the road, into the trees, and began to pick his way through the ruins.

Lime Street. What had the place been? Had people really lived here long ago? Why here . . . in the middle of the countryside? Had there been a factory nearby, or a mill? There was no evidence of how the street had come to be there . . . or of how it had come to be abandoned and left to the trees.

Rennie entered a crumbling house through its shattered doorway. There were still traces of floorboards. Weeds and coarse grass covered the ground area; fallen stones had acquired a mossy velvet covering. There was no roof on this house; no roofs on any of them. All open to the sky and the wind and the weather. Rennie picked his way carefully through the long grass and stood in the centre of the house.

Who had lived here? He tried to conjure up a picture of the family. But all he could see was his own family, his own childhood. He kept walking, making his way down an overgrown back lane, weaving slowly in and out of the houses.

It had been hard to be black where he was born. Bad enough to be white in an overcrowded, neglected, deprived and slum city, with no prospect of work for fathers or mothers. But being black seemed to compound the sin. He had learnt to be hard; had learnt how to handle himself. Over the years it had stood him in good stead. He had never allowed himself to get close to many people. First Eddie, and only then when they were kids because he had once saved his skin from a good hiding. Colour had meant nothing to Eddie; he had never made reference to it. Only Eddie was close . . . and then Florinda . . . and . . .

. . . and now the hard man had fallen. He had allowed himself to be close to a woman because she had seemed special, and she had told him that he was special to her. Then she had left, and he had decided then and there that it would be the last time he would ever be hurt by a woman again. He would be the hard man again; act the hard act. Last night, Eddie had betrayed him. He had sent that . . . that *thing* . . . to his room to prove his point. And Rennie had given in, had fallen in with the fantasy, had allowed the old hurt to return. It was a double betrayal . . . because he had also betrayed himself. Florinda was gone, and that was the simple fact, no matter what Eddie could conjure up. He should have known better. Now, Rennie felt soiled. He felt unclean and . . . hollow.

He kept walking, climbing across another ruined doorway and into another open-roofed house. Once again, the ground was thigh-deep in couch-grass and tangled weeds. But in the centre of the house grew a lime tree. And Rennie remembered their first arrival at the House on Lime Street and his observations of the other houses amidst the trees; houses with lime trees growing in the houses themselves. It had seemed impossible then. It must surely still be impossible. He walked across to the tree. Its branches swayed in the cold wind, fumbling at the sky. He touched the rough bark of the bole and looked up. The tree was about forty feet high. How the hell could that be? How long did it take a lime tree to grow to that height? How old were these houses? Surely not as old as the trees? This didn't make a great deal of sense . . . like everything else that had been happening recently.

Rennie smacked the bark with the flat of his hand; solid and high and heavy. He found himself thinking: *So people come and go, they build their places and they live there and then they leave. Sooner or later, the grass and the weeds and the trees grow right back again.* The thought seemed more potent than he could explain. He also found himself thinking of pavements . . . and of how they could be cracked apart by a single clump of grass growing beneath. Just like now, with these houses and these trees. The trees had . . . gobbled up the houses on Lime Street after the people had gone. To him, it seemed as if they possessed an intelligence. People came and went . . . but the trees were always here.

Again, his thoughts returned to the past; and to dirty back alleys and street fights and thoughts of making something of his life. He walked on, continuing to pick his way through the ruined houses.

And as he walked, he could not shake off the feeling that had crept up on him recently: that there was more to Eddie's new-found power than he had told him; that somehow Rennie himself was privy to parts of a puzzle; that although Eddie had told him about the Government research in that House, there was *more* to it than that. He was walking through part of the puzzle now − the ruined houses. They seemed to hold a key to . . . something. His dreams seemed to be trying to tell him something about it, too. But as he walked, he could get no nearer to arranging the jigsaw into an acceptable pattern.

Rennie walked all day through the ruins, down one side of Lime Street and up the other, back to the House.

When he finally arrived at the main gate, the strange dogs allowed him entry without challenge. They watched him pass and their unnatural demeanour further unsettled him.

It was as if they wanted him back in the House.

He re-entered.

15

'*Rennie?*'

'*For God's sake, Florinda. Leave me alone.*'

'*You don't mean that. You know that you want me.*'

'*Florinda . . .*'

'*Shhhh . . . Love me, Rennie. Love me.*'

Outside in the night, the limes sighed; their weaving shadows caressing the silhouettes of two lovers.

* * *

'Does it still hurt?'

'Sometimes. Only when I think about it.'

'So? You know the answer, don't you?'

'Yeah. Don't think about it. I know.'

'Come on. She *is* real. She's as real as you are. When you want her . . . she's there. It's like not having lost her at all.'

'I don't know, Eddie. I'm confused.'

'It's okay. Don't think about it. Just accept it for what it is.'

'It took me a long time to get used to . . . used to . . .'

'I know . . . it took a long time to get used to losing her. Now the pain comes back a little after each time. But that'll go, believe me. You don't have to have that pain again, because as long as I've got the power, I can always bring her back.'

'I don't know what's real any more.'

'Like I said . . . I'm the one who creates reality. There's no such thing as fantasy any more.'

'I need another drink.'

'Lister! It's party time again . . .'

16

The visitors came on the following day.

The first limousine arrived at the security gate at 7.15 pm, as instructed. The guard had been briefed to expect them. He ticked off the names of the occupants on his list: Brinkley and Johnson — both worried men.

As the car slid past the gate and into the grounds of the House, they exchanged nervous glances and then fixed their attention on the House itself.

Brinkley could not get the thought of cricket bats out of his head. The memo and the terror of that especially convened 'board meeting' were still imprinted on his mind, together with Bishop's bloody death at the hands of Sheraton's minder. Brinkley had believed himself set up; fingered for sacrifice — but death had passed him by this time. But he had taken Sheraton's point and, as Head of the Extortion and Drug Trafficking 'arm' of Sheraton's enterprise, had pulled out every stop to find and eliminate Brinkburn.

Until last Thursday.

Until the time he'd come home late to his luxury apartment wanting only to have a drink and relax.

Until the time he'd gone into the kitchen for ice and found that . . . that . . . *thing* . . . standing there waiting for him.

Brinkley loosened his collar as the car slid on towards the House, remembering that tattered, ragged scarecrow of a thing which had stood in his kitchen; that patchwork Guy Fawkes dummy of a thing standing six feet tall like a man and made of the kitchen curtains, the towels, the dusters, torn wallpaper, broken glass, bin liners, carpet, Domestos bottles . . . and the sharp and disintegrated fragments of kitchen appliances, crockery and splintered glass.

Most of all, he remembered the thing's voice when it had spoken to him; a voice of filthy water in black, detritus-clogged drains.

'*Mr Brinkburn sent me, Brinkley. You've been bad, haven't you? And you'll do anything to make things better, won't you? Because if you don't, I'll have to hurt you, won't I? Gooodd . . . Now, this is what Mr Brinkburn wants you to do. He wants you to speak to your business friends abroad. He wants you to make confidential contact and you must persuade them to send their most important people here . . . to this country. Mr Brinkburn wants to meet them. Sheraton is finisssshed. You know that, don't you, Brinkley?*'

Brinkley had nodded, like a child.

'*Your partner, Mr Johnson — Sheraton's Prostitution man — is also being visited. He'll be contacting his own top men . . . just as you're going to do. And you're going to tell them that Mr Johnson and yourself are the ones who are challenging Sheraton for power. When your friends come, you're both to bring them all to Mr Brinkburn.*

'*Your foreign friends will want to do business with you, won't they? They'll want to retain their connections with the new bosses. So . . . be a good boy. Telephone your friends. Mr Brinkburn will be waiting for you. When everything is ready, when you've made the arrangements with Mr Johnson for all your foreign friends to visit . . . all on the same day, at the same place . . . Mr Brinkburn will be in touch to tell you where the party is going to take place. But you mustn't tell tales, Brinkley. Because you know what'll happen to you if you do. Don't you?*'

Brinkley remembered how the thing had flexed claws that were made from compacted knives and forks . . .

The limousine pulled up outside the House, as instructed, and Brinkley looked at Johnson again. He knew that one of Brinkburn's things had also visited him and that, together, they'd made the necessary arrangements. But Johnson wouldn't talk about what he'd seen.

Seconds later, Lister escorted them up the stone staircase, past the stone lions and into the hall. A banquet had been prepared in the central room. Lister escorted them inside, poured their drinks and left them to chat. The two men whispered nervously to each other throughout, as if in preparation for what they assumed would be a gruelling and intensive interview.

At 7.30 pm, the other limousines began to arrive.

There would be four of them, each containing two men and one driver. In the first, Jonathan Crandall, from America. In the second. Alfredo Andinaro, from Italy. In the third, Willi Brecht, from Germany. In the fourth, Henri Lefèvre from France. Each of the men with a bodyguard and driver; each of them summoned by Brinkley and Johnson.

By 8.00 pm, the central room buzzed with expectant conversation.

'Wake up, Rennie. We've got visitors.'

Rennie felt a hand roughly shaking his shoulder; dragging him unwillingly back from his familiar dream of a Caribbean beach; moreover, a beach which he now shared with Florinda. He slapped out at the hand and the voice. He wanted no intruders; he only wanted to dream.

'Come on, wake up.'

Through sleep-blurred eyes, he saw the shadowed figure standing over him in bed; recognised the voice but could not put a name to it. The empty wine bottle he had been cradling like a sleeping infant fell to the floor with a *clunk*.

'. . . leave me *alone* . . .'

And then anger began to germinate inside him. Who the hell was this? Who the hell did he think he was, bursting into his bedroom; invading his privacy *and* Florinda's privacy? He reached out for her — and touched a handful of empty black lace. And then, of course, everything came into focus with the familiar sick and hollow emptiness which he was trying, day by day, to drown with alcohol.

'You've got five minutes to wash, shave and get dressed. There's a party waiting for us downstairs.'

'No more parties, Eddie. I'm sick to death of parties . . .'

'Not *that* kind of party. This one's special.'

Eddie moved to the bedroom window and looked out. Beyond, the lime trees swayed and hissed in the wind. He smiled and stretched . . . contentedly. Rennie groaned and climbed out of the bed.

'Okay . . . what's the big deal about *this* party?'

Eddie moved back to the bed and clasped Rennie firmly by the shoulders, shaking him from his lethargy like an indulgent parent with a recalcitrant son.

'It's special, my son . . . because *Sheraton*'s people are downstairs.'

'Sheraton!' Rennie's lethargy evaporated instantly. He shook his head. '*Now* what the hell are you doing? Sheraton's people? *Here*?'

'Everything's in order, Rennie. I'm in control. Now come on.'

* * *

With trepidation, Rennie washed, shaved and awkwardly threw on his clothes. His days and nights had become a continuous fog-blur, a wine-induced safe-feeling with Eddie, as always, in control. It helped him to accept the fantasy – and as long as he kept himself well topped up, he was happy with 'Florinda'. Instinct was now trying to force him to throw off that blur, to come to terms with the fact that, according to Eddie, some of Sheraton's people were downstairs. He refused to be shoved into taking an active part. Eddie was in control and knew what he was doing. Far better for Rennie to stay in the safe blurred place and let him get on with it. Still befogged, Rennie walked out onto the landing.

Eddie was standing, six steps from the top of the landing, facing downstairs. One hand was holding onto the banister, apparently for support. His head was bowed. He seemed unsteady. Rennie stepped quickly forward, feeling the fog begin to clear as anxieties started to crowd in. And as he moved forward, he heard Eddie say:

'. . . smaller . . .'

But he could not see Eddie's face or assess his emotion. He reached forward. Abruptly, Eddie turned to face him – and in that one horrifying moment, Rennie expected once again to see that mask-face which he had once thought he'd seen. In a split second, the terrible image of that flapping-gowned teacher thing from his dream jumped into his mind.

268

And then the image was gone. There was no horrifying mask.

There was puzzlement. A dying and fading puzzlement. The kind of puzzlement without terror that might register on a mountain climber's face as the ledge he reached for crumbled in his fingers and he fell back.

Falling, thought Rennie. *He's falling*.

Now the puzzlement was wiped away by another expression — an almost jubilant expression — of confidence and assuredness. Eddie laughed and nimbly mounted the stairs again, slapping Rennie heartily on the shoulder.

'Ready for the party?'

The confidence obliterated the surfacing anxieties in Rennie's breast. He allowed himself to slide back into the fog.

They descended.

18

Brinkley helped himself to another whisky and looked nervously around the room. In the centre, a long table had been laid: with twelve places. His inner anxieties demanded that he examine every square inch of that room. It reminded him again of the day when Sheraton had gathered together the 'board members' to teach them all a lesson. If somebody produced a cricket bat, he couldn't be sure that he would not run from that room screaming. He downed his drink and hoped that the others would not notice. So far, it seemed to him that Johnson was handling this situation far better than he. After all, Johnson had seen the same kind of horror that he had; he'd also been visited by . . . something . . . that he wouldn't talk about in detail. But they both knew what they had to do. He looked at his colleague mingling with the foreign representatives whom Brinkburn had demanded, via his . . . Frighteners . . . that they should invite. For an instant, his eyes caught Johnson's . . . and now he saw for a split-second as their eyes met, that the Fear was there . . . the terror at what he had also witnessed . . . but Johnson was concealing it better than he was, that was all. He forced himself to smile, turning away as someone nudged his shoulder. It was Lefèvre. The Frenchman's minder kept close, scanning the room.

'So, my friend,' began Lefèvre. 'When do we find out what this is all about?'

'Very soon, Henri. We're waiting for someone.'

'Lefèvre grunted and accepted the vodka which Brinkley proffered. 'I've come a long way, Brinkley. I am hoping

. . . *we* are hoping that the meeting will be a profitable one. There is a lot at stake here.'

'I'm sure that everything will be made plain very shortly. I'm sure you'll have a lot to tell the management at your end.'

' "The old order changeth, yielding place to new"?'

'You could say that.'

'And Sheraton?'

'Sheraton is finished. You know that. You've heard what's been happening.'

'Yes . . . we've heard. And you've both made your continental cousins very nervous.'

'Well I'm sure that after today's meeting, you'll be able to report back with confidence.'

'I certainly hope so, Brinkley. I certainly hope so.'

Lefèvre turned to talk to his Italian counterpart, Andinaro: a small, balding man with rubber jowls. Brecht overheard them and joined in, their minders hovering on the outskirts of the conversation.

Bloody foreigners, thought Brinkley, downing his whisky and moving to join Johnson.

Johnson beamed a smile at the crowd of visitors, but then hissed under his breath at Brinkley as the latter began to pour another drink.

'For God's sake, Brinkley. Pull yourself together.'

'What?'

'It's written all over your face how scared you are. If they get wind of that, who knows what their twitchy minders might do?'

'So you're *not* scared?'

' 'Course I'm bloody scared!' Johnson smiled again and raised his glass in a toast at one of the guests. 'But what choice have we got but to go through with this?'

He moved closer, smiling through gritted teeth at a passing minder: 'Look . . . we've talked this through. We don't know what the fucking hell is going on, but we know what Brinkburn can do. We've seen it. And I don't want any more of those . . . things . . . coming back to visit me. There's

271

nothing we can do. We've just got to go through with it.'

Brinkley gulped his drink nervously, trying to force a smile on his grey face: 'All right, all right. I don't want to see those things again, either. We've done what he asked. We've got them all here, without Sheraton knowing about it. But you realise what's going to happen to us if she finds out? She'll think it's *us* behind all the aggro, not Brinkburn. Maybe . . . maybe that's what Brinkburn wants.'

'Brinkburn wants Sheraton dead, and as far as I'm concerned, he can have her that way. It's a question of what happens afterwards. Look . . . he's got the power, he's got the muscle to do these things. He wants to take over and, for my money, he *can* have everything. If we play our cards right, we'll be okay. He'll be the new Head of Industry. But he's got to have people to work under him. So if we can keep our noses clean and do what we're told, we'll be okay. Who knows? With what he can do, maybe things'll be better . . . maybe it'll be better under Brinkburn than it ever was under Sheraton. Once he's got her out of the way, once he's at the top, things can go back to normal. If it keeps on, everything'll be gone. If it stops *now*, if Brinkburn can convince the frogs and the eyeties . . . well, we're home and dry, aren't we?'

The double door opened, and they turned to see the old guy who called himself Lister opening it. Two men walked into the room: the first one was white, in a long black raincoat. He was smiling broadly as he entered. Behind him followed a black guy who looked as if he had just woken up. All eyes turned to the newcomers.

'Good evening, gentlemen.'

Brinkley recognised that voice immediately and downed his drink again: 'Brinkburn,' he muttered under his breath.

The minders turned to the newcomers, forming a protective circle around their masters. Eddie laughed; a gentle, rebuking laugh for naïve children.

'All right,' said Crandall, turning back to Brinkley and Johnson. 'Who the hell is *this*? You said there'd be no strange faces.'

Johnson stepped forward anxiously, remembering his part in this performance.

'Gentlemen, this is Eddie Brinkburn.'

'Who?'

'Mr Brinkburn is the . . .' He struggled to find the words.

'. . . the successor to the throne,' finished Brinkley.

Eddie laughed again. 'Thank you, Mr Brinkley. Very apt. I like that.'

Rennie fired a quick glance at Eddie. Did he *mean* that?

Lefèvre's ready smile seemed to have dissolved. 'I don't like mysteries,' he said. 'I think it's time we got down to talking business, don't you?'

Eddie walked past them, the minders turning together in one, smooth, almost choreographed movement to follow his progress. Nervously, Rennie followed close behind, wondering whether their tailors made special arrangements for cutting additional cloth for the inside pockets. There must be enough firepower in there to knock out a small army. They reached the table. Eddie stood at the head, whispered, 'Sit next to me,' to Rennie and then turned back to the others, spreading his hands wide to indicate that they should join him. 'Take a seat. As you said . . . it's time for answers.' Lister was hovering near the door. 'Mr Lister will see to your drinks. We'll dine later, if that's all right.'

Ready for their cue, Brinkley and Johnson began to usher their guests towards the table. Grudgingly, unprepared for a strange face at the proceedings, they moved to the table and sat down, each with a protective minder beside him. All except for Crandall's man . . . who remained sentinel-like at the door. Eddie beckoned him to join them; the man remained impassive. Eddie smiled indulgently, nodded in acceptance and sat down.

Now what? thought Rennie.

19

At 6.00 pm, a detachment of thirty-five armed men had arrived at the main road which turned into Lime Street. 'Territorial Div 23.15' was stencilled on the side of their camouflaged lorry, and with a Territorial Army barracks only fifteen miles away down the road, the truck had drawn no inquisitive stares. It was an ordinary sight on this stretch of road, just a bunch of yahoos enjoying their weekends away from the bank or the building site to act out their macho fantasies.

But this lorry was not owned by the Government, and it did not contain semi-professionals.

At 4.30 am that morning, a Cessna light aircraft had flown over the House on Lime Street. Photographs of the surrounding area and the security patrols had been taken. At 6.15 pm, a further three detachments of twenty men, also disguised as Territorial Army soldiers, had moved from temporary bivouacs on the north, east and west of the House on Lime Street. Deployed amidst the lime trees and the ruins of Lime Street, all four detachments had observed the arrival of the five limousines and had kept their ground, observing their passage through the main security gate on their way into the grounds. Each man in each detachment knew the name, age and origin of each of the limousine's occupants. Each man was also fully equipped with the latest state-of-the-art weapons – weapons, moreover, which Her Majesty's Government could never afford for each of its own professional, let alone semi-professional, soldiers.

At 7.45 pm, according to plan, each of the detachments had begun to move in on the House on Lime Street.

* * *

Now that all the guests were seated, Eddie stood up again and began to walk around the table. He stopped beside Lefèvre, placing a hand on his shoulder, almost paternally.

'So you're wondering why you're all here? Good! Well . . . first of all, I want to thank Mr Johnson and Mr Brinkley for carrying out my orders to the letter. That's what I expect. I'm sure you'll agree that I can be very persuasive. I have ways and means of getting what I want.'

* * *

The Southern Detachment moved quickly through the tangled undergrowth and the fallen stones and decay of Lime Street, on either side of the rough track on which they had observed the limousines travelling. They were joined by scouts from the East and West Detachments, who had been reconnoitring the surrounding area to ensure that Brinkburn had no back-up of any kind, no concealed security or firepower. There was none. At the crossroads ahead, there was one security 'hut' with three men and two dogs. Four other pairs of security guards, it was known, would be patrolling the electric fence somewhere else on the estate at this very moment. It would be up to the other detachments to identify their positions and also to ensure that there were no further security units hidden in the trees out of the sight-lines of the previous photographs taken from the air.

* * *

Eddie continued to move around the table. This time, he stopped beside Crandall, the American, also placing a hand on his shoulder. The fat American looked at the hand in disdain, then brushed it roughly aside. Eddie laughed quietly and continued:

'First of all, let me tell you who I am. My name . . . as Mr Johnson pointed out . . . is Eddie Brinkburn. That name

275

is probably not familiar to you. That's no matter. It's a name that you'll come to know . . . and respect.'

'You're full of shit so far, Brinkburn,' said Crandall laconically, lighting a cigar.

Eddie smiled and continued. 'Shit and humble beginnings. Let's talk about that. Let's talk about families, and love, and . . . death.'

* * *

Watches were checked at 8.00 pm. The East, West and North Detachments had located the other patrolling men and their dogs. There were no other security units in the trees. Men slid through the grass in perfect military precision to the fences. Clamps were inserted on the wire, the current was broken, the wire cut. A dozen high-powered rifles were trained on each of the patrolling guards and their dogs. At the main gate, the Southern Detachment waited for the appropriate signal; their own weapons were trained on the secuty unit and the men and dogs within. There were to be no more subtle manoeuvres. The area was clear for miles around. The entire operation from now on would take no more than fifteen, perhaps sixteen minutes.

* * *

'A garage mechanic?' said Lefèvre. 'Are you talking in riddles?'

Eddie smiled.

'So you're out for revenge?' said Andinaro. 'And that's what this whole thing is about. *La Vendetta*? How the hell are we expected to believe this bullshit? It could be a load of crap! How are you organised, big man? Where's your sources? Where's your muscle coming from? Who the hell are you, anyway? No one here has ever heard of you. Now you want us to believe you just turned up out of nowhere and can turn Sheraton's operation upside down single-handed . . . with just the spade to help you? That's a load of shit.'

Eddie continued to smile indulgently.

'I've got the power,' he said.

Brinkley was beginning to sweat. He did not like the way they were reacting.

To Rennie, it seemed as if all the wine he had consumed since arriving at this godforsaken house was now oozing slowly out of the pores of his skin. He could feel the tension, and even his befogged senses had started to respond. Maybe Eddie *was* in control, but Rennie didn't like the look of all the heavies in the room. Despite everything of which he'd seen Eddie capable — the power, the ability to conjure up Frighteners — how the hell would he have time to do anything if somebody decided to turn nasty? These men were *hard*. Anyone could see that . . . and if guns started to be pulled out, Rennie couldn't see how he was going to avoid catching at least one stray bullet. He sat stock still, hand gripping the arm-rest of the chair out of sight, praying that Eddie could keep the lid on everything.

And then the sound of the first explosion reached their ears, following by the rattling outpouring of machine-guns and small arms.

The effect on the 'party' was instantaneous.

The minders moved swiftly, again with that orchestrated swift and purposeful motion, to protect their own people. The men pulled away instantly from the table as if it was somehow electrified; chairs tipped to the floor. And now, as Rennie had predicted, there were suddenly guns in evidence. Every one of the heavies had levelled weapons at Eddie, Brinkley and Johnson . . . and himself. He threw his own hands up to his head as another roaring explosion reached them. Over the sound of gunfire and roaring detonation from outside, Rennie could hear screaming now, too.

Eddie smiled again, calmly. Each gun was now trained on him. Overhead, the lights dimmed as another explosion rocked the estate. Rennie looked frantically from Eddie to the watching men. At the door, the American's minder was trying to open it while still keeping his gaze fixed on Eddie. The door appeared to be locked. Rennie looked at the other two men still seated at the table. Even Johnson's display of confidence had vanished, his face wearing the same look of terror that Brinkley had been trying so unsuccessfully to hide. They, too, had their hands raised above their heads.

'All right!' shouted one of the minders. 'We're getting out.'

'No way out,' said Eddie calmly, in a voice that was too quiet to carry, but which Rennie picked up. He looked at Eddie . . . and the terrible feeling that he was looking at something else, not Eddie, came over him as abruptly as cold sweat.

'The bloody door's locked!' shouted Crandall's man.

'Then shoot it out!' yelled another.

Crandall's heavy stood back and took a two-handed aim at the door lock.

This time, Eddie's voice was raised: 'It's no use. I'm whole now. You can't use it.'

'*Shit!*' Crandall's minder dropped his gun before he could fire, wringing his hand in pain. 'It's . . . *hot*!'

'They're all hot,' said Eddie in that matter-of-fact voice.

This time, there was a simultaneous chorus of pain as the minders hastily dropped their weaponry to the carpet. Each man hugged the hand that had been holding a weapon and uncontrolled panic began to register strongly on faces that had once been confident.

Rennie looked back at Eddie in disbelief. This was new . . . he had never seen him perform like *this* before. Eddie smiled. 'Hot, eh?' he said.

Another roaring explosion sounded from outside, and this time the lights flickered and went out.

Rennie inched back in his seat. Brinkley dived from his chair and lay trembling in the corner, curled up in a foetal position. Johnson remained where he was, frozen in fear . . . while the others in the room shifted uncertainly from foot to foot.

'What am I *paying* you for?' shouted Andinaro at his minder. And the man suddenly lunged across the room towards the table again, arms pushed forward like a springboard-diver to take Eddie by the throat. Something *sparked*, like a live cable suddenly spitting out blue electricity for a millisecond in the darkened room. And, somehow, in a blur of jumbled movement, the heavy flew through the air and hit the wall at the far side with incredible force, like a man hit by a speeding, invisible car. Rennie heard the *dunching* soft wet crack of broken bones ... and Andinaro's man rebounded to the floor, inert and lifeless.

Rennie looked back at Eddie in awe. At last, he saw what he had feared all these weeks.

Even in the darkness, he could see that face. It was the mask again, the feral, death-white mask of something that was not Eddie. The eyes were glittering like black marbles, and as another explosion momentarily drowned the sound of gunfire and screaming, an orange light blossomed in the window, revealing the face to all in the room. It was a human ... yet *not* a human face. It was a dead face ... only the eyes seemed alive, and with a hideous, powerful and *knowing* life.

'Who's next?' said the face, and this time Rennie knew with absolute certainty that it was not Eddie Brinkburn speaking.

The crowd of men in the darkened room remained rooted to the spot, the flare of the explosions outside making their shadows dance and leap.

'No one?' said the face again. 'You disappoint me. Particularly you ... Mr Crandall and Mr Brecht.'

Rennie looked back from the monstrous apparition standing at the table to the two men he had mentioned. Was it just his fancy, or did the men seem to be even more agitated than the others now?

'After all,' the Thing that was *not* Eddie continued, 'all the activity outside is *your* doing, isn't it?'

'For God's sake *do* something!' screamed Brecht at his own minder. The minder prevaricated, hopping between decision and indecision, his eyes darting from Brecht to the corpse on the floor and back to Eddie.

'Such indecision,' the Shadow said. 'And such betrayal.

279

All around me. You, Brecht . . . and you, Crandall. You conspired with Sheraton, didn't you? After you'd received your messages from Brinkley and Johnson? You thought to betray me. Outside . . .' the Shadow gestured almost regally to the window. Now, the noises of gunfire and screaming were dying. '. . . Sheraton's servants are *being educated*.'

And now, Rennie remembered the men and dogs guarding the estate. So uncommunicative, so bloody strange. At last he understood where the security firm had come from. He looked up at the Shadow by the table, and almost pissed when it smiled . . . a terrible, cracking, white smile . . . and looked down on him as if it had read his thoughts.

'Yes, Rennie,' it said. 'I *made* them. And they're *entertaining* our visitors at this very moment.'

'It wasn't me!' said Crandall, stepping forward. 'Look it wasn't me. I'm not important . . . I'm not . . .'

'Betrayal,' repeated the Thing, turning its attention back to the crowd of gangsters. 'Even the gentleman who is still seated here at the table . . . and the child crying in the corner, of course . . . are part of that betrayal.' The thing turned to Johnson, cowering at the table, ignoring the snivelling tears of Brinkley as he whimpered in the corner. 'You *knew* that these "representatives" from abroad were *not* the people I wanted. When they arrived, you *knew* that they were lackeys from abroad, sent by the important ones in Sheraton's organization. I told you . . . my visitors told you . . . that only the important ones were to come.'

'For God's sake . . .' bleated Johnson. 'We did what you wanted us to do. We made the calls. We did the convincing. If Sheraton got wind of it . . . it wasn't our fault. Honest to God . . .'

'God?' sneered the Eddie-thing.

'We *did* what you wanted, for Christ's sake!' stuttered Johnson. 'If you've been betrayed, it was them . . . not us.'

The Shadow turned away from the men at the table. Outside, the sounds of gunfire and explosions had ceased. Somewhere close, something was burning. The colour and

280

shadow of the flames was reflected in the window . . . and the shadow of the Thing that stood at the Last Supper table dominated the room. There was no indecisive hoping from foot to foot now, no attempts to get away from the room, no attempts to grapple with their host. Every man remained rooted to the spot, facing that table; as if their host was now somehow in charge of their every movement and their every action. Rennie, too, was bathed in the orange light that invaded the room; its bursting and flaring hid the details of the Shadow that stood beside him; hid the details of that mask-face, and for that he was grateful. But he, also, was frozen; rooted to his seat in the way that a snared fly remains rooted in the web, hoping beyond hope that the spider . . . the ruler of that webbed lair . . . will ignore him and sup upon the other, juicier captives ensnared within.

'Crandall,' said the Shadow. 'Come here.'

'No . . .' said the fat American, but the word was not a defiance. It was a plea.

'*Come here*,' said the Shadow again.

And this time, Crandall stepped forward, looking down in utter bewilderment at the leg which had taken the step as if it had acted of its own accord. A fractured relief flooded Rennie: relief that Eddie . . . no, not Eddie . . . that the *Thing*, had centred its attention upon Crandall, and not upon him. Crandall took another step. He was a man learning to walk on artificial limbs; his torso writhed and swayed upon them, trying to exercise control . . . but they were not his to control, and they continued to walk . . . step by awkward step . . . towards the Shadow at the table. Desperately, with terror clearly visible in his eyes, Crandall swung from side to side on the pivot of his renegade legs, looking backwards at his colleagues.

'. . . help me . . .'

But no one would . . . or could . . . move forward to help him.

Rennie watched him come, his stark, terrified face livid with the reflections of burning from beyond the window. It was Judgement Day in Hell . . . and the Thing that posed as Eddie . . . was the Judge. Crandall had been summoned. At last, he reached the table, before Eddie. The upper part of his body was straining away from the pivot of his legs, away from the tall, dark Shadow in front of him.

'Messengers,' said the Shadow in a sibilant parody of Eddie's voice.

'. . . I'm not supposed to be here . . .' said Crandall in a childlike voice.

The Shadow reached forward easily across the table towards him. Crandall began to twist his head from side to side . . . and a peculiar metaphor occurred to Rennie, completely inappropriate to the terror of the occasion. Crandall was a reluctant and rebellious child. The monstrous Shadow before him was the parent. And the parent was going to feed that child with something that he did not want to eat. When the hand was fully outstretched, Crandall's body began to bend forward at the waist towards it — quite obviously against his will. And this time he began to scream hoarsely. The others remained motionless, frozen like waxworks in a burning museum.

Rennie waited for the gushing of blood.

There was none. The Shadow caressed Crandall's face. As it did so, his eyes closed. The parent had sent the child to sleep.

'It doesn't really matter how important or unimportant you are, after all,' said the Shadow. 'You're here. And you can serve my purpose when you return to where you came from.'

Crandall's eyes flew open.

Although there was no obvious physical transformation, Rennie knew instinctively that Crandall was nevertheless *changed*. There was a kinship now about his face, a white death-mask kinship with the monstrous Shadow which presided at the table.

Please don't look at me. Not at ME! thought Rennie, afraid now that even his thoughts could be heard in this hellish room.

And Crandall turned away from the table, away from the

Shadow, to face the other occupants of the room. It seemed that he had control over his actions again.

'. . . Fucking *hell* . . .' said someone, somewhere in the shadows.

Brinkley's weeping in the corner took on a renewed urgency. The smell of his urine was acrid in the darkened room.

Crandall began to move slowly towards them, step by slow step, head cocked to one side. Smiling . . . and with a horrifying *purpose* about his movements.

Now, the terror which had held them all bound seemed to relent. There was an instant response. The three remaining minders all had the same idea at once. They elbowed their way to the side tables by the nearest wall. In a blur of shadowed movement they seized the nearest available weapons: table knives, forks and a silver candelabrum. Rennie watched the others quickly follow suit. Plates skidded crashing to the floor.

Crandall continued to move slowly forward.

'I want to *touch* you. That's all . . .' he said in a voice that was almost too quiet to hear, but the menacing sibilation was clear. 'Just to *touch* you. The way he *touched* me . . .'

'Stay where you are, Crandall!' warned Andinaro.

Lefèvre began to curse in French.

Brecht pushed his minder in front of him, urging in German: 'Don't let him anywhere near me . . .'

The Shadow laughed. 'Good . . . *Cabaret*!' It turned and, in one swift, liquid black movement, drew the curtains across the glowing orange windows. All light vanished. The room was plunged into utter blackness.

And the screaming began.

Rennie knew now that it must be a dream. He'd drunk too much wine again. All the horrors which he had been privy to since Eddie had emerged from prison had been too much for him. They had invaded his dream place. He knew that he must fade out of this dream and into another — he'd often had the power to do that as a child when the nightmares became too bad; when the dark shadow began to rise at the foot of your bed calling your name, all you had to do was ball your hands up into fists and screw them into your eye sockets, curling up safe in your bed, away from that shadow.

As the screaming continued . . . and the tearing and the shattering of glass and china, and the sound of Brinkley's desperate wailing tears . . . Rennie knew that he must escape now from this dream in the way that he had escaped from that attack in the showers in prison. He was hearing the same noises now that he'd heard then, and it was time to escape again before he became too closely involved in this nightmare ever to get away.

He screwed his fists into his eye sockets and bent forward until the backs of his hands touched the cool tablecloth.

The horrified and agonised screams faded, as if the owners had fallen screaming into a bottomless well.

Rennie slid away into a safe black place.

20

And afterwards, when the screaming had eventually ceased, the Shadow at the table drew back the curtains again; admitting the leaping, dancing shadows to the room and revealing the five silent, motionless silhouettes standing there amidst the jumble and stains of what else now occupied the room. The Shadow looked back once, briefly, at the man who slept in the cradle of his fists at the table. And then it looked back at the silhouettes. For a long time, it looked.

When, at last, it nodded, the silhouettes turned silently away.

The door was now unlocked, and opened soundlessly at their approach.

The figures crossed the hall. Again, before them, the front door opened and admitted them to the night. The scenes of slaughter and carnage within the grounds of the House on Lime Street drew no response from them. Silently, each figure moved to the limousine in which it had been delivered, pulled out the corpse of the driver who had brought it to the House on Lime Street, climbed into the driving seat and started the engine.

Shapes . . . and shadows . . . were still clearing the remnants of carnage from the driveway.

The figures in the limousines waited until a path had been cleared. When this had been done, the limousines slid slowly back the way they had come, tyres crunching on gravel. They passed the unmanned security gate, which swung open gently on the wind. There was movement beyond, movement in the lime trees. Shadows and shapes were there too, clearing away any evidence of what had transpired that evening. The silhouettes in the limousines ignored this activity. Purposefully, the limousines slid down Lime Street . . . as the trees on either side whispered and danced in the evening winds.

At the crossroads, where Lime Street joined the main road, the limousines took different directions which would lead them to the appropriate airport or railway station. There was no parting conversation, no waved acknowledgement.

But all had the same singular purpose.

21

It was time to wake up. Rennie knew it. It must be daytime by now. There were no more screaming, tearing sounds. He could hear birds singing somewhere at his back. Still bent forward over the table, head resting on his fists, eyes screwed shut, he began to analyse just exactly where he was and what was going on before he opened his eyes. He had experienced this before . . . and the pain was always almost too much to handle when he opened his eyes, expecting to be in one place, and finding himself somewhere else.

It had happened in prison. He would wake, with those dreams of an unknown Jamaican beach still fresh in his mind. And the grey, bleak walls of the prison cell would face him.

He would wake with the memories of Florinda still warm and happy inside him. And then he would see the empty black lace.

He had woken from his drugged sleep on a sofa to find himself in another nightmare of Eddie and his dead family.

He had woken from his bed and his dreams of ragged flapping black things, and faceless children and abominable things in laboratory bottles . . . only to find himself elsewhere, in the place where his nightmare had been set.

He did not want to open his eyes now, after a nightmare to end all nightmares, to find himself in a worse place than he'd been before.

He listened.

He heard only the birds outside; an ordinary, early morning sound.

He lifted his head gently and cautiously. His arms ached; there was a crick in his neck and he had a headache. He had obviously been asleep for a long time. Daylight was trying to creep in under his eyelids. Still, he waited. There was an unfamiliar smell in the air: a warm and cloying, scented smell . . . like stale food. He turned his head slowly and cautiously to the right, still keeping his eyes closed lest something be watching his movements.

Slowly . . . very slowly . . . he opened his eyes. The dark mass at his right came into focus.

It was Eddie. He was on a chair next to him, slumped forward and asleep. As Rennie watched, he too opened his eyes. But there was no nightmare here. It *was* Eddie . . . not something obscene which merely hid inside his body. Eddie blinked. Rennie saw his tongue move within the pocket of his cheek, probing gums and teeth and — by the resulting grimace — not liking the taste he found there. He blinked again, his eyes glazed . . . and then he saw Rennie.

'Rennie . . .?'

'Is it over, Eddie? Is it daytime?'

'Yeah, it's daytime. What the hell are we . . .?'

Eddie sat back groaning, rubbing his head. He began to scratch . . . and then Rennie saw him freeze. He braced himself against the table, pushing himself away. Rennie looked quickly to the centre of the room to find out what had shocked him. Somehow, the room was still blurred. The pale creams and pastels of the newly decorated walls were gone, replaced with a chaotic jumble of ochres and crimsons. Rennie shook his head again, sitting back and rubbing his eyes. They still ached. For some reason, he seemed to have been sleeping with his fists pressed into his eye sockets. He looked again. The room was still confused. And then his vision came into focus.

The banqueting table had been overturned; the torn tablecloth and twisted candelabra were scattered on the floor amidst a mess of broken china and jumbled cutlery. Wallpaper had been ripped from the walls; it hung in long streamers. Rennie could see clawmarks on the paper and

288

the gouged plasterwork. Chairs were overturned and shattered. It seemed as if a bomb had gone off in the room; miraculously, they had both somehow survived the blast. Rennie became aware that Eddie was standing now, weaving slightly, passing a trembling hand across his forehead.

Wine, thought Rennie. *There's wine all over the place* . . .

And then when Eddie said '. . . Oh, Christ . . .' Rennie suddenly realised that it was most definitely not wine which had been splashed all over the walls, floor and ceiling. It was blood.

He lurched back from the table, and stood in something soft. Not wanting to look, but looking anyway, he saw, in the corner on his left, the ragged mass which had once been Brinkley; still huddled in a foetal position, his back shredded and gleaming. He blundered away from it, round the table, and whirled . . . trying to find somewhere to stand that was not splashed with crimson. There were shredded things on the floor which he did not want to look at, identify or stand in. Uttering hoarse cries of disgust, arms spread like a dancer in mid-pirouette, he looked back at Eddie. He was standing with one hand braced on the table to steady himself, the other hand across his mouth, staring at the ravaged room and its grisly decoration. And despite the very human look of horror, doubt and confusion on his face, all Rennie could think about was the mask-face of the Thing that hid inside Eddie's body as it had stood there on the previous night, dealing out death and destruction.

I am whole, it had said.

Rennie turned and blundered to the door, refusing to look down at the soft things he was treading on. The door handle was wet and slippery . . . but it slid open when he tugged. Reeling on the door jamb of that stinking, charnel-house room, he staggered into the hall. Behind him, he heard Eddie weakly call his name, just before he swung the door savagely shut behind him. The sound of its slamming seemed to echo throughout the House.

Lister was standing in the middle of the hall, looking at him.

Dressed in a stained boiler-suit, his head was bowed, but his eyes were fixed on Rennie from beneath those wild eyebrows. Shoulders hunched, hands behind his back, there was an air of expectancy about him.

'Lister . . .?' Rennie moved towards him. For once, there seemed to be an intelligent glimmering in his eyes; an awareness there which Rennie had never seen before. 'What the hell is going on . . .?'

Lister stepped back, shaking his head warily as Rennie moved closer.

'Don't be afraid, man. It's me.' Rennie looked back at the closed door from which he had just emerged. 'It's just me . . . just . . .'

He had started to turn back to Lister when the old man stepped forward briskly, wielding the broken length of pipe that he had been hiding behind his back. Rennie had no time to avoid it as Lister laid it savagely along the side of his head.

22

Am I awake or asleep again? dreamed Rennie.

It was dark. But he was unsure whether it was still the darkness of sleep. The difference between waking and sleeping, dreaming and being, had long since ceased to have its definitions for him. Did he want to find out? Wasn't it always much better recently to stay where you were and ask no questions? When he attempted to make sense of everything, when he tried to put everything into perspective, he always found himself stepping out of one bad dream and into another.

There was physical discomfort in this dream. The side of his head throbbed, his ear was stinging furiously. He was lying on his back; beneath him, he could feel cold, hard earth. He took a handful of it, feeling its gritty dampness on the skin of his palm. Were these the sensations of a dream or was he truly awake? His back was aching. He was cold. When he groaned, the sound of his voice seemed to press back on him . . . as if he was in a confined space. He struggled up on one elbow, feeling the site of the pain in his head with the other hand. There was a dried and cracked coating of old blood there and a scabbed lesion. Memory came back.

'Lister . . .' His weak voice bounced back with greater strength from the stone walls that surrounded him.

'Yes?'

Rennie rolled on his side and from there into a sitting position, nursing his head. Lister was sitting on a packing case in the gloom ahead of him. He still nursed the length of broken pipe in his lap. Now, Rennie was aware of his surroundings.

He was in the cellars beneath the House.

'Drink?' asked Lister, and before Rennie could answer, he threw a bottle at him. Rennie flung up a hand to ward off the projectile; miraculously, he caught it smartly by the neck. It was brandy. He struggled into a better position, resting his back against another grime-covered crate. He rapped the bottle neck against the side of the crate, snapping off the stem, and drank deeply. It burned in his guts.

'Lister, you bastard! What the hell . . .?'

'I wasn't sure.' His voice seemed different. It seemed so much more in control than it ever had before; so much more *sane*. 'After what happened last night, I didn't know if you were real or not. Didn't know whether it was you . . . or only something that looked like you.'

Rennie drank again. The details of the cellars were coming into focus at last. Now, he could see the rough stone arches and passageways on either side; the running walls, the wine racks covered in cobwebs, the packing cases, the filth-encrusted earthen floors.

'I'm sorry,' said Lister guiltily, looking down into his lap and realising that he was still holding his improvised weapon. He dropped it to the ground with a hollow clang. 'I wasn't sure. I am now.'

'Well . . . I *feel* real.' Rennie groaned again, struggling to his feet and sitting on a crate. He took another draught.

'I should have given you Amontillado instead of brandy. It would go with your name.'

'What?'

'Your name, Montresor. "The Cask of Amontillado".'

'What the hell are you on about?'

'He's a character in the story . . . by Edgar Allan Poe. Very appropriate down here. In the wine vaults.'

'You're different.'

Lister paused, slowly rubbing his hands up and down on his knees, looking at Rennie in the darkness.

'Yes, I'm different. I'm . . . *me* again.'

'What the hell is going on, Lister?'

'Hell. Yes. *That's* what's going on.'

Rennie paused to swallow another mouthful. The pain in his head was fading.

'I've been freed for a while,' continued Lister. 'Something *big* happened last night. Something that released whatever it is that lives in these walls. It's got something else to think about now, it's not so bothered about me for a while.'

'Riddles and more fucking riddles . . .'

'No. No more riddles. I don't know how much time I've got, maybe just enough to tell you what's really happening here. I know what Brinkburn's told you . . . and it's not the whole truth.'

Rennie laughed. The alcohol was beginning to take effect. 'The truth? What's that, then? Don't tell me . . . *you're* behind it all. You're the butler here, aren't you? And everybody knows that the butler is always the one whodunnit.'

'The butler? No. I'm not the butler . . . or the caretaker . . . or the handyman.'

'Then what the hell are you?'

'I own this House.'

Rennie paused in mid-swallow, then wiped a hand across his dirty face.

'Of course you do, man. Of course . . .'

'Don't humour me! There isn't enough time. This House is mine. And it's been mine ever since the . . . Government . . . moved out.' Lister looked down at his feet, found another bottle and threw it at Rennie. 'Here!' It landed roughly at Rennie's feet, but did not break. 'More brandy. Drink as much of it as you like. But listen very closely to what I have to say.'

'Okay, Lister. Okay. You're the Storyteller. So tell me a story.'

'Brinkburn has told you about the Government experiments which took place here on prisoners. He's told you about what they called the "Jekyll and Hyde" effect. That's all true. He's told you how the scientists using this place were able literally to change people's minds . . . change their souls . . . and how they could separate the duality of man, eradicate the "Evil" impulse. That's true, also. But he's lying when he calls it simply negative energy, easily controlled. Because the fact is, Montresor . . . he is *not* in control. It controls *him*. It only allows him to think that he's in control at the moment, to suit its purposes. Are you listening?'

Rennie drank again: 'I'm listening.'

'All of the "Evil" energy that was drained from those people didn't dissipate. It was absorbed into the very fabric of this building; the bricks and the mortar and the wood. If the experiment had been carried out anywhere else rather than here, it *would* have dissipated. But not here. Because this House is an . . . evil . . . place. It has a history of evil. It has always attracted evil to itself. Some very bad things have happened here over the years. This House was many things before the Government acquired it. It was once a boarding school. There was a terrible scandal then. Several of the boys were said to have absconded over the years, vanishing without trace. It was later found that one of the masters − a monstrous sadist − had abused and killed them. He buried them here − in this cellar. The House was also once owned by an earl; completely insane, he tortured and imprisoned people here for years before he was discovered and hanged. He buried his victims out there in the forest, where the lime trees grow.'

'Lime Street . . .'

'There are mine workings not far from here. An industrialist, who owned the House after the earl lost possession, built a community here for his workers. There was a terrible disaster . . . a cave-in . . . dozens of men were buried alive. The industrialist committed suicide here, in this House, and the mining business died too. The remaining families moved out, back to the city. Lime Street fell into ruin and the trees reclaimed it.'

'Those bloody trees . . .'

'You've seen them, haven't you? You've seen them

growing out of the ruins even though it's impossible? Those trees were *never there* when I first bought this House. They've grown since. It's as if . . . as if . . . those trees have rooted and grown from each of the bodies buried out there . . . the murder victims and the dead miners. There's a legend about that, you know. About lime trees growing from the graves of murder victims. It appeals to the House, I think. It likes to make unreal things real. It has always done that . . .'

'You're not making a lot of sense, Lister.'

Lister snapped back quickly; his words coming out in a torrent: 'There is a long, long history to this House. The site on which it stands . . . this very ground . . . was claimed in ancient manuscripts to be "accursed". It has always *attracted* evil things to it. I believe that it attracted the Government scientists engaged on the project here to suit its purposes. It absorbed the "Evil" energy from those prisoners, from those child rapists and murderers and psychotics, and stored it within itself. But more . . . much more . . . than that. Because, as the experiments continued and the negative energy of those hundreds of people was absorbed and assimilated . . . the "Evil" took on a *personality*!'

'Lots of big words, Lister. Lots of . . .'

'Don't you see? All the Evil bled from those men has combined. It was assimilated together into one massive energy source. The House was like a battery, absorbing the energy over the years. At the peak of its power, that energy "jumped" from the House, into the mind of that child-man Duncan . . . and was imprisoned. It desperately needed a living host, but chose the wrong man. Since that time, it's struggled to be free. To find a new host. Now, it's inside Brinkburn. So far he's been using it for his own purposes, but it's been growing stronger all the time. It's been allowing him to *think* that he's in control of it. But he's not. Very soon, Eddie Brinkburn will simply cease to exist and the Thing within him will have taken complete control. Those scientists . . . and this house . . . have literally created a Demon.'

'The thing inside Eddie is a *Demon*?'

'What's in a word? There never was any such thing before. But now, we've created the very Devil himself.'

When Rennie spoke again, there was no casualness about his voice; his words were low and serious. 'All right, Lister. All right . . . So tell me, what are you doing here?'

'I bought the House after the Government people moved out. I knew nothing of the scandal then, of course. And I also knew little of this House and its history.' He began to laugh; as if it was the greatest joke in the world. His laughter spluttered into silence. Drawing breath, he continued.

'I used to be a very successful entrepreneur. Yes, I know how I sound. I know how ridiculous it seems. But it's true. I always wanted a country place like this when I retired. The price was right . . . so I bought it and moved in.' The old man's voice had begun to tremble. Rennie drank carefully now, more controlled. 'My wife died shortly after we moved in. Heart trouble. But she'd never had a history of it. I became depressed, very depressed. And that's when the House started to work on me . . .' Lister drew breath; in the darkness Rennie could not see his face and could not be sure whether it was a sob or a sigh; its echoes hissed sibilantly amidst the rough stone arches and away into the darkness. 'A large part of the Evil left this House in Duncan, but there was still a residual Evil in these walls. And like everyone who has spent any length of time here, it got into my mind. It tortured me. It gave me dreams. It showed me . . . things . . . Just like Brinkburn, I've seen things in dreams. I've seen *everything* . . . but it's been very selective about what it's shown to Brinkburn. He is the host, and it's had to nurture him, make him feel in control. Brinkburn was attracted back to the House. Now that he's here, he is absorbing that residual power. The Evil is bleeding what remains from the House into itself, into its *personality*. Last night . . . he infected those men with that Evil. They're his disciples now. They've gone back to their own countries to spread their contagion. There was a massive energy surge

296

last night. For the moment, its attention is . . . elsewhere
. . . That's why I can talk to you now . . .'

'So what the hell do we do?'

'Do? There's nothing *I* can do. But you've got to get away
from this place. You've got to find the people who began
this experiment. You've got to tell them what's happened.
There's a name in my . . . dreams . . . Callender. *Sir* James
Callender. He was involved in this project in a big way. Find
him and tell him . . .'

Above, the cellar door swung open. A shaft of brittle light
spilled down angular stone steps. Lister drew in an alarmed
breath; it hissed away into the darkness. Rennie swung the
jagged bottle up to his mouth, felt it cut into his lip as he
drank: one, two, three full swallows of brandy.

A figure stepped into the light at the top of the stairs.
A gaunt, angular shadow spilled over the worn steps. Rennie
looked up at last.

'You down there, Rennie . . .?'

The figure slumped against the door jamb, hand to face.
It was Eddie . . . the *human* Eddie . . . and he still seemed
on the verge of collapse. Rennie pushed himself away from
the packing case, aware that Lister was frozen in position,
head down, hands cradled in his lap; like a child due for
a scolding.

'I . . . been dreaming . . .' mumbled Eddie, his low voice
carrying impossibly far in the depths of the cellar. 'Bad
dreams . . . help me . . . help . . .'

'*Get away from here! Now!*' hissed Lister.

Rennie looked back. Lister's head was still down, refusing
to look up.

'Oh God, Rennie . . . please . . . help me . . .' Eddie
clutched at the jamb, his knees beginning to buckle.

Despite the fear and the horror and the knowledge that
something from Hell was living inside Eddie's body, Rennie
hurried up the stone steps, still clutching his brandy bottle.
And despite the nightmares and the death and the blood,
he grabbed Eddie by the arm and pinioned him against the
door jamb until he could look straight at his face.

297

'Is it *you*, Eddie? IS IT YOU?' His strained voice caught in his throat like a sob.

'I'm getting . . . getting . . .'

For God's sake don't say 'stronger'! Don't say 'whole'! . . .

'. . . smaller, Rennie. I'm getting smaller inside.'

'Come on.' Grimly, Rennie threw Eddie's arm over his shoulder and dragged him away from the jamb. Below, Lister was on his feet now, shouting: 'No! No! No! No! For Heaven's sake, get away from here! Get away now! Don't you see? Don't you? Why the hell do you think you've lasted so long? Why do you think that it hasn't killed you by now? It's because Brinkburn's kept it at bay, kept it away from you!'

'Fuck you, Lister!' Rennie shouted back over his shoulder as he dragged the now semi-conscious Eddie into the hall. 'He can beat it! He needs me!'

'You bloody fool! Eddie Brinkburn hardly exists any more. It nearly has complete control of its host. When that happens . . .'

'It's not going to happen!' Rennie leaned Eddie against the hallstand. He groped feebly at it for support.

'You idiot! You insane *idiot* . . .'

Rennie strode back to the cellar door. He grabbed it.

'Then that makes two of us.' He swung the door savagely shut. Its echoes crashed and reverberated in the arches and recesses of the cellar.

Turning back to Eddie, Rennie grabbed him again and carried him to the stairs, pausing only to look once in the direction of the charnel-house drawing room. The door was shut. Gritting his teeth, his eyes on Eddie's pale, sweat-beaded face, he began to drag him up the stairs.

23

Eddie dreamed.

And in his dream, he seemed to see the shadow of a man standing at a banqueting table. There was fire behind him, bright orange flames licking at the sky. And because the figure was in silhouette, he could not see its face. The figure was talking to him, telling him something important, but he could not understand the words.

Now, it was summer. Tracey was sitting in that folding chair she liked so much, in front of the flats, watching the kids playing. She was smiling at him as he stood on the front pavement, also watching. Everything was just fine. He'd come home from the garage, still wearing his overalls. No doubt he'd be due for a reprimand at not having washed and changed. They'd just got a new three-piece suite on hire purchase. They could ill afford it. Eddie was putting every spare bit of cash into a savings account. But hell — she'd wanted it so badly. Tracey wouldn't want it marked. The kids looked up, aware now of his presence. Russell whooped, throwing a bright orange plastic ball into the air. Jane saw him next and joined in the chase as they ran towards him, welcoming him home. He stooped low to catch them.

But now they were gone. Kneeling down, arms still held wide to greet his kids, Eddie looked up towards Tracey in puzzlement. She was still sitting there in the folding chair, but there was something different about her. Her face was too white, much too white. He could see the dark hollows of her eyes even from here. He began to walk towards her, alarmed now, but there were lead weights on his feet, slowing him down.

'I'm sick, Eddie . . .' she said.

'I know, love. I know.' He struggled to reach her.

'I can't wait. It's eating me.'

'I know. We'll pay for private treatment. As soon as I get the money . . .'

'The waiting list . . . the waiting list . . .'

Eddie howled at the sky as blackness descended and wiped away the dream. He raged at the Health Service waiting list, at the Government. And a confusing succession of images unfurled in his mind. Images of men strapped to operating tables, thrashing and crying out. Images of scientific equipment, of lime trees, of prison. Of a House surrounded by those trees and a crazy old man . . . a crazy old man who was somehow a threat. In the blur of images, he saw the old man conspiring with his friend, Rennie. Conspiring about what . . . and with whom? And then he saw the burnt-out flats and the garage; he saw three open graves and rain pouring as coffins were lowered into them; he saw a faceless figure standing in a tower of black stone high over a Victorian London. He soared up like a bird to the figure in that tower as it laughed and looked out over the city which it had claimed as its own. Now, he knew the identity of that figure within his dream as he hurtled upwards through boiling black clouds to meet it.

'*Sheraton!*' yelled Eddie. '*I've found you, you bastard. You can't hide from me any more!*'

The faceless figure was standing on a balcony, curtains flapping around it as it held its arms wide at his approach; laughing, laughing, laughing. Eddie grabbed for the balcony and clung there, his power of flight now gone. The faceless figure had long dark hair. It stepped forward. And as it did so, a face began to form. Eddie strained to look against the howling wind as the features began to take shape; as the contours began to mould and fix in that face of clay. When it was complete, the face laughed again, wild and mocking.

'A woman . . .' said Eddie. 'You're a woman. Is *that* why I couldn't find you? Because you're a woman?'

Sheraton laughed again, standing back.

Beneath Eddie, the balcony crumbled and snapped. Thrashing wildly, screaming, he fell from the tower. The dark street below rushed up to meet him.

'*Tracy, Tracey, Tracey!!*'

There was no impact. A greater darkness swallowed him, like a black and bottomless sea. And as he sank, his rage swelled and grew.

'*Sheraton, you bastard! I know you now! I KNOW YOU NOW!*'

24

'I know you now!'

Eddie sat bolt upright, startling Rennie. He gripped him by the shoulders and forced him back down onto the bed.

'You're all right, Eddie. It's okay.'

Eddie slumped back, breathing heavily.

'Eddie, listen to me. This is important.' Eddie groaned and turned over onto his side. Rennie pulled him back, shaking him by the shoulders. 'Wake up, Eddie!'

'I'm awake . . . I'm awake . . .' Eddie rolled to a sitting position, rubbing his head.

'Do you remember last night?'

'Last night . . .'

'Come on, Eddie. Snap out of it. Do you remember?'

'Yeah, I remember . . .'

'That . . . *Thing* . . . came out of you. But were *you* in control?'

'In control?'

'Think, Eddie. Think! It's important.'

'Of course I was in control!' Eddie clambered to his feet. 'I'm always in control. We . . . I . . . got rid of Sheraton's filth.'

'It was you? *You* did it?'

'Yes, yes, it was me. Me!'

'But Christ, Eddie. It's like a butcher's shop downstairs.'

'*Look . . . I . . . mean . . . I* was in control. But *they* did it to themselves.'

'How long before this all stops? You *can* stop it, can't you, Eddie?'

'Of course I can stop it. It's okay, Rennie. Really. I've nearly finished. It's nearly all over.'

'What do you mean?'

'I've found Sheraton. At last I've found her.'

'*Her?*'

It's a woman. Not a man. All this time I thought it was a man. I was looking in the wrong places for the wrong person. Don't ask me how or why it matters whether Sheraton is a man or a woman. But it does. And now I *know* her.'

'So now what happens?'

Eddie turned to look at Rennie. 'Pass me that bottle.' Rennie handed it over and Eddie drank deeply. 'We're both going to get pissed. 'Cause pretty soon it'll all be over.'

'You're sure about that, Eddie? You're absolutely sure?'

Eddie smiled. It was the Eddie of old.

'Absolutely.'

25

It's starting again, thought Lister. *I can feel it.*

Montresor had slammed the door shut, plunging the cellar into blackness again. And it had seemed to Lister that the echoes would never end. Even when those echoes in the cellar died away, there were still echoes in his head . . . different echoes. On the previous evening, when hell had broken out around him, the House's control over him had temporarily slipped away. Staggering blindly away from the fire and the blood and the horror, he had found the cellar door and plunged into its blackness. Deep down in the bowels of the House, he had found himself again.

Now, it seemed, he was once more losing control. He could feel it, creeping around the edges of his mind; seeping into his brain in the same way that the nitre in the cellar walls was seeping through the bricks and mortar. He staggered to one of the walls, head held in his hands.

No . . . I won't have it . . . You can't come back. I won't let you.

He shook his head madly. Reality was blurring at the edges now; he could see a series of disjointed images in his head. He could see . . . could see . . . a classroom full of schoolboys, all silently standing and facing front, while something horrible pointed at a blackboard. He could see fire and blood . . . and his wife, lying in bed, arms thrust out in front of her in *rigor mortis*, mouth frozen in a silent scream at what she'd seen, at the Thing that had frightened her to death. He could see . . . a man . . . Eddie Brinkburn, with his fingers clawing through a frame of steel bars. He was wrenching at the bars of his cell, wrenching and screaming. The face began to change in the darkness, its features flowing and altering into a face from nightmare. Now, it was no longer Eddie Brinkburn; it was the face of some monstrous Thing, imprisoned inside *him*. A prison within a prison. More flames and blood and screaming . . . and now Lister could see dead bodies being thrust into roughly hewn forest graves, their arms flapping horribly as they fell; spadefuls of earth being flung over them . . .

'No!' yelled Lister, whirling around. He flung himself back at the cellar wall, headbutting it to clear his mind of these horrifying and dreadful visions. 'No! No! No! I won't let you . . .'

. . . and now he could see a pit, deep below the earth. And there were men there; men in miner's helmets, the weak lights from those helmets swinging wildly in the darkness as they tried to run away . . . away from the beams above them which groaned, and sagged . . . and collapsed with a grumbling roar. Lister could feel the weight of rock and soil on him, could feel it stuffed into his mouth, suffocating him . . .

He reeled again, staggered across the cellar and blundered into a packing case. Bottles shattered as he fell over it. He rolled on the soil, clutching his head.

And then he heard them coming up.

They were beneath him now, in the earth. He could hear them. The boys and the miners and the torture victims. They were struggling up through the clay and the soil and the worms; clawing their way up into the cellar from underground. They had been sent for him at last.

Lister pounded at the soil.

'No! You can't . . .'

But they were still coming. Very soon, the first putrescent hand would claw its way up through the cellar floor and fasten on him. Then another, and another. Lister staggered to his feet again, looking back to the cellar door.

And then he laughed, looking down again and listening as the House's dead scrabbled upwards to meet him. It didn't matter where he ran, the House had claimed him. He could never get away. And whether or not the dead beneath were really crawling back, or whether it was just another of the House's tricks — making the unreal seem real — it didn't matter. With peripheral images whirling around his mind, for an instant — at the core of his being there was a shaft of blinding clarity. He might return to his horrifying twilight world as House Caretaker, or the House might kill him. But there was a third option. There was another way to gain release.

With the whispering, scrabbling sounds of undead fingers beneath his feet, Lister walked back to the overturned packing case. Madness was only seconds away. He bent down and retrieved a shattered brandy bottle. Standing, he looked back at the cellar door.

'It's up to you,' he said sadly. And then, with a mere hint of amusement as the scrabbling reached a frenzy in his mind: 'For the love of God, Montresor.'

Looking up at the dripping ceiling, he drew the jagged bottle viciously across his throat.

26

Rennie was drunk and starting to feel good again. The horrors of the previous evening were being safely anaesthetised into a safe, manageable place. As he exchanged stories with Eddie about the old times, and drank, and laughed . . . he also quickly skimmed over what Lister had told him earlier. He believed the most part of what the old man had told him and, given that, he knew that anyone with the sense God had given them should be miles and miles away from this House by now. But, as he talked and laughed with Eddie, he was also watching him; testing him, searching his face for any sign that the mask was still there. It was a matter of control. Hadn't Lister himself said that Rennie had been protected by Eddie? And despite all the death and the horror, none of it had touched Rennie at all. Only once, in the beginning, had Eddie failed to exercise control and so put him at risk. But that had been in the beginning, when Eddie was still learning how to control his power.

When the laughter subsided, Rennie steeled himself, took another drink and struck home to the subject:

'Lister says you've turned those forcign guys who were here into "Disciples". He says they've gone back to their own countries to spread . . . "contagion". That right?'

'Bollocks! The old guy's out of his head. They're still downstairs. All of them.'

'It . . . you said last night that they would serve . . . your purpose . . . when they returned to where they'd come from.'

'That's crap. They're all down there. I'm going to get

Lister to get rid of the mess downstairs. Bury all that shit out there in the ruins.'

'Where the lime trees are?'

'Yeah. Why not? Good cover there.'

'Doesn't it . . . sicken you, Eddie? Doesn't any of it turn your guts?'

'Listen, Rennie. I've told you before. Those shits downstairs . . . or what's left of them, anyway . . . *they're* the Evil ones. They're the ones who are filming and peddling kiddie porn, they're the ones who're making a living out of other people's misery. And up until now, no one's been able to bring them down. No one's been able to make an impression. Not even the police. No one! No one that is . . . until me. They deserved everything they got downstairs. I didn't do a thing. I used the power . . . and they tore themselves apart. Believe me, the world's a better place without them.'

'So now you know who and where Sheraton is?'

Eddie nodded vigorously. 'When Sheraton's dead, this is all finished. We're going to Jamaica.'

'Okay, Eddie. Okay. But when Sheraton's dead, what happens to the . . . power? What are you going to do with it?'

'I'm going to get rid of it.'

'And how the hell do you do that?'

'It's easy. I just don't use it. I squeeze it out of me. Like I said, Rennie, I'm in control. Once we're set up, once we're safely away and have as much cash as we need . . . I can snuff it out. I know how to do it.'

'You're sure?'

'I'm sure. Now pass me the bottle.'

'When, Eddie? When are you going after Sheraton?'

'Sooner than you think.'

27

Twenty-five men, loyalty dwindling, guarded the grounds of Sheraton's most recently acquired bastion. Three times in the last month there had been a change of properties. The high-rise penthouse overlooking the city had now become too open for Sheraton, too vulnerable, too easily accessible. When yet another similar high-rise administration building of her company had burnt to the ground, she had decided to move. The other two properties had been 'acquired' from within the dwindling ranks of her own operation. None of them had been satisfactory. And as Sheraton's lack of control became more apparent, as her temperament became more dangerous and illogical in the wake of the ever-increasing succession of attacks on her organisation, Sheraton Inc itself had continued to disintegrate.

She couldn't settle tonight . . . like most nights now.

The video she had been watching in the main lounge made no sense to her; just a jumble of images with no narrative, no sense. She snorted more of the cocaine, aware deep down inside that she was addicted now, but refusing to acknowledge the fact. It was only a temporary respite, to relieve the tension. When the Brinkburn business was completely resolved she could pay for any medical treatment she might need to get rid of the habit.

She began to pace the floor again, checking the reinforced window each time; looking out through the curtains across the lawn to make sure that her men were still patrolling there. After a while, there was a change of 'guard' at the ornamental gate giving access to the grounds of the house.

The drug began to take effect, flooding her with new optimism. Now, the room didn't seem so much like the prison cell that all her other rooms in all her other houses had seemed to become. Even the crumpled newspaper on the sofa didn't bother her now. She picked it up again and read the headline.

'*A New Age? Are the Days of Organised Crime Over?*'

It no longer infuriated her in the same way that all the other newspaper reports had done. It only served to amuse her. Words, only words. In fact, the Days of Eddie Brinkburn would soon be over. Now, thanks to her American colleagues, she had found out where Brinkburn and his people had been hiding. It had taken substantial funds and persuasion to develop and plan her strategy. But it was worth it. More than worth it, in fact: it was vital. Brinkburn had succeeded in bringing her carefully established organisation to the verge of collapse, something the authorities themselves had been completely incapable of doing, even on an international level. How Brinkburn had managed to do that still remained the great mystery. No doubt she would find out after he had been completely obliterated. Only the best men had been chosen for the task, with orders to take Brinkburn alive if possible but to leave nobody else alive, to raze the place to the ground and get away quickly before drawing any attention.

Maybe there were lessons to be learnt from the Brinkburn situation which she could use to rebuild and strengthen Sheraton Inc? That was it! A New Age . . . just like the newspaper said. But not in the way that they meant. This would be a New Age for Sheraton Inc. Learning from the ashes of Brinkburn's destruction, interrogating Brinkburn to learn his sources of power and strength (a personal interrogation, of course), her organisation would become stronger and more powerful.

'It's a *learning* process . . . that's it exactly,' she said aloud. Her optimism enfolded and reassured her. She moved to the telephone. It was answered immediately by one of the six minders next door.

310

'Yes, ma'am.'

'Any news, yet?'

'Nothing yet, ma'am.'

'Well . . . that's all right. There's time.'

'Yes, ma'am.'

She replaced the receiver and poured herself another large brandy. 'Just a matter of time.' She began to make new, optimistic plans.

* * *

'Think they'll do it?' said Sewell to his colleagues after he had replaced his own receiver.

' 'Course they'll do it. She's sent in a fucking army.'

'And what if they don't?'

'If they don't . . . you're gonna see a clean pair of heels. Mine.'

'It better work. Those drugs are sending her out of her skull. If it doesn't work, there's no telling what she'll do. Best not to be around her.'

'Bloody Hitler . . .'

'Hitler hasn't got a look-in on her.'

'Just pray that telephone rings with good news.'

28

Sewell stepped out into the fresh morning air, looking up at the sky. It had a bruised-peach look to it this morning, with ash-grey streaks. Just recently, he had spent a lot of time looking at the sky. He had never realised that there were so many colours. And each time he looked, it made him feel uneasy. Things were different somehow, he could sense it. Things had changed . . . were changing . . . and they were not changing for the better. He had first taken an interest when Brinkburn's attacks had begun, and the news had begun to filter back with uneasy regularity about the warehouses and cathouses that were being burned down. It seemed to him that the skies had taken on a different colour then. When he scanned the evening skies, he could swear that they were reflecting another burning part of the business. He had never seen those wide red gashes in the clouds before.

Bruised peaches, he thought again, rubbing his hands together. *And ash-grey. Ashes . . . ashes . . . I wonder what else has been burnt today?*

He laughed. He must be turning into a poof or something. Only poofs thought about things like that. He looked down at his hands: great calloused hands that had seen a great deal of street action. He was twenty-five years old, but looked thirty-five. He rubbed the most recent gashes on his palm, caused when he had crushed that glass at Sheraton's request. He shook his head. She was a dangerous bitch. A dangerous and clever bitch. One step out of line, one indication that she wasn't getting 101 per cent loyalty . . .

and he was finished. Just another name to add to the roll-call of those who had fallen out of favour and suffered badly . . . *very* badly . . . as a result.

Crazy bitch.

At least he'd stuck it out so far. Things had got pretty bad, but he had stayed fast. And that must hold him in good stead for the future in Sheraton's organisation, when so many had already cut and run. When Brinkburn was sorted out once and for all by Sheraton's miniature army, she would set about pulling the pieces together again. Everything would be gravy for him then. Wouldn't it?

Sewell looked out across the lawns of the house to the front gate. Twenty-five men . . . armed, of course . . . patrolled the house and its grounds at all times on a shift-system. On his far right, under the trees, was some kind of pavilion or groundsman's hut where the men not on duty slept. *Just like the army*, thought Sewell as he walked across the lawns towards the gate. He grinned, thinking of the time he'd come across his old friend the sergeant in an East End pub. His old friend the sergeant, who'd given him such a hard time when he was doing his bit for Queen and Country. At closing time, he'd waited for the old bastard in the car park behind the pub. The git had even walked over to him . . . never even recognised him . . . and had asked if he had a spare cigarette. The dispenser in the pub was broken. Sewell had obliged, carefully taking the packet out of his inside pocket and handing one across. When the bastard opened his mouth to put the cigarette in, Sewell had moved quickly with a square right-hook punch to the jaw . . . just the way he'd been taught. It was an old Kray Brothers trick he had picked up. The jaw was instantly shattered. When the old bastard had gone down, Sewell had spread his legs wide and jumped on his knees. Both legs had broken with the sound of wet tree branches.

Still grinning at the memory, Sewell lit a cigarette and blew out smoke contentedly. He reached the gate. Curly Green was standing there with his back to him, staring out at the rough road which led up to the gate. His hands were thrust

313

into his camouflage jacket, blond hair ruffling in the chill morning air. There was a promise of bad weather in that wind. Curly was a good boy, his cousin's son. And Sewell had managed to get him a job in the firm. *Call me Sewell, boy. Don't call me by my first name. Not professional, know what I mean?* Sewell could see the bulge under Curly's jacket which betrayed the Uzi he was carrying, and smiled. For an instant, he toyed with the idea of creeping up behind him and giving him a scare. The idea was quickly discarded. Everyone's nerves were shot to hell by what had been going on recently. The last thing he wanted was a full clip of bullets in his guts. Announcing his arrival would be a much better idea.

'Okay, Curly? How's it going?'

Curly turned and smiled in recognition.

'Quiet.'

'Good . . .'

Sewell looked out beyond the gate, drawing heavily on the cigarette and pinpointing the other men walking around the house. There was an enclosing stone wall all around the two-acre estate.

'Pete . . . I mean, Sewell.'

'Yeah?'

'I was talking to Johnny Gordon yesterday. Know him?'

'Yeah, I know him. Organises a ring of pushers up Brixton way.'

'He was telling me he was there when Eddie Brinkburn hit one of the drug factories down at the docks. The whole place was torched. Six guys burnt to death . . . but he got away.'

'Yeah, I know about that. Johnny's an okay fella. So what?'

'Well . . . like you say, Johnny's okay. And I know we're not supposed to listen to any of the crazy stories coming back about Eddie Brinkburn's Frighteners. But last night in the pub, Johnny had a few too many. He was saying . . . the things that burned the place and killed his lads. Well, they weren't human . . .'

314

'Look, Curly. I've told you before. Don't listen to that garbage. If you know what's good for you, just don't listen to it. And if you value your health, you won't pass any of it on. Those orders come from the top . . .' Sewell stabbed his finger back at the house. 'You're family, Curly. So take some advice and shut it!'

'But Johnny . . .'

'That's enough, boy. It's all shit. Just forget . . .'

And then Sewell became aware of the noise. Insubstantial, distant . . . but somehow disturbing. Curly opened his mouth to speak again, but Sewell held a hand over his mouth, cocking his head to one side and listening.

'Hear that?'

'What?'

The noise was a susurration of sound; a distant rumbling, like the grumbling approach of water from a burst dam. Sewell moved to the gates and looked out down the road. The trees on either side swayed slightly in the wind, branches rustling . . . but there was no sign of anything coming. Sewell looked up into the sky again. A cold, flinty sun was dissolving the peach and the grey. He wondered what he expected to see there. Some kind of change? No, but Sheraton had mustered a small army to take out Brinkburn's operation. Might it not be possible that he had sufficient muscle to retaliate with some kind of air strike? Choppers? Sewell quickly scanned the house and its grounds.

'I can hear it now,' said Curly at last, sensing Sewell's uneasiness and drawing his Uzi. 'Rumbling or . . . something . . .'

'Something's coming,' said Sewell plainly. 'Get the others out of the bunkhouse.'

Curly ran towards the groundsman's hut, head twisting from side to side as he moved, looking for the source of the noise. Sewell began to shout to the nearest men patrolling the perimeter wall. They too, were aware now of the sound. Sewell withdrew his own weapon, a Czech CZ 75 9mm pistol, and returned to the gates, scanning the road again.

He began yelling orders as the off-duty men spilled from
the bunkhouse.

* * *

'What is it?' Sheraton screamed down the telephone.
'What's that noise?'

'We don't know, ma'am. Sewell's taking care of
everything outside.'

Sheraton slammed down the receiver and crossed to the
French windows. Twitching the curtain out of the way, she
looked out across the lawns and the men in camouflage
milling about. They were looking around urgently as they
ran: at the perimeter walls, at the sky, at the gate. The
rumbling noise was increasing in pitch by the second, its
source still unknown. She could feel it now, in the window-
sill on which she was leaning; a faint, trembling vibration
in her fingers. She pulled her hand away quickly as if she
had been scalded, backing away from the window until she
was in the middle of the room.

'Do something!' she yelled at the walls. 'Do something,
you bastards.'

* * *

Curly rejoined Sewell at the gate.

'Where the hell is it coming from?' he shouted.

Sewell shouted orders at the men nearest him. 'I want a
protective circle around the house. And I want everyone else
to find cover. It may be an air strike.'

'It's Brinkburn, isn't it?' said Curly in alarm. 'I knew it.
I knew it was going to happen.'

'Keep on this gate, Curly!'

'Johnny said Brinkburn's things aren't human, Pete. He
said nothing can . . .'

'Will you get back to the bloody gate!' Sewell threw him
hard at the iron railings. Curly fumbled around, the snout
of the Uzi protruding through the railings and aiming down
the road. He could feel the growing rumble of sound
reverberating in the gate itself.

'Tanks!' He yelled back.

'Where?' Sewell spun in alarm back to the gate.

'No, I mean *maybe* it's tanks. Maybe Brinkburn's got a whole bloody army or something . . .'

'Cover the gate, boy! And keep your mouth shut!'

Sewell scanned the skies again and began to move away, back to the house.

'Sewell! You're not leaving me here, are you?'

'Stay where you are, Curly.'

'But I'm family . . .' His words were drowned now by the roaring, grumbling sound. The gate, the walls . . . even the ground . . . seemed to be trembling as the sound became the noise of an earthquake or an erupting volcano. Sewell swung his pistol from side to side, scanning the sky, looking around him to see the circle of men backing away towards the house, also looking for the other men who had taken cover by the peripheral walls and in the shrubbery. It was an air strike. It had to be.

Something exploded on the ground not ten feet from Sewell.

The velocity of the blast spilled him over. He clung to his pistol, wriggling around to see that a geyser of water was shooting up from the concrete drive. Seconds later a sewer grating clanged to the ground, splitting the concrete pathway. The water showered him. It stank. Sewell clambered to his feet as the geyser began to shrink away.

'The sewers . . .'

And then the other sewer gratings around the house and in the grounds began to burst upwards with a series of detonating roars. Geysers of filthy, detritus-clogged water began to spew from a dozen places at once. Fountains of sewer filth began to shower Sheraton's men in an obscene parody of the delicate, rotating garden-watering machines that had once spun so lazily on this lawn. Somewhere, Sewell heard a burst of machine-gun fire. Men were milling about in confusion. Back at the gate, a last sewer grating juddered and exploded into the sky with tremendous force. Yelping, Curly ran from the gate towards him, showered in filth. He

317

whirled as he ran and fired back at the gate; a blurt of flame.
The bullets ricocheted crazily from the iron railings as the
eruption subsided.

'Curly! Save it!'

The geysers of sewage dwindled away to bubbling troughs.
Everything seemed to be soaked in the filth − the lawns,
the concrete path, the men themselves, still milling around
on the grass, trying to train weapons on what seemed to be
an invisible adversary. But the grumbling sound had
vanished. Only the quiet hiss now of running water and
broken drains.

Sewell skipped over to the shattered hole from which the
nearest sewer grating had exploded. Water was still coughing
and bubbling, as if there was an obstruction down there.
The smell was appalling. He reeled away from it, hand over
his mouth. *Bombs in the sewers? They trying to gas us out,
or what?* He looked over at the shattered grating, embedded
in the concrete driveway, grateful that it hadn't landed on
him. Curly joined him at last.

'What's going on, Pete?'

'You tell me.'

The drain coughed again; an ugly belch of muddied water.

Curly moved to it, looking down in disgust. He hopped
to one side to avoid another bubble of muck as it burst,
spread and sluiced away down the concrete drive. 'Shit!'
The drain assented at once, vomiting more of its contents
onto the drive.

'What do we do now?' shouted one of the men from the
house. Sewell looked over. Everyone was still extremely edgy,
despite the fact that the threat . . . whatever it was . . .
seemed to be over, or had never been. He looked back at
Curly, who was still making disgusted noises but still looking
down into the broken drain. Was that all it was? Some kind
of accident in the sewage system? Some kind of gas build-
up? Ruptured pipes? He cupped his hand to his mouth and
began to shout back at the others that they should move out
and recce the perimeter walls. His voice dried and his
automatic swung up when the other noise began.

It was Curly.

He was screaming.

At first, Sewell thought that he had snagged or somehow cut his foot on a piece of the shattered grating. There was muck and shit on his legs. He'd got too close and stood in the drain's belching filth. But why was he continuing to make those distressed little boy sounds? Why was he bending down, clutching at the leg nearest to the broken drainhole? Sewell stepped forward to help him. He must be caught. And then Curly started to claw at his ankle, frantically tearing with both hands at the filth on his foot. Sewell stopped in his tracks.

There was more than filth on Curly's foot. Something had come out of that sewer and fastened on his ankle.

No . . . that's not possible.

An arm had emerged from the drain; an arm which seemed to be composed entirely of filth and muck and sewage. And the clutching, shit-encrusted hand that also looked like a claw had fastened on Curly's ankle.

Curly hammered at it. Sewell saw filth and detritus splash from it on impact, but the grip was relentless. The drain made another choking noise. More raw sewage spewed out, splashing Curly; a small tidal wave of it raced away down the concrete path. Sewell knew with absolute certainty that something was coming up out of that drain.

With no more pause for thought, he stepped briskly forward, chambering his automatic.

'Get it off, Pete! GET IT OFF!'

Sewell stood uphill of the drain. Curly was looking up in agony and terror, straight into his face. Sewell glanced down. A head and shoulders were wriggling upwards out of the drain. A head and shoulders that were completely covered in sewage, rotting vegetation and excrement.

'Lean back, boy!'

Curly twisted away in agony, the fingers of the 'hand' buried through sock, shoe leather and into the flesh. Sewell took one more step forward as the figure in the drain struggled to rise in another gushing wave of filthy water . . . and then he opened fire.

The first shot blew away the top of the figure's head. Sewell saw it burst apart, splattering Curly like mud. Another encrusted arm flopped from the drain and braced on the concrete paving. *Not possible*, thought Sewell, and fired again. The second shot blew the figure's head completely away from its shoulders in a spray of filth. *That's not a human head*, Sewell found himself thinking, and fired a third shot as the headless figure began to heave itself out of the drain. The bullet punched a slopping hole straight between its shoulder-blades. Sewell could see right through it, could see Curly's desperately writhing legs as the thing emerged with a *sucking* sound. In a flashing instant, Sewell had a childhood impression. That sound was just like the sound you made when you stood in deep mud and tried to pull out again, with the mud gripping tight on your boot.

Mud pies, thought Sewell . . . and emptied the entire clip into the thing's body. Sewage and filth splattered him. Curly was screaming again, and Sewell could not be sure now whether he hadn't caught one of those bullets. Shell cases spun in the air, clattering on the concrete. Sewell stood back out of the cordite cloud.

The thing was still standing, waist high, in the drain. Its left arm was still braced on the driveway; muck eddied and pooled from its 'fingers'. Curly still thrashed and beat at the other 'hand' and 'arm' which held him, like a landed fish. The thing was immense. And its torso was riddled with holes. Even now, those holes were slopping and running . . . and filling up, like impressions in mud. Refusing to believe it, Sewell watched the squirming, writhing activity on top of the thing's shoulders; watched the sewage remoulding like clay, reconstituting itself. He fumbled for another clip for his automatic, looking down only briefly. Beyond him, all hell was suddenly exploding around the house. His head jerked up. Men were running and firing; the explosive, shattering roar of sub-machine-gun and automatic fire rent the morning air.

The thing before him in the drain had not been alone.

Other clay-mud shapes were crawling out of each of the shattered drains.

'Pete!' screamed Curly. 'For God's sake, don't leave me here.'

Sewell looked back. The thing's head had somehow been completely reconstituted. He jammed the clip home into the automatic and steadied it again as the thing lifted Curly up into the air by his ankle. He whirled helplessly.

And then the clay man turned its head back towards Sewell.

He recognised that clay/sewage face immediately. Some diabolical sculptor had taken the raw sewage and fashioned it into a perfect image. The clay visage smiled as the figure turned bodily to face him, swinging the still-screaming Curly with it. Sewage oozed and bubbled around its waist as it turned.

'You're not him. You can't be him . . .' said Sewell, his finger pausing on the trigger.

The thing's smile broadened. Filth and muck slid from its jowls onto the concrete drive with a thick smack.

'What's the matter, Sewell?' It's voice was a liquid gurgling nightmare from the deepest bowels of the sewer. *'Don't you recognise your old sergeant?'*

'Oh God, Pete! Do something!' Curly thrashed again, trying to twist upwards against gravity to the grip on his foot. Blood was seeping down his leg. The thing seemed to notice him again. It smiled . . . and Sewell could only watch, frozen in horror, as the thing brought its other arm up slowly. Curly saw it coming and began to scream more hoarsely, slapping out ineffectually.

The thing took him by the throat. His screams were choked off with a squawk. Smiling again, the clay man brought him almost lovingly to its broad, stinking breast and cradled him there in its filth. And then, still smiling its ghastly runnelled, flowing-clay smile, it pushed him roughly down to its midriff; and then thrust him even farther downwards, hand over careful hand . . . into the drain.

321

Curly's juddering feet vanished from sight, one of his shoes plopping from the swilling filth. It began to sail away down the drive on a tide of sewage, like some ridiculous boat.

'*Now he's where he belongs,*' said the sewage thing. It braced its hands on the concrete and finally began to pull itself out.

Sewell screamed at the immensity of the thing and emptied the clip into it.

'*Shouldn't have broken my legs, Sewell,*' it said.

He never had time to reload.

29

'What's happening?! *What's happening?*'

Sheraton slammed the receiver down again. There was no answer; had been no answer for the past fifteen minutes. When the first explosions had gone off outside, one of her men had looked round the door to tell her to sit tight; they were going to check everything outside. She had screamed at him like a wild animal to get out. He had broken one of her direct instructions. No one was to see her. She was to be left alone in her rooms. All contact was to be made by telephone. He had quickly vanished.

When the sub-machine-guns and small arms fire had begun, she had started to scream again. And again, and again; becoming hysterical when the sounds of her own men screaming had reached her ears.

It was silent now.

And no one was answering the telephone.

She looked from the receiver to the French windows, seized by two conflicting impulses: an impulse to move to those curtains, pull them aside and find out what was happening; and an impulse of sheer terror telling her to keep away from those windows at all costs. She gave in to the latter, backing away into the centre of the room.

Something was going to happen. She could feel it.

She scanned the walls, the ceiling, the outside door, the door leading into her bedroom. Inexorably, her attention was drawn back to the French windows.

Something outside was turning the handle, behind the curtains.

It's locked! Go away! It's locked!

And then, with a grinding snap, the handle was snapped off. She heard it clatter on the patio paving.

The curtains billowed slightly as the windows were opened.

There was a gun in the drinks cabinet drawer, six feet or so from the curtains. But her terror would not allow her to cross the room. She remained rooted to the spot, attention fixed on the undulating velvet hangings.

A hand appeared in the central fold between the curtains.

Oh, God . . .

It crept over the fabric, fingers clutching.

I never really wanted to hurt anybody, Daddy, I was always a good girl. Oh, God . . . don't hurt me . . . don't . . .

And then Eddie Brinkburn stepped smartly into the room, smiling.

'Barbara Sheraton, I presume.' He flipped the curtains close behind him, as if he'd just appeared on stage like some kind of magical act.

Sheraton flinched, hands bunched into fists before her; white face staring. She recognised Brinkburn's face immediately. He was wearing a dark raincoat; his hair was tousled and he hadn't shaved recently — but she would have recognised his face anyway. It had haunted her dreams. Now, at last, he was here.

'Brinkburn . . .'

'One and the same.' Brinkburn stepped casually into the room, hands in jeans pockets. He looked around, smiling, as if he'd come to buy the place. After a brief examination, he moved to the drinks cabinet. Did he *know* that there was a gun there?

'Nice,' he said, looking back.

'Help yourself.' Her voice sounded calm and totally collected.

'Thanks.' He popped two cubes from the icebox into a glass and poured a large brandy. Still smiling, he strolled calmly to the sofa and sat down, as if he were just visiting.

He sighed . . . as if he'd just put in a hard day's work, and then took a sip of the brandy.

Sheraton moved to the padded leather armchair which faced the sofa, and sat down.

'My men outside?'

Eddie shrugged ruefully and then shook his head, as if mourning the passing of dear acquaintances.

'All gone . . . I put the Frighteners on them, I'm afraid. Everything you've ever had − all that filth − it's back in the sewers where it belongs.'

'So you've won after all? You've finally got what you want.'

'Almost.'

'I don't know how you've done it − but you have. The Garage Mechanic. Mr Fixit. How *did* you fix it, Brinkburn?'

'That would be telling.'

'So you've won and I've lost. Are you going to kill me?'

'What do you think?'

'I think so. I think you intend to do something nasty. Put your Frighteners onto me.'

'So you believe in them now?'

'What else can I do? However . . .' She crossed her legs, lounging back in the chair. '. . . there's another alternative.'

'And what's that?'

'You don't have to kill me. You've got everything you wanted. You've got your revenge and you've brought Sheraton Inc to ruin. But whatever you may be, whatever power you have . . . you're still an amateur in this game. You're not a professional. You could have it all. You *have* it all! But you don't know how to manage it, how to run it − the way I do. This is my life. And I could help you.'

'You don't have anything to bargain with, Sheraton. You're finished now.' Brinkburn took a mouthful of brandy and swallowed hard, grimacing at the burning in his gut. 'You took everything away from me. My wife and my kids, everything that meant something to me.'

'But you did that to me, too. You took my brother away — that's what started this whole mess. Look . . . all right . . . we've *both* taken the best things away from each other and there's no bringing them back.'

Eddie smiled and drank again.

'So why don't we come together? If you kill me — then you've been successful in that you've destroyed Sheraton Inc completely. But you don't need to do that now. With my help in re-establishing the business — *your* business — I could make you, and your black friend, very wealthy. Do you know what it's like to be rich?'

Eddie finished off his drink.

'Here . . . let me get you another.'

Eddie proffered his empty glass. Sheraton slowly rose from the armchair, took it, and began to stroll casually across the room to the drinks cabinet.

'There are *other* ways to start again, you know.'

'Other ways?'

'I know how much family means to you. That's what it's all about, really, isn't it? I come from a big family myself. All dead now. And I can understand how you feel. You've lost a family — I could give you a new one. I could even give you children myself.'

Eddie's smile wavered. 'A fate worse than death?'

'No, not for me. I could be just what you want me to be.' Sheraton reached the drinks cabinet and put down the glass. 'It's worth thinking about. More money than you could conceive.'

'Conceive . . .'

'Never having to want anything again' She slid open the cabinet drawer at the same time as she unstoppered the brandy decanter. 'A new family.' She reached inside and felt the cold black metal. 'A new beginning. A New Age!'

She whirled from the cabinet, levelling the gun.

Brinkburn was standing in the centre of the room, looking at her. There was a wistful smile on his face.

'It's too hot,' he said calmly. 'You can't use it.'

Sheraton yelped. The gun twitched from her fingers and bumped to the carpet. She staggered back, hands behind her and bracing on the drinks cabinet. 'How . . .?'

Still smiling, Eddie walked slowly across the room. Sheraton's enforced casualness appeared to have gone forever. She continued to stare wildly from the gun on the floor to him as he approached. Eddie clucked ruefully, stooped and picked up the gun. 'See? Not hot at all, really.' He opened the chamber and slowly removed the shells, dropping them one by one onto the carpet. 'No need for guns. No need at all . . .'

Sheraton stepped forward urgently, her movement making the bottles and decanters on the drinks cabinet shelf rattle.

'Please, Brinkburn. Please . . . I'm begging . . .'

'Just like my wife and kids begged? Just before you torched my house. Just . . .'

Sheraton lunged forward, her left hand curling around his neck, her right hand jabbing the carving knife she had taken from the drinks cabinet shelf hard under his ribs — to the hilt.

Eddie convulsed, his eyes starting from his head. Sheraton held firm . . . and twisted the knife hard, literally carving it across his body.

'Thought you fucking *had* me, Brinkburn? Thought . . . *you* . . . *were going* . . . *to give it to me. Didn't* . . . *you?!'*

Eddie made a gargling, choking sound. The empty gun fell from his hand. At last, the blood came. It sprayed and gushed around the handle; black-red arterial blood, spurting over Sheraton's powder-blue blouse. But she continued to hold fast as Eddie crumpled slowly and judderingly to his knees. As he descended, she continued to carve the knife upwards.

Eddie knew that he was dying. He could see the blood erupting in surges from him, could see it slopping and streaming over Sheraton as she held him fiercely, like a madwoman. Her glittering eyes seemed marble-black; he could hear her grinding teeth. The pain could not register — shock had deprived him of that — but he knew with a

327

fading yet intense horror just exactly what she was doing. He could feel himself coming apart; could *feel* his internal organs for the first and last time in his life sagging and spilling from the opened sac of his torso. He tried to scream. Black blood spouted from his mouth instead of his voice.

'Wanted to stick it in me, Brinkburn? Well . . . what does it feel like *now*?' Sheraton twisted one last time as Eddie collapsed finally to his knees, jerking the knife from his body with an audible rip. She stood back. Eddie clutched at his body, hugging it tight, trying to keep himself whole. The blood gushing through his fingers and from his mouth widened the dark pool in which he knelt. Sheraton began to laugh, throwing the bloody knife into a corner.

Eddie could feel something essential *fading* inside him, as only a dying man could recognise. He looked up at her, and laughed. It was a crimson, gargled laugh. So this was what it was like to die? He began to swallow as hard as he was able, swallowing the blood which still jetted from his stomach and ruined torso into his mouth. Gagging and spluttering, knowing that death must be only seconds away, he began to force out words.

'It's . . . guh . . . guh . . . *good*. I wanted . . . to . . . feel like this. I wanted . . . to take . . .'

Sheraton snorted in disdain, turned and poured herself a large brandy.

'. . . it as far . . . as I could.' Mists were beginning to cloud his eyes. 'I'm duh . . . duh . . . dying. That's . . . what you wuh-want.' Sheraton threw down her brandy in one gulp, face mocking and disdainful.

'So die, Mr Fixit.'

'Guh . . . glad . . . you didn't . . . make it easy.' A bubble of blood surged from his nostrils and mouth. He spat it out. A great buzzing sound had descended on him. Darkness was almost complete.

'Tuh . . . time to . . . go. Goodbye, Sheraton. See you . . . see you . . . *in hell*!'

And Eddie withdrew his essence from the butchered wreck on the floor, just before the darkness became too complete

328

for him *ever* to get away from it. In an instant, he snapped himself away from the most perfect thing he had ever created with his new-found, always developing and increasingly sophisticated power. For the very first time, he had been able to project himself into one of his creations.

Sheraton turned to pour another brandy, heard movement and turned back to Brinkburn again.

The empty glass rolled across the cabinet shelf and clunked to the carpet.

Brinkburn was beginning to stand up; smiling, eyes alive and filled with a glittering humour. He was wiping one hand across his mouth as he stood; wiping away the black-red blood from his chin. Sheraton was only feet away from him; she could see the carved and butchered body, the glinting, spilling pinkness of intestine and gut. He laughed. The sound came from the monstrous gash in his torso — not from his mouth. There was nothing of Eddie Brinkburn in that laugh.

And then the thing's face began to contort, twisting and stretching into a tight rictus, the skin pulling away from the teeth. The sardonic grin flowed and writhed like pink plasticine. The entire face was now alive in a fluid shape-changing turmoil. Only the eyes remained unchanged: cold and gleeful . . . and waiting.

'The flesh is clay and the clay is flesh,' said the thing.

And when the changing and the restructuring and the reshaped flesh had resumed its normal shape, Sheraton began to scream as Sewell's bloodied corpse stepped towards her, arms raised.

She began to scream.

'Mr Brinkburn likes to take advantage of available raw material,' said the Sewell thing by way of grinning explanation. Sheraton blundered back from the drinks cabinet and into a wall. She was hemmed in. There was no exit.

Its face was changing again as it came. She could see the pink-white flesh being kneaded and stretched like bloodstained dough by an invisible baker or sculptor. The change was quicker this time. Now, when she recognised the face, she could not stop screaming.

'Frightened, Barbara?' asked Bobby Sheraton, her baby brother.

He picked up a corkscrew from the cabinet shelf as he came, raw sewage spilling from his mouth.

'Come on, baby,' he gargled. 'Make it hard.'

30

'Come on, Eddie,' said Rennie. 'Wake up . . .'

Eddie still lay sprawled on the bed, unmoving. Rennie took another drink from the brandy bottle, screwed the cap back on and bumped the instep of Eddie's foot with it. But still he did not move.

Rennie had been sitting on the floor, his back against the wall. Now, the small of his back was aching. He pushed himself to his feet and swivelled his back, groaning. When he checked his watch, he supposed that Eddie must have been asleep for half an hour. He had complained of feeling tired after drinking Lister's brandy; his voice had become slurred and drifting. 'Shhhhcraton . . .' had been his last word before he drifted into unconsciousness.

'Too early for drinking, I suppose,' said Rennie. 'Pubs aren't even open yet.' He moved back to the bed again, swinging the bottle against Eddie's foot. 'Wakey, wakey.'

Eddie groaned and turned onto his side.

'How about breakfast? I'll give Lister a shout. He's still down there in the cellar.'

Eddie groaned again.

Rennie walked to the window, looking out across the estate. It was the first time he had done so since the horrors of the previous evening. The electric fence was broken in a dozen places. Smoke still drifted across the open space and into the lime trees beyond. There were black burnt patches on the grass. But there were no bodies. And there was no sign of the security guards. In a reflex action, Rennie unscrewed the cap and lifted the bottle to his lips.

31

And Eddie flew back from the thing which he had temporarily occupied, leaving it to finish its task. He flew back at impossible speed through a fog of images. He was a high-jump diver, arms spread in the swan-dive as he hurtled back horizontally to the House on Lime Street where his body lay. Faces swam at him as he plunged onwards. Tracey's smiling face, huge as a film star's face on a cinema screen. He plunged into that face, its image rippling away like shattered water. Jane and Russell called his name, flashed by and vanished. It was all right. When he got back, he would relinquish the power eventually, but not before he had brought back their images to stay with him forever. They would never leave him again. He had lost nothing. He had been revenged . . . and he had everything back the way it was before.

'Jamaica,' said Rennie. 'Wonder if I'll like it after all?' He hoped that it was going to be as good as the Jamaica of his dreams . . . even without Florinda.

Eddie could see himself now: lying on his bed. It was as if he was floating above it, looking down. Rennie was drinking from the brandy bottle, staring out through the window. All Eddie had to do now was glide down and slip back into himself. It was easy. He moved downwards.

'Come on Eddie.' Rennie turned back to him. 'Rise and shine.' He laughed as he watched Eddie roll onto his back again, raising both arms slowly as if trying to embrace something from above.

And Eddie saw his body lift its arms up to accept him

back. He slid downwards and saw the face smile as he entered . . .

But something was wrong. He sensed it immediately as he entered that embrace. Something was already there . . . inside him . . . and as it embraced and enfolded him he struggled to assert his self-identity within his own body. It was loathsome − it swarmed and roiled within him, holding him fast and suffocating him.

'No . . . you can't . . . this is me, me, ME!'

'Too late,' said something inside. And in a moment of startling clarity, Eddie knew three things. He knew that he had only been allowed to believe that he was in control. He knew that his inability to find Sheraton had nothing to do with her being a woman. The Thing which he had inherited from Archie Duncan − the Thing with the power − had hidden her whereabouts from him to prolong the vengeance, the blood, the death and the horror while it fed on it all and grew stronger. At last, it had allowed him to find her; just as he could have found her from the very beginning. And with that knowledge, Eddie knew the third and terrible thing.

The Thing within was strong enough now to act and live independently. It had his body completely now. Screaming and thrashing and dwindling . . . dwindling . . . Eddie's personality began to dissolve . . .

It was in possession.

'. . . make plans now.'

Rennie smiled again as Eddie sat up, eyes closed.

'You been listening to anything I've said?'

Eddie was sitting up straight now, his legs over the end of the bed, eyes still shut.

'Eddie?'

Rennie moved to him, bending down to look directly into his face. Sweat was beading on Eddie's brow.

'Hello, Eddie? Anybody in there?' asked Rennie, smiling.

And then Eddie opened his eyes.

Utterly mesmerised, liquid fear flooding his body, Rennie could only stare into those glittering, bottomless hell-hole eyes. He could not move. Inches from those hideous and terrifying mirrors which were not Eddie Brinkburn's eyes, he could hear the sound of a terrible screaming echoing in his head and did not know whether it was his voice or not. And as he stood there in terror, held by eyes that could dispense madness or death or worse, he saw changes taking place on the periphery of his vision; changes in Eddie's face. Gaunt shadows were etching themselves around those eyes – as if someone was holding a bright light over their heads and slowly moving it. The flesh became corpse-white. The shadows flowed and shifted as the face behind Eddie's face emerged. Even before the change was completed, Rennie knew that it was to become the death-mask face that he feared so much.

'Oh God, Eddie . . .'

'Rennie,' said the Thing, directly into his face. Its voice sounded and stank of the grave. Its simple, one-word identification of him was intensely dreadful. It was more than a simple word. It identified the very essence of his self. He knew that it *knew* him – body and mind, heart and soul. In the instant that those eyes had opened, the Thing within Eddie had stripped him bare and lovingly claimed him. It knew every secret part of him, every worst fear. Those eyes – and that voice – told him in that one word of identification that all he could expect was the embrace of the grave and an agonising eternity of torture worse than he could ever have imagined.

It reached out and touched him on the shoulder.

'Another messenger,' it said.

And Rennie felt the dark blossoming in his gut; knew that what the Thing had done to Crandall, it was now doing to him. Somehow, he was nine years old again and the horrifying face before him was a demonic dentist, holding that horrible rubber-taste mask over his face; delighting in his terror as the gas filled his lungs and his belly. As that terrible face filled his vision, he could feel that gas liquefying his guts, filling him with its evil essence. It spread quickly from his lungs and belly into every vein and artery.

'You're getting smaller, Rennie . . .' said the voice, like

some mad theatrical hypnotist. *'Smaller . . . smaller . . .'*

But in that dwindling, in that shrinking of his essence, which was reflected not in a diminution of terror, but in a massive escalation of fear and horror, Rennie recognised something kindred. Like a man lost overboard in a sea of blood, he thrashed for that something which had momentarily surfaced and then submerged beside him unseen. He plunged downwards for it as waves crashed over his head, found it and hauled its waterlogged essence to himself.

A face swam up to meet his own.

Eddie Brinkburn's face.

In that instance, Eddie recognised him and seized him in a mutual and desperate embrace. His eyes were lost, glazed and idiotic.

'You said you had control, Eddie! You promised me.'

They began to sink. In the dwindling, shrinking essence of his individuality, Rennie felt a spark of something other than fear and horror, something indefinable and insubstantial. Momentarily, the 'shrinking' abated.

'Don't worry,' said Eddie. 'Let it take over. You'll be all right . . .'

The insubstantial feeling solidified as they trod blood in the sea of madness. Now, Rennie knew what that feeling was; a small part of him was astonished at it, even in the presence and the immediacy of his death, madness or worse. It was rage. And it was a flame that fuelled itself. He seized Eddie tighter.

'Eddie, you bastard! You really did it to me, didn't you? I don't mean a fucking thing to you! Nothing!'

'Not me . . . not me . . .'

'After everything we've been through? You've lied to me! You're just as evil as the things you say you were fighting against! You've turned *me* into your bloody filth!'

'Not me . . .'

'So drown me! Tear me apart! Snuff me out! Only take me away from you. Kill me! Even being dead is better than being here with you and what you've done . . .'

335

A wave of blood swamped them and pushed them downwards. Rennie could feel some hellish current pulling at his body. His eyes and mouth were filled with blood. But there was more to death than an end to existence. He could feel the sucking black pit beneath which was dragging them downwards in a whirlpool. Beyond that pit lay worse fear and horror than he could imagine. He could not move. He could not thrash out. The black pit yawned.

And now he was kneeling on the floor in Eddie's bedroom. Eddie was sitting on the edge of his bed, one hand placed on his shoulder. The hell-pit eyes were gone. Rennie was staring directly into the human eyes of Eddie Brinkburn; eyes that were brimming with tears. Rennie could see their coursing track down his cheeks, a droplet even now beading and falling from his chin.

The surging, rapacious blossoming in Rennie's arteries and veins was no longer there.

'What . . .?'

Eddie's grief-stricken, bloodshot eyes blinked. In that instant, Rennie could see the glass-metallic reflection of the Thing's eyes; like the second layer of some fiendish and feral beast. Was this some further sick and dreadful trick? Had the Thing brought him back only to torment him in some more horrifying way?

'No!' Eddie blinked again. Rennie seemed to hear it. And this time, it was Eddie's human eyes again. But they were eyes that reflected a different and dreadful inner hell. Rennie felt the grip tighten on his shoulder. When he looked directly into Eddie's eyes there was an acute awareness of things inside and things beyond; an awareness that was conveyed to Rennie of the limited time . . . the *seconds* . . . available.

'I've taken it away again. It's gone out of you. Get away, Rennie! For God's sake . . . GET AWAY!'

Something electric, like a static shock, seemed to jump in the air between them. Rennie fell back, scrabbling away until his back was against the wall. Eddie's voice faded away to a groan of grief and fear. Spittle slipped gossamer-like from his mouth. He began to rock backwards and forwards, like a man grieving for the loss of someone important. Rennie knew that he was mourning the loss of himself.

Seconds . . .

Rennie clawed himself upright, eyes still fixed on Eddie as the rocking increased.

'Eddie . . .?'

Seconds . . .

Eddie blinked. His pupils and irises vanished, instantly replaced by those hellish cataracts.

Rennie blundered from the room. Behind him, Eddie began to howl like a wounded animal. Rennie hurled himself down the stairs, bouncing from the banisters. Half-way down he slipped and finished his descent in clumsy cartwheels. Winded and sprawling at the foot of the stairs, he looked up expecting to see . . . something . . . descending after him. There was no one. And the howling had stopped.

Rennie hurtled through the outside doors. Running full tilt, he launched himself down the stone stairs. The stone lions seemed to swell on either side of him. He reached the bottom in three long, leaping strides.

And then he ran. Without looking back, without looking from side to side for evidence of the previous night's horrors, he ran.

The guard-post at the front gate had been gutted by fire. The gate was shattered and swinging on one hinge, just the way it had done when they had first arrived at the House on Lime Street. Breath catching in his throat in crazed sobs, Rennie ran wildly past the gate and out into Lime Street.

Although he expected it at any second, nothing emerged from the lime trees or the ruined houses on either side.

He ran.

Soon, the House on Lime Street was lost to sight behind the trees.

PART FOUR

SAINTS
AND DEMONS

'If each, I told myself, could but be housed in separate identities, life would be relieved of all that was unbearable; the unjust might go his way, delivered from the aspirations and remorse of his more upright twin; and the just could walk steadfastly and securely on his upward path, doing the good things in which he found his pleasure, and no longer exposed to disgrace and penitence by the hands of this extraneous evil. It was the curse of mankind that these incongruous faggots were thus bound together — that in the agonised womb of consciousness these polar twins should be continually struggling. How then, were they dissociated?'

The Strange Case of Dr Jekyll and Mr Hyde.
Robert Louis Stevenson (1886)

1

Jason Conway, fourteen years old and brutalised by both mother and father since his birth, clambered over the allotment wall and crouched there until the sounds of police sirens began to die away.

It had been easy. Easier than the others.

The old woman must have been ninety, if she'd been a day; and it had been a simple matter to follow her, wait until the streets seemed clear and then cross the road to ask the time. When she'd started to say that she didn't have a watch, he'd moved in and grabbed the handbag. The old bitch had tried to hang onto it, screaming; so he'd been forced to give her a good kicking — and with each kick he delivered to her head, he imagined by turns that it was his mother's or his father's head.

He'd run across the estate to the allotments, ducking and weaving through dense shrubberies and crumbling garden walls until he knew that he was safe. He was in an enclosed space now; a forgotten patch of wasteground between two allotments. The wall he'd clambered over was about seven feet high and he was in a vee-shaped patch, the rough planked walls of two allotments at either side, each as high as the stone wall. In this space, about forty or fifty feet at its broadest across the wall, the allotment holders had taken advantage of the opportunity to dump rubbish. There was an old sofa here, stuffing hanging out of its sides, the skeletal frame plainly visible, like some strange kind of animal brought down by hunting night creatures, its foam rubber entrails pulled out by hungry teeth and claws. A rusted wheelbarrow lay on its back in a filthy pool. The rest of the wasteground had been given a unique and undulating geography by mounds and hummocks of matted garden refuse.

As the sirens died away at last, Jason looked in the handbag, discarding the rubbish until he'd found the cash. Seven quid. Not much. But better than nothing. Shoving the money into his back jeans pocket, he threw the handbag aside and stood up.

And then froze.

The sofa had been turned right side up — and someone was sitting on it, watching him.

Confused, Jason looked from side to side. An allotment owner? A *copper*? No . . . not a copper. This guy was in his mid-thirties, with dark hair and wearing a black raincoat. He was lounging back on that tattered sofa as if he was having a quiet night at home or something. One elbow was casually propped on the arm rest, his chin cradled in the cup of his hand. And he was smiling. That smile only seemed to confuse Jason further. Light was somehow reflecting from those eyes — the way he'd seen those Easy Rider type sunglasses reflect light in old films; or one of those night-life documentaries on television where some hunting night creature's eyes were reflected in a torch beam.

'Hello, Jason,' said the man.

Confusion turned to panic. Something about all this was wrong and he knew that his best defence from the confusion of this strange man on the sofa, who knew his name — was flight. Jason spun round and lunged back to the wall.

But somehow — it was as if he had never turned at all. He was still facing the man on the sofa. Again, he froze in confusion.

The man stood up, smile widening, mirror eyes gleaming. Jason could see himself in those eyes as he approached and the man said:

'Spent your whole life running away, haven't you? Now's the time to stand; now's the time to get your own back.'

'Who . . . are you?'

The man paused for a moment, head cocked as if thinking; mirror eyes still on him. Jason was captured in the reflection of those eyes and he knew now that he could never escape. There was fear in that realisation — but also a kindling of the same elation he had felt when he'd stuck the boot in on the old lady. Did he truly *want* to escape?

'I never had a *name* before,' said the man at last. 'Everybody's heard of me, though, everybody's seen me; some have experienced me, some have lived me. Now that I'm whole I suppose I do need a name, don't I?'

Jason tried to speak; tried to say in the midst of the paralysis and mounting excitement and dread inside him that he didn't really care what the man's name was.

'I know,' said the man, approaching again. 'A rose by any other name . . . you can call me Brinkburn.'

The man was standing directly in front of him now, looking directly into Jason's eyes. And Jason could see that those eyes were mirrors after all, as he'd first thought. Things were happening in those mirrors: naked bodies twisting and contorting and *doing things*. He wanted to be there in those mirrors with them.

'You want to get even with the old bastard? You want to pay your mother back?'

Jason nodded awkwardly, barely in control of his neck muscles.

'And Uncle Billy. I *know* you want to get even with Uncle Billy.'

'. . . yes . . .'

'Then let me touch you, Jason. Once I've given you the power you can get even with them . . . and with everybody else you touch. Do you want that?'

Eyes glinting with tears, Jason nodded again.

The Thing in Eddie Brinkburn's body reached out to place a hand on his shoulder.

2

Elwyn Gray replaced the telephone receiver and stared at it for a long time, trying to think of something — anything. But the fear growing in his gut told him that this time there was no way out. He examined the details of his office, looking for an answer. But no answer presented itself. He had been embezzling money from the firm for years . . . and this time he had been found out.

His gaze transferred to the outside window. Eight storeys up, a window ledge outside. A *cliché*? Despite the numbness, Elwyn laughed. Yes, of course it was a *cliché*. Of course, it was ridiculous. But wasn't it far better to go with the current? Wasn't it far better to stand up now . . .?

Okay, I'm standing.

Wasn't it also far better to walk round the desk . . .?
Like this?

. . . yes, just like that; and move over to the window?
The window lock's been painted over, hasn't it? I'm sure it won't open.

Of course it opens. You know it opens.
Oh, yes . . . but it's cold outside. The wind feels cold. Won't it feel colder when I'm falling?

You won't feel anything. The whole thing is ridiculous, remember? Now, just step up onto that window ledge . . .
Pigeon shit. On the window ledge. Shall I slip on it . . .?

How ridiculous! See what I mean? It's all a stupid, stupid joke.

Elwyn laughed and braced himself against the sides of the window, lifting one knee.

Someone touched him on the shoulder.

Bewildered, his sense of the ridiculous evaporating, he turned slowly. But somehow, the sudden jolt which threatened to bring him back to reality was dismissed by that hand on his shoulder. Elwyn completed his slow turn and looked directly into the glass eyes of the man who had come up behind him.

'Wouldn't you rather get even?' said Brinkburn.

3

The hotel was a fleapit. The door, window frames and sills had not seen a lick of paint for years. But it was cheap, and out of the way. Above all, no one was likely to ask any questions.

The building had four storeys, and in his five days there he had neither seen nor heard another guest. Meals were delivered to his door, but the money was running out fast and very soon he would need more.

Rennie knew that it was a bad move to return to the city, but he had been irresistibly drawn back. It was where he had been born; it was really the only place he knew. And if he was going to die, then far better that he should die where he belonged. He moved to the window again, picking up the cardboard clown's mask that he had found in the gutter on his way back here. Was he going to need it again? Cursing, he threw it across the room onto the bed. Rennie Montresor, ex-con, still a criminal. With no one to turn to for money, no family or friends he could approach for fear of drawing Sheraton's attention, he had put on that mask and surrendered to what fate had decreed he should become. Using the revolver he had taken from Eddie, he had robbed a small grocer's shop. Seventy-five quid, in all. He felt sick about it.

Sighing, he looked out onto the grim and dirty street from his second-storey room. He had escaped from Eddie . . . but he was not free; could never be free. There was nowhere he could hide. It was just a matter of time. All he could do was wait.

Down there, in the street and beyond, Rennie could feel Eddie's presence.

No, not Eddie's presence . . . its *presence.*

It was out there now. He could feel it like death pressing against the window pane. He could sense that the city had changed since their departure from it. He could sense the Thing's essence in the bricks and mortar of the street, in the factories and the tenements; in the burnt-out factories and the orange-grey ashes of a smouldering sky.

Most of all, he could see the reflection of its presence in the frightened faces in the streets below. He could sense its presence between the lines of every report in the newspapers that were delivered to his hotel room door. He read and reread the major concerns about the apparent decay in the fabric of society: the crime rate, the soaring murder rate and the civil unrest . . . all escalating out of proportion. He listened to the television debates. People were now too frightened to go out at night because of the rise in violent, motiveless crime. The burning of schools and the death of children. Riots. Open gang warfare. He listened to two intellectuals pondering the possibility of curfew and even martial law. He read about and listened to the reports from abroad: a mounting and horrifying video-frieze of mass murder, riot, disaster and wholesale slaughter for which participants, onlookers and socio-political analysts could provide only hazy and ill-defined reasons. The unseen, brutal face of a Great Murderer was Abroad in both senses of the word . . . and also here, now, stalking the streets. Rennie alone knew that face, and that knowledge made him want to dissolve weeping and hopeless. He listened to video prophets heralding the arrival of the New Age and tried to make sense of their rantings. But he could see no conviction or firmly held belief in their faces. He could only see Fear.

Rennie's nights were sleepless. He would watch the night creep over the city and listen to the sounds of the police sirens out there in the darkness, screaming madly on their way to a new scene of carnage.

He moved slowly and wearily back to the bed. How long?

347

How long before it came to claim him? How long before the Frighteners were put on *him*? He scooped the clown's mask from the bed and lay down, looking at the ceiling.

God in Heaven.

He had been inside it. It had been inside him. As he had begun to drown in that hideous sea of blood, it had laid claim to his soul. It *knew* him in a horrifying and hideously intimate way. But it had been a two-way experience. Because now, he knew *it*. Just before the last vestiges of Eddie's humanity had managed to propel him out of the Thing's grasp — at the last moment — he had seen the true Nature of the Beast. He knew its darkest secret.

And that secret filled him with misery and hopelessness.

Should he get drunk again? Was that the best way out? To get so drunk that he was unconscious or simply didn't care when it came to get him? And then he thought of the days he had spent in the House on Lime Street, getting progressively drunker to hide from his fears . . . fears that had been realised. Eddie had lost control and the Thing inside him had been growing stronger all the time. A spark of rage kindled in him. He kicked himself from the mattress, silently raging. Was this the way his life was to end? Lying on his back in some decrepit hotel? What the hell had his life been about anyway? Did it have to be so valueless? He knew with absolute certainty that he was going to die . . . but was he just going to accept it?

He struggled to remember the name Lister had given him. Cullender? No . . . not Cullender. Callender. Sir James Callender. Was there any point?

Yes, thought Rennie. *There's a point. At least I can tell the stupid bastards just exactly what they've done*.

He walked back and looked out over the city.

Once, it had belonged to Sheraton. And then, to Eddie. Now, it belonged to something else.

4

They weren't listening to her. She could tell. All eyes were fixed on the clock above the bloody blackboard, waiting for the bell that signalled the end of the last lesson.

All those years at teacher training college, all the optimism and the ambition. And here she was, thirty-four years old, divorced and trying to interest this bunch of twelve-year-old cretins in a subject in which none of them had an interest and which could not possibly have any bearing on or use in their future life. Geography!

She could feel the seconds ticking away, could sense the children's mounting agitation as the time crept closer. She could feel those seconds ticking away like a heartbeat inside.

It's my life that's ticking away, you little swines!

Should she manufacture something to detain them? More homework? Find something to be offended about? Keep two or three of the sods back for *bona fide* detention?

Tick . . . tick . . . tick . . . tick . . .

'Agriculture is the main industry of this country, and . . .'

We were childhood sweethearts. Everybody knows that childhood sweethearts don't divorce.

Tick . . . tick . . . tick

'After the destruction caused by the Second World War there was a great drive to . . .'

Deputy Head Teacher at least at my age. Not still sweating it out here to no purpose.

Tick . . . tick . . .

'The Government reforms meant that . . .'

Shrivelling up, wasting away, no purpose, no meaning.

349

. . . Tick . . .

The school bell rang. The thunder of slamming desks and scuffling feet began.

'You will *wait*!' She swung back from the blackboard with wild fury on her face. Her certain expectancy of the children's reaction fuelled that rage.

The slamming and scuffling stopped. She could feel her rage boiling out of control. But the heat beneath that bubbling pot was being turned down rapidly and the rage fading away as she looked over that sea of blank and patently uninterested young faces.

The silence was palpable.

Nothing she could say would give her what she really wanted. She *wanted* them to stay.

'Class dismissed.'

The thundering began again. Laughing, giggling, jostling figures bundled from the classroom, their enthusiasm lying beyond the walls of this room.

The classroom was soon empty. And silent.

She could taste chalk dust in the back of her throat as she stood a long while facing front. When at last she sat down in that stifling silence, she buried her face in her hands and wept.

When she had cried it out of her system, for the time being at least, she reached down for her handbag, intending to retrieve a Kleenex — and became aware of the shape standing in the doorway. Her heart leaped in shame; she could feel the blush on her cheeks and neck. She saw the legs first — the legs of a man. *Oh, God, no!* 'Not that pompous prat Statton!

She raised the Kleenex to her mouth, trying to hide her embarrassment as she sat up straight again. The figure was not Statton, the head teacher, or any of the other teachers. This man was a stranger. A stranger with shining eyes.

The dark and terrifying fear which had haunted her for years was now vividly real — the fear that one day she'd be caught alone and attacked in one of these empty

350

classrooms. Each rape headline held a particular dread for her.

She stood up quickly as the man walked into the room. Her chair clattered backwards.

'Who . . .?'

'School's out, teacher,' said the figure as it strode towards her.

'Stay away from me! I'll scream!'

'No you won't,' smiled the figure. 'Not when you see how young you can be in my eyes.'

Why can't I move?

'Look at my eyes. Beauty's in the eye of the beholder.'

'I . . . I . . . yes, oh yes!'

'Tomorrow, my love, you can teach so much more.'

Soon, by the following morning, she would be ready to show her pupils a new geography.

A Geography of Hell.

5

The flat was damp. There were great creeping stains on the floor and ceiling. The carpet looked as if it might have been laid in the 1960s: great whirling floral patterns that were completely worn down to the weave in places. The wallpaper seemed to have been glued to the walls with spit and threatened to peel away in great patches at any second. The water, gas and electricity had been cut off. Indeterminate filth and grime covered the bare window panes, letting reedy early evening light into the flat — one room serving as living-room and bedroom; one bathroom with a shattered basin and a broken cistern.

In a word, it was squalid.

And the squalor excited him.

As she opened the door into the flat and he had his first viewing of it, he felt the already latent sexual excitement inside burgeon. He felt hard now; and it was a hardness that felt good, felt *potent*. Barely able to wait, he entered behind her.

'Shut the door, then,' she admonished. Dutifully, he shut the door as she took off her coat and threw it onto the rumpled bed which took up most of the room. He came quickly behind her, groping. Laughing, she pushed him off.

'What's the matter?' he asked 'Why . . .?'

'So you're going to last thirty minutes? Not at that rate, pal.'

'But I'm paying . . .'

'All right, all right. But give me a chance to go to the little girl's room first. It's cold on the bladder out there in the street.'

'Oh . . . sorry . . .'

'Why don't you take everything off? You want it in the bed?'

He tried to answer 'Yes', but his dry voice simply made a croaking noise in his throat. She laughed, moving forward and stroking her hand over his penis. He moaned then, praying that he could last. She laughed again and left the room, banging open the toilet door. She groped for the light cord and then remembered that there was no electricity.

'Shit!'

She closed the door behind her, hearing the rustle and fumble of her punter slipping out of his trousers.

Thirty minutes? she thought. *More like thirty seconds.*

Smiling at the easy money and the fact that she could be back out on the street, hustling up more trade, in just a few minutes, she groped in the dark for the toilet bowl.

And put her hands on a face.

She drew in breath sharply for a scream, but a hand that was somehow *not* a hand was suddenly clamped over her face. An arm that was also too insubstantial to be a real arm was snaked around her waist, holding her firmly. She could not move. In terror, she could only stand in the darkness with her hand on that marble-cold face. It was coal-hole dark in that toilet; she could see no details of that face, no details of the man . . . for it was undoubtedly a man who held her.

'*Shhhhhhhh* . . .' said the face. And now she could see faint light where the face's eyes must be; small glinting reflections, like reflections in ebony.

'You all right in there?' she heard the punter ask faintly from next door.

And then the hand was taken away and she heard her own voice say:

'All right, love. You just get yourself ready. Shan't take a moment.'

'*Love me.*'

353

The face moved closer in the darkness towards her own.

* * *

The bedsheets stank but it didn't matter. How many other men had been here? What had they done with her? The thought was akin to the squalor and it kept him rigid and potent beneath those stained sheets. He felt his heart begin to hammer again when the toilet flushed with a muted roar and the bathroom door opened.

She walked slowly into the room again, smiling. She was naked . . . and he moaned again in expectancy as she crossed to the bed. She licked her lips deliberately and lasciviously as he eased himself into a semi-sitting position.

'Want you . . . to look . . .' he moaned.

She pulled back the covers to look down at his paunch, the bulb of his penis straining over-optimistically to reach his belly button. Still smiling and without asking what he wanted to do, she quickly straddled his body and took his stiffness in her hands. He gasped in surprise.

'Protection?' he asked.

'Not tonight.'

Hurriedly, she guided him into herself and sat down hard, her face and its sickly sweet breath in his face. She was cold inside; so shockingly cold that he drew breath again as he was totally enclosed and gripped. But with the coldness there was control and he knew with absolute certainty, as she began to move up and down, that this time . . . for the very first time . . . he was going to get his thirty minutes' worth.

Her dark hair cascaded over his bald pate, her breath hissed in his mouth as she worked . . . and any concept of time was lost in the exquisite *now* of what was happening. He was completely hers to control and she could give him everything.

'Never knew . . . it could be . . .'

'Good, isn't it?'

'Oh . . . yes . . . good . . .'

The sensuous smile on her face was gone in the darkness now. Her features were serious, working hard on the

354

rhythm, chewing her lip. She said something, too low to be audible, and he asked:

'What?'

'. . . smaller . . .'

'I'm not . . . so small . . . am I?'

The smile was back again. She began to ride harder, and he dismissed what he had obviously misheard as he felt his climax rising. Was it thirty minutes? Was it . . .? *It doesn't matter! It doesn't . . .*

And that exquisite blossoming began, rising from his loins, spasming his entire body, convulsing him. He had never experienced an orgasm like this before. Its intensity was consuming him. The pleasure seemed to be pouring *in* from the slut above him, rather than outwards from him and into her.

Gasping, he fumbled for the fifty pounds in the crumpled trousers beside the bed.

* * *

Afterwards, when he had gone, she stood naked in the darkness looking at the toilet door.

The cold draught of dirty night air from one of the living-room's shattered window panes gusted around her legs. Five ten pound notes whispered across the threadbare carpet on unknown destinations.

The Thing inside her smiled and looked around for her clothes.

It had sent him out as a bearer of something much more potent and permanent than syphilis, gonorrhoea or AIDS.

Now it was time for more customers.

6

Sir James Callender — sixty, with blue-white hair that revealed how jet black it must have been in his youth — felt less like a Knight of the Realm today than he had ever done.

Wearily, he parked the car in the garage of his country home — twenty tidily planted acres and very *knightly*, he had always thought — and closed the outer doors. Solitude was something he had always valued, but today he wished that he did have the retinue of staff others expected of his position, rather than just a housekeeper. Tonight, he needed to feel that there were people around him.

He let himself into the hall from the garage door and made his way into the drawing room, dropping his briefcase on the chair beside the telephone. He paused briefly to examine the photograph of his wife next to the telephone. Lovely Liane, dead these twenty years.

'The old fart's home again. Remember the High Flier?'

He smiled ruefully, stroked the photograph and looked round. Wall-to-wall taste and elegance which would have delighted Liane. Tonight, he could not savour it. He poured himself a drink and looked at it. Silence lay heavily like a suffocating blanket. At least back at the Institute there were people; no matter how jaded and restricted the research over which he now presided — at least there was activity. He walked slowly to the French windows, flanked on either side by eight-foot high bookcases, standing at right angles to the wall because it looked like a library and made him feel . . . well, comfortable.

He sipped his drink again, reflectively.

And then a black man stepped out from behind one of the bookcases, holding a book.

'Remember the House on Lime Street?'

Callender whirled in alarm, almost spilling his drink. Rennie tipped the cover of the book and read: ' "My devil had long been caged, he came out roaring." Nice.'

'What the *hell* are you doing in my house?'

'*Dr Jekyll and Mr Hyde*. Pretty appropriate, isn't it?'

Callender moved quickly towards the telephone.

'Don't try it,' said Rennie, raising the gun in his other hand.

Callender saw it and stopped, alarm quickly spreading on his face.

'Look, I don't have any money here. There's a safe over there. Look inside if you want . . . you'll find absolutely nothing of value.'

'I don't want your money, Callender.' Rennie shoved the book back into its slot on the shelf and moved into the centre of the room. Callender backed away.

'Then what do you want? Who the hell are you?'

'Sit down, Callender.'

'You can't . . .'

'*Sit down!*'

Callender sat awkwardly on a padded armchair as instructed. Rennie moved to the sofa opposite him, sitting casually on the arm. 'Like I said before . . . remember the House on Lime Street.'

'You're a prisoner.' Callender began to nod in understanding at last.

'An *ex*-prisoner.'

'And you've come for . . .'

'Revenge? No. Thank God your whole operation was well wound up before my stretch began. You and your brain-washing bastards didn't have a chance to work on me. But that's why I'm here. I want to talk to you about the "Jekyll and Hyde Syndrome".'

'I've got nothing to say to you, whoever you are. I'm sure you've heard of the Official Secrets Act.'

Rennie tapped the barrel of the gun. 'And I'm sure you've heard of a Smith and Wesson .38. Know what size hole this can blow in your guts, Sir James?'

Callender seemed somehow more at ease now. He sat back. 'You don't seem to me to be the sort of man who would use that gun.'

'Believe me, I wasn't. But I am now. Lots of things have happened to me since I was inside. I've seen things you wouldn't believe possible. There are things out there . . . things that will probably kill me. So I'm on borrowed time, you might say.'

'Look, my housekeeper will be here soon . . .'

'You're alone. What's wrong? I only want to talk.'

'So talk.'

'I know all about your research, all about what went on at Lime Street. I know about Archie Duncan.' Callender seemed to flinch uncomfortably. 'I see you're familiar with the name. Duncan killed some of your people and the plug was pulled on the research because of the fear of scandal. Isn't that how it goes?' Rennie sat on the sofa, cradling the gun in both hands, keeping it aimed squarely at Callender's midriff. 'But first things first. As we're sitting comfortably, I'm going to tell you a story. I'm going to tell you it all.'

Rennie talked.

And when he had finished, night had descended.

7

'So now you know,' said Rennie at last.

Callender had sat silently throughout, knitting his fingers into a cats-cradle. His face lay heavily in the shadow of oncoming night and Rennie could discern no emotion there. There was a pause when Rennie finished speaking. Callender gave a small library cough and motioned to the lamp on the small table at his side. 'Do you mind?'

Rennie nodded. Callender switched it on. Even though he was now sitting in an orange spotlight, Rennie could still see no response to his story on Callender's face.

'Now what?' asked the older man.

Rennie looked down at the Smith and Wesson in his hand, gave a small, rueful laugh, and then threw the gun across to Callender. The old man caught it in surprise.

'Now you can call the police. You're right . . . I could never use that thing.'

Callender weighed the gun thoughtfully in his hand as Rennie sat back, massaging his neck. His muscles were tense and aching. Slowly, Callender stood up and moved to the telephone. His eyes remained on Rennie as he lifted the receiver. Rennie's eyes were shut; he seemed completely unconcerned about what Callender might do.

'You can't expect me to believe any of this. You're obviously well advised about the research programme which took place. But I don't understand why you expect me to swallow all your nonsensical fabrications.'

'Look, Callender. I don't care what you believe. I came here to tell you, that's all. Whether you believe that there's an ulterior motive or not doesn't bother me. You screwed up, Callender. You and your people. That's all there is to it. And things are going to get much, much worse.'

'What are you getting out of this?'

'Once you've turned me in, the worst that can happen is that I go back to prison. As good a place to die as any.'

Callender replaced the receiver.

'I'm starting to believe that *you* believe this baloney. But you can't expect me to believe . . .'

'You can believe what you like. It's all the same to me.'

'I'm intrigued. I can't work out your motive.'

'Maybe I don't have one. Maybe I'm telling the truth.'

Callender leaned against the table, Smith and Wesson still aimed at Rennie.

'Do you mind if I search you?'

Rennie stood up wearily. 'You've got the gun. Why should I mind?'

Callender moved across as Rennie turned his back on him, holding his hands high. The older man began to search his pockets and waistband. Rennie laughed. 'This is like being inside again. What you expecting to find? Bugs?'

'Exactly. Now, if you don't mind . . . just to be on the safe side, we'll move into the kitchen to continue our conversation You're not wired, but you may have had time to wire the room.'

Rennie lowered his hands and turned. 'So lead the way.'

'After you. Through the door there.'

Rennie acceded, stopping briefly beside the whisky decanter. 'You mind?'

'By all means.' Rennie picked it up and headed for the door.

The kitchen was almost as big as the drawing room. Gleaming and immaculately fitted. Rennie laughed at the extravagant luxury. 'Where I come from, a family of six would give their eye teeth to *live* in a room like this.' In the centre of the kitchen, he turned back to see Callender moving to the sink. Still with both eyes on Rennie, he turned on the cold tap.

'You want me to do the washing up?'

'A precaution. If the kitchen is wired, it'll drown the conversation.'

'Neat. You should be on "Mission Impossible".'

'All right. Who sent you? Fulwell? Greaves?'

'Those names mean nothing to me. Nobody sent me.'

'They were colleagues of mine during the research. They knew how . . . troubled I was about the terms of reference of the research, how interested I was in the unexpected psychic developments.'

Rennie took a tumbler from a shelf and poured himself a large whisky. Callender raised the gun threateningly. Rennie paused, looking at the gun. 'Believe me, you'd be doing me a big favour . . .' He swallowed the whisky, grimacing at the burning sensation inside. 'I'm sure that Eddie . . . *it* . . . has much more interesting things planned for me.'

'You're trying to tell me that we conjured up . . . a *demon*?'

'No, I'm not. For a scientist, you're not very quick on the uptake, are you? Call it . . . negative energy. In big grown-up type words . . . an accumulation of negative energy drained from human subjects (not bad for a garage mechanic, eh?) . . . and stored in that fucking House like . . . like a battery. It discharged into Archie Duncan – and then into Eddie.'

'You called it Evil? Like the Devil? Satan? Lucifer? What?'

'You still don't get it, do you?' Angrily, Rennie poured himself another drink. 'It's not the Devil, it's not a demon. I was *inside* it. It . . . touched me . . . and I felt it like I've never felt anything before. I know what it is, all right. It's not Satan, not Lucifer . . . not anything like that. That's the fucking joke! That's what means there's no hope for us.'

'Then what . . .?'

'It's *human*, Callender. That's all. Human.' Rennie paused to drink again, the words costing him great effort;

361

familiar nausea gripping his bowels and stomach at the thought of the horrible, intimate embrace of the Thing. When he spoke again, the anger had gone from his voice; he sounded dreadfully weary. 'You're the philosopher, not me. But this Thing . . . it's the dark side of *us*. All of us. It's the human energy behind every atrocity, every massacre, everything bad about us. It's . . . what's his name, that crazy Roman guy? Caligula. It's Auschwitz. It's death and torture and all the other things we call "evil". You distilled it, Callender. You gave life to a spiritual cancer. You and your clever bastards distilled it, and it created its own *personality* . . .'

'Evil personified. You're saying it's incarnate and intelligent. Independent, active and sentient − with supernatural powers.'

'Big words, Callender. Not sure I understand all that. But you're on the right track, at last.'

'No . . . no . . . I can't accept that. There is no such thing as spiritual evil. And we certainly haven't harnessed it in the way you're suggesting. It's impossible . . . impossible . . .'

'Open your eyes, Callender. It's started already. Can't you see what's happening on the streets? Eddie's Frighteners are out there now. And they're spreading and getting stronger.'

'The negative energy you talk about was dissipated from the subjects. We were only interested in the positive side of man's nature. There were indications which promised exciting possibilities: of *developing* man spiritually, not *regressing* him. And supernatural powers . . . well, really, that's all late night movie material.'

'Duncan? What about Duncan?'

'Psychotic and retarded. Nothing supernatural there. Our work was . . . well, sensitive . . . After the Duncan incident, it's not surprising that the Government withdrew funds and enacted statutory . . .'

'You're frightened!' said Rennie at last, realisation dawning. 'You're saying all these things, but you know I'm right. You don't believe a word of what you're saying, do you? *Do you?*'

'That's enough. I'm calling the police. Back in the drawing room.' Callender waved the gun in the direction they'd come from.

'You stupid jerk. I've told you how it is. And I know you believe it, even if you won't admit it. Go ahead, then. Make your call.'

8

Rennie let himself be taken back to the room they'd just left, allowing himself only one backward glance as they re-entered. 'Nice tour you're giving me of the place,' he said without humour. He kept on walking, stopping at the bookshelves again and running his fingers absently over the spines.

'Don't try to get away,' said Callender, picking up the telephone receiver once more.

'Don't be stupid. I've got nowhere to run.'

A book slipped from its place and fell to the floor at Rennie's feet. He picked it up and smiled ruefully. '*Dr Jekyll and Mr Hyde* again. Neat.'

'Hello, police. My name is Callender. Sir James Callender.'

Rennie opened the book randomly again, and read aloud: ' "Instantly, the spirit of hell awakened in me and raged." '

Callender saw Rennie look up at him as he spoke, saw him pause and then open his mouth to speak. And then he saw the look of doubt spread on his face; a look of doubt which was somehow now becoming an expression of *pain*. Callender heard the voice on the other end of the line, saying something that he could not make out . . . and then understood the reason for the strange expression on Rennie's face. He could feel it now — in the air.

He was smothered in an oppressive *heaviness* which instantly reminded him of his time abroad before monsoon weather, but was much, much worse. And getting worse by the second. He saw Rennie put his hands to his ears, as if trying to block out some noise. But there was no noise . . . only a swelling feeling behind the eyes that was beginning to hurt him now, too. The air had somehow become vibrant; he could feel it, could taste it. His vision stretched like elastic and he reeled, grabbing at the table for support.

Rennie was moving fast across the carpet towards him now, with alarm on his face, arms outstretched. Was he trying to get the gun? Callender brought it up, feeling that swelling inside reach a crescendo, hearing Rennie say 'Something's coming . . .' He quickly levelled the gun at Rennie's head, squeezing the trigger.

The effect seemed immediate. There was a shattering detonation. But he knew instantly, in the split-second that he was hurled to the floor, that it was much too loud and too powerful to have been caused by the gun. In a blur, he saw the French windows at the far end of the lounge and the bookcases on either side of them erupt in a chaotic, explosive cloud of shattered glass and shredded paper. The cloud engulfed Rennie. Something hard, like splintered wood, cracked across the bridge of his nose, and for a while he drifted away from his body into that roaring, erupting chaos.

The blast caught Rennie squarely, lifting him off his feet. Savage pain, like liquid fire, seared his back. His coat was shredded instantly, jagged triangles of glass embedding in his flesh. *I'm in the car! Eddie, watch the pram, for Christ's sake!* In a ridiculous freeze-frame, Rennie saw Callender on the floor below him, and thought: *You're not Eddie.* The roar of the explosion smothered him then, and he collided with the sofa, sending it spinning away as he bounced from the deep-pile carpet and sprawled awkwardly across the fender. He lay there, arching his back and gasping at the agonising pain in his back. He knew that it was flayed.

The roaring subsided into a low grumbling, but now the room was filled with a great wind which appeared to be gusting in through the shattered French windows. Back still arched, feeling that he was on fire, Rennie struggled up on one elbow and looked back.

A whirlwind had appeared in the room. Where the French windows and the bookcases had exploded raged a spinning, twisting column of debris. Torn books, madly undulating masses of torn bindings and paper spun and twisted amidst sprays of broken glass and shattered wood. Rennie saw Callender begin to clamber to his knees, mouth open and gasping against the gale. The mirrors on the wall, the framed painting, the glasses and the bottles on the bar began to shatter explosively one by one. The glass chandelier overhead suddenly blew apart, showering them with more glass.

Rennie clutched at the marble fender, hauling himself painfully to his feet. He pushed a hand behind him, feeling the shredded fabric and his gashed skin. When he brought it back to his face, it was covered in blood. Beyond, the maelstrom continued to suck in all the debris around it. The spinning vortex of torn books, glass and broken wood was making a mad, susurrant, flapping sound, like a massive flock of hellish birds on hell-bound wings.

Senses now returned, Rennie looked at that maelstrom and *knew*.

Something was beginning to take shape.

Over the insane flapping and rending of the sucking wind, he heard Callender gabbling: '. . . a bomb? A *bomb*? . . .' and thrust himself away from the fireplace. Without thinking, mind and bowels and sick apprehension focused on the whirling wind and its ever-solidifying centre, he blundered forward and seized the floundering Callender under the arms. He hauled him to his feet, despite the agony in his own back. Callender was still dazed, unresponsive to his grip. Rennie yelled out loud, thrusting one of Callender's arms over his shoulder and hauling hard.

He cast one long look back at the whirling, ever-solidifying vortex.

'Eddie, for God's sake, Eddie . . .'

The howling, spinning vortex was taking on a rough but distinct man-shaped form.

'What . . .?' began Callender, now focusing on what was taking place.

'It's one of Edd . . . it's Frighteners!' shouted Rennie, dragging Callender towards the door. 'Nothing for you to worry about, you bastard. You don't want to believe it . . . maybe it'll go away.'

Gaining bulk and substance, the thing within the whirlwind began to be cognisant of its creation. With intent, it mustered and breathed. And then it stepped into the room.

Rennie burst into the hall, still dragging Callender.

'My car . . .' struggled Callender. '. . . my car . . . in the garage.'

Rennie kicked the hall door shut with one foot and dragged Callender back to the kitchen, now resenting his dazedness. 'Come on, come on . . . WAKE UP!' In the kitchen he pitched him forwards like a sack of potatoes, uncaring of where and how he might fall; aware only on his peripheral vision of the solidifying, walking, sickening *something* only yards away from them in another room. Callender grabbed at a worktop, hand wavering to his head. Already, a bruise like a kiwi fruit was forming over his eye.

Rennie slammed the kitchen door, breath tortured. Leaning against it, he shouted: 'Garage, garage, garage! Where the fuck's the garage, Callender?' On the other side of the door, the raging wind seemed to have died to a whisper. But something in the hall was walking with a heavy and *rustling* tread. Callender seemed to have rallied. He pushed himself towards the side door which Rennie had observed earlier. His propulsion and weight snapped the door open with a shuddering thud. Rennie followed hastily, brought up sharply when Callender braced himself on some kind of stair rail at his left and stabbed out with his right hand at a light switch on the wall. Their bodies collided roughly, the light came on and now they were clattering down a small wooden flight of stairs into the garage. Breath whooping in his lungs, Rennie swung back and slammed the door, fumbling for some kind of lock. His fingers found a thick bolt in its clasps. He shoved it home hard, skinning his fingers, finding the end-piece in its hasp and flicking it down. He plunged down the stairs.

'*No, no, no, no . . . no! I'm breathing too hard. I'm panicking. I'm going to lose it. I'm going to die. Slow, slow, slow . . .*'

The garage was three times the size of the one that Eddie and Rennie had owned, with Callender's car parked sedately and snugly on the inside, nose up against a workbench strewn with unknightly, cobweb-ridden junk. Rennie passed Callender at the foot of the stairs, lunging for the car.

'Keys, old man! Give me the keys!' He whirled back to Callender, hand thrust out.

Callender fumbled weakly in his pocket, and then remembered. 'I haven't got them. They're on the table by the telephone.'

Rennie moaned. 'Garage door?'

'On the same key ring.'

'Oh, *fuck!*' Rennie dashed to the garage doors, hitting them hard with the palms of his hands and wincing at the pain in his back. The doors rumbled, but remained locked. He stabbed higher up. The doors did not budge. And behind them, the door from the hall leading into the kitchen burst asunder with an explosive crash. Callender whirled from his support on the banister at the foot of the stairs and backed off. After the crash, nothing . . . only silence. Mind spinning, swamped with a horrified dread, Rennie moved back to Callender's car, bracing his hands on the boot.

'It's outside,' whispered Callender. 'I can hear it.'

Something heavy and sharp scraped deliberately and slowly on the door to the kitchen.

Rennie heard something laugh on the other side. Fear seized him. It was laughter that he recognised.

'Oh no, no, no . . .'

'*Don't you love me any more?*' whispered Florinda, in an echoing voice from behind the door.

Oh no. Florinda. Oh God in Heaven, not you.

'*You've loved me before. Love me again.*'

Callender looked at him in confusion.

'*Eddie's waiting for you at Lime Street, Rennie. He sent me for you.*

'You evil bastard!' yelled Rennie. 'You're not real!'

Something bumped against the door. The bolt shuddered in its hasps.

'*Is there anything in the dark, Rennie?*' asked Russell. *Are you sure that there's nothing in the dark?*'

'. . . no . . .' Rennie heard himself say.

'*But there* IS!' The door shuddered and cracked.

Rennie banged his hands down hard on the boot. 'You're not real! You lying bastard, you're not REAL!'

'But . . .' Callender turned back to Rennie. 'There's a mistake. There must be. It's a woman, and a child.'

'It's *death*, Callender.'

'How can we stop it? There must . . .'

'We can't stop it. It's not human. I've seen how he makes these things — from junk, from bits and pieces, *anything!*'

And then a thought flashed through Rennie's mind. A flashback to the time he'd answered Russell's question about things in the dark by saying, *That's just storybook stuff.*

'Storybooks,' said Rennie, moving around the boot of the car. 'Books . . . books . . . is that what you've done, Eddie? Is *that* what it's made from?'

Something slammed hard against the door. One savage and bluntly confident blow. Rust flaked from the hinges.

'Get out of my way!' Rennie shouldered Callender to one side, lunged to the rough workbench in front of the car and swept its contents savagely to one side. Glass shattered, dust flew. He grabbed at some decayed and blistered rubber tubing, fumbled for a tatty wine-rack. There was one cobwebbed, unbroken, empty bottle there. He seized the tubing and the bottle by its neck.

I thought you wanted to die, said an internal Mickey Mouse voice. *I thought you were going to tell him, then lie down and let it happen.*'

Like hell!

Another blow on the door; splintered cracks of light began to appear.

'What are you doing?' shouted Callender, eyes flicking from the door to Rennie and back again.

'Shut up!'

Rennie ran back to the car, dumped the tubing and the bottle on the floor and began to twist off the cap on the petrol tank.

RENNNNNNNNNIIIIEEEE!' screamed a voice that was neither woman nor child, nor even human. The entire door frame juddered under the next savage blow; the cracks bulged and widened.

Rennie looked back at the door, awaiting an explosive tornado such as had demolished the French windows and bookcases. The cap rattled to the ground. Rennie shoved the hose into the car's tank as far as it would go, ducking down swiftly and shoving the other end into his mouth. He sucked desperately: once, twice, three times.

The garage door *cracked!* Something long, like a ragged arm, burst through a splintered aperture. It writhed, twisted . . . and was rapidly withdrawn again.

'What are you *doing*?' Callender blundered towards Rennie.

Rennie drew breath, keeping his thumb over the end of the hose. 'Books . . . paper . . . maybe it'll burn.'

'Paper?' shouted Callender. Another shattering blow sent a spar of the door's panelling whirling into the garage. '*Paper!* How can something made of paper hurt us . . .?'

Rennie hurriedly slipped his mouth over the hose again and sucked. Almost immediately, his mouth was filled with petrol. He gagged and spat it on the floor, holding the hose away from him. Some of it splashed down the side of the car before he nipped his thumb over the end of the tube. Another shuddering blow, and another length of panelling whipped into the garage. Callender ducked to avoid it. Rennie plucked the wine bottle from the floor and shoved the hose into its neck. Instantly, it began to fill with petrol.

No, no, no . . . I'd rather do it myself . . . in my own time . . . I don't want to die. I don't want to die.

He discarded the hose in a spray of petrol, running back to the bench in front of the car. There were rags there; dirty, grease-smeared rags. He grabbed them, stuffing them into the neck of the petrol-filled bottle. Standing back now, looking up the stairs at the splintered door, beyond which he could see an indistinct but horrifying form, he knelt quickly, placed the bottle on the ground and fumbled for the matches in his pocket. His hands were shaking badly; a dozen of them fell from his clumsy fingers. *Come on!* He struck them together, hands still shaking as he applied the flame to the rags.

The upper half of the garage door imploded. At last, they had a proper view of the thing. Rennie heard Callender moan, 'Oh, my good Christ . . .' as the ragged, compacted, man-shaped mass thrashed at the remaining wood. Rennie felt like crying, he could feel it like a child inside. It was the same feeling he had experienced before in the presence of Eddie's Frighteners; only this time, his fear and hopelessness threatened to overwhelm him as he moved to the foot of the stairs below the thing. He could see the stiff, *papier-mâché* no-face of the thing with its hollowed eyes and statue features as it tore the remnants of that door apart with its ragged black-white arms of compacted pages, broken wood and glinting glass. It stepped through the ragged gap and paused, looking down.

Rennie was swamped by the horrifying presence of the thing. He could not move . . . and he knew that he would only be able to stand and watch as the thing descended the stairs, took him by the neck and tore him apart.

'Eddie . . .' His voice contained a childlike plea.

The thing placed one ragged foot on the top step and began to descend.

And then the burning rag in the neck of the wine bottle flared on Rennie's wrist. The stabbing pain shocked him from his paralysis.

'Burn, you bastard! *Burn!*' He flung the blazing wine bottle at it.

The bottle shattered on its chest. With a crackling *whump!* the thing's upper torso and head were instantly wreathed in a surging blue and yellow flame. Its arms flailed; sparks and burning paper flaked from it. But it continued its awkward descent.

Rennie grabbed Callender and pulled him roughly to the car. Gritting his teeth, he jerked an elbow at the side window. Once, twice . . . and the glass cobwebbed. Three times, and it crumbled inwards. Leaning in, he flicked the lock button and yanked the door open.

'Get in!'

'The garage doors . . .'

'*Get in!*'

The thing was still clawing at the ever surging flame, trying to beat it out as it came. Was its vision obscured? Rennie spun to the front of the car as Callender climbed inside, and yanked the bonnet open. The thing blundered against the wall, sparks and soot flying, and then against the wooden stair rail, snapping it with one flailing arm of fire. Rennie fumbled at the transmission wiring. The engine coughed into life.

'Rev the engine, Callender! Rev it!'

Callender frantically did as he was told. The engine began to roar, exhaust fumes coughing into the garage. Rennie slammed the bonnet shut, made ready to hurl himself into the car . . . and then saw the blazing flurry of motion, fireballing in his direction. The thing had reached the foot of the stairs and launched itself at him, arms held wide to embrace him in fire.

Rennie cried out, throwing himself away from the bonnet to the far side of the car. In a headlong, blundering lunge, the burning man-shape collided with the car, rocking it on its suspension. Flame transferred to the overspill of petrol on the car's side. Rennie remained flattened against the wall as the thing groped with burning arms across the roof of the car, trying to reach him. Rennie choked on smoke and slid farther away along the wall. The thing tried to compensate, lunging at him as it moved towards the front of the car, intent on seizing him.

He was almost at the rear of the car, ready to skip round it, when Callender slammed the gears into reverse. Rennie flattened himself against the wall again as the car roared away . . . leaving him completely exposed.

Callender, you bastard!

He ran wildly across the garage, seeing that the thing had been caught off balance by the car's departure. It had fallen to the floor in a blazing mass, but was even now clambering awkwardly to a kneeling position in its wreath of flame. The car, still burning on the passenger side, slammed into the garage doors, buckling the metal. The hinges screeched. Rennie whirled to look, seeing the car roar forward again, brake . . . and then screech back into the doors, buckling them further and shattering the rear window. Callender repeated the manoeuvre again and again, screeching and impacting. The guttering flame on the side of its bodywork was snuffed out.

Now completely smothered in roaring orange flame, the shape stood upright again. Arms weaving, it turned in Rennie's direction.

Rennie collided with the far wall, wincing at the pain in his shredded back, gasping for breath. Garden tools clattered at his feet. Was the thing slowing down? Was it?

The stairs?! Or the garage doors?!

Rennie headed for the stairs, but even slowed down, the thing was already blundering across the garage and would be on him before he could reach them. Running back towards the car would still bring him within the shape's burning embrace. In agitated desperation, Rennie scrabbled at his feet for the garden tools, his fingers connecting with a rake.

'*Come on!*' He flung the rake sideways in a whirling arc. It slapped against the thing's blazing torso, the impact sending up a showering cloud of sparks. Behind it, he heard the car slam into the garage doors again; heard the agonised, rending screech of the hinges. The thing was still coming, arms weaving. '*Come on . . . come on . . . come on . . .*' Rennie clawed at the floor again. The shape was less than twenty feet away. '*Come on . . .*' The spade felt like a weapon, and as he stood up with it in his hands, something

373

profoundly instinctive blossomed in him. Something that transformed stark terror, and the certain knowledge that death was a second away, into a desperate aggression. Something that made Rennie scream, *'Come!on!THEN!'* as he lunged forward to meet the thing's blazing approach, wielding the spade like an axe.

The blade bit savagely into the side of the thing's neck, all Rennie's weight behind that blow. Sparks and burning paper *whumped* in the air as the thing staggered to one side, dislodging the spade. Rennie screamed again bringing the spade back on its upswing, the flat of the blade slapping squarely into the thing's face. It tottered and stood back.

Rennie lost his mind then.

Screaming, he swung blow after blow at the burning shape, each staggering lurch backwards . . . *backwards* . . . fuelling the primal instinct inside him. Dodging flailing, blazing arms, he continued to hack at it. Roaring, he two-handedly drove the spade like a pike into its chest and ran hard; shoving, shoving, shoving.

The burning mass collided with the workbench at the end of the garage. Tottering, it flailed out again and connected with the spade's shaft. The spade was wrenched from Rennie's hands; it spun clattering away. The thing began to rally, looming gigantically over Rennie as he stood there, sobbing and now drained by his attack of any further initiative.

'GET OUT OF THE WAY!' yelled Callender from the car's driving seat.

Rennie whirled as Callender shifted gears again and the car screeched forward directly towards them. Rennie spun to avoid it, but not quickly enough. The front wing clipped him, scooping him up and rolling him headlong out of the way. The car smashed into the burning man-shape and ploughed right on through the workbench. It collided with the garage wall in an explosion of splintered wood, a firework display of gushing orange sparks and black smoke. The thing was pinned against the wall, arms still thrashing weakly on the buckled bonnet. Rennie hauled himself to his knees and shouted, 'Yes! Yes! Yes!' as Callender screeched into reverse once more, and the burning, ragged shape began to lose its form in a crumbling, flaming mass. The car squealed to a halt and then roared forward again, tyres spinning as the shape tried to rise on disintegrating legs.

For a second time, the car slammed into the garage wall. The Frightener exploded on contact, like a collapsing bonfire. Sparks and burning paper showered the air. Dense black smoke enfolded Rennie as he staggered to his feet and Callender reversed out of the burning debris at the foot of the garage wall. The car stopped, engine growling like a vengeful beast. On the verge of collapse, Rennie hauled open the rear door and fell across the seats.

Callender thrust into reverse again. The car roared backwards, the rear door slamming. This time, the garage doors buckled and collapsed on impact. The car hurtled out of the garage, taking the doors with it. Smoke gushed out after them.

Callender executed a brutal, screeching three-point turn. Battered, burnt and with metal trimwork squealing in protest, the car headed down the drive towards the gates.

From where he lay, bouncing on the back seat, Rennie became aware of the sound of sirens from somewhere ahead.

'Police,' said Callender from the front.

'You still . . . you still going to turn me in?'

'No, I don't think so. First, we'll get you to a doctor.'

'Callender?'

'Yes?'

'Don't believe for one moment that it's over.'

'I believe you.'

The car stopped. Rennie could see blue light dancing on its ceiling.

And then he slept.

9

Extract: La Stampa, Italy

The Police Commission's Executive Committee, with special government powers, have as yet been unsuccessful in their attempts to discover the exact reasons for the violent internal conflict currently taking place within the Mafia. Despite several testimonies from ex-Mafia 'capos' who have sought government protection in recent weeks, no evidence of a specific bid for control within the ranks of the Mafia is apparent.

The current wave of violence resulting in the deaths of so many long-established Mafiosi has now, it seems, extended to other parts of the community in a wave of senseless and brutal violence . . .

Extract: New York Times

'Is this the beginning of a New Age?' the English tabloids have been asking in recent months. The American public, observing the violence with which the Anglo-organised-crime network has been tearing itself apart without any apparent initiative for that destruction from the police, has perhaps been asking itself the same question. And from that question comes another question: could we also hope to be so lucky on this side of the water?

In recent times, we have seen the development of 'organised crime' in England on the lines of the American model. In 'Gang Warfare: A Probe into the Changing pattern of British Crime', Judge Gerald Sparrow observes that the English gang leader has 'rationalised crime. He is no longer a brilliant lone operator. He and his friends are highly organised, highly specialised, and they represent a new challenge to society as a whole, far more menacing and a good deal more dangerous than any challenge to law and order in the past. For the first time in our rapidly changing pattern of British life, that gang leader now emerges as a secret figure, but perhaps in the years to come, with waxing wealth and increasing power, as a public figure rivalling the tycoon and politician.'

Judge Sparrow's words were prophetic. But the reasons behind the sudden and apparently self-destructive purges within English criminal society have so far been resistant to analysis. Now, of course, we are seeing the same developments in American organised criminal activity. Something is happening in the Underworld. The drug barons, the extortionists, the corrupters, the highest-of-the-criminal-high in our own cities have caught this strange and mysterious 'disease' from their English counterparts. What is happening? How is the hysteria generating itself? Even now, as in Italy and Germany, we can see this carnage spilling out onto the innocents. Motiveless, brutal murder has always been a feature of the disease in our society, but this disease is a rampaging epidemic, completely out of control.

Extract: Le Monde, France

The cloud of poisonous gas released by the generator explosion in Peralt now covers a one hundred kilometre area and continues to spread. Emergency measures to disperse the deadly toxic chemical continue but there are major concerns about the consequences of any weather variation such as rain or strong winds, which will only serve to escalate this terrible threat. Speculation that the explosion was not accidental, but was caused by a terrorist attack, are still unsubstantiated.

10

'What does it want, Montresor?'

'Want?'

'This thing must have a purpose. Now that it has full power, now that it has a personality, it must want something.'

'It wants nothing, Callender.'

'Dominion? Is that what it wants?'

'It has no great plan. It simply exists to destroy. I thought you understood all this, by now. It takes pleasure from death, from pain . . .'

'Then we must obliterate it.'

'And how do you intend to do that?'

'We'll obliterate Lime Street, with missiles if necessary.'

'It'll never allow you. Believe me, I've seen what it can do. It can even stop time if it wants to.'

'Preposterous.'

'Yeah, just like Paper Men.'

'We'll wipe that House out, along with Brinkburn . . .'

'It's not Eddie, any more. He's long dead. Even if you could launch some kind of attack on the place, are you trying to tell me that *you've* got the power to do that? *Sir* James Callender with his finger on the red button? Good old *Sir* James who was shunted into a corner after the research went wrong.'

'We have to talk to the right people about this. We have to explain what's going on . . .'

'You're still full of shit. Who the hell's going to believe us? *You* wouldn't have believed *me* if Eddie . . . I mean, the *Thing* . . . hadn't sent that thing to get me.'

'We've got to try.'

'Yeah . . .yeah . . . but we're on borrowed time, Callender. Don't forget that. We got away once, but it can send something else at any time. And this time, it's not just me it's after . . . it's you.'

'All right, Montresor. I believe you. But before we start, there's somewhere I want to take you.'

'Where?'

'Not far from here. It won't take long.'

'You going to tell me where?'

'No. When we get there, I'll explain.'

'Why should I want to die when life's so full of fun? A *mystery* trip, for crying out loud.'

11

'Peter, sit up straight and pay attention. Now that's a *good* boy. Neal? Are you listening? Good . . .'

She moved back to the blackboard, smiling.

'Now does anyone know what this is?'

'*It's Treblinka, Miss.*'

'Good, well done, Janet. And what happened there?'

'*Nice things.*'

'Yes, that's right. What kind of nice things . . . Tony?'

'*People were tortured and killed. Lots of people.*'

'That's good. Now . . . let's look at the next picture. Does anyone know what *this* is?'

'*Mi Lai.*'

'Yes. And next?'

'*Hiroshima and Nagasaki.*'

'And what is the truth, my darlings?'

'*The truth is that all shall die, all shall suffer.*'

'They fly by night and look for children without nurses, snatch them from their cradles and defile their bodies. They are said to lacerate the entrails of infants with their beaks and they have their throats full of the blood they have drunk.'

'*All is without hope. All is death. All blood, all pain . . .*'

She smiled as she stepped down from the blackboard, waving her hands at the class as if conducting an orchestra. They joined in with her as she reached beneath the desk to retrieve what she had put there earlier.

'*Do lurk in shrines, in roods, in crosses, in images: and*

*first of all pervert the priests, which are easiest to be caught
with bait of a little gain.'*

She picked up the petrol can and unscrewed the cap. Still
smiling, she began to walk down the centre aisle, splashing
the petrol on the floor and on the desks.

*'To work we miracles. To appear to men in divers shapes;
disquiet them when they are awake.'*

When the can was empty, she took out the matches and
began to strike.

*'Trouble them in their sleep; distort their members; take
away their health; afflict them with diseases.'*

She clapped her hands in joy when the match flared. She
dropped it at her feet and joined in again as the flames began
to surge and spread in the classroom.

'Only to bring them to some Idolatry.'

The flames hungrily devoured.

12

He had travelled this street before when the urge had become too much. He hated it because of the way it made him feel afterwards. But he loved it, too. Loved it because of the way it made him feel: breathless, excited, mouth dry, face perspiring. And, of course, it was a dangerous place to be. Dangerous not only for his health, perhaps (wasn't he a vigorous campaigner in favour of the Government Health Warnings on television), but also for the threat to his position should he ever be recognised. So . . . hating and loving it, he cruised the street in the car he always hired especially for the occasion, and felt the sweat beading on his body, felt the shirt clinging to his back under an expensive Savile Row suit.

Tonight, the street seemed different in a way that he could not immediately discern. Still the same late night peep-shows, take-away food shops, dirty garbage-strewn alleys, run-down shops and leaking gutters. Still the same promising shadows in doorways; the others, not so shy . . . to use an inappropriate and unbusinesslike word . . . standing in the glare of neon, waiting for custom.

What was it that seemed so different, then?

Their faces. That's what it is. Realisation dawned at last. He strained to look at each new face as he cruised. They all watched him passing, but made no attempt, as they usually did, to flag him down and make their bids. All the faces seemed to hold the same curiously *blank* look. In the neon lights, it seemed as if their eyes all glittered with that same alien amusement. Perhaps he was over-tired, perhaps even over-excited.

He stopped the car and rolled down the window.

A girl in a black leather skirt was sitting on the cill of a decrepit foodstore frontage. Dyed blonde hair, heavy mascara, tattoos on both arms. She looked at him with that strange blank look, deep-set eyes glittering. She unnerved him, but not enough to prevent him leaning out of the window and saying:

'Hello, my name's Tom.'

'No it's not,' said the girl.

He smiled nervously, not sure now whether he should roll up the window and drive on; maybe call it a night and go home to his wife and hot cocoa and the late night film on television.

'But it doesn't matter.' The girl pushed herself from the cill and walked slowly over to the car. The movement of her hips under that skirt dispelled his uncertainty. She moved slowly round the bonnet, trailing black varnished fingernails across it until she had reached the passenger door. Her leather skirt rode up, revealing more thigh as she climbed in and slammed the door. Still somehow unable to look at the girl's eyes, he said:

'I like it oral.'

'So let's find a quiet place.'

Fingers trembling, he shoved the gears into first and cruised off.

'Oral for an orator,' she said, when the car had reached the end of the street.

Oh God, she knows me! She recognises me!

She caressed his hand on the steering wheel, and he could feel a tingling *something* in that touch that was infinitely promising; so promising that his fears were immediately allayed. He felt that touch surging and blossoming in his veins like some forbidden and exciting drug.

'Let me give you something interesting to take back. Something from my Ministry to your Ministry.'

He drove on, uncaring.

Behind them, two dozen faces watched them depart into the night. When the darkness had enfolded them, the faces smiled and turned back to the street as one; waiting for more, even if it might be less important, custom.

13

They had been travelling south for twenty minutes when Rennie said, 'Nice car.'

'Thank you,' said Callender from the driving seat. 'Good value for money, too.'

'Never worked under one of these before.'

'Ah, yes. You were a garage mechanic.'

'One of the best. But Eddie was the one with the golden fingers. Grease fingers.'

'Grease fingers?'

'Same as green fingers for gardens. Grease fingers for engines.'

'Oh, I see.'

'Come on, Callender. Where the hell are you taking me?'

'It's really best that I show you. How's your back?'

'Okay. Your people did a good job on it.'

They continued the drive in silence, but now the journey reminded Rennie of the drive Eddie and he had made to the House on Lime Street. There had been mysteries then; mysteries and unanswered questions. It was the same now. It was like some kind of pattern, some kind of ritual. He shifted again in his seat to get a more comfortable position for his back, and decided to go along with the flow of it. Even the tree-lined avenue along which they were travelling reminded him of Lime Street.

Lost in day-dreams, none of them pleasant, he became suddenly aware that they had arrived at a wrought-iron gate. Two men in uniforms were moving towards the car. More uncomfortable reminders of Lime Street and the things that had only looked like security guards. Rennie read the sign on the gate behind the approaching men: *Janus Corporation*.

'Janus?'

'For Janus . . . read Callender.'

The men reached the car as Callender rolled down the window and proffered an identity card. The first man took it, examined it and handed it back.

'Good afternoon, Sir James.'

'Hello, Bob.'

The guards waved back at the gate. It began to open, operated apparently by invisible hands.

They drove through, continuing down another tree-lined drive towards a single-storey building ahead. It looked bland and innocuous.

'Looks like an old folks' home or something,' said Rennie.

'That's what you're supposed to think.'

'Must have some pretty freaky old people in here if you have to have guards on the place.'

'Just security, that's all.'

As they approached the white stone building, Rennie half expected to see two stone lions at the top of a stone staircase; just to make the comparison complete. There were none . . . but there were two further security men standing at the main entrance. Like their counterparts at the gate, they approached as the car drew near. Callender stopped the car again and proffered his card.

'How come I don't need one?'

'This will do for both of us.'

'Pretty shitty security, if you ask me.'

'It's served us well so far.'

With the car parked at the entrance, Callender led Rennie through the main reception doors past the security men's post, and into the building. It had the antiseptic smell of a hospital.

'What's it like, being rich?' asked Rennie as they walked, feet ringing and echoing in the cool, blue-tiled corridor.

'You think I'm rich?'

Rennie spread his hands, gesturing at the building around them, as if this provided conclusive proof.

'Yes . . . I suppose I am. Never thought about it. What's it like being poor?'

'Doesn't matter who's rich or who's poor. Who's black or who's white. Who's right or wrong. The way things are going, we're all going to be dead meat soon, anyway.'

'Maybe not.'

They had reached the end of the corridor. There was an office there, and a large padded door with a security window. A slight, balding man with spectacles emerged from the office carrying a clipboard. He appeared agitated when he saw Rennie.

'I don't understand, Sir James. Do we . . .?'

'It's all right, Desmond. Let us in, please.'

Grudgingly, the man moved to the padded door and pressed a button at the side of the window.

'You're hiding something here,' said Rennie.

Callender merely smiled.

'Something dangerous.'

'You're right when you say I'm hiding something, but you're wrong about it being dangerous. They're not dangerous at all.'

'They?'

The security window opened. For an instant, a woman's face was framed there. Dark hair, pale face, dark eyes. A businesslike, no-nonsense face. The window was flapped shut again. Rennie heard some kind of internal mechanism being operated within the door, and then it opened.

Callender walked ahead, beckoning Rennie to follow. Desmond remained behind as the door was closed again behind them.

Rennie was immediately aware of a low vibration in the air, almost too low to be audible, but registering nevertheless. The entire room seemed to be filled with an invisible but surging power. There was a pervasive violet light in here, too. The same kind of light that Rennie remembered from nightclubs: the kind that made white shirts glow.

Hi-tech, he thought, looking round. *A hi-tech hospital ward*.

There were twelve beds in all: six at either wall, facing each other. And the beds contained six men and six women, all apparently asleep, all of them wired up to appliances at their bedsides. Rennie could see the drip-feeds in their arms, the wiring on their foreheads and bodies, connected to machines that registered heartbeat and vital signs. There were as many men and women in attendance, all wearing sterile white and all apparently unconcerned about his presence; concentrating instead on the job in hand, whatever that might be. Instantly, Rennie was reminded of the House on Lime Street and the dreams he had experienced there. He vividly remembered his dream of Archie Duncan thrashing and screaming on a hospital bed. Now, he knew what was happening. He turned back.

'Callender, you bastard. You're doing the same thing here that you did at Lime Street.'

'That's right, but there's a difference.'

'More poor bastards. More of your bloody brainwashing . . .'

'There's a *difference*, Montresor!'

'What difference?'

'These people are volunteers, not prisoners. You may not believe this . . . but I was never happy with the morality of the Lime Street operation.'

'Oh yeah? So unhappy that you just kept on doing it anyway? It never occurred to you that you should stop it?'

'These people are here of their own free will. The Government knows nothing of this continued operation, and has no control over us here. This is a private institute . . . *my* institute. When the Government withdrew the Lime Street funds, we continued on our own.'

One of the men attending the 'patients' looked up from his work and saw them. Whispering quick instructions to one of the other female 'doctors' beside him, he hurried over. Slight, with neatly parted ginger hair, he had a glow of satisfaction on his face that widened to a broader smile, revealing bad teeth.

'How is everything, Menard?' asked Callender.

'Remarkable, Sir James. Remarkable . . .' It was clear that Menard was much more interested at this moment in Rennie. He held out a hand. 'You must be Mr Montresor.'

'Doctor Menard,' said Callender by way of introduction. 'He's the real guiding light here. The developer of the serums which have resulted in the effect which we've perhaps over-dramatically labelled the "Jekyll and Hyde Syndrome".'

Rennie made no move to shake his hand. Menard appeared unperturbed. 'Its formulaic title is almost unpronounceable, so I'm afraid that melodrama prevails. I've read Sir James' report based on your experiences. Fascinating.'

'Yeah, that's one way of describing it. So you're not content with what happened at Lime Street, you want to make it all happen again here.'

'Oh no, no!' Menard appeared genuinely concerned. 'What happened at Lime Street was an aberration, albeit a fascinating one. When we have more time available to us, I want to discuss with you this principle of an inanimate building being able to store this released energy in the way you describe. But that is not our prime concern here. Our concern is . . . always has been . . . to liberate man.'

'Don't lecture me.'

'No lecture, Mr Montresor. But you know by now the inescapable truth that man is not truly one, but two. We've managed to harness man's psychic self, his soul . . . even if we're still not sure how the effect is actually produced. After the . . . setback . . . at Lime Street, we continued with the research. We had no reason then, you see, to suspect that Duncan's psychotic attack was in any direct way connected with the dispersal of "negative energy" . . . to use your own phrase.'

'Not mine. Lister's.'

'Who?'

'It doesn't matter.'

'There has been no accumulation of that negative energy here. It has been successfully dispersed.'

'We carried on with the research,' continued Callender, 'because we believed that by eliminating the negative energy and developing the positive psychic emanations observed in our volunteers, we could bypass the evolutionary process and develop the latent spiritual powers in man.'

'According to computer analysis,' Menard took over again, 'the people you see here, in these beds, have acquired spiritual and psychic powers which it will take us . . . as a species . . . three million years to develop.'

'Don't you see the value, Montresor? We can never expect to survive in this world to achieve our . . . our sainthood. We're on the verge of destroying ourselves. But if we can develop this wonderful talent, if we project ourselves three million years into the future and avoid the holocaust which we're currently heading for, what wisdom and power we'll have.'

'Saints,' said Rennie quietly. 'You're making saints.'

'Yes . . . yes . . . I suppose we are, if you put it like that.'

'But you've also created demons, Callender. I've seen them. And the greatest Demon of them all is walking the streets.'

'I want you to talk to Menard. I want you to tell him again everything that has happened to you. He already has my report, but I want you to give as much detail as possible. There are a number of scientific . . . tests . . . which I want you to . . .'

'I'm not volunteering to be one of your guinea pigs.'

'No, no . . . nothing like that. But with Menard's guidance, and with the facilities we have available, perhaps we can find a solution to what has happened at Lime Street.'

Rennie turned to the people lying on the beds. The youngest seemed about eighteen years old, the oldest perhaps seventy.

'Saints and demons?' laughed Rennie. 'No . . . no . . . just human. That's all. Just human.'

'Human, yes,' replied Callender. 'But humans as we *will* be . . . not as we are now.'

'Your saints don't seem very active, Callender. Shouldn't they have heavenly smiles and haloes, or something?'

'Therein lies our quandary . . .'

'They're comatose,' said Menard. 'Or in some kind of state related to coma. We can't be sure.'

'They've been like that now for two years,' said Callender. After the advancement of our work . . . after Lime Street . . . our volunteers began to show signs of astonishing, absolutely astonishing, abilities. After a while, there appeared to be a change in their perception patterns. Conversations became . . .'

'Abstract,' continued Menard 'Shortly afterwards, they drifted away from us . . . into their current state. Vital signs have remained normal, very healthy. But ECG readings since that time have indicated substantial dream activity, much more than one might expect, in fact.'

'Maybe they just got bored with all your long words,' said Rennie.

Menard gave a fragile laugh.

Rennie began to walk past the beds, looking at each of the volunteers in turn, as if he was some kind of doctor on duty.

'Must have lots of fancy drugs here, Callender.'

'As I say, I want you to liaise with Dr Menard on . . .'

'Do you have any of the drugs like you see in the movies?'

'What?'

'You know the kind I mean. The kind where you bite down on a capsule and seconds later you're dead. That kind.'

'Well, yes, there are drugs which can . . .'

'Do you have any here?'

'Yes, but . . .'

'Then I want some, Callender. I'll talk as much as you like to Menard. Not that it's going to do much good in the long run, but I'll do the talking. But I'll only do it if you give me something that'll kill me quickly.'

'What in hell for?'

'Like I keep telling you, it's only a matter of time before Eddie sends another Frightener after me. I'm not going to sit and let it tear me apart. You get my drift?'

'Very well. Menard will prepare something.'

'Good. I suggest Menard makes up two prescriptions, Callender. Know what I mean?'

'I know what you mean. But I'll take my chance.'

Rennie laughed ruefully.

14

And Crandall — Eddie Brinkburn's American disciple — begat Shirley Miller, an airline stewardess en route to America from England, who begat John McAndrews, advertising executive, who begat Billy Fenimore, truck driver, who begat Kenneth Grigson, agriculture wholesaler, who begat Donna Hart, prostitute, who begat Donald Starley, who begat Mathew Donall, farm labourer, who begat Annie Donall, farm labourer's wife, who begat Donnie Maxwell, farmer, who begat Al Floret, proprietor: 'Al's Diner', Phoenix, Arizona, who begat James Paisley, Chief Engineer A1 Security clearance, Nuclear Commission.

When it was good, Crandall looked at the sky and said:
    'Do it. Do it, now.'

Smiling, James Paisley . . . Chief Engineer A1 Security clearance, Nuclear Commission, Phoenix, Arizona . . . withdrew the rods.

With the equivalent of one million tons of TNT, the fireball of the nuclear explosion seemed brighter than the sun at noon to observers fifty miles away. Its heat charred the skin and blinded everyone out in the open air. Cars, buses, houses, hospitals, garages, burst into flames. The blast wave instantly transformed sheets of glass, gates, concrete slabs and other structures into a deadly rain of debris. Radiation slashed invisibly through cloth, concrete, metal, wood, flesh and bone. The blast wave and the fireball generated hell-

*winds, fanning fires on the periphery of the blast, linking
together in built-up areas as they were fuelled by blast-
damaged gas mains, petrol stations, paint and furniture
stores. The firestorm would rage until everything
combustible within its area was consumed. Particles from
the burst began to float down in a radioactive blanket of
fallout, ten miles wide and sixty miles long, following the
direction of the wind.*

*Alfredo Andinaro, Willi Brecht and Henri Lefèvre looked
at the sky in their own countries and felt the change in the
air thousands of miles away. They felt the new power surging
in their spirits; the new, blossoming and limitless power.
Smiling, they began to give their own instructions . . .*

* * *

Jason Conway finished doing what he had been doing to
his father's body and wiped his face, leaving a bloody smear.
Grinning, he walked back to the bedroom and shoved open
the door with his foot.

The room had been redecorated. And the donors to that
decoration lay on Jason's bed. Underarm, Jason flung his
father's head at the atrocity that lay there. With a wet smack,
it rolled and nestled between Jason's mother and Uncle Billy;
mouths open, eyes staring from their ragged lovers' embrace.

Jason thought of the things that had to be done. He
turned back into the living-room, walking purposefully
through its chaotic, crimson décor and into the kitchen. He
began to piss in the sink. And then he froze, looking up at
the sky.

It was time. He could feel it. The power was upon him.

Zipping himself up, the last vestiges of his personality and
humanity swilled away from him like the urine swilling away
down the plughole. The Thing inside him was at last truly
born. He headed for the kitchen door.

* * *

Elwyn Gray, embezzler and failed suicide, also felt that

394

change in the air. He released the grip on his employer's wife's neck and let her fall to the floor. Dressing again, he looked out of the bedroom window at the sky. There was no change to be observed by the naked eye; but the stark power that burned in his guts recognised the signals and began to spread and engulf from within.

Time to get even, said the Thing inside.

'Thank you,' said Elwyn as he died.

And then the Businessman headed for the street.

* * *

Burnt and charred, but still alive, the schoolteacher stood in the field behind the blazing schoolhouse and listened to the sound of fire engines drawing near.

'Can I go yet?' she asked, her cindered tongue crumbling in a charcoaled face.

Yes, you are dismissed.

'Th . . . ank . . . you . . .'

Her passing spasmed the fire-ravaged corpse only briefly.

It turned and began to stagger away across the fields towards the city.

* * *

In the time she had spent on the streets, she had learnt one golden rule: honour among whores. There was no need for independents to be competitive, no need for the girls to fall out among themselves. It was different when pimps were involved, of course. She had fallen foul of them before, and knew that their own areas of operation were clearly marked. But for the single girl, trying to earn a living . . . well, why should there be any hassle? Punters were punters. And there was plenty of work around here, without pimps getting involved. The only one who had tried it on by using his muscle had ended up with his baby-making muscle slashed. Since then, no problem. Working girls shared things in times of trouble.

And she had shared her special something with the other girls on the streets. They were all one now. Passing on the message to all who cared to come and fuck at the well.

When the change came over the sky, they all felt it as one. They felt it down in the streets waiting for custom. They felt it in their rooms, pausing in the middle of transactions, to their clients' dismay; felt it in the cars, motels and homes of their clients. They looked to the sky and were fulfilled.

It was time.

15

'It attacked you?' asked Menard. 'Brinkburn's . . . Frightener, as you call it, attacked you both in Sir James' home?'

'Yeah,' replied Rennie, losing patience. 'It did act a little pissed off.'

Menard cleared his throat and gave a weak smile. 'I've discussed this with Sir James, of course. And he's told me more or less what you've just told me. But there is the possibility . . . the possibility . . . that what you *thought* you saw didn't really happen at all. Perhaps some kind of hypnotic effect . . .'

'You've had people up at Callender's home by now. Haven't they seen the damage that's been done to the place? Those French windows, the bookcase. Hell, the thing tore its way through at least two doors. If Callender hadn't rammed the fucking thing to death with his car we would never have got out of there alive.'

'Yes, the damage to the house has been examined. But there's nothing there to give complete credence to what you say. There's considerable damage. But nothing to indicate the intervention of a . . . shall we say, *supernatural* presence.'

'Look! It was there, right? It wanted me dead. This is like another bloody re-run of my conversation with Callender. What does it take, Menard? Another one of Eddie's Frighteners to burst in here? Is that what it takes?'

'I'm not denying that there's something very extraordinary taking place. But I'm just making suppositions

397

that perhaps what you thought you saw was the result of . . .'

'Yeah, yeah. Hypnosis. Everything I've seen, everything that Eddie's done was all fantasy stuff. Even the gashes in my back, right? So all the glass they picked out . . . that was fantasy, too. Right?'

'Maybe a bomb of some kind?'

'But your "people" didn't find any evidence of a bomb, did they?'

'No.'

'So what the hell are you talking about?'

'Tell me again about that night in the street, just after Eddie was released from prison. The night that Sheraton's people tried to set him up.'

'When I saw that thing climbing out of the car engine . . .'

'Saw?'

'Don't try and make me say "thought I saw", Menard. That thing was real.'

'Sorry. Please continue . . .'

16

The Whores walked the streets, hunting for customers.

No need for the night now; no need to hide. No need to be wary of the police; no need to solicit. Only hunger. And the need to feed that hunger. There were changes in the sky, in the air. The Time was Right. In broad daylight they displayed their wares. And the first to meet them — those who did not die — ran screaming and blind and tainted from their approach.

Looking for lovers, they walked. They took the eyes that saw them, and the hideous progeny that sprang from their wombs also hunted in the alleys and the streets for food.

The terror and the death began to spread rapidly.

* * *

The Teacher entered the housing estate bordering the city, looking for pupils. They were easily found, but not so eager to learn. She taught of fire and of death and blood. She spread her lesson to the houses on either side of the street as she walked. Windows exploded, flame blossomed and raged within. People ran shrieking from her class in flames. All she saw as she walked learned their lessons and ran screaming to spread the word. The city drew her. She knew that her sisters were also abroad. They were hungry for love as she was hungry to teach . . . and the city was so full of people who needed to be loved and taught.

Charred and twisted, she moved on through the estate towards the city.

Spreading the word.

17

In life, the Businessman had been taught that the body corporate was the god which he should worship. The Corporation, the Business, the Amalgamation, the Company . . . was all. It owned him body and soul. In a unified and corporate business strategy was power and strength and the main goal in life. He was a cog in the machine, one small part of that body corporate. It was also the body corporate that had led him to open the window and put his foot on the sill, ready to surrender himself to the sky. Down below, his own corporateness, his own wholeness, would be sundered and disintegrated on the blood-splashed pavement. His wholeness would be instantly disassembled in that final concrete embrace. Now . . . he knew a different truth. Strength lay in disassembling, in returning everything to its constituent parts. The body corporate was a Lie.

So now he walked the streets, like his sisters, and preached a new business religion. It was his place, his purpose in his new life to disassemble those persons who tried to run screaming from his approach. It was his task to return them to their own constituent parts.

Behind him, the trail of dismembered limbs, heads and internal organs bore testimony to the Truth of this new Business Religion.

He Walked.

18

And the others walked with them. The Boy who had killed his mother, his father, and Uncle Billy knew now, with his power upon him, that they had escaped his justified wrath. They had escaped from the ruined flesh in the bedroom. Their spirits were hiding. Hiding in every man, woman and child on the streets. And he knew that only when every last hiding place, every flesh-cage, was destroyed . . . only then would Justice Have Been Done. So he walked the streets, calling their names and destroying all he met in whom that Bastard Family were hiding.

19

Rennie felt it first.

Menard's irritating questions were becoming too much, and he felt urgently in need of a drink. The presence of the 'capsule' in his pocket provided a curious kind of security, although he had pushed its use to the back of his mind in an abstract way. Now, his irritation and depression were focused very sharply on a sense that *something* had happened . . . was happening.

'There's a very strong correlation,' continued Menard, 'with Haitian practices. The term "voodoo" is a kind of movie cliché now, isn't it? But it's all to do with the power of the mind, of course. As I've been saying. If a victim "believes", then the power of suggestion, of "hypnosis", can provide exactly the desired effect. That has always been the problem, of course. The refusal to acknowledge that this kind of psychic power has . . . well . . . *power*. Here at Janus, we've . . .'

'Shut up, Menard.'

'. . . discovered that there is an untapped . . . what?'

Rennie held up his hand, rising from the padded leather seat. He looked at the windows, saw nothing, and then at the ceiling.

'Do you think . . .?'

'Shut *up*!' snapped Rennie again, and this time Menard was silent. 'Don't you *feel* anything?'

'What do you mean' "feel"?'

'I don't know . . . I mean . . .' Rennie moved to the windows again and looked out. There was nothing to be seen

402

but the night-shrouded green fields behind the Institute. He turned to Menard again, and this time the feeling swelled inside him, in his stomach. It was like the times he had been out on the town with Eddie after a hard day's work and they'd had too much to drink. When he'd got home, he'd slumped on the bed and everything had started to spin in the darkness. 'The Whirling Pit', Eddie called it. It was the feeling you got just before you knew that you had to be sick. And Rennie had that feeling now . . . 'the Whirling Pit' inside, even though he hadn't had a drink for a while. It was a sickening, cramping, spiralling feeling. The only way to be rid of it was to throw up.

He staggered back to his seat, caught a brief glimpse of Menard's concerned face. And then . . . instead of being sick . . . the feeling inside him resolved itself into something else.

The ground beneath their feet seemed to judder.

Menard staggered. Rennie slumped into the seat. Overhead, the lights flickered. Menard looked round in confusion, and this time Rennie grabbed his arm and felt the feeling inside finally heave out of him like a last nauseous spasm of something bad that had to come out before he could ever feel better again. The feeling was accompanied by a shuddering rumble. The room seemed to shake. Somewhere, something *cracked* in the foundations of the building . . . and the lights went out.

'A power failure,' said Menard in the darkness. 'The emergency supply will come on . . .'

'It's worse than that,' said Rennie instinctively. 'Something really bad has happened somewhere. Something really bad.'

'The subjects!' Menard blundered in silhouette to the door and yanked it open. There was no illumination beyond. 'Where the hell is the over-ride? It should be on by now.'

Rennie pushed himself to his feet and blundered after Menard as he stepped out into the corridor. 'You're not fucking listening again, Menard. Something *bad* has happened. *Is* happening . . .'

Menard plunged ahead into the darkness and Rennie followed. Somewhere, an alarm was sounding. Rennie could hear clattering footsteps in other corridors, and raised voices, but all he could see was the blundering silhouette of Menard ahead as he set off down the pitch-black corridor. 'Where are the over-rides? Where the hell are they? The subjects are on life-support systems. If they fail . . .'

Another silhouette collided with Menard. They grabbed at each other to avoid falling in the darkness. Behind, Rennie collided with them both.

'Desmond?' said Menard. 'Is that you?'

'What the hell's happened, Dr Menard? It felt like an earth tremor.'

'More than a tremor,' said Rennie. *How the hell do you know these things?* 'That was a nuclear device. Somewhere up north.'

'What do we do?' asked the silhouetted Desmond in a voice approaching panic. Menard pushed him to one side and continued along the corridor 'What do we *do*?'

Rennie followed the shadow in front of him, dodging the indistinct figures which milled around them. He had lost all sense of direction when Menard suddenly halted in the darkness, flung open a door and cursed. At last, Rennie realised where he was. They were standing by the security door giving access to the ward where Callender's 'volunteers' lay asleep. The small glass office next to the door, which should have contained someone on duty, was empty. Menard turned back to the door and banged on the window-slot. There was no reply. He slapped at the door itself, his blows flat and ineffective. Bundling back into the glass office, he stabbed at an intercom link with the room next door.

'This is Menard. Let me in.' The intercom was dead. 'Damn it!'

Rennie heard movement and looked back at the door. Someone inside was operating the manual system. Menard pushed past him as it swung open. Before it had completely opened, he squeezed swiftly inside, and Rennie followed.

The once intense violet light had dimmed considerably. There was a bare glow from overhead. Instantly, Rennie became aware of the urgently raised voices and of the bustling activity. The life-support machines had all failed. The team of technicians, doctors and nurses were moving hastily from patient to patient in the gloom. Menard rushed to join them.

Rennie was pushed to one side by a woman in a white coat. He reached out to steady himself against a wall, listening to the tight, hurried instructions being issued, and watching the bustling activity. Someone grabbed his arm. He turned and saw that it was Callender.

The floor beneath his feet seemed to heave again and he knew by the sudden, split-second gap in activity that the others had felt it, too. The lights overhead flickered and somehow became stronger, throwing out more detail. The life-support machines were still inactive.

'It's a nuclear bomb somewhere,' said Rennie. 'Or a power-station melt-down.'

'Brinkburn?' asked Callender, face grim.

'Yes.' Rennie grabbed at Callender's coat sleeve. 'My God, Callender.'

Somewhere in the ward, a woman screamed.

Callender shoved Rennie to one side and stepped forward. Rennie saw that the other personnel in the ward had frozen, their attention centred on what was happening on one of the beds. The doctor in attendance there was standing back in alarm, and Rennie recognised her face immediately as the one he had seen in the window-slot on his first arrival at the 'ward'. The lights overhead fizzled and spat again, making shadows swell and leap. Now, Rennie could see what it was that had so alarmed that female doctor to make her cry out . . . and what also held the others spellbound.

The patient in that bed was sitting up.

It was an elderly woman, perhaps seventy or seventy-five years old. Her white hair was shoulder-length, ruffled at one side where she had been sleeping. The bedclothes had fallen away to reveal her clean white shift. Even from this distance,

Rennie could see that the woman's eyes were bright, clear and alert. She was looking straight at the woman doctor by the bed. There was no evidence in her expression that she had just woken from a sleep of many years. She turned from the shocked doctor to the others in the room, head cocked to one side as if listening. Her sweeping gaze rested on Rennie . . . and it seemed to him that her examination lingered there slightly longer than on the others. She turned back to the doctor. And now that instant of surprise was gone. The doctor moved back to the bed and reached for her arm as the others in the room also began to advance. Rennie felt Callender begin to move forward, too. An impulse made him grab his arm, stopping him.

'No . . . wait . . .'

Callender stopped and looked back at him in puzzlement. And then Rennie saw the woman doctor take her patient's arm. The effect was instantaneous. The old woman looked up into the doctor's eyes . . . and the doctor slumped heavily at the side of the bed into an awkward sitting position. Rennie seemed to hear the air whoosh out of her lungs as she fell. The old woman continued to look at her. The doctor was not unconscious. She seemed captured by the enigmatic look on the old woman's face. Incredibly, the doctor was *smiling* up at her drunkenly. Her hand fell away from the old woman's arm.

Callender tried to pull away, but Rennie held fast. 'Look, Callender!' he hissed. 'Look what's happening.'

The other patients in the other beds were all beginning to sit up now.

There was no gradual awakening process. As if at a given signal, each of the other eleven patients was sitting slowly up and looking at the doctors surrounding them. And somehow Rennie knew that they were all, each and every one of them, *aware*.

'What's going on?' Menard pushed past his astounded colleagues to the nearest bed. The teenage boy there regarded him wistfully as he pulled aside the bed covers and began to rise. As one, the other patients began to do the same.

Menard reached for the boy, his fingers brushed against an arm . . . and he fell to the side of the bed.

Rennie pulled Callender back as some of the other doctors and nurses tried to intervene, tried to restrain the patients from rising. But each touch had an instantaneous effect. Deprived of strength, each of the braver doctors or nurses slumped to the floor, a vacant smile on their faces. The others backed away as the patients climbed from their beds, looked only briefly at each other, and then moved into the centre aisle between the beds . . . as if ready for some strange kind of inspection. Rennie and Callender watched as they began to look at their bodies, at their feet; holding up their hands before their faces as if this was some wondrous kind of development . . . to have a body, to be able to move.

The remaining doctors had reached Callender now, and milled in confusion. Six of their other colleagues were still slumped or kneeling beside the beds, where they had been touched; vacant, anaesthetised smiles on their faces.

The elderly woman, the first patient to wake, was looking across at them again. And, once more, Rennie had the feeling that she was looking directly at him.

'What do we do, Sir James?' asked a voice.

'What the hell . . .?' began another.

'*Shut up!*' Rennie shoved past them and walked to the centre aisle, feeling a new atmosphere in the air and knowing . . . just *knowing* . . . that something else was going to happen. The elderly woman watched him approach. In one uncanny movement, the others also raised their heads and looked at him, too.

Rennie stopped, looking directly into her face. There was a word to describe her expression, a word that had eluded him, but which now registered profoundly. As a child, his mother had used that magical word to describe the look on the face of the plaster saint in her bedroom.

Serene.

'It's Time,' said the old woman. She was the only one to speak, but Rennie seemed to hear echoes of other voices in that one voice.

'Time for what?' he heard himself ask.

'The Time . . .' said Menard from the floor at Rennie's left, and he turned to see the doctor struggling to pull himself up on the bed. Unlike the others touched by the patients, Menard was not smiling vacantly. To Rennie, it seemed as if he had received some kind of shock, as if he was suffering some kind of hangover as he clutched at the counterpane and hauled himself up onto the bed.

Rennie turned back to the woman, waiting for an answer to his question. Her face still held the same serene expression which, he could now see, was shared by the others. Each face had that same *look*. There was a kinship there, and Rennie knew without any doubt that each knew what the others thought, felt what the others felt . . . and all had the same purpose. Behind him, he heard the clattering sound of running feet from the darkened corridor beyond the security door, knew that the security men were on their way.

'Come away, Montresor.' Rennie heard Callender's voice, but did not turn. There had been a wealth of meaning in the woman's two words. He had asked a question . . . and although he feared what the answer to that question might be, he meant to hear it. 'Come away. Don't let them touch you, for God's sake. Heaven knows what's happened to the others . . .'

The sound of the security door slamming shut behind him made Rennie whirl in alarm. Callender and the remaining staff had also been taken completely by surprise, inching away from the door. Callender moved quickly to it and began operating the manual control. Instinctively, Rennie knew that he would not be able to reopen it. Rennie whirled again, looking at the twelve men and women in their pristine white shifts. A dark-haired man with a shaving cut on his cheek, caused no doubt by the slip of an attendant nurse. He looked innocuous, a respectable man-in-the-city, perhaps a chartered accountant. An eighteen-year-old girl with blonde hair. How old had she been when the experiment had begun? A woman in her middle-twenties with a pale, pale face and pursed red lips. A middle-aged Indian, with bristling eyebrows. And all of them with that same serene expression.

Rennie knew that it was they who had shut the security door. He exchanged a glance with Callender as the remaining staff began to hammer on the door, afraid now of what they were trapped in with, panic beginning to register in their calls for assistance. Callender made no move to join them, offered no instructions or advice. He simply returned Rennie's look, and watched . . . as Rennie turned back to the twelve, walking slowly up to the old woman until he was so close to her that she could easily reach out and disable him the way that the others had been disabled.

'Time for what?' he asked again.

'Time,' said the woman . . . and turned away from him to face the wall behind. The other eleven turned with her, in one perfectly choreographed movement. They walked slowly down the centre aisle, filing out at the end of the row of beds until they were in a single line facing the blank pastel wall.

'What do you mean?' shouted Rennie after them. 'What do you *mean*?'

The overhead strobe lights began to fizzle and splutter again, sending long streaked shafts of violet light over the ceiling, making shadows leap and rear once more.

'It's going to happen . . .' said Menard weakly from the nearby bed. Rennie moved quickly to him, seizing him by the lapels of his laboratory coat, searching his face for answers.

The hissing began.

Like escaping steam at first, it reminded Rennie with sickening clarity of the prison washroom and the billowing clouds which shrouded Archie Duncan and Eddie as the maniac had asked, '*How much do you hate?*' But this hissing was rapidly growing louder, filling the ward. The light overhead was flickering more violently now, and Rennie looked up from Menard at the strobes. The sound was sibilant and intense. With a spluttering crack of sparks and thin smoke, the strobes disintegrated in a rain of fine glass

409

splinters. Rennie covered his face as the brittle rain showered on the beds and the tiled floor.

But the room was still being zagged by flashes of bright light and the hissing had changed from the sound of rain on live coals to a susurrant, throbbing rhythm. Rennie dropped Menard back on the bed, shaking fine glass from his hair as he turned quickly to the source of that pulsing light. It was coming from the twelve white-robed 'volunteers' who were standing with their backs to the ward, facing the wall.

No, not from the twelve . . . but from the wall itself.

The wall was suffused with a throbbing, growing light. And as the pulsating, hissing sound became almost unbearable and all detail of the wall itself was dissolved by its brilliant white inner-light, Callender's staff began to shriek, claw and hammer at the security door. Rennie shielded his eyes, the twelve figures at the far side of the room now only indistinct silhouettes. There was no heat emanating from that light, but he knew that looking directly at it could burn out the lenses of his eyes. He turned away, eyes screwed shut, hand covering his face. He turned his back on the light and pulled Menard from the bed, dragging him round to the other side and dumping him on the floor.

'*Time for WHAT?*' he yelled above the noise and the frantic cries of the others. He had seen that look on Menard's face when he had recovered from the boy's 'touch'. Even now, he could tell by the doctor's glazed eyes, from the astonishment still registered on his face, that he had new answers for this crazy phenomenon. Menard groped out at him ineffectually. Rennie shook him by the lapels, letting go with one hand and slapping him hard across the face. 'TIME FOR WHAT, YOU BASTARD?' The blow seemed to shatter Menard's daze. He focused on Rennie's face at last, squinting at the throbbing, hissing light on the other side of the bed. Callender was beside them now, kneeling down and restraining Rennie from delivering another blow.

'Time . . . for . . . what?' asked Rennie again, each word accompanied by a shake of the lapels.

'We've done it!' shouted Menard, struggling to sit up as he shielded his eyes. 'We've succeeded!'

'Succeeded in what?' Callender was shielding his eyes with one hand, trying to catch some kind of glimpse of what was going on at the far side of the room. The intense, throbbing light had obliterated all sign of the twelve silhouettes.

'We were right, Sir James. They've developed ahead of us Three million years ahead. In the right circumstances, in three million years, we could evolve into what they are now. We thought they were comatose, Sir James. But they weren't! Don't you see . . . they've been in a *chrysalis* stage!'

'What the hell are they doing?' shouted Rennie.

'Doing . . .?'

'For God's sake, snap out of it!'

'. . . God's sake . . .?'

'Come ON!'

'They're . . . reacting . . . reacting to the things you told me about, Montresor. The things that are out there now, walking the streets. They're reacting to them . . . to the Evil that's been released from Lime Street. That negative energy . . . that Evil . . . is out there now. I believe you, Montresor. I believe you now! That Evil means to destroy everything. That's all it exists for. But they . . .' Menard pointed feebly to where the twelve had been hidden by the brilliant, throbbing light. '. . . *they* . . . they're positive energy. They're *us*, Callender! They're us in three million years' time, in the same way that those . . . those Frighteners . . . could also be us in three million years' time. The positive and the negative. Now . . . now . . . they're reacting to that threat. They're reacting to . . .'

The hissing, throbbing sound swelled in a great balloon of noise. Rennie felt his eardrums pop.

And then with a great roar, the far wall blew out in an explosive shower of shattered concrete and hurtling, spinning debris. A cloud of smothering, choking plaster dust gushed into the ward.

Rennie stood up, waving the dust away from his face and eyes. There were hysterical cries and sobbings from the security door. The plaster dust billowed and began to dissipate. Twelve indistinct forms were walking slowly out through the ragged gap which had been blown in the ward wall.

'They're still alive . . .'

A new light was spilling into the ward from that demolished wall. Streaks of guttering, glowing red were shafting through the falling plaster dust. Rennie gagged, flurried at the air in front of his face again and squinted to watch as the dust swirled away and that new red light flooded the ward. Beyond the gap, the twelve . . . untouched by the blast . . . were walking in silhouette into what seemed to be a hellish landscape. Rennie could see ruined, blazing buildings, flames leaping and curling into the sky; could see smoke billowing and clouds of sparks dancing in the air as roof timbers caved in and masonry collapsed into . . . into what? A street?

'My God, that's not possible,' said Callender. 'There's nothing but fields out there.' Now, in the distance, they could hear the sounds of crowd panic, of screaming and shrieking.

Then Rennie recognised the black tower on the skyline, surrounded by burning buildings and framed against a flared, burning sky.

'That's the Post Office Tower, Callender.' Somewhere behind it, a building exploded with a detonating roar. Smoke swirled around its base. 'It's London.'

'No . . . no . . . that can't be possible. London's thirty miles away.'

Details of the ruined street ahead were becoming clearer now as the plaster cloud finally wisped to nothingness and the twelve silhouettes walked away from them. A shop window out there exploded, showering the street with glass, but the figures continued their slow advance, apparently untouched.

'They're going to find Them,' said Menard from the floor.

'They've got Power, Sir James. They've created their own *rent* in reality. They've . . . warped the distance between here and London. They've gone to confront Them. It's Time . . .'

'Menard,' said Callender. 'Time . . . for what?'

Menard's broken spectacles reflected the red glare from the hellish city beyond the gap in the wall.

'Armageddon, Sir James. Armageddon.'

Rennie was walking forward now, stopping to lean on the last bed and staring out of the ragged gap at the burning city. Callender helped Menard to his feet, looking back only briefly at his remaining staff beside the security door, still hammering and shouting for help.

Menard shoved Callender aside and blundered past him towards Rennie.

'We've brought it forward. Our research has brought it *forward*!'

He reached the last bed and tried to push past Rennie to the hole in the wall. Rennie shoved him back hard so that he sprawled across the bed; then he turned back to look out onto the street. The twelve figures had almost blended into the guttering shadows. Somewhere in the city, there was another rumbling explosion of collapsing masonry, and Rennie could feel its vibration in the tiled floor beneath his feet. Loose bricks and plaster crumbled and fell from the gap before them, and in the shimmering dust around the rim, Rennie seemed to see a lingering phosphorescent glow, a residual trace of the brilliant light that had initially flooded the ward and blown out that hole. It fizzled and spat there in the cracked brickwork and the tattered, flapping plaster.

'You've really fucking done it, haven't you?' said Rennie as Callender drew level. 'You and Menard.'

'The End of the World . . .'

Menard sat up again, shaking his head, rubbing his eyes. 'When the boy touched me, I *felt* it. I felt it all. This is . . . amazing . . . it's, yes it's . . . *liberating* . . . it's turned my thinking inside out.' There was something akin to joy on Menard's face now as he looked through that crumbling

413

archway into Hell. Rennie felt utter revulsion at that joy; he wanted to go up to Menard and show him just how repellent he found him.

'No, no . . .' said Callender. 'I can't believe that . . .'

The street before them suddenly heaved and cracked. A gaping fissure zig-zagged across its breadth, splitting tarmac and rending concrete slabs. A water main beneath the street split apart and a geyser of water showered into the air. On both sides of the street, windows exploded. A shop frontage collapsed. Rennie and Callender grabbed at the bedstead for support, but Menard had jumped forward again, eyes glowing, and was staggering towards the hole in the wall.

'No, Menard!' Callender heaved himself after him, grabbing to stop him reaching the gap. 'Come back!'

Rennie remembered the spluttering residue of the 'light' around the edges of that hole, and knew instinctively that there was still a residual and dangerous power there; he leaped after Callender just as he caught Menard. They struggled awkwardly.

'Let me go, Callender! I need to see. I need to KNOW!' Menard lunged through the shattered aperture, Callender still clinging to the sleeve of his laboratory coat, just as Rennie seized Callender by the shoulder.

'DON'T . . .' began Rennie.

The effect was instantaneous. They were all touching, and the power was still there within the walls, ebbing and dissipating . . . but still there. Like an electric shock, it surged in Menard, transferred to Calender and from there to Rennie. Menard was instantly gone from Callender's grasp, the shock of the contact hurling Callender to the debris-strewn floor. Rennie was slammed against the side wall, the burning agony in his hands rapidly transferring to the recently flayed flesh on his back. The air was knocked from his lungs as he collapsed on a jagged pile of rubble.

In the twenty seconds of the remaining ebb-tide of that power, all three saw the same scenario. All three saw what it was that the 'volunteers' were now responding to on the streets. All three were given a concentrated, mentally injected awareness of what was happening in the city. In those brief seconds, they received a horrifying feedback, like a super-speeded visual tableau of death and horror and blood.

They saw the horrors of burning, charred flesh. They saw mutilation, they saw dismemberment, they saw what the Frighteners were doing in the streets, they saw what was to come. They saw perpetual night and torture and horrors too hideous to contemplate, where true death was something to be longed for as an escape, but nevermore attainable. They felt the anguish, the pain, the terror and the desolation. The knowledge and the awareness coursed through their veins like fire . . . and when the residual power left the walls, it finally left them as well.

Rennie turned over and threw up. He heard Callender dragging himself away from the gap in the wall. There was no sign of Menard.

There had been no move from the people at the security door to help them, but Rennie became aware of new, bustling activity over there as he dragged himself up on a nearby bed. He retched again, his stomach reacting to the horrifying images which had been implanted in his mind. Gasping, he looked up to see that the security door was opening. The white-coats were scrabbling to get out, and Rennie looked across to where Callender had pulled himself to a sitting position. His expensive Savile Row suit was split under the arms and he was covered in plaster dust. A thin stream of blood was creeping down from his eyebrow.

'All those people, Montresor. God . . . so much *death*.'

Rennie stumbled across to him, seeing the security men pushing through the door at last and striding down the ward towards them.

'Menard?' asked Rennie.

Callender pointed at the jagged archway.

Beyond, Rennie could see that Menard was out there in the street, dodging the cracks in the pavements and the road, skirting around the ragged fissure in the middle of the street from which gushed a fountain of dirty water.

'Menard!' shouted Rennie. The scientist looked back in

their direction. 'Come back, you idiot!' Pausing only briefly, Menard turned again and hurried off in the direction that the twelve had taken. On the skyline, a fountain of liquid fire roared into the air, setting nearby roofs ablaze. Menard's shadow leaped gigantically across the street in its glare, then he had skipped into a side street and was gone.

The first of the security men reached them. Rennie shrugged off assistance and moved to Callender as two uniformed men began to help him to his feet. Rennie could see their confused faces as they stared out into a street where none should be.

'So many people,' said Callender in a voice cracked with sorrow. 'So many people . . .'

'You got another car outside?' asked Rennie.

'What . . .?'

'A car? Another car?'

'Yes . . . yes . . . a Volvo . . . in the drive . . . but . . .'

'Give me your car keys,' demanded Rennie. He wiped a tattered sleeve across his brow.

The faces of mothers and babies, perishing in flames. The knowledge that something somewhere was taking enjoyment from it.

'What . . .?'

'Your car keys, Callender. Give them to me.'

Eyes torn from living heads, screaming voices begging for mercy.

The security men were helping Callender to one of the beds, propping him there, and standing back at the jagged gap with its leaping fire-shadows and its collapsing street.

Men and women burning in a new Hell. Burning the way that Tracey and the kids burnt. And something laughing, laughing, laughing.

'Come on. Give me the keys, man.'

Callender groped in his jacket pocket and handed them over.

'What are you going to do?'

Rennie took the keys, weighed them grimly in his hand and looked back out into Hell.

The Thing inside Eddie Brinkburn, waiting to be born so that it could create this new Hell. Carefully nurturing its host, waiting for the day when it would be in control and could savour all this death and horror and destruction.

'Where are you going, Montresor?'

Rennie looked away from the street, back at Callender. He tossed the keys in his hand and then gripped them tight.

'I'm going back to Lime Street.'

20

Rennie drove on the outskirts, avoiding the Hell which he knew was taking place in the city.

Callender's second car handled well. The little traffic that he encountered as he drove on the outer roads screamed past with no regard for road safety or traffic signs — people escaping like bats out of hell from the horrors they had witnessed behind them. Fire engines, ambulances and police cars were the only traffic heading *towards* the city. The sky was glowing red and that colour reminded him of the photographs he'd seen at school of London in the blitz.

He kept to the small roads, avoiding the inevitable police road blocks and the snarl-ups.

And as he drove, he heard conversations from the past.

How much do you hate?

Really. No joking, Rennie. This is the last. Once we've got the cash. I'm giving my share to that private clinic. Tracey'll be okay. And then . . . phfttt! . . . that's it. No more deals.

How much do you hate?

They killed them, Rennie.

Russell asking: *What's it like being black, Rennie?*

How much do you hate?

I hate! I fucking hate! Hate, hate, hate!

Look, Rennie! I need you man. You're going to be part of this. We've always stuck together. For years, man! I owe you a lot. You got done over as much as me for that petrol station business. It was three years of your life, too. We're not letting Sheraton get away with it. Those bastards took

three years out of your life, three and a half out of mine
— and they fucking murdered my wife and kids. Rennie!
They killed them! Burned them!

 Hate . . . hate . . . hate . . . hate . . .
 I'm in control, Rennie. I'm in control.
 HATE!

Rennie pulled the car over onto a grass verge. He was on
an isolated but familiar road. Strange winds whipped the
grass as he flung open the door and lurched out, dashing
to a broken fence and leaning over it. He vomited, retching
over and over again . . . unable to bring anything up. The
fear which had taken up residence in his guts would not come
up. It clung down there, its tentacles fastened in his innards.
He swung away from the fence, collapsing on the grass verge
and looking up at the sky.

Unashamedly, his distress erupted in weeping. He had not
cried that way since he had been a child. Even then, it was
discouraged and he had hardened himself against the luxury
of tears. But now, he gave vent to it, howling his pain and
anger and distress at that sky.

It was an alien sky. There were colours there he had never
seen before. There was a strange wind blowing now; a bitter
wind that seemed to hold a promise of invisible fire. Was
there movement in the ground? Could he feel the trembling
sensation in the soil, bearing witness to greater horrors
taking place many miles away?

He rose to his feet again. The tears subsided to sobs, and
he knew that his grief and his fear could not be exorcised by
weeping. He knew what lay ahead of him, and what he must
do. There was a distant thundering and grumbling behind
him; the sound of a great storm rushing outwards from the
city. He looked along the country road which would
eventually lead him to Lime Street. The sky above the tree
line was also a livid burning red. And that redness was even
now discolouring as black clouds rose from the earth to meet
it. Rennie climbed back into the car and sat for a moment
drawing in deep breaths, tasting the bitterness of bile. Then
he rammed the gears into first, and set off again.

21

Callender stepped through the jagged gap in the Institute wall . . . and into the burning street.

He looked back once, mind still trying to adjust. Back in the ward, he could see the scattered beds, the rubble and the shrouding of plaster dust. He could see the security door, wide open to the wall. The security men had gone. He had despatched them on false errands. And Callender knew that beyond that farthermost corridor were the grounds of the Institute, and green fields beyond.

Now, he was in a street in the centre of London . . . thirty miles from the Institute. Its sundered wall seemed to blend perfectly with the surrounding buildings, as if it had always been there. He staggered on the rubble which had burst from the wall, and then turned back to face the shattered street.

'*I have to see,*' Menard had said. '*I need to know.*'

Callender was drawn by that same need as he crossed the street to an unfractured pavement, turned up his collar against the hissing spray of the burst water main and hurried on into the shadows. The sky was still erupting, the air still full of the sounds of devastation and wholesale destruction. Seeking the greater realities, Callender turned off the main street and into the trembling, groaning alley which Menard had taken earlier.

22

Rennie stamped his foot on the brake.

The car screeched to a halt on the rise which overlooked the main road leading down to the crossroads . . . and thence to Lime Street.

Flinging open the door, he climbed out and walked to the grass verge, looking down. Now he knew what the black clouds rising to meet the red sky had meant. That blackness was smoke.

Lime Street was burning.

The entire forest surrounding the House was ablaze; a roaring forest fire, with waves of twisting smoke and showering sparks rising from that great sea of flame.

'You're still there,' said Rennie aloud. 'I know you're still in there.'

He walked back to the car and climbed in. Seconds later, the Volvo had crested the rise and was heading down the main road towards the forest fire. Smoke swirled and drifted across the road, twisting and undulating in the outermost tree boles on Rennie's right. The air was filled with a great roaring and crackling. The smoke became denser as he neared the crossroads, sweeping from the trees across the road and over the bare fields on his left.

The corroded sign was still there: '*Lime Street*'.

Rennie swerved to face the avenue on his right and stopped the car again. The lime trees on either side were burning furiously and reminded him instantly of the time he'd been taken to the cinema by his mother to see *The Ten Commandments*. The parting of the Red Sea had been the most spectacular thing he'd ever seen. The immensity of it had thrilled and alarmed him. It was like that now, looking down Lime Street. But instead of water foaming and rearing on either side of a riverbed, there was fire . . . roaring and leaping in a great wall of raging flame on either side of the track that was Lime Street. Whirlwinds of smoke and sparks spun and gushed in that gap between the flames. Even in the car, Rennie could feel the blasting heat.

Rennie had lived in the House long enough to know that this was the only entrance. He had seen the extent of the forest fire from the rise overlooking the road, and knew that there was no other way in.

'Oh, God . . .'

Fear cramped his stomach again.

How much do you hate?

He revved the engine furiously, eyes fixed on Lime Street and its burning gauntlet of trees.

How much . . .?

'Bastard!'

The Volvo screeched across the road and roared into the swirling smoke tunnel ahead.

23

Menard had lost all sense of direction, had never really known where he was anyway.

The streetlights had all gone out. Apart from the burning buildings he passed, the only illumination was coming from the sky — great fiery canyons, splashing hellish red reflections and stark angular shadows as he moved through the deserted streets. And everywhere around him, he could hear the sounds of fire and of collapsing masonry, of people screaming. But although he followed the sounds, dodging the rubble, the falling sparks and the shattering shop windows . . . he could still find no one.

He kept moving, running the length of another shadowed street where steam gushed from the gratings. A building at the far end had collapsed. He squinted up as he ran, trying to catch sight of a street name that might tell him exactly where he was. There was none. He dodged into another side street, heard an explosive crash and shattering of glass followed by more screams. There was a greater light ahead, at the end of this street. He ran towards it. At last, he could see people in front of him. They were running down the main street. A department store was ablaze, providing this stretch of street with a light that was almost as bright as day. He could see the raging flame gushing from the store frontage, as a screaming crowd ran past it. He ran faster towards that street, seeing a scorched sign above the department store frontage: 'Oxford Street'. Gasping, he reached the end of the side street and stepped out into what had once been a main street crowded with taxis, buses and other traffic. Now it was swarming with people, hurtling past him from something that was happening farther down on his right.

He dodged collision with the crowd, fighting against its flow to find out what it was that they were trying to get away from.

The crowd began to thin. A young woman collided with his shoulder, spinning him around and knocking him to the pavement. Senses reeling, he pulled himself to his feet again and saw something appalling.

Someone was running towards him. A young man in a business suit, still clutching a briefcase as if it was some kind of protective charm. And the man was burning from head to foot as he ran, eyes boiling in his blackened face, mouth opening and closing as he lumbered towards him. Gasping, Menard stood aside as the man blundered past in his wreath of flame, patches of burnt clothing falling sootily to the pavement in his walk. Menard watched him for a full minute, watched until he collapsed to his knees and then slumped forward, the impact with the pavement snuffing out the flame. His corpse smouldered like a yuppie's dying barbecue. The horrid fascination of it had mesmerised Menard. Suddenly released from the spell, he realised that the running crowd had passed on. He was alone now in the street. He turned.

There was a solitary figure farther down the street, standing on the pavement about fifty yards away in a pile of rubble that had once been a burger bar. The building had exploded, burnt and spilled out across the street. A whirlwind of dust was swirling around the figure's feet as it seemed to stand, straight and erect, watching the departing crowd.

Here was the Answer.

Menard began to walk towards the figure, seeing at last its details. It was a man, a middle-aged man. He was wearing an ordinary dark business suit, not unlike the suit of the burning apparition that had just run past Menard. He began to quicken his pace, knowing that the man had seen him now and was awaiting his approach.

'Menard!'

He whirled in mid-stride to the source of the voice and saw another figure emerge from another side-street, groping at the brickwork for support. He recognised him immediately, even from a distance. It was Callender.

'Leave me alone!' Menard kept on moving, his pace changing to a trot. 'I don't need you!'

'Menard! Keep away, you bloody idiot. You don't . . .' Callender's voice disintegrated into a coughing fit.

Eyes glazed with mad glee, Menard laughed and ran on. The middle-aged man in the business suit was patient. Menard knew that he had more answers, knew that he could teach him so much. Now, he could see the man's face, the askew tie, the wisps of hair dancing around his balding pate. The dust vortex was still swirling around his feet and it seemed to Menard that the man was smiling as he finally reached the rubble-strewn pavement and clambered towards him. Menard staggered on loose bricks and fell to his knees. The man stood above him now, only six feet away.

Somewhere behind, Menard could hear Callender shouting to him, but the words made no sense. The only sense, the only truth, the only Answers, were to be found here after a lifetime devoted to the false altar of empirical science. He had sensed those new realities in the boy's touch back at the ward, had seen more in the flashing ebb-tide of power which had rushed through his body when he'd first stepped out into that burning street.

He looked up at the man's face and tried to find the right words. None would come. But he could sense the awesome power in that very ordinary figure above him, and the only words he could find came trembling from his lips.

'I could be you.'

'*Yes*,' said Elwyn, Prophet of the Body Disassembled. '*In Time*.'

'You've turned my thinking . . .'

'*I know*,' said Elwyn, stepping forward. '*We've turned your thinking inside out*.'

Menard nodded vigorously as the figure loomed above

him. It reached out and placed a blood-crusted hand on his shoulder.

'*Menard?*'

It was wonderful that it should know his name.

'*Do you like irony?*'

'Irony . . . I don't . . . I . . . yes . . .'

'*Good*,' said Elwyn.

And Menard shrieked from a bloodied mouth, hands flying to his face as he staggered erect again. Blind and in desperate agony, he hurled himself away across the rubble, bloodied fingers clutching and clawing at a face that had been turned *inside out*.

Still screaming, he vanished into the night.

The Prophet continued its slow walk up Oxford Street in search of new converts.

24

The Volvo hurtled into the smoke wall and was swallowed.

Rennie fought to keep control of the steering wheel as the car jolted and shuddered on the rough track, engine roaring. The first cloud of smoke broke apart, and now Rennie could make out the track ahead. On either side, the lime trees were being consumed by that raging fire; he could see their skeletal outlines as the car raced onwards. Already, it was difficult to breathe.

Another gushing cloud of smoke enveloped the car, and the track was lost to sight. Now, he was driving blind with the steering wheel twisting in his hands. He snapped out of his mind the horrifying possibility that the car might leave the road and he might drive straight into that inferno, colliding with the trees.

Please, God . . . Please, God . . .

The smoke was sucked away again, and this time he knew that he was in Hell. The hungry, devouring flame towered high on either side of him. He could see the shadows of the ruins that had once been Lime Street deep within that blazing inferno. The car hit a rut and bounced out of it, front wheels leaving the ground. Rennie twisted at the steering again as the car hit the track, suspension juddering. Somewhere under the bonnet, he thought he heard something tear.

Come on, come on, come on . . .

Smoke swallowed the car again, and this time he had a vision of one of the limes finally cracking apart in the flames and falling across the road. He saw in a split-second, in his mind's eye, just what would happen. The car would collide with that fallen tree and slew off the road into the fire. The doors would be jammed. He would scream and beat at those jammed doors with flesh sliding from cooked hands as the interior of the car became an oven. His eyes would boil and burst in their sockets.

No! No! No!

The engine was making an ominous noise as he pressed his foot on the accelerator. There was little oxygen in here now and he could feel the heat on his body. His shirt was soaked in sweat. He could imagine the paintwork blistering and bubbling as the car roared on and . . . and . . .

Is there something moving around in the trees?! Are there people *in there?* He could see ragged silhouettes amidst the burning trees, moving slowly and awkwardly in the blazing ruins.

No . . .

He looked ahead again, refusing even to catch a glimpse of what it was that moved in that hellish inferno. How long before the super-heated petrol in the tank exploded and turned the car into a hurtling firebomb? Another smoke cloud swept over the windscreen.

How long is this road? For God's sake, HOW LONG?

Something reared in front of the car, lunging through the smoke and slamming down hard on the bonnet in an explosion of sparks. The impetus of the car swept it over the roof, spilling it into the road somewhere far behind.

A man? A burning man?

In pain, Rennie jerked his elbow away from the door handle, feeling the metal burn his flesh. There was another smoke whirlwind ahead and fire so close to the car on both sides that he might be driving right into Hell itself. And in the dreadful moment when the smoke hit the car again . . . Rennie believed that he wasn't in Lime Street any more. He believed that he had been tricked, that the Thing had led him here and that he was, quite literally, driving into the middle of a furnace from which he could never escape.

He was going to burn.

The rubber casing of the windscreen was melting, black

428

streamers flowing over the glass and obscuring what little view he had. The windscreen wipers disintegrated and blew away. He wrenched at the wheel, crying out loud, and saw the paint bubbling on the bonnet before him.

In his imagination, he saw his hair catch fire, saw himself letting go of the wheel and scrabbling insanely at his head as the car slowed to a halt and the upholstery spontaneously ignited. He saw the petrol tank rupturing at last. He saw his clothes erupt into flame, saw himself clambering out of the car like a human fireball. He saw himself trying to run back down the road and collapsing to disintegrating hands and knees after only a few feet.

He was going to burn.

And then the car burst through the smoke vortex and hit the smouldering road ahead hard, in a spray of shale which slashed across the windscreen. Rennie swung up an arm to protect his face, expecting the glass to implode, expecting flame to gout inwards. But none of this happened. In front of him, the fire-wall had vanished . . . and he could see into an empty, flame-free clearing.

Shouting, he twisted at the wheel and the car roared around on burning tyres towards a familiar blackened gate. Something under the bonnet *spanged!* and steam began to gush from the radiator grille. Gravel spurted from the rear wheels as the car hurtled through the gate and skidded to a halt a hundred feet from the fire-wall.

Rennie tried to open the door; something in the lock mechanism had fused in the terrific heat, and it resisted. He kicked at it hard; once, twice . . . and the door squealed open. Clambering out, he sprinted from the car, the sound of the forest fire behind him like the sound of some gigantic and continuous avalanche. The heat beat on his back as he ran, gasping for breath; finally he spun round to look. Smoke curled from the roof and bodywork of the Volvo. Behind it, on every side, he was horrified and awed by the spectacle of the burning forest: a great rumbling, orange-red wall of flame. He turned slowly, sweat pouring from his face, scanning the immensity of that fire barrier and its monstrous sky-curtain of smoke. And when he had completed the turn . . . he saw what he had come back to at last.

The House was standing in the middle of the clearing, surrounded on all sides by the burning trees. Stark and spectral, it waited for him. Dante or Doré could have created this house, standing in the centre of this infernal arena, untouched by the fire that raged around the perimeter fence.

And Rennie knew that the House was looking at him.

He vividly remembered his first impression of the hellish place; remembered how the House seemed to have a face. Fire-red light was reflecting and glinting in its window-eyes. Shadows were leaping on the vines and creepers that crawled on the House's frontage like the sinews, veins and tissue which comprised that monstrous visage.

Behind Rennie, there was a coughing roar.

He turned quickly to see that the petrol tank in the Volvo had finally erupted. The car had vanished in an exploding fireball. He ducked as the bonnet flapped high into the air, clattering to the driveway.

There was no way back.

He turned to face the House again. There was a new expression in the mad, glittering window-eyes of that face. It was a look of monstrous pleasure.

Rennie walked towards the House.

25

Callender staggered through burning and ruined streets, trying to avoid the mad rush of the crowd, stepping over burnt and dismembered bodies.

The horror had numbed him.

The first nausea and terror caused by the sight of what that . . . that *thing* had done to Menard, had been rapidly followed by a succession of horrifying and soul-jarring sights in the street.

Men and women, somehow impaled on the tips of street lamp posts, like the engravings he had seen in books of Vlad the Impaler's victims . . . speared alive on stakes. Some of those people were still alive.

Severed heads on street railings.

People who ran, burning.

Gaping fissures in the middle of streets, containing the entwined corpses of a deep and compacted pulp of humanity.

In distress, Callender skirted the edge of just such a fissure as steam arose from it. He crossed to the other side of the rubble-strewn street, wincing when something nearby collapsed with a roaring grumble and the ground trembled underfoot. There was a shattered shop frontage there; sheets of glass lay like cracked ice, the sign above swung crookedly: 'Super-Sex'.

He needed somewhere to rest, somewhere safe. There was no fire nearby; whatever destruction had been visited on this part of the street had been completed. The Angel of Death had touched it and moved on. Callender reeled on the

...ntered doorframe and looked inside. Shadows guttered on shelves. There were soft-porn video boxes scattered all over the floor. Torn magazines flapped in the wind. Callender stepped through into the shop, glass cracking underfoot. There was a check-out a little deeper in the shop. He walked over to it and rested there, one hand on the open till. Five and ten pound notes fluttered there under a clasp, untouched.

He took deep breaths, head bowed, eyes screwed shut. *Menard, with his outlook turned inside out.*

Callender looked at the jumbled frieze of naked flesh on the floor of the shop, at the haphazard montage of torn magazine photographs. He had seen similar torn montages in the streets, but those jigsaws had been red, not pink.

Something scurried in the dark recess of the shop. Startled, he looked up. Only magazines, flapping in the wind.

Another sound, this time from the street, and Callender looked out through the shattered shop front to see a woman standing there watching him.

She was young, perhaps twenty or twenty-five, with deep-black eye shadow, red spiked hair and a pale face. She was wearing a leather skirt and fishnet stockings. Callender pushed himself up from the cash register. The girl stood silently watching him, apparently in shock . . . perhaps she was drugged. Her arms hung at her sides, and she had handfuls of something wet and jumbled that dripped on the pavement.

'I can't help you,' said Callender. 'I can't . . .'

The girl stepped forward. A sheet of glass underfoot shivered and cracked. She smiled and held out her hands to him.

'*Shopping for something, love?*' Her voice was the sound of many voices, swirling and echoing out of that red, red mouth in a horrifying, powerful bass. A wind blasted into the shop as she spoke, sending magazines whirling into the air. '*You don't need to shop. I've got everything you need.*'

Callender stood back, bumping against one of the video

shelves. At last, he could see what she was holding in her hands.

They were eyes. A jumbled, bloodied mess of human eyes. Blood dripped between her fingers as she moved towards him, droplets of blood plucked from her hands like black caramel by the wind.

But it's going to cost you to look . . .

Too terrified to stir, Callender could see movement under that leather skirt, a movement that had nothing to do with the wind that accompanied her. There was something alive under there, something between her legs. Something that squirmed and writhed, and finally *plumped* from her onto the glass and rubble. It contorted and wriggled there, blood-pink and skinned. It was the size of a baby . . . but not a baby.

It was a rat. A skinned rat. And as it wriggled and found purchase, its glittering, marble-sized eyes found Callender. Light glinted on small, needle-teeth. It squealed.

And in a dream, Callender heard that squeal answered from the street, saw dozens of the monstrosities begin to stream over the rubble from outside and into the shop.

'*Love me*,' said the girl.

Her skirt was rumpling and moving again as she prepared to give birth once more. The dream snapped back into real-time and Callender was able to move. He blundered round to the other side of the cash register, uttering hoarse cries of revulsion. But he was not fast enough. This was real-time now, not slow-motion dream-time. A swarming horde of the purple-veined, skinned-pink rats flowed leaping over the rubble. Squealing and leaping over one another to gain purchase, they began to fasten on his legs. He could feel their needle-teeth and claws tearing through the trouser material, puncturing his flesh. Blundering away, knocking over a shelving cabinet, he slapped out at the things, trying to dislodge them. Already, their claws were snagging on the hem of his jacket. The strongest were leaping high and fastening on his pockets and waistcoat. Whirling, stamping and slapping out, Callender was barely aware of the

433

woman's echoing, unearthly laughter. A rat leaped from a shelf, clawing in his hair. He plucked it away with both hands, feeling its hindlegs raking across his cheek, and slammed it down hard on the shop counter. It squealed and bit in his grasp as he pinned it there with one hand, unable to stop them now as they swarmed up his legs and body, hunting for his eyes. Seizing a half-brick from the counter he began to pulverise that squealing, wriggling monstrosity.

They wanted his eyes. They would take his eyes.

But!Not!This!Bastard! Not this one!

His eyes were clouding in a blood-red mist, his ears hurting at the shrill, high-pitched squealing of the clinging, climbing mass which meant to reach his face and fasten there, bringing him down. The thing in his hand was limp now, but he kept on hammering at it. This one would pay for the others.

But somehow, the nightmare was beginning to fade.

The pulped and bloody mess was still under his hand on the counter. He was still wielding that brick and smashing it at the abominable thing, even though whatever life had motivated it was gone. He was still uttering short, hoarse cries of revulsion and terror with each blow. But the scrabbling, biting mass around his legs and on his body was leaving. Wiry, sharp legs were kicking away from his shredded thighs. He could feel the blood there, warm and flowing.

Staggering back, letting the bloody mass and the half-brick drop from his hand, Callender turned to see the woman walking out onto the pavement. The squirming mass of skinned rats flowed over the rubble behind her, disappearing in a scrabbling frenzy into the street.

The Whore walked out into the middle of the ruined street, smoke swirling around her. It was as if Callender had never existed. He watched her turn her head to the left as she walked, her attention taken by something down there. She stopped at the ragged fissure, turning in that direction as steam from the cracked road wreathed her and chased skywards in ragged shrouds with the smoke.

434

Callender was at the shop door now, holding onto the window frame and looking where the Whore was looking.

At the other end of the street, he could see that there was another woman, about a hundred feet away and walking slowly towards the Whore. He strained to see through the shifting smoke. The woman was dressed in white, her shadow leaping gigantically down the street as another explosion shattered the skyline behind her and another building began to burn. Her white hair was whipping in the wind.

Even before he could see her properly, he knew that it was the elderly woman patient from the Institute, the first one who had woken from 'coma'. It was the woman who had said: 'It's Time.'

And as the elderly woman approached, and the Whore waited with ghoulish amusement, Callender could feel the power building in the air between them. Unconscious of his action, he was stumbling out onto the street now, awestruck and bleeding. The rat-things had gone as if they had never existed. Staggering on the rubble, he watched the elderly woman stop in the middle of the street, facing the Whore . . . and the power between them was building so fast and was so immensely tangible, that it took the breath from his body. There was nothing to see, only the two women standing fifty feet apart on the blitzed street, smoke swirling between them, sparks raining from the sky. But Callender could feel it, and knew that when it reached its pitch on both sides, a Fight would begin to end all Fights. He reeled to the near wall, moving hand over hand down it and away from the Whore towards the other woman. He remembered that woman standing with the eleven others before the Institute's ward wall; remembered how that wall had been blown out, and what the hole had become. What other destructive forces were being mustered on either side? What were these women about to hurl at each other?

He stopped when he was directly opposite the older woman. Her gaze was fastened on the Whore, her face still serene. But the power was beginning to affect Callender's vision. She seemed blurred now, as if some great vibration was shaking his optic nerves.

He was present at the moment of a Confrontation like none ever seen before. And a greater instinct within him made him stagger from that cracked brick wall and stumble to the woman with the white, whipping hair and the serene face. He reached her, was only inches away now but could not touch her as she stared directly ahead. The street was beginning to shiver as the power began to reach its crescendo. Swaying, Callender searched her face for protection, and instinct made him say:

'Love me . . .'

But the woman's face was unchanged. The Confrontation was All.

'Please . . . look . . . you're a saint, or something. Aren't you?'

There was no noise, but the building sensation was beginning to make his head hurt. His ears were ringing, blood was beginning to seep from his nose.

The woman seemed unaware of his presence.

'You're a *saint*! You're supposed to be on our side. That's what saints are *supposed* to do . . .' His words were carried away by the wind and the smoke and the terrifying power.

Callender staggered away, eyes still fixed on her, knowing that he had to get away before the power erupted and he was consumed in it. There had been no refusal to acknowledge his existence: the woman was simply unaware. And in that certain knowledge, Callender felt the deepest distress and desolation that he had ever experienced in his life, greater by far than the loss of his wife. Because now he knew that everything had been taken out of human hands. The Confrontation would take place here . . . and all over the world. Wherever there were Saints, wherever there were Demons. This was a matter for higher powers. Positive and Negative. Good and Evil.

And to the Positive, mankind was infinitely less than a bystander.

The New Mankind and the struggle to define it, even in

the face of total obliteration, was All. The Old Mankind, that primitive and powerless clay, was already three million years distant and forgotten.

There was no hope.

Callender ran.

The blast of that erupting power began when he was five streets away, and it knocked him flat to the pavement. Torn and bloodied, he rolled onto his back and felt the ground shuddering under the terrifying explosive impacts and psychic screaming that was taking place in that Confrontation. There were no stars visible through the dense pall of smoke above.

He stood up again and joined the milling, chaotic crowds.

Everywhere, it seemed, he could hear the exploding detonations that were the evidence of other Confrontations taking place in the city. There was nowhere to run.

But he ran anyway.

26

Rennie reached the foot of the stone staircase which led up to the main entrance of the House.

He looked up. The stone lions were still standing guard at the top of the stairs. Shadows were moving and writhing on their snarling stone visages, making it seem as if they were alive and waiting. Sick with fear, Rennie wondered if they really *were* alive. He had already seen what the thing inside Eddie Brinkburn could do. Were they standing guard there, waiting for him to ascend? Were they waiting for him to reach the top of the stairs, so that they could fall on him and tear him to pieces?

Rennie began to walk up, like a man climbing stairs to the gallows, gaze fixed on the stone monstrosities. He was finding it more and more difficult to breathe. He remembered what he'd been told about the fire bombing of Dresden in the Second World War, how the air in the city had been sucked away and devoured by the raging firestorms. Fists clenched, he arrived at the top step and waited. The lions remained where they were, snarls frozen, bodies motionless.

Beyond them, he saw the entrance doors. They were wide open.

He advanced, with the noise of that great avalanche of fire all around him. More shadows danced and fluttered beyond those doors. He could see dead leaves in there, being scooped and flurried by the wind. With utter conviction, he knew now that he had been allowed to return; knew that the Thing could have killed him at any time, but had been playing with him. Like a cat with a mouse.

He entered — and the smell assailed him before he could fully take in the changes that had occurred since his departure. It was the smell of things long dead. He remembered the carnage that had taken place on the evening before he'd left. What further carnage had there been since then?

The once luxuriant décor had now returned to its former state of deterioration. The chandelier lay shattered in the middle of the hall. Hanging glass fragments chimed in the wind. There were dark splashed stains on the walls, the floor and the detritus-strewn marble staircase on his right. The doors were all shattered, burst asunder by some great force. One of them swung creaking on one hinge in the wind.

Rennie looked up.

There was a great jagged hole in the ceiling, thirty feet wide. And as he looked, he could see that there was a similar hole in each of the floors above, even in the roof itself. He could see the smoke roiling and guttering in the sky above the House. It seemed as if a bomb had ploughed through the roof, blasting a hole clear through to the hall. But why no hole in the hall floor? Why no rubble? No . . . the hole hadn't been blow downwards. There had been an explosion of great force *upwards*.

A movement at the top of the staircase caught his eye. A figure was shambling away from it into the upper shadows.

'Eddie?'

Rennie skirted the shattered chandelier, his footsteps echoing on the marble floor. Grasping the rail at the bottom of the staircase, he looked up again and listened. There was no further movement or noise. He started up the stairs, looking nervously on all sides as he climbed.

At the top, he looked out across the landing and saw nothing; looked back to his right, and down through the great hole in the floor to the hall below. There was no movement down there but the rustling leaves, shifting in the wind. Looking ahead again, he thought he saw a shadow move by the door leading into Eddie's bedroom suite. The door creaked slightly.

Oh God, Montresor . . . what the HELL are you doing? he asked himself, as he walked slowly towards that door. He braced himself there, heart hammering, breath tight in his lungs. His teeth chattered. Clamping his jaw firmly shut, he walked into the bedroom.

Eddie was standing in his black raincoat, his back to Rennie. He was looking out of the window at the far side of the room. It was a familiar pose. Rennie remembered how he used to stand at the window of the flat, looking out into the night, searching the city for Sheraton.

'Eddie?'

He stood waiting for a reply, but Eddie did not turn.

'I'm back, Eddie.'

Slowly, he walked into the bedroom and across to the figure by the window. There seemed to be a weary resignation in that stance. And as Rennie drew near, he seemed to see Eddie's shoulders rise and fall, seemed to hear a sigh.

'Are you okay? Are you . . .' Rennie placed a hand on Eddie's shoulder, and Eddie turned round at last.

Rennie screamed, recoiling from the sight before him.

It was not Eddie. It had never been Eddie, even though it was wearing his raincoat. Rennie was staring at the rotted face of a corpse. The eye sockets were ragged and empty, the skin yellow and leprous. The skin had rotted and peeled away from the mouth, revealing a grin of yellowed teeth. And despite the sickening decomposition, Rennie still recognised that face.

It was Lister.

Lister's dead grin widened as the lower jaw dropped . . . and he began to laugh. Peals of raucous, mocking, hysterical laughter. Flakes of skin began to peel and drop from his face as the effort of laughter stretched and tore leather-tough facial muscles. In moments, he would literally laugh his head off.

Lister flung his raincoat aside, revealing a rotted torso.

440

His ribs crawled with indeterminate, maggot-white living things. Rennie fumbled in his coat pocket and brought out the gun he had been carrying for so long but had never used. He had brought it to use on Eddie, to what effect he had no idea. But he was prepared to use it now to blow that thing to pieces if necessary. The laughter turned into a choking, crackling sound. Lister's arms began to spasm like some mad puppet. And then the corpse caved in upon itself, the rotted flesh no longer able to hold to its skeletal framework. The impact on the floor was sickening. Lister's head cracked open like a cantaloup, spilling grey matter. Leprous hands clenched and unclenched.

Rennie gagged and whirled from the abominable sight.

And then he froze as the terror overcame him.

Arms braced on either lintel to prevent any escape, the Thing that had been Eddie Brinkburn was standing in the bedroom doorway, waiting for him.

27

Callender ran with the crowd, allowing himself to be swept along in its mindless, headlong path.

He had lost all sense of time and place and meaning.

Almost exhausted, he allowed the crowd to carry him wherever it went. Each time the screaming reached a new intensity on either side and the crowd veered in a different direction, he knew that it was reacting to new horrors in the streets. He did not look up. He did not want to see what was happening. Head down, he staggered on, struggling to keep his feet. Beneath him, he stumbled on rubble or bodies trampled underfoot. He knew that if he fell, it would be only moments before he was trampled to death.

'*Where's Andy? Where's my Andy*' screamed a woman in his face, as they ran. Callender shook his head, still looking down, struggling to keep his place in the crowd and avoiding the flailing limbs of his companions. The woman screamed again and lashed out at him before pushing on. Her elbow stabbed under his ribs, knocking the breath from his body. Callender collapsed to the pavement, hands flying to his head. Someone behind fell over him and he knew that in a few seconds a pile-up would begin and he would be simultaneously crushed and suffocated. People were running over him now, feet stamping on his back and his shredded, bitten legs.

But now, miraculously, the crowd had surged on past him.

He had been one of the stragglers, exhaustion finally taking its toll as he slowed down. He took away his hands from his head and looked up. Ahead of him, there were people running on. He tried to move, but there were pains in his chest now, pains that numbed his chest and arm. Was this the way it would end? A heart attack?

There was a roaring detonation up ahead, where the people were running. A great blossoming orange cloud of flame silhouetted the fleeing figures, and as the crowd parted in disarray, screaming, he saw that a Wimpy Bar at the end of the street had exploded. Fire raged within, gushing out of the shattered doorway and across the pavement.

Even as he watched, he could see a figure moving within that blazing furnace. Was it human? Slowly, the figure stepped out of the fire and into the street. As it did so, Callender could see the flames dancing round it, and on it . . . and *in* it. The thing that had emerged from the fire might once have been human, but was human no longer. It was a charred and blackened corpse, its skeletal frame almost completely consumed, but still somehow alive. Callender saw it open its arms wide, heard it say in a hellish and echoing voice:

'*Let me teach you.*'

Liquid fire was spurting from its fingertips, the arms somehow like hideous flame-throwers. And that flame was falling on the heads and shoulders of the men, women and children who still milled in confusion in the street, trying to get away. Burning shapes began to blunder awkwardly into each other in a pyrotechnic dance of death. The others who had managed to escape the fire began to run to other streets, where other hellish lessons awaited.

When the burning bundles could no longer stand, the charred corpse began to walk on stick-insect legs amongst them; studying its pupils to make sure that lessons were being learnt. The thing began to laugh, great echoing peals of laughter. And it was laughter that he recognised: the same sound had issued hellishly from the lips of the Whore.

Callender buried his face in his hands and wept. The pains in his chest were crushing. The hideous laughter swelled and then began to die away. When it spoke again, Callender felt the fear return.

'*I knew that you would come.*'

Had it seen him? Was it even now staggering towards him on its charred stilts of bone, ready to teach him the same lesson? *Please, God, no!*

He looked up.

The corpse-thing was still standing on the pavement in front of the burning Wimpy Bar. The roaring flame of the blazing furnace behind it looked like some kind of entrance to Hell. A movement on Callender's right made him look across. A figure was stepping out from one of the side streets, picking its way over a smouldering pile of rubble towards the Wimpy Bar. The corpse-thing's attention was centred on this figure, and Callender recognised the white shift of the newcomer. It was one of the Institute's 'volunteers'. He remembered the eighteen-year-old youth who had been the second to awaken.

The youth walked calmly to the centre of the street, his back to Callender, facing the charred horror in front of the furnace. And already, Callender could sense the familiar building of power in the air between them that meant another Confrontation was going to take place.

He looked across to the other side of the street. Could he drag himself over there to safety? He made no effort to do so. He knew that the pains in his chest and arm, the fire in his legs and the utter exhaustion, would not allow him. This time, when the street was torn apart in the Confrontation between that unstoppable force and the immovable object, he would also be torn apart.

Calender's head dropped to his pillow of rubble. The pain swelled in his chest . . . and he fainted.

28

Rennie could only look at that face in terror as it smiled and said:

'*Welcome home.*'

He had seen and feared that face before. First, when he had caught snatched glimpses of the countenance crawling beneath Eddie's own face; then, when it had emerged in full to tear Sheraton's visitors apart; and finally, when it had swallowed Rennie and consumed Eddie. He had sensed the presence of that face everywhere in the city; on the streets, hunting and feeding in the alleys. Knew that it *knew* him . . . and that it could have taken him at any time. He had merely been lucky with the monstrosity that the Thing had sent to Callender's home, the Frightener that had been smashed to pieces in the garage. It had always been only a matter of time. And that time was now.

But if Rennie had feared that face before, he stood now in absolute, terrified immobility. Its power had grown . . . and there had been further changes in that face.

The skin was almost a luminous white, stretched taut over the facial bones, hair hanging lank at either side of the face. There were pockmarks and craters on the face. The eyes were hell-black and shining. And there was absolutely nothing left of Eddie Brinkburn in that Face from Hell as it began to laugh; great echoing shouts of monstrous laughter, the same laughter that had issued from the mouth of Lister's corpse. The piercing noise of that laughter broke Rennie's paralysis and he raised the gun, his arm feeling as if it did not belong to him. Hopelessly, he pulled the trigger.

The gunshot joined the crashing echoes of the Thing's laughter. When Rennie had fired five shots into it, those echoes were still bouncing around the House when its laughter had stopped. Rennie had known from the beginning that the gun would have no effect.

The Thing pushed itself from the doorway and strode gigantically into Rennie's vision. Shrivelling inside at the almost palpable power that surrounded it like an aura, Rennie was dimly aware that it was wearing Rennie's own clothes which he had left behind in the House; his own long Oxfam greatcoat flapped about it like wings.

'*No way to greet an old friend,*' it said, taking the gun from him with one hand and seizing him by the throat with the other. The face hissed directly into his own and Rennie tried to scream at the abominable *closeness* of it, but could only give a strangled gasp as the Thing turned and strode back out of the room, dragging him effortlessly behind like a man dragging a sack.

Sparks exploded behind Rennie's eyes, the sound of the encircling fire outside was raging in his head as he felt himself being swung round and lifted bodily from the floor. His feet were no longer on the ground. He clawed at that steel-cold grip on his throat . . . and then the Thing threw him clean across the landing.

In the stunned blackness that followed his impact with the far wall, Rennie knew that this must be a dream. When he woke, everything would be back in its proper place again. When his eyes opened . . . seconds, minutes, hours later? . . . he knew that he was concussed and waited for his double vision to focus. It did. But there was no respite in that awakening.

The Thing was still standing in the bedroom doorway, looking at him and grinning. It was still holding his gun in one hand and now, disdainfully, it threw that gun across the littered landing. It vanished from sight down the ragged hole in the floor and Rennie heard the metallic crack and skitter of its impact on the marble floor below.

Rennie crawled to his knees, facing the Thing. How could

446

he ever have thought that the resolution to this nightmare could be as simple as the gun? There was only one other thing to do. One other thing, before that . . . that . . . Evil Bastard swallowed him whole and threw him into its Hellpit forever. He would do and say what he had really come to do and say.

'Eddie,' he asked quietly. 'How much do you hate?'

The Thing braced itself in the doorway again and laughed.

'*You've been meddling in my affairs, Montresor. Haven't you?*'

'How much do you hate? Come on, Eddie. Tell me.'

'*I'll have to punish you for that.*'

'Don't you hate what this fucking thing has done to you? Don't you hate what it's doing out there on the streets to other mothers and their kids?'

'*Punnnnissssssssshhhhh!*'

'I don't believe that you're dead, Eddie. I don't believe that there isn't some small part of you still in there.'

The figure held out one hand, pointing it at Rennie.

Something invisible had seized Rennie's right arm. He tried to resist, but was powerless as his arm was dragged up from his side until it was held parallel to the ground from his shoulder. The force held his arm there, moving to the clenched hand. He gasped as his fingers were made to open out.

'It needs a living host, Eddie. A *living* host. That's what Lister said. You can't really be dead. You must be in there somewhere . . .'

Rennie felt the pressure in his extended forefinger and knew what was going to happen before it happened.

'Noooo!'

With a crunching *snap*, his finger was torn from its socket by the invisible force. No pain he had experienced before had been like it; liquid fire flowed down the length of his arm. Blood spurted from the socket, pattering on the floor. His arm remained outstretched. He could not move. Gasping in agony, he could see that the Thing was grinning.

'Eddie, you . . . cowardly bastard! Come out of there! Come out . . . and face me . . .'

Snap!

Rennie screamed as another finger was torn away.

'*Prying eyes and meddling fingers. First the fingers, then the eyes.*'

'You're . . . you're a joke Eddie. You always were. All the time you were working for Tracey's operation, all the time you . . .'

Snap!

Rennie's renewed scream dissolved into sobbing, but his arm was still held in the invisible vice.

'. . . all the time you were thinking about Tracey and the kids when you were in prison. All the time you were grieving for them when they were burnt. Well *that* was the joke. Because they were never yours to grieve for, Eddie.'

Snap!

'Ohhh, Christ! Tracey . . . Tracey was laughing at you. *I* was laughing at you.'

The grip was gone and Rennie hugged his hand, blood running from it thick and fast. He looked up in agony. The Thing was still grinning insanely.

'You idiot, Eddie. You stupid idiot. What do you know about grief? All the time you were grieving in prison, missing Tracey and the kids . . .' Rennie doubled over, groaning and hugging his mutilated hand again. He straightened up, gritted his teeth and continued. 'You knew nothing, Eddie. *Nothing!* That's the big joke. Because Tracey loved *me* − not you. We'd been screwing for years. For years!'

The invisible force plucked Rennie from his knees, lifted him bodily and hurled him at the head of the staircase. Spinning awkwardly, he slammed into the balustrade and began a bone-jarring descent, body rolling, legs twisting. Half-way down, he kicked his leg through a gap in the marble banisters. His fall was arrested. Still hugging his hand, he rolled to his feet and clattered down the remaining steps to the hall. His impetus and weakness were too great.

Combined with the shock, his legs gave way and he sprawled on the hall floor.

Still grinning, the Thing began to descend the stairs.

Rennie rolled onto his back and forced himself to sit up, watching it as it came.

'*What do you prize most, Montresor? Fingers? Eyes? Or something else?*'

'Here's another joke for you, Eddie. Listen carefully, man. Because I'm talking about the kids. The kids!'

'*Yes, perhaps something else.*'

'You stupid bastard. They were my kids not yours! Think about it, Eddie. Use what's left of your stupid mind in there and tell me that you hadn't thought about it. Never notice their *dark* complexions, you jerk? It was staring you in the face and you couldn't see it.'

It reached the bottom of the stairs and advanced on him.

'Now tell me, Eddie . . . tell me . . . How much do you hate, now?'

'*Eddie's dead. And you have to be punished.*'

'We were laughing at you, Eddie. Laughing.'

'*Yes, there is something you value more, isn't there?*'

Rennie felt that invisible pressure moving to his legs now as the Thing approached. It was pinning them to the floor as surely as if a concrete slab had been laid over them. The pressure increased and Rennie uttered a hoarse, guttural yell when something in his left leg snapped and a stinging which quickly turned to numbness flowed from his knee to his hip.

'She loved it, Eddie. She loved every bit of it.'

The power on his legs began to move. Slowly, they were pulled apart. When he was spreadeagled, Rennie felt that pressure begin to move towards his crotch . . . and knew what was going to happen.

'You coward! You fucking coward! You going to let it do your job for you, Eddie? Don't you hate me enough to do it for yourself?'

Something invisible but made of ice seized his genitals.

'Eddieeee! You . . . you . . . She loved it. She couldn't get enough! She . . . *Sheeee!*'

Rennie's scream echoed up through the jagged hole overhead. His head jerked up towards it, and as his vision began to fade, it seemed that the hole was now a spinning, undulating whirlpool. The fire in his groin was consuming him. He was burning. And now, like smoke, he seemed to be drifting up towards that whirlpool. Dimly, he was aware that he had been seized by his coat lapels and was being dragged across the marble floor. For some reason, he had not been gelded. Dimly again, he was aware that he was no longer screaming, but that something else was screaming directly into his face as he was hauled upright and slammed against a wall. That something began pounding him against the wall, again and again.

'You bastard, Rennie! You (*bang!*) stinking (*bang!*) bastard!'

'Eddie . . .?'

'I'll (*bang!*) kill (*bang!*) you!'

'Eddie, is that you? Is it *You*?'

The grip on his lapels was suddenly gone, and Rennie collapsed to the floor. He tried to look up and focus on the figure that was looming over him, but it began to lash out again, kicking him.

'I'll . . . bloody . . . kill . . .'

'Eddie! For God's sake, EDDIE!'

The figure backed off, sobbing. At last, Rennie's vision came into focus.

The face was still hellishly white and drawn, still horribly pocked and wasted, with hair straggling across the eyes. But it was a face that Rennie recognised. It was the face of Eddie Brinkburn. And as he stood there, looking down on him, sucking in great sobbing mouthfuls of air, eyes filled with hate, Rennie heard again in his mind the words that Eddie had said in the flat in Windsor Street.

'There was something inside *Archie. I don't know what if was, or how it came to be there. But there was something . . . something that was locked inside him. It* jumped,

*Rennie. It jumped out of him and into me . . . and it had
something to do with the way I was feeling. Archie kept
asking everyone how much they hated. Remember that?
That's all he could say: "How much do you hate?" Well,
at that time, right at that moment . . . I hated everything
the way that nobody's ever hated in their lives. And . . .
whatever it was . . . my hating that way made it able to jump
out of Archie and into me.'*

Rennie had made it happen. Hate had been the emotion
that the Thing had been seeking to escape its initial
imprisonment in Archie Duncan. And Rennie had used that
same hate to draw Eddie out.

Still sobbing, Eddie collapsed to his knees in front of
Rennie.

Hugging his mangled hand, Rennie crawled to him,
dragging what he knew was a broken leg.

'It's not true, Rennie. Tell me it's not true.'

Rennie scrabbled furiously in his pocket with his one good
hand for the thing he'd put there earlier. '. . . not true, Eddie
. . . not true . . .'

'She loved me, didn't she? The kids were mine, weren't
they?'

'. . . yours . . . She loved you.'

Where the hell was it? He prayed that it hadn't been
crushed.

'Oh, God, Rennie. Oh, God . . . no . . . it's coming back.
It's coming back!'

Rennie saw shadows begin to crawl on Eddie's face again.
At last, he found the small tablet in his pocket, no bigger
than an aspirin or a pain killer. He pulled it out — the
greatest painkiller of all. It was the cyanide capsule prepared
for him by Dr Menard, the capsule that he had been going
to take after he'd shot Eddie. He held it up to Eddie's face.

'Eddie . . . here . . . here . . .'

'God, Rennie. What've I done?'

'Here, man! Do it . . . DO IT!'

Eddie blinked, and in that split-second when his eyes
reopened Rennie could see that they were hell-black again.

The thing inside him was recovering possession. Eddie grabbed Rennie's outstretched hand.

'I'm sorry, Rennie . . . sorry . . .'

Eddie stared at his hand with those hell-black eyes. Was it too late? Had the thing regained possession?

'Fix it, Eddie. Fix that bastard forever!'

Eddie looked at him again, directly in the face, and smiled.

Rennie knew that it was too late.

And then Eddie plucked the capsule from Rennie's hand and pushed it roughly into his mouth, biting down hard.

Rennie gasped and pulled away, crawling back until he was against the wall. Was it still too late? He had fired five shots into Eddie when the thing was in full possession and they had made no impression. Would the same thing happen now with the cyanide?

Eddie convulsed. One shuddering spasm.

'Please, God . . .'

His eyes were screwed shut, his jaw clamped shut.

'Please . . .'

And then Eddie leaped backwards from his kneeling position, choking and retching, trying to spit out what had already been swallowed. His arms were thrashing at his sides as he staggered back into the centre of the hall. Great roaring noises were spewing from his mouth . . . and now Rennie could see that his face had become the hideously white, hellish visage of the Thing. There was no sign of Eddie Brinkburn in that face. It flung its head back and howled upwards through the ragged gap in the ceiling, its rage echoing and reverberating throughout the house. A whirlwind of dead leaves and dust began to swirl around its feet.

Rennie began to crawl across the littered marble floor, praying that he could find the one thing that might save him.

The gun.

His plan had worked backwards. He had intended to shoot Eddie and take the pill before the Thing could jump to the only other living host available – himself. Without

452

a living host in range, the Thing must surely dissipate and die. He knew that the gun was down here somewhere. It had taken the gun from him and thrown it through the hole in the floor. He had heard its impact on the marble below. But had he fired five shots, or six? Five, it had to be five!

'Please, God . . . please, God . . .'

He could see something black on the floor, not far from the double doors.

The Thing had ceased howling, and Rennie looked back.

It was no longer thrashing and choking. It was standing still and silent in the middle of the hall, looking at him as he crawled. And he knew that it *knew* its living host was going to die. As he watched, its eyes began to glow with the same boiling white light that he had seen in Archie Duncan's eyes, just before it had jumped into Eddie. Rennie twisted his head away, knowing also that his own eyes were reflecting that hellish glow as the Thing began to prepare for its new host. That glow was misting his vision. Crying out loud, he tried to focus on that black object as he reached the shattered chandelier and began to crawl over its jagged fragments, still hugging his mutilated hand and dragging his broken leg. He could feel the power building in the air between them as it prepared to jump.

The chandelier clattered and jangled as he pulled himself in agony towards the black blur on the marble floor ahead. Was it the gun, or a piece of wood or stone?

'Please . . . please . . .'

He dared to look back, seeing that the Thing's eyes were glowing at the peak of their intensity. Dust and leaves still swirled around its feet. Its lips were drawn back in a hideous and expectant smile. It didn't need hate to transfer this time. It was strong enough, even though its present host was dying.

Eyes still held by that unearthly glowing light, Rennie heaved himself over the broken glass, clutching for the object. Fingers scrabbling, he saw that light was also beginning to spill from its nostrils like luminous smoke.

And then the Thing jumped.

Eddie's body collapsed to the marble floor.

Rennie felt the power in the air as his fingers connected with cold, dark metal. He felt that sickening presence blast into his own eyes in an implosion of light. He could see nothing now but that horrifying glow, and he was drowning in it. The Thing swarmed into him. It took possession of his nervous system. Instantly, he felt it exploring his heart, his lungs, his kidneys. He felt it in his gut and in his groin. He felt it pulsing in every vein and artery, rushing with his blood to explore every fibre of his being. After that instant circuit of his body, it returned to his eyes . . . and exploded into his mind. It planted its essence there, laying its eggs like some hideous mind-spider. Instantly, the roots of that evil spread and grew and entwined in his soul; a cancerous spiritual growth that began to eat and consume him.

Rennie screamed. The pain in his hand and his leg was nothing compared to the hideous thing that was happening to him now. The scream dispersed the luminous glow that had blinded him, but he still could not see clearly. The Thing inside shifted and settled, as if it was trying on a new coat it found to its liking. It was deeply rooted now, and Rennie could feel himself dissolving away.

Squirming in agony, he held the metal object to his face, trying desperately to focus.

It was the gun.

You don't need the gun. Throw it away.

'You don't have me yet, you bastard!' Rennie barely had control of his hand. He began to curl his finger into the trigger guard.

It's no use now. You're mine.

'. . . don't . . .' Rennie could feel himself on the edge of a hellish pit. A wind was sucking at him and he could feel himself about to plunge into that nightmare place from which there was no return. The gun didn't matter. Nothing mattered. There was no bullet left in it. And the world was finished anyway. This hellish thing would see to that. The pit yawned beneath him.

And somewhere inside, a voice seemed to ask him: 'How much do you hate?'

Rennie reeled back from the edge of the pit, crying out hoarsely. He couldn't allow it . . . he *wouldn't* allow it.

Raising his fingerless, mangled hand he savagely punched the marble floor with a wet smack.

The pain was hideous . . . and it propelled him momentarily back from the pit and into the hall again. His vision began to clear, and he turned the gun to his face.

YOU DON'T NEED IT! THROW IT AWAY!

'You Bastard!' Rennie writhed on the floor, pain eating him, and tried to get the gun barrel to his mouth.

'Rennie! No! Over here!' It was Eddie's voice.

He twisted his head to look, and through the haze he could see that Eddie was somehow standing again. And he was beckoning urgently to him now.

'It's still here, Rennie. It's a trick. It's still in me.'

'No . . . I don't believe you . . .'

Another figure was swimming into focus on Eddie's left. It was Lister, wearing his pink dressing-gown, shambling past Eddie with his wild hair fluttering in the wind. Dead leaves flurried and danced. 'Don't listen to him. It's me, Montresor. *Me!* I'm dead . . . you saw that I was dead . . . and it's hiding inside me. Shoot me, Montresor! Shoot me and put an end to it.'

The gun wavered from Rennie's face as he squinted into the haze.

'It's always been in me,' said a dark, cowled and insubstantial figure on Eddie's right. It was wrapped in folds of dark linen, like a monk, its face hidden. The voice was slow and dragging, like a record running down. Even through the blur, Rennie recognised it as the hideous flapping thing from the classroom of his dreams. 'Use the gun, Montresor. Use it on me.'

'Here, Rennie!' shouted Eddie, beckoning again. 'Do what you came to do, for God's sake!'

'No, no, no!' Lister began hopping from foot to foot in that agitated manner he knew of old. 'It's me! Me!' Rennie's gun began to waver from Eddie to Lister to the now silent cowled figure.

'Help me, Rennie,' said a voice that he knew only too well. Florinda was standing by the double doors, summer dress blowing in that dead wind. Her hair was dancing around her head.

'It's *in* me, Rennie. It's raping me, using me, possessing me.' Her voice dissolved into hopeless tears. Rennie turned the gun on her. 'Kill me, Rennie. Please kill me. Kill me so I can be free.'

Rennie groaned. 'Free?'

He looked at the other three figures, and then back to Florinda – gun wavering. He spat blood on the floor.

'What a fucking laugh.'

He chose.

Aimed.

And pulled the trigger.

29

Callender awoke.

The pains in his chest had subsided to a dull ache. His legs still throbbed, and there was a band of pain across his temple where it rested on its brick pillow. He looked up, his vision misted. Flame shadows reflected back, orange-black. Sparks drifted from overhead.

But there were no exploding detonations, no rumblings in the street beneath him . . . and no screaming.

He remembered the Confrontation that had been about to take place between the youth and the charred corpse-thing before consciousness had left him. He remembered feeling that invisible build-up of power in the air. But there was no trace of that power now. There was no sound but the hissing roar of burning buildings.

But there was an air of terrifying expectancy.

Somehow, the devastation had momentarily abated. Callender had the instinctive feeling, as his vision began to clear, that something was happening somewhere . . . and whatever it was, the consequences could be even more devastating.

His body was taking time to obey motor instructions. Slowly, he began to drag himself from the pile of rubble in which he lay. It felt as if he was crawling out of his grave. Steadying himself, he looked around at the devastated street. Ahead of him, bodies still burned and smouldered on the pavements. A sickening smell of incinerated flesh drifted across the street. But his attention quickly focused on the two figures who were still standing facing each other at the end of the street.

The youth's hospital gown was blowing in the wind, his hair ruffling. Beyond him, the corpse-thing was standing motionless, framed against the still-burning Wimpy Bar like some waxwork from a Chamber of Horrors.

They were waiting for something.

And Callender was drawn to them, uncaring now of himself as he staggered down the street on legs that were still reluctant to carry him. He did not question why he was drawn to them. He only knew that he must see.

The sky overhead still glowed red, reflecting the burning city. But despite the rumbling, crackling roar, there was an underlying *hush* that made Callender's heart beat fast.

He reached the youth and stopped, looking at his hair as it ruffled in the wind. Slowly, he moved round to see his face. The boy was awake, his eyes still fixed on that corpse-thing. But he was absolutely still. He did not even seem to be breathing. Callender turned, staggered, and looked at the charred monstrosity. It was impossible to tell whether the thing had been a man or a woman. Impossibly, its eyes were intact; swollen, white, cataract eyes that remained fixed on the youth. Both figures seemed unaware of Calender. Flame shadows leaped and crawled on the three figures in the street as Callender looked up to the sky, as if expecting to see some answer there.

'*Callender?*' said a voice that he knew.

He whirled back to where the youth stood.

'Montresor!'

Now, Callender could see that the youth's face was darkening and changing. In horror, he knew that a transformation was taking place. Had the balance of power in the Great Confrontation somehow been shifted? Was this Saint going to become a Demon? The change was rapidly complete . . . and now he knew that face.

The face of Rennie Montresor had somehow been superimposed on the boy's.

Stupefied, Callender staggered up to the youth, staring directly into his face. There was a gaping bullet-hole in

458

Rennie's left temple. The lips moved again, and when the boy spoke, it was with Rennie's voice.

'*Callender?*'

Was he alive?

'*No.*'

'Then how . . .?'

'*The right choice, Callender.*'

Rennie's face began to dissolve. There was another sound behind Callender, the sound of something dry and fragile shattering and skittering on the pavement. He whirled on unsteady legs to see that the corpse-thing had fallen to the street and shattered there in a ruined pile. Callender turned awkwardly back to Rennie. But his face was gone. There was only the youth's face now, and Callender watched in stunned fascination as that face began to glow. It rapidly became too bright for him to look, its luminosity obliterating the boy's features until there was only an oval pulse of intense white light. Callender backed away, hands across his eyes. Through shading fingers, he looked back to see that the youth's entire body was now suffused with that intense glow. And Callender recognised that light. It was the same light that he had seen back at the Institute, just before the 'volunteers' had blown out the ward wall and stepped into London.

The light began to emit a hissing roar, and Callender staggered farther back, feeling no heat but afraid of what might happen. The hissing began to build in intensity, so loud now that Callender had to clap his hands over his ears.

The roaring abruptly terminated with an echoing *SNAP!* and Callender saw a great luminous ball shoot skyward like some gigantic, brilliant firework. It was gone . . . and the boy collapsed to the street.

Callender moved forward quickly, turning the boy over. The face still held the same serene look that he had seen on the other Institute patients. But the body was lifeless.

Callender looked up

A brilliant comet of light was arching into the burning night sky above them. And as he looked, he could see other tracers of that same light erupting from all over the city; all rapidly arching towards each other in a glowing cage. On a strange impulse, Callender quickly counted them. There were twelve.

The tracers of light connected simultaneously in a detonating roar of brilliance and power. For an instant, a great ball of energy hung over the city. It seemed to throb and pulse there. Callender had to shield his eyes again, heard another explosive roar, and looked back to see a single blazing white comet streaking off into the night sky. The light and the noise swiftly diminished and he watched it vanish into the heavens with something approaching a profound sadness and longing and loss.

It was over now. Callender knew it with utter conviction. He knew it somehow from Montresor's face, superimposed on that of the youth. The negative energy . . . the Evil . . . had been taken away, and because it was no longer present, there was no need for the Confrontation. There was no need for that positive energy . . . that Good . . . to stay. There was no place for it here. No place for the New Mankind now that it had developed beyond the Old Mankind. Callender watched the light fade to a dwindling speck. Where was it going? Nowhere so trite as Heaven, perhaps . . . but wherever it was going, he wished with all his heart, and with a great emotion clutching at his throat, that he was going with it.

But he could not. And neither could the survivors of this Old Mankind. Not for another three million years, perhaps, not until evolution could take its course.

Callender looked around at the burning streets.

What had happened elsewhere in the world? Had the same ravaging Confrontation taken place in a dozen other countries? Was it possible, then, to rebuild from the ashes and learn from what had happened? Could they rebuild in the knowledge that there was a spiritual side to man, or would the Old Mankind learn nothing from this and continue its course to self-immolation? God, no . . . he could not bring himself to believe that the latter could happen. Not now. Not any more.

What had happened to Montresor and Brinkburn? What had happened to avert the Confrontation?

Callender heard Rennie's last words again: *'The right choice, Callender.'*

The right choice.

Saints or Demons? In those final moments, had Montresor . . . and even Brinkburn . . . earned their own right to choose? Callender remembered Montresor's words when they'd first met and he'd tried to explain the nature of the Evil: *'It's not the Devil, not a Demon. It's not a Satan, not Lucifer. That's what means there's no hope for us. It's human, Callender. That's all. Human.'*

'The right choice,' said Callender aloud. 'Saints or Demons?'

He looked at the sky, searching for a sign of the vanishing comet.

There was none.

'Or perhaps only Human, after all.'

The right choice.

In the rebuilding, which way would the Old Mankind choose?

Only time . . . perhaps three million years of it . . . would tell.

F. PAUL WILSON

REBORN

'This is war! Evil such as the world has never known is coming. Satan in human form, here not just to claim our lives but our very souls as well!'

The Last Will and Testament of Dr Roderick Hanley, Nobel Prize-winning geneticist, had left Jim Stevens a fortune and a Long Island mansion. As importantly to Jim, adopted as a baby, it revealed the identity of his natural father.

But that was when his pregnant wife Carol began to dream the terrible dreams. While in the city, a band of Charismatics, led by the wandering monk Brother Robert, became possessed of the knowledge of the coming of a great Evil.

The true, awful nature of the inheritance was about to be made manifest . . .

Reborn is the first of a three volume sequel to F. Paul Wilson's horror bestseller *The Keep*

'Strong emotional narrative and a wonderful sense of mystery'
Fear

HODDER AND STOUGHTON PAPERBACKS

STEPHEN GALLAGHER

RAIN

LUCY ASHDOWN IS A GIRL WITH A MISSION — to find the driver who ran down and killed her sister Christine.

Now she has a lead and she's off to London.

Joe Lucas is as dedicated as Lucy. His aim is to bring her home.

In the dangerous night-world of the West End, violence and corruption lurk just below the neon-lit surface. With Joe no more than a heart's beat behind her, Lucy steps eerily into her dead sister's life, and a race against time.

'Stephen Gallagher is in the top league of new generation thriller writers'
James Herbert

HODDER AND STOUGHTON PAPERBACKS

CHARLES L. GRANT

STUNTS

When the night wind blows across Salisbury Plain, imagination plays strange games and shadowed figures tap at snug cottage windows.

At Halloween in small-town upstate New York, preteen witches Trick and Treat in borrowed black while the sheeted dead gibber and giggle through the safe streets.

But when the shadow of the wolf falls on a man, death comes to life within him, he grows to hate all creation and all he hates must die.

Then it is the true time of killing is come . . .

HODDER AND STOUGHTON PAPERBACKS